NIGHT RUNNERS

A Novel by

Rodger J. Bille

Illustrated by
Carol Van Wagoner

© Copyright 2006 Rodger Bille.
All rights reserved. No part of this publication may be reproduced, stored in a retrieval system, or transmitted, in any form or by any means, electronic, mechanical, photocopying, recording, or otherwise, without the written prior permission of the author.

Note for Librarians: A cataloguing record for this book is available from Library and Archives Canada at www.collectionscanada.ca/amicus/index-e.html
ISBN 1-4120-8007-x

Printed on paper with minimum 30% recycled fibre. Trafford's print shop runs on "green energy" from solar, wind and other environmentally-friendly power sources.

Offices in Canada, USA, Ireland and UK
This book was published *on-demand* in cooperation with Trafford Publishing. On-demand publishing is a unique process and service of making a book available for retail sale to the public taking advantage of on-demand manufacturing and Internet marketing. On-demand publishing includes promotions, retail sales, manufacturing, order fulfilment, accounting and collecting royalties on behalf of the author.

Book sales for North America and international:
Trafford Publishing, 6E–2333 Government St.,
Victoria, BC v8t 4p4 CANADA
phone 250 383 6864 (toll-free 1 888 232 4444)
fax 250 383 6804; email to orders@trafford.com
Book sales in Europe:
Trafford Publishing (UK) Limited, 9 Park End Street, 2nd Floor
Oxford, UK ox1 1hh UNITED KINGDOM
phone 44 (0)1865 722 113 (local rate 0845 230 9601)
facsimile 44 (0)1865 722 868; info.uk@trafford.com
Order online at:
trafford.com/05-3005

10 9 8 7 6 5 4 3 2

OCTOBER, 1929

Without warning, machine gun bullets whipped from the dark, shattering the side window of the boat just in front of him. Don wrenched the wheel and jammed the throttle of the Ghost forward so violently that Al was thrown from the rear deck where he had been getting ready to unload a few cases. There was no time to take a breath before the frigid water enveloped him and no way to know which way the surface lay. He struggled to overcome the panic that would kill him if he didn't surface in a few more seconds.

"God help me, help me to find the way up! And please forgive me for the greed that brought me to this hellish watery grave if I can't make to shore," Al shouted in his mind. His body relaxed and in a few seconds a swirl of the rip tide threw him half clear of the surface. He caught a glimpse of light from a cabin at the south end of Salmon Beach and got his bearings. Striking out towards where he believed the shore to be, he soon realized he was being swept south faster than he was heading east to safety. Above his pounding heart and the splash of his strokes he could hear the bellow of the Ghost's exhaust and the scream of her supercharger disappearing toward Rocky Point. Don had left him to drown! Or didn't he realize what had just happened? Further thought was cut off as the beam of a searchlight swept just over his head and picked out the rip rapping of rock that held intact the shore bordering the railroad track. His destination was under surveillance, probably by whoever had shot up their boat. Could it get any worse, Al wondered? He was soon to find out.

INTRODUCTION: NOV. 26, 1924.

Hubbard grinned as he read the Seattle Times headline for "King of the King County Bootleggers Nabbed". His former boss and the whole crew of one of his several boats had been arrested down at Des Moines. Another boat, the Eva B, had been boarded by Canadian authorities just a month previously and the boss's elaborate Seattle home had been raided only nine days earlier. "Roy Olmstead, his hot-shot attorney, all the gang and maybe even Elise, are going to jail this time," Hubbard thought, aloud. "The Prohibition Administrator for Washington State, Mr. Lyle, has got to be one happy man today. And all on account of me! I may be a snitch, but I ain't going to be the one in jail."

Hubbard knew that Olmstead, a former Seattle Police Lt., never allowed his boat crews, drivers or warehousemen to carry guns. Unlike his Eastern counterparts he didn't believe that smuggling liquor was worth spilling blood. So, though Olmstead was bound to figure who ratted him out, Hubbard felt reasonably safe. Even after being arrested three times, Olmstead didn't give up his $200,000 per month business until he and 20 other of the 90 defendants were convicted almost 15 months later. He got four years on McNeil Island Penitentiary and an $8000 fine. He appealed clear to the Supreme Court, claiming his right of privacy was compromised by the wire taps on his phones. Of course, his chief attorney was in prison with him, so he lost and served his time. His wife, Elise was acquitted even though the prosecutors claimed she was giving the boat crews coded information through her evening radio broadcasts of children's readings from their personally funded radio station. [That station, KFOX later became KOMO the ABC affiliate for Seattle.] She continued her community service, catching the attention of Franklin D. Roosevelt, who later gave Olmstead a full pardon and ordered a refund of his $8000 fine and court costs of over $2200! After Roy declared himself a Christian Scientist and began a prison ministry, Hubbard was relieved more completely, because you never knew when a guy might get sore about losing such a lucrative business.

By February of 1926, there were many small timers scrambling to quench the thirst for liquor left by the incarceration of the King of the King County Bootleggers and his crew of boat pilots and truck drivers. Into this situation blundered two talented young boat builders and an ambitious woman from a different time.

CHAPTER ONE : SEPT 12, 1928

The early September night was dry and crisp, unusually so for the Pacific North West, as Don and Al emerged from the lush greenery of Wright's Park onto Sixth Avenue and crossed to J Street. They were half way home from the Stadium bowl and the opening game of the 1928 Tacoma High School District football season.

The young men lived next door to each other in the tall, narrow row houses that lined the modest area between 7th and 11th Avenues on J St. It was a working man's community, close to the street car lines that ran down to the industrial tide flats, where mills and wharves gave employment to many trades. [Some of the upper floors of the row houses sported a view of the city that claimed one of the world's best deep water ports.] Immense log rafts waited, in those waters, to crawl up the metal chain ladders to be fed into screaming headsaws, where they became lumber to be shipped across the world. Felled stands of Douglas fir arrived behind tug boats almost around the clock to feed the hungry sawmills. Freshly harvested grain from eastern Washington and Oregon heaped in train cars were being off loaded into the Fisher Flour Mill. Boat building and repair facilities of varying sizes attached themselves conveniently to the many piers. It was busy port, bustling with the prosperity of the late 1920s, a place of opportunity in the town that had designated itself: "The City of Destiny".

"Our Tigers sure whipped those turkeys from Lincoln tonight, didn't they? Looks like we're off to a good season, don't you think, Al?"

"Yeah, but they aren't really 'our' Tigers anymore, are they? We're out of there and on to bigger things now," Al replied.

"Hope so, but scraping and washing boat bottoms is not my idea of bigger things. It wasn't bad summer work, but I'm not looking forward to climbing under dripping boat bottoms all winter. Do you think the boss will get us into the plant and start helping on one of the new boats, or at least doing some topside stuff or finishing work soon?"

"Probably, if we blow our own horn a little; let him know we already built a good looking tender in shop class last year and are capable of turning out work as good as most of the journeymen," Al guessed.

"If we only had some capital to start our own place, I've got a great project in mind. Something that could put us in the seat of one of those new Model A Roadsters or maybe even something faster, like a new six-cylinder Dodge," Don said, wistfully.

"Good luck! Our folks have all their money socked into the stock market and we're working for four-bits an hour. Not much chance of breaking out on our own for a while yet, but what's your big idea anyway?" Al asked.

"A thirty footer, a design that's not only fast but able to handle rough water and still operate in the shallows in a very quiet mode. A special purpose boat that certain people would pay a premium price for," Don answered, his grin wide enough to be quite evident even on the poorly lit street.

"Oh man! You're dreaming of the perfect rum runner, aren't you?"

"Want to see my ideas on paper? Come up to my room and I'll show you a plan that will get your heart pumping!" Don gushed.

As they approached Don's home, Al asked, "Has somebody moved into the house across the street? I haven't seen anybody in there for awhile, but there's a light on in the top floor bedroom opposite yours."

"Not that I know of, but I bet we can find out, if you remember what else I've got in my room besides the boat plan and my home-brew crock," Don said with a knowing wink.

It was almost 11 o'clock and Don's parents were already in their second floor bedroom as the boys climbed quickly but quietly to the attic dormer.

"Phew! That brew of yours is getting awfully strong. Is it going to be drinkable this time or are we going to use it to kill weeds again?" Al joked.

Ignoring his friend, Don went to his closet and produced a pair of very powerful German made binoculars, which both boys had made use of in their teen years to spy on certain young ladies that lived in similar houses on their street. They had never actually caught much bare flesh through the lenses as it seemed that the girls in question either pulled a roller curtain down or were just out of view at the critical moment of exposure. Nevertheless, the boys had never given up hope and they remembered the drill now.

Being sure his own light was not showing, Don focused on the rather bright light from across the street. Soon handing the binoculars to Al, he said,

"It's a girl and she's looking into something like a box that glows kind of bluish. I can't figure what it is, can you?"

"No, but now she's typing on a kind of flat typewriter that seems attached to the lighted box. Then she waits a few seconds and types some more. I haven't got a clue what she's up to. The light's kind of weird; makes her look funny ,- - I mean, odd, you know," Al replied.

"Wonder who she is and how she moved in without someone in the neighborhood noticing? She looks about our age or maybe a bit older. What do you think, Al?"

"I'd say older unless she's got a lot of makeup on. Hey, the light's getting dimmer and it looks like she's going to go to bed or something. Mmm, oh crud, she ducked out of sight," Al complained.

"Let me see," Don demanded and Al handed him the binoculars.

"Yeah, they always turn out the lights before we see any skin. The box is still glowing though, just dimmer, so I can't make out much, but I think she popped into bed," Don mused.

"I need to hit the sack too. We're scheduled for a half day tomorrow, so I'll check out your plans after work, okay. I'll let myself out real quiet like, so your folks don't wake up. See you on the 7:30 trolley," Al said as he made for the door.

"Yeah, good. If I can wake up early enough, I'll check out our new girlfriend and report any progress when I see you," Don replied.

"Progress? That's a funny way of describing 'peeping tom' antics!" Al said, with his hand on the knob.

"Well, for the record, let's just say it's investigating a strange phenomena, okay?" Don replied, as Al took his leave.

CHAPTER TWO: SEPT. 13, 1928

Jill jolted awake, suddenly aware of bright sun streaming through her dormer window. "I must have forgotten to lower my blind," was her first thought. But there was no blind, just a common old style roller curtain loosely attached to the upper window edge. Its tattered look made its operation quite doubtful. Her computer glowed faithfully; in fact, the web page of old newspaper articles that she had been scanning was still open. She hesitantly crawled from the warm covers and immediately found herself shivering as she reached over to shut down the computer. The room felt frigid. Had dad turned the thermostat down for some reason? She knew he hated how much the ancient house consumed in utilities, but this was ridiculous. A glance at her watch told her she had slept a full eight hours, but her body felt like it had been much longer. She knew a trip to the bathroom would certainly help. Going to the closet, she pulled on a flannel robe and headed down to the second level bathroom next to her parents bedroom. The stairs creaked and felt oddly different as she started to descend. What had happened? The stairs had no carpet! Slightly marred varnish was their only covering.

"I'm cracking up. I'm cold, I've got to pee and I feel crappy. Maybe I've got the flu or something," she complained aloud, now running down the stairs and into the open bathroom. "Whoa! What happened in here?" Jill came to a sudden stop as she surveyed the foreign sight.

The new tile her father had lovingly installed was gone as were the new fixtures. Back in place, it seemed, were the pedestal sink and the archaic toilet with the water box mounted high above the stool, its pull chain dangling. The floor tiles were small white hexagons with thin black edges. The jetted tub was missing. In its place was the rust stained, claw footed monster she remembered her grandmother bathing her in as a very young child. She collapsed to the floor, gripping the stool, nausea and confusion overcoming her. After a half hour of crying she washed up with cold water, dried on her robe and, shivering, climbed back in bed and tried to encompass herself in sleep. Even the blackness of the bed clothes could not shut out an awareness of her changed circumstances. Finally, hunger and curiosity overcame enough of her fear that she emerged. She dressed warmly in slacks and a sweater before taking a first, hesitant peek from her window.

Antique cars were parked irregularly along the block, seeming to match the old row houses somehow. "It looks like a movie set," she thought, "And I seem to be a part of it." Once more she descended the stairs, slowly taking in the emptiness of the place. It was a nice old house, rather worn, but it was not the home of her parents. It was very much the home of her grandparents, at least as much of it as she could remember. Only it was almost empty; all but her bedroom and even that had changed since she had gone to sleep, just a few hours ago.

"Am I stark raving mad? Have I lost all my marbles? Is somebody playing a terrible, cruel joke on me? Am I in some kind of time warp? Oh, God help me, please!" she cried. It was the first plea she had made to God since she was a child and she had prayed for her little dog Charley to live after being hit by a car. Charley had recovered, with the help of an expensive veterinary doctor and lived until just two years ago. Would God help her now? Somehow, she felt she couldn't drum up the faith that she had as a child. She collapsed into the single kitchen chair, laying her head on the wooden table. She cried for a time before hunger temporarily overcame grief and confusion. Arising, she was not really surprised to find the modern appliances replaced by a true ice-box, rather than a refrigerator, a wood range in place of electric and an under sink cabinet where once resided a dish washer. Of course, the ice-box was empty. She headed for the door, beginning to think more of food than her ridiculous circumstances. The door key didn't fit!

"What else is new," she thought. "Oh well, there's sure not much to steal is there? Except my computer. My only connection to reality. Oh, God, please protect it!"

******

Don and Al were making fast work of the three block walk home from their trolley car stop on Sixth Avenue. The Saturday morning had gone quickly as they finished the copper bottom painting of a fifty foot tug boat on which they had been working Friday. As they neared home, Don looked ahead and said, "Isn't that the girl from across the street that we saw last night?"

"You probably saw more of her than I did! I went home, remember," Al said flippantly.

"Yeah, wise guy, but I didn't really see anything that you

didn't and this morning she must have still been asleep when I got up, because I didn't see any life over there then," Don shot back.

"Okay, okay! She's heading our way, so maybe we can get acquainted. What do you think?" Al asked.

"I think that we'll probably scare her off unless we act like gentlemen. I'll go first," Don replied.

Before Al could answer, Jill had closed the distance and yelled to them, "Hey, you guys, is there a place near that a girl can get something to eat?"

"Wow, she's a brave one, eh?" Al muttered under his breath. "A real flapper; look at her short hair and she's wearing pants!"

As they drew near enough for normal conversation, Don said, "Hello, I'm Don Grant and this is Al Nelson, we live right over there," pointing to their respective houses across the street.

"Hi, I'm Jill. How about directions to a restaurant or fast food place?"

"Uh, I don't about fast food, but most of the restaurants are down town. The Sixth Avenue trolley goes right by a couple of them. Say, are you our new neighbor? I saw a light in the old Gardiner place last night. Hadn't heard that anybody had moved in, though."

"Yeah, well, I guess I'm new. It's my grandparent's---oh, never mind. I need to get some lunch, really starving and nothing in the fridge--uh, ice box this morning," Jill stammered.

"Well, I'm sure my mom has more than enough to go around for lunch, if you'd like to join us," Don said smoothly, as Al winced at his friend's forwardness.

"No kidding? I mean you don't even know me. I really don't think I should impose," Jill said rather hesitantly.

"No better way to get acquainted, neighbor. Mom will be glad to have another lady to converse with. Dad works Saturdays and I'm the only kid left at home and I work some on Saturdays too. Come right in. It'll be just fine."

As fast a worker as ever Al thought, but he only said, "I'll catch up later. I'm sure mom's got lunch ready and I promised pop to get some wood cut today. Very nice to meet you Jill and welcome to J Street!"

"Yeah, thanks, Al. See ya," Jill said, trying to remember her manners.

"Guess the paper got here late this morning," Don remarked as he scooped up the newspaper and opened the front door with a wide flourish. "Come on in."

Jill sucked in her breath and almost lost her balance as she glanced at the date of the paper in Don's hand. September 13, 1928--it couldn't be true, but it was!

As his mother appeared, Don started to introduce Jill. "Mother this is Jill--Uh, from across the street. Jill this is my mother, Mrs. Grant. Say, --- are you all right?"

"You look faint child. Here, come into the kitchen and sit down. May I get you a glass of water?" June Grant was taking over as only a mother could.

"I'm sorry--I feel really funny. I'm sorry. I don't know what's wrong with me!" Jill blurted out as she fell into the chair proffered by a baffled Don.

"My dear, I don't hold with spirits much, but I have a prescription for some medicinal brandy, this being Prohibition and all, and I believe you might just need a wee drop. Donald, get Miss Jill a jigger of your father's brandy."

Mrs. Grant was a tall, thin lady with the pale complexion of her native Scotland. After her first husband had died in the war, leaving her with two boys at home she became a nurse in an English Army hospital. There she met the ruddy complexioned, but handsome American soldier who, after his recuperation, swept her and her boys off to the United States. The wet climate and greenery of Tacoma was much like her native country, which she appreciated. Their neighbors were a mixture of Scandinavians, a few fellow Britons and second generation Germans. Her kind nature made all who met her feel welcome, as did Jill, who relaxed after sipping down the potent jigger of "medicinal" brandy.

"You are looking some better, my dear. Would you care to take some tea and scones with us now? I make the raspberry jam myself, you know. The berries are the best the Puyallup Valley can grow. I assure you my boys find it most tasty," she coaxed, soothingly.

Don took Jill's hand, gallantly leading her to the small formal dining room and being sure her chair was firmly set under her. "Mom's right, Jill. Her scones are super!"

"I'm sorry to be such a bother," Jill stammered. "I'm going through some difficult changes in my life just now. You're both very kind, thank you very much."

"Tell us about yourself, my dear. Are you moving into that big place alone? It's been empty some time now. I'm sure there are many things that my Don or his friend Allen might be able to help you set straight. They are very handy, you see. Boat builders, they want to be and those that build boats can do about everything that needs to be done, I'm certain." Mrs. Grant busied herself with pouring the tea and passing the scones, jam and heavy cream.

"Well, I expect my parents will be along soon---or as soon as they come back from---Uh, traveling. They're traveling abroad just now. Dad's retired," she tried to explain, lying not coming too naturally to her--yet. "Mmm, these are good!" being truthful now and feeling much better as she finished her third scone and second cup of aromatic tea. "Thank you again."

"Say Jill, since your ice-box is still empty and the ice man doesn't deliver until Monday, maybe you'd like to have some dinner down town with me tonight and take in a movie after? There's one of the new 'talkies' playing, Broadway Melody with Bessie Love. It has singing and dancing as well as comedy. Might make you feel better! What do you say?" Don was bubbling over.

"I thought you and Allen had planned the evening together?" Mrs. Grant leaned in close, nudging her son meaningfully.

"Well, yeah, sure. Safer that way, huh, Jill? A lady as pretty as you undoubtedly could use two guy friends to fend off the lugs, right?"

"Donald, mind your manners," his mother scolded, but playfully.

"I can take care of myself, ma'am, but, sure, that sounds nice, Don. If it's okay with Al," Jill said in her most demure manner. She had just realized that if this was truly 1928, her credit cards, debit card and even her modern dated cash would not buy her sustenance! What downer this was going to be until she could get her hands on some current money. Until then---

"Al, oh, wow, he'll be grateful to have somebody besides me to talk to. He isn't much of a ladies man, you see, maybe too nice a guy or something. But he's smart and he has big plans for us, him and me, I mean. We're going to be boat builders. I'm the designer and he's the money man, the guy who has the business plan. You'll like him, but remember, I saw you first!"

"Donald, you are embarrassing both Miss Jill and me. Behave yourself!"

"It's okay, Mrs. Grant. I know he's just kidding. I can hold my own with the guys. Actually, I think they are both much nicer than others I've known."

"I'm sorry, Jill. I get carried away sometimes." Don took her hand gently and said, "I'm your friend, new, but still your friend and I promise to be a gentleman. I would never want to disappoint my mother, or you," he affirmed.

"Thank you, that's sweet," Jill said, giving his hand a small squeeze and thinking, maybe, just maybe, 1928 was going to turn out all right. Maybe, that is, if she was really back in 1928 and, if so, that she was stuck here.

Dinner was actually just clam chowder at a small cafe near the waterfront that dished out large portions of plain, but tasty local cuisine to dock and mill workers at bargain prices. The gilt and glamour of the Pantages Theater made up for the lack of sophistication of Broadway Melody. Jill had changed into a skirt, blouse and jacket and felt that she fit in well with the movie goers around her. Though she had never heard of Bessie Love, Jill overheard comments that Bessie was sure to be nominated for best actress. Afterwards, at Don's suggestion, the threesome hiked the three blocks to the Olympic behind Rhodes Brothers department store for a double scoop cone each. Jill couldn't remember tasting such rich ice cream in her life.

Later as they swung off the trolley for the three block walk home, Jill announced, "Thank you for a great evening, guys. I feel much better now. I couldn't have gotten through this day without you."

"Great! Then how about coming for Sunday dinner at my place?" Don asked. "Mom always puts on a good spread when we have company."

"Thanks, Don. I really appreciate the offer, but I don't want to be a pest."

Before Don could protest, Al chimed in, "Good! Then you can come to my house, meet my family and I'll get to have something special. My mom loves to show off her Swedish heritage to guests and dad is always has a good story for new friends. Does three o'clock sound good for you?"

Thinking again of her empty ice-box and lack of current money, it wasn't a difficult choice. "I'd be happy to accept if you'll let me exchange the invitation. Once I get established, I mean," she agreed.

"Sounds fair. Anything that Don and I can do to help you get established, as you put it? Got enough firewood or coal? We've got plenty of wood scraps that we salvage from the boatyard," Al added.

"And we could loan you a bag of coal until you get a delivery. I know there is a bit of cord wood left in your back yard, but with the nights getting colder, banking the furnace with coal will hold the fire until morning," Don suggested.

As they mounted the steps to her front porch, Jill began to feel a little wary as to how to conclude the evening. Gathering nerve she said, "I'd invite you in, but I actually only have one chair and a kitchen table, so---. And, I don't know when I can pay you back for your hospitality. It may take me a while to find a job because I don't know anybody here but you guys."

"Hey, we've got connections!" Don burst out. "First thing Monday we'll get some introductions arranged. What kind of work do you want?"

"We do know a lot of people, Jill. Don and I met some pretty well placed Alumni when we were playing football for Stadium. I was quarterback and he was our prime receiver, so we caught a lot of attention--along with most of the passes," Al laughed, depreciatingly at his own joke.

A couple of jocks, but still nice guys, Jill thought. Never happen in my time! Aloud, she said, "I'm impressed! Well, let's see: I can type over 60 words per minute, I'm good on the phone, I'm really fast on a 10 key--Uh--adding machine, I mean. I'm able to deal with people well, so I guess a receptionist or office clerk situation would fit me."

"Well, we know the bosses at Cox Machinery and Atlas Foundry, but I'll bet a girl like you might do best at Brown and Haley Candy. Cliff Haley is a close friend of ours and his dad owns half the place. What do you think, Don?"

CHAPTER THREE

Jill awoke late Sunday morning in a much calmer frame of mind than she thought possible. The sunny skies of yesterday had given way to high clouds, but it seemed warmer somehow. Nevertheless, she dressed in her heaviest sweater and jeans in preparation for trying to start a fire in the basement furnace. As promised, Don had already left a bag of coal and another of wood scraps on the back porch. She dragged them downstairs one at a time then went to the wood shed in the backyard for an armload of larger cord wood. In her previous life Jill's parents had been avid campers and stream fishermen. Thus, Jill had little trouble in getting a fire started in the old furnace. However, it took a bit of figuring on how to set the bottom draft and the chimney damper to keep the initial fire building and not smoking. By the time she had brought a few more armloads of cordwood downstairs, added a bit of coal and slowed the intake draft it was past one o'clock. As she glanced out her bedroom window she noticed several families returning from church services.

While setting out a change of clothes, she thought aloud, "I need a real bath before I go to dinner with Al's family. I can't go looking and smelling like this! I hope I can stand the cold water long enough to get clean."

To her surprise and relief, the water began to run warm from the tap of the old claw foot tub. She wasn't aware that the furnace had coils that heated the water quickly when the fire was set. Pouring in some bubble bath she had found in her clothes drawer she reveled in the luxury of the huge bathtub. An hour later the water had cooled and she found herself, once again, drying on her terry cloth robe.

"Got to buy some towels and a whole bunch of other stuff as soon as possible. No use camping out if I'm stuck here," she thought aloud again as she tried on clothes to see what might adapt best to the late twenties era.

Al's mother had prepared Swedish meatballs, sweet potatoes laced with brown sugar, green beans flavored with bacon and onions, a tart apple pie and coffee strong enough to peel one's skin. Jill was stuffed and still Mrs. Nelson was insisting that she have another piece of pie.

"Yah, you need to keep your strength up dear, thin little thing that you are," the stocky woman implored.

"Momma, I think she's just right. Let her relax a bit," Mr. Nelson chided his wife. "Leave a bit of room for some of my cherry wine a little later. We make it from our own trees. Royal Anne, they are. Sweetest you'll ever taste and good for you, regardless of what those old Abolitionists try to tell us. Right, Al?"

"Yeah, dad, but you don't want to broadcast that we make alcohol here. There's too many snitches around these days. We don't need G-men knocking down our doors," Al said, half joking.

"What we do in our own home is no business of the government, Al. No damn business at all!" Mr. Nelson fairly exploded.

"Arnie Nelson! We have a lady present. Watch your language, please", Mrs. Nelson scolded.

"Sorry Mamma. Sorry Miss Jill. Just gets my goat that we have to tip toe around about what we drink because of some goody two-shoes teetotalers that don't know their ---Oh, forget it. Sorry," Mr. Nelson sputtered.

"Not a problem, Mr. Nelson. My dad says worse things about the bureaucracy than that! I'm originally from Olympia, so I've heard plenty about politicians. And please, just call me Jill. Gardiner is my last name, but I prefer Jill."

"Well Jill, Al tells me that you are looking for a job. That so?"

"Yes, sir. I'm going to start looking tomorrow. I hear business is going well in Tacoma, so I hope to land something quickly," Jill answered.

"I'm sure you will, young lady. I think you got what it takes. Now, are you ready for a sip of my latest crop of fermented cherries or are you going to be one of those teetotalers that we were discussing?" the older man challenged.

"I turned 21 last year and took the occasion to celebrate with champagne that some friends brought to my party. I found that a little goes a long way, but a little is probably just right, thank you," Jill said forthrightly.

"Mom is still cleaning up, so I'll do the honors Dad. You and Jill sit tight," Al admonished, as he headed down to the cellar.

The phone rang briefly from the back of the house. Mrs. Nelson came in and said, "Jill, you have a call. The phone is on the wall by the back door."

Startled, Jill could not conceive who might be calling her in a strange house in a different time. She walked tentatively to the back hall and quivering inside, picked up the dangling receiver and said, "Hello?"

A tinny, but familiar voice answered, "Hi Jill, Don Grant here. It's all set. You have an interview at nine tomorrow with Mr. Haley at the candy factory. Do you know where it is?"

"I think so. Isn't it down on 25th Street by the overpass?"

"It's on 25th Street where it's always been, but there's no overpass there," Don answered. "You can take the trolley down town and then transfer to the Pacific Avenue line and walk from Pacific. It's only a few blocks"

Jill was mortified at her mistake; the overpass hadn't been built until a freeway spur to downtown had been added in the 1990s. But she did know where Brown and Haley was. She had loved their Almond Roca and Turtles candies since she was old enough to chew. "How did you arrange the interview already?" was all she could think to say.

"Nothing to it when you're famous!" Don expounded. "Kidding aside, Jill, they need somebody sharp like you. When I told Cliff how fast you could type, he couldn't believe his luck! You're a shoe-in kid, a sure thing. Thirty-five cents an hour and all the candy you can eat. What a swell setup. But don't forget to bring some sweet stuff home for your pal here, okay?"

Thirty-five cents an hour. How would she survive? A crazy thought entered her head: She would have to live on candy! "Thanks, Don. You've been a great help. I won't forget. Bye."

Later, after Al had seen her back to her door, a totally unnecessary, but gallant gesture, she thought, she stoked up the furnace and headed up to her garret bedroom. With no television or radio, she booted up her computer to see, if by some mysterious chance she might get some tunes from the internet.

"This is crazy. Internet won't be around for over 60 years. I need to be thinking of how I'm going to be eating without selling my body," she muttered to herself. "But it was still on this morning. I must have some connection to the future. Maybe, I can e-mail somebody to come rescue me."

More craziness, she knew, her mind cluttered with the absurdity of the situation. As the computer came to life, she let her mind drift to a movie she had seen a long time ago. The late Christopher Reeves in "Somewhere in Time". He had wished himself back to another era, falling in love with a woman he had seen in a picture. Then he had found a coin from his own time and lost his love as he returned to the present. She stopped short and reached for her purse. Yes, there were a few coins and several bills that she had gotten from an ATM machine at the mall Friday. She poured them out, and sat looking at them wondering if concentrating on one of them might return her to 2001

"Wow a quarter minted in 1918! That's a rare coin." She examined another coin, a 1926 penny. Unfolding the currency she was dumbfounded to find they all were produced previous to 1928! She had taken out $300 and only spent $25 for a skirt and blouse on sale at Penny's. Disappointed as she was about the early dates, she knew $275 might go a lot farther in her present era. But it wouldn't be enough for what she had in mind.

CHAPTER FOUR

Don had kept an eye out the window Sunday evening and after seeing Al say goodnight to Jill he stepped out on the porch and yelled to him, "Looks like you're through entertaining. Come on over and look at the boat plans."

They excused themselves from Don's parents who were listening to their favorite Sunday night dramas in front of a huge Philco radio and climbed up to Don's room. The whole floor was covered with large scale drawings. Don was an excellent draftsman and Al could see at once that this was a very imaginative project.

"How do you like the 'W' bottom shape? See how it protects the prop and shaft in shallow water yet should allow good speed in rough conditions," Don said.

"I agree, but it won't be easy to build ribs to that shape. Do you think it will have enough lift to plane or will it mostly displace the water?" Al asked.

"Both! At low speed it will cut through easily with minimum disturbance and with enough power it will lift well enough to plane. See the shallow shaft angle? The engine will be very far forward, allowing lots of cargo area aft. The cargo and large, bilge mounted fuel tanks will keep the hull attitude quite flat. That and the forward mounted cabin and windshield should give good visibility, which will be really important running at night or in lousy conditions." Don stated.

"You're pretty sure of yourself for such a radical design," Al argued.

"Look at this," Don beamed as he produced a model boat. "I've tried this in a fast running stream out at Point Defiance. It's weighted to resemble a typical load of, say 75 to 100 cases, 200 gallons of fuel and 2500 pounds of engine. It's going to work!"

"Wait," thought Al, doing some figuring in his head. "That's about $2000 worth of cargo, $40 in fuel, but several thousands of dollars for engine and running gear. You're talking more money than we're ever going to come up with, pal," Al stated frankly.

"We'll figure something out. There're still some of those Sterling engines from the war that are cheap and make enough horsepower. As for the cargo, there're plenty of guys willing to front the money for that. Since Olmstead and all his boats are out of the picture the demand exceeds supply and the profits could be 100%."

"The Coast Guard has some boats that will make almost 20 knots now and a few faster small boats they've confiscated from runners they've caught. What kind of speed do you think this boat could make if it had to make a getaway run with a full load?" Al asked.

"With the right prop and a good Sterling, 25 to 30. With a lighter engine like a Scripps maybe 35, or with the best, a Duesenberg, probably over 40. Ray Moore, over at Tacoma Avenue Garage, claims the Duesenberg brothers have a supercharged, mostly alloy, eight cylinder, overhead cam engine that will outperform anything in the country. Says he has a connection to get one and could fit a marine manifold and gear box to it for about $3000. That would include an underwater exhaust cut-out for silent running," Don explained.

"Gee, how many other people know we're going to try and build a rum runner, Don? We could get in trouble before we actually sell the boat!"

"Relax, Al. Ray would be building this himself if he didn't have a wife and three girls to worry about. He'll do it for almost no profit just to know he could build something better than anybody else. He's a perfectionist. You should see what he's done to his V-12 Packard. Just the sound of it will scare the pants off anybody trying to race him! He's our guy if we can dig up the loot," Don proclaimed. "Start thinking, partner; this could put us on the map."

Cautiously, Al examined Don's drafts. Finding no flaw and a great deal that appealed to him, he finally said, "The more I study your plan the more I like it. In fact, I can't wait to get started, because if we can find the money to build this baby, while the market is hot, it's sure to sell. Of course, if it wasn't going to be used for rum running, it would be a boat very few people could afford to own or run."

CHAPTER FIVE

As soon as her computer booted up, Jill returned to the Google site she had been researching Friday night. It seemed like an eternity ago. Had it really been only two days? In fact was anything real? Maybe this was just a long, weird dream caused from reading all the computer files about the "Roaring Twenties" era she, admittedly, had been enthralled with since hearing tales from her grandparents. They had lived in this very house from 1931 until they died. Her parents had inherited the place and had been pouring money into it for almost 15 years. It had been her home until she went to college in Olympia three years ago.

"I'm supposed to be starting my final year next week," she thought aloud. "Instead of interning at Merrill Lynch I'll probably be answering phones and licking stamps for Brown and Haley. At 35 cents an hour. Ouch!" She laughed despite herself at the incongruity of her situation then focused on a newspaper headline from October 1929 coming up on the screen. As she scanned the coverage of the stock market crash, a feeling of hope, rather than despair, crept into her mind. If the stock market went down, it had to have gone up previously. If there were losers, there must have been winners. All she had to do was find the data for 1928 and 1929, put everything she could dig up on the winners and get out at the high! In the present market, a person could buy stock with only 10% margin, leveraging a small investment greatly if a stock was continuing to gain. If her computer could access the old stock quotes, she could make a nice little nest egg because stocks were set to rise 40% before the crash next year. She worked until her eyes no longer could focus, printing out copious notes, all the while scheming how she could implement her plan.

After only five hours sleep, Jill hit the street running, making good connections on the trolley rides. She stopped only long enough to buy a pastry from a corner cafe on 25th and Pacific and ate as she walked the remaining blocks to the candy factory. The aroma of warm chocolate and roasted nuts assailed her olfactory senses from a block away. The storefront and offices were as she remembered them as a child, but brighter without the shadow of the overpass that would obscure the light some 60 years in the future. She had dressed as sharply as she thought prudent, her skirt perhaps only a bit immodest, determined to make the very best first impression possible. Jill hoped that she could use her looks as well as her skill to command a salary better than the 35 cents per hour that Don thought might be the going rate. Fortunately, she was interviewed by the senior Mr. Haley, who fancied himself the best judge of new talent, particularly nice looking young women. After an initial appraisal, he passed her off to his personal secretary for a test of typing speed and dictation accuracy. Jill could actually type 90 words per minute on a computer, but knew the old mechanical typewriter couldn't respond that fast. She went for absolute accuracy, realizing that one couldn't delete and retype errors. Her shorthand was less accurate, but her exceptional memory allowed her to fill in what she might have missed otherwise. After a reasonable wait for her assessment to reach the owner; she was rewarded a position in the pecking order just below his personal secretary. She would be working 50 hours per week at 40 cents per hour. "Twenty dollars a week isn't going to help much in cornering the stock market. There has to be a way to take advantage of the insider knowledge I have," she thought as she boarded the trolley for home that evening. Deep in thought she almost forgot to get off the trolley at 11th Street where she walked up a block to shop at the Market Street grocery. For just over four dollars she bought enough food and staples to last two weeks; so much that she could hardly manage to board the 6th Avenue trolley carrying a cardboard box with another sack heaped on top.

  "Looks like we'll be riding the same trolley home at night," Al Nelson called as she struggled up the steps. He came forward and took the box from her as she gave the conductor the fare.

  "My lucky day all the way around," Jill said giving him a dazzling smile.

  "Did you get the job, then?" Al asked as they sat down together.

  "Sure did, thanks to you and Don. And now you get to help me carry the groceries home too-- - if you want to, I mean," she stammered, realizing how forward that might sound to a person like Al.

  "I'll be more than happy to Jill. In fact I have something to bring over to you as well. We got a coal delivery early this morning and I got an extra 100 pound sack to keep you going until you get a paycheck. Don is bringing home another bag of wood scraps later tonight to start your furnace or use in the kitchen stove."

  "You guys are really spoiling me, but thank you! Does Don

work a later shift than you at the boatyard?" she asked.

"No, he's talking to a man about renting a shed near where we work now, a place where we can build a boat on our own. A very special design that Don thinks will sell for a good profit," he replied..

"That sounds really exciting. When are you going to start?"

"Just as soon as we can come up with cash for the materials. It won't take much to start the hull but we'll have to find somebody to front us the money for the mechanical stuff and fittings. Those are really costly, you know."

"Looks like we're in the same boat; pardon the pun. I've got some real good information on stocks that could make a lot of money, but only a small amount to invest and at $20 a week salary, not much prospects to put in much more," Jill said.

"Isn't that risky? I know a lot of people are making a ton in the market this year, but it's got to back down sometime, doesn't it?" Al said, his brow wrinkling.

"Let's talk about it tonight over dinner at my house, okay? Maybe we can help each other with our projects. It'll just be hamburgers but I owe you and Don at least that much. Do you think he can come over too?" she asked.

"Try and hold him back! Sorry, but Don is the competitive type to say the least and I think he's quite enamored of you, Jill. He'll be there. What time?"

"Give me an hour or so to get some heat going and change, okay?"

"Sounds terrific! Here's our stop. You take the bag and I'll get the box." Glancing up at the lowering sky, he urged, "Looks like we better hustle. I think it's going to start raining again."

Just as the old school clock on the living room wall chimed seven, Don and Al knocked at the door. Jill hustled out from the kitchen and found Don with a burlap bag of wood in tow and Al with a bag of coal dragging from one hand and a dish in the other.

"Wow, look at you guys! Thank you for the fuel. What's in the pan?"

"Mom's fresh apple pie, just out of the oven. She always bakes two, so she sent this one with us, knowing you're a working girl now," Al answered brightly.

"Smells good in here. So you can cook too, huh?" Don quipped as they entered the kitchen, now cozy from the fire in the wood range.

"I can manage. Nothing fancy, just the plain American standby with a German name: Hamburgers. I forgot to order ice, so I needed to use up the whole package, so I hope you guys are hungry," Jill said. Pointing to the rickety chairs around the table, she said, "Lucky I found some more chairs out in the shed or we'd be eating on the floor, but be careful or you might! Go ahead and dig in."

The boys had no problem in consuming three hamburgers each and half the pie, all the while questioning Jill on the experiences of the day. Don congratulated her on getting a better salary than he thought she might, but warned her to watch out for "Roman" hands and "Russian" fingers of the male help in the company.

"Mind your manners, Don. Jill is a lady and they'll treat her as such," Al said protectively.

"No offense taken, Don. Like I said before, I can take care of myself and I can put the brakes on if anybody gets out of line," Jill said with feeling. "I'm a black belt in Karate. I've won some tough matches, even against some men."

"Karate? What's that?" Don asked, somewhat bewildered.

"A form of martial arts," Jill replied less forcefully, knowing she had forgotten who she was, or at least where she was in time. "Eastern stuff. Not too well known around here I guess. Enough about me. Tell me more about your boat building project. Al says you've dreamed up a unique design, Don. Our family has always had some kind of boat kicking around. What kind of rig are you thinking of building?" she asked, trying to move the conversation away from herself.

"We're not just thinking, we're going to build it and soon. This evening I arranged to rent a building to work in." Seeing Al eyeing him, Don waved him off, saying, "This is news to you too, Al, but it's only $10 a month and we can start gathering materials right away now. It's just a block from work, which will be handy until we can go at it full time."

"Sounds reasonable. Tell me about your boat Don," Jill urged once more.

"It's a 30 foot, high speed, utility hull that will be able to operate in shallow water. The unique feature is the 'W' shape of the bottom which allows the prop and shaft protection from obstacles. It will also cut through the waves easily. It'll take more power than a flat or semi-vee bottom to plane, but the ride will be far more stable in choppy conditions. It has a large carrying capacity aft with the cabin far forward for better visibility. With a light weight, high output engine, I expect it might be capable of over 40 knots," Don explained.

"That's faster than most boats these days, isn't it" Jill asked.

"Most, I guess," Al said, wishing Don wouldn't be so explicit in details. "You were going to talk about your ideas on the stock market," he suggested, trying to steer the conversation away from the proposed boat plan.

"Fellows, I have to be very frank. We barely know each other yet, but I know the times we are living in. I think all three of us want to take advantage of the current boom in certain commodities, right?" she asked openly.

"Who doesn't?" Don asked. "But what does one thing have to do with another? We want to build a special boat. You want to play the market. Where's the common denominator?"

"Do we want to go there, Don?" Al inquired, feeling uncomfortable sharing his dreams of ill gotten wealth with someone that he wished would have a good opinion of him.

"I do," Jill said simply. "From the reading I've been doing lately it sounds like you're going to build a boat that can carry whiskey down from Canada. Something faster and more elusive than is now available. You need money to build it, right?"

They looked at each other, then both nodded and she went on. "I have some special information about the stock market. I need money to manipulate it for profit before it loses its value, which may be in the not too distant future. We have similar goals, maybe lacking in ethics, maybe even illegal. I'm willing to take some risks to make a better future. I think you are too. I'm sure Don is."

Sensing his discomfort, she turned to Al, "How about you? Please don't be bashful. I intend to be your confidant as well as your friend. You both are very special to me already. You both have ambition, brains and compassion. If I seem forward to you, it's because I've been raised differently. I don't want to be the boss, but I do want to rise above what we have now."

"What do you say to someone with so much passion for life, Al?" Don whispered hoarsely to his friend. "I say, let's go for it!"

Al wanted to say, "I love you Jill, you untamed tiger!" Instead he simply muttered, "All for one and one for all."

They clasped hands and immediately started brainstorming the plan that would alter their lives completely, for better or worse.

CHAPTER SIX

A week later the trio had put together a cache of $2000, an amazing amount, considering their position in life at the time. Ray Moore, proprietor of the Tacoma Avenue Garage, and a very willing accomplice for any scheme that he thought might grease his palms with greenbacks rather than real grease, had ponied up $500. He had been promised a 25% return and an eventual order for a Duesenberg racing engine to work his magic on. Coworkers of Don and Al's at the Foss Tug and Barge repair shop kicked in $400 on the promise of a 25% return by the first of the year. Jill easily talked Cliff Haley, her boss's playboy son, to pitch in $600, which was more than she thought possible. The boy's parents came up with the balance. Working at her computer Jill compiled reams of notes of stock transactions from 1928 and 1929 and immediately plunged into trading with vigor. She knew that Radio Corporation of America was headed straight up as was Standard Oil of New Jersey. Electric Bond and Share had been climbing steadily and would continue to do so for some time. General Motors was kicking Ford's butt with the Chevrolet, Cadillac and new Pontiac divisions. Jill knew that would change when the upgraded 1929 Model A Fords came out and planned to take every bit of advantage that her foreknowledge would give her. She shamelessly charmed a young broker at the local branch of J. P. Morgan, and, though she was a new client, he saw, in the first few weeks that she was picking only winners and allowed her to invest on margin. She soon had leveraged the original $2250, which included her own $250, into over $15,000 in stocks. She planned to sell just enough to pay back the outside investors then buy as much more as possible during the pullback that would occur in early January. Ray Moore wanted to let his $500 ride since it quickly increased by more than the promised 25%. Impressed by Jill's ability to make his investment grow and the two young men's enthusiasm to build their uniquely designed boat, Ray asked to join them as a partner. At their weekly Friday evening business meeting a few days before Christmas, Don asked Al and Jill to consider Ray in their future plans.

"Ray could bring a lot of experience to the table and maybe some more capital as a partner," Don suggested.

"He's more of a self taught mechanical engineer than a garage owner. He's also a guy who seems to take a lot of chances. I wouldn't be surprised if he was using that souped-up Packard of his to tote some whisky for local bootleggers. Kicking in that $500 didn't seem to faze him," Al mused.

"Fellows, I think we should take a long look at the risks involved in bringing anyone else into our confidence. Our stock market gains are probably not going to attract much attention. Lots of others are doing well too. The bubble will burst at some point and we will have already taken our winnings before it does. I think we won't be noticed much then; just chalked up to good luck and good timing by those that know us. But building and selling the rum-runner could make us stand out if more than the few that put it together are involved," Jill cautioned.

"The thing is kids, I think that Ray is a guy who could make the connection we need to sell the boat for a large profit," Don argued.

"You have a point there and he is already involved in supplying the engine and marine conversion if everything goes right," Al agreed.

"Why don't you let me check him out first before we bring him in further? About how old do you think he is? He lives on J Street too, doesn't he?" Jill asked, thinking of what a computer biography search might turn up.

"Are you going to add detective work to your other occupations as stock trader, secretary and financial adviser to up and coming boat builders?" Don joked.

"Maybe I am. Maybe there's a lot more to me than meets the eye Mr. Smarty pants Grant," she teased.

Don looked at Al knowingly, nodded, and said, "Yes, I'm sure there is. For instance, what is it that you do so late at night? Regardless of how late I go to bed myself, I see a bright, odd looking light coming from your window."

"Oh, do you spy on unsuspecting young women's windows at night, you naughty boy?" Jill asked, trying to act unconcerned that she might be observed using an instrument that came from over 60 years in the future.

Flustered but still very curious, Don replied, "Not since I was 15, but Al and I have both wondered why the light from your window looks so different and if you sleep with it on or something. Not prying, we're just curious."

The thought of Don watching Jill at night brought a pang of

jealousy to Al. He squirmed in his chair. Although he was just as curious about what sort of machine that Jill had in her room, he wished Don would just drop the stupid inquiry.

But he didn't. "You've never showed us the rest of your house. You've seen my room. How about a grand tour to see where you study out your next move to conquer the financial world?" Don persisted.

"A lady doesn't take gentlemen to her boudoir, unless she's not a lady, of course. Right, Al?" Jill parried, almost sure that Al would come to her rescue.

"Absolutely, my lady! Forget it Don, as long as Jill turns out the kind of positive results that she already has, I'm in her corner," Al rejoined. His brain was saying silently, "I want to be in your corner always Jill. Maybe someday you'll see me as more than a partner." Then he blushed deeply as he caught Jill staring at him as if she had overheard his thoughts.

They finally agreed that Jill would check out Ray in an undetermined way and report her findings in a couple of days. She also let them expect a hiccup in their stock holdings in a couple of weeks.

"Don't worry fellows. I'll have us covered and we'll be out of debt to our fellow workers real soon, I promise. See you on the trolley in the morning. I'm going in early to get some extra filing done before the phones start ringing, so I think we better call it a night, okay?"

As the two friends drifted over to Don's house to go over the latest rendition of their boat plan, Don asked, "How does she do that stuff? She hasn't missed on one stock! Do you think she's physic or something?"

"I think she might be," Al said, adding, "but I hope she's not."

"Because, she could read your thoughts, right? You love sick pup!"

"Does it show that much?" Al asked, more than a little embarrassed.

"I guess so! Hey, she's a great looking bird. And she's smart, real smart. Smart enough to keep me on my toes and out of her hair. I think she only likes me because I'm your friend, and, of course, I bring her lots of scrap firewood!" he said laughing. "Yes, she can read you like a book, Al. And she enjoys every moment of it. The older woman playing with her young lover."

"She's only 22! That's not old, ---and I'm not her lover,

anymore than you are. Although I bet you wish you were. She's our partner, our neighbor and our friend. We should keep it at that, right?" Al sputtered.

"Right, Al. I don't have a problem with that. In fact, Jill set me up with a gal from the candy factory for tomorrow night. Says if I treat her right, I'll probably get an invitation to the company Christmas party next week. Might be a good place to make some other kind of connections; you never know." Seeing Al looking nervous, he added," That leaves it wide open for Jill to invite you as her date. It's going to work out nicely, Al. Don't fret"

They mounted the stairs to Don's room and began going over what they hoped were the final draftings before the boat could be laid out in full dimension. An hour later as Al started to leave, he saw Don looking over at Jill's window.

"Let's not start that again, shall we?" he said sharply.

"Hey, cool it! Jill always has her window shade down. I'm not trying to peek at her fine body. I'm just darn curious as to what she's doing." Don retorted.

Jill worked later than ever that night. She began by doing a search for a Ray Moore, who Don thought might be in his late forties and lived less than two blocks from them. The only item she found that seemed to match was an article from the Tacoma News Tribune in October, 1951. It stated that Ray Moore, chief millwright for Puget Sound Plywood was killed while, presumably , cleaning a gun at his home. He was survived by a woman described as his foster sister. The Tacoma Police Dept. was looking into the circumstances because Mr. Moore was known to be an excellent marksman who cared for his weapons carefully. She found nothing further in later newspapers.

"Very odd indeed," Jill thought aloud, as was becoming her habit when engaged with the computer. "No mention of his wife and daughters, apparently no follow up investigation and he was living with another woman. Our Ray seems to be a man of many facets. At least he doesn't seem to have any criminal record, so maybe we're all right bringing him in, at least as a silent partner."

It then occurred to her that it might be wise to check for criminal records of Donald Grant and Allen Nelson, born about 1908 or 1909. But if she found something negative, what could she do to prevent it? Could events already recorded be changed? What about herself? How did she fit into history? She was becoming part of others lives. That meant she most likely was altering the futures they otherwise would have built.

"I'm going in circles, just like everybody else that's tried to get a handle on time. It's too scary to consider looking into the boys' future or my own," she decided, speaking only to the computer.

With that decision made, Jill went back to gleaning every last bit of information she could find about the next few months in the stock market. After that she studied tales of the rum running trade, paying particular attention to those runners that were caught, where they were caught and how their capture was made by the authorities. The biggest bust to date was of Roy Olmstead, billed as "The King of King County Bootleggers," in 1924. The fact that he and his associates were arrested three times in just over a month, in entirely different locations, led Jill to believe he was ratted out by an informer that was very close to the operation. Sure enough, digging further, she found that Al Hubbard, who had been with Olmstead from the start, had cut a deal to lessen his own sentence. Olmstead's empire of large and small vessels, trucks and warehouses had been seized. Only his radio station, the first in Seattle, remained intact. However, the liquor suppliers in Vancouver and Victoria, B.C. were very much still in business. The restaurants of Seattle, Tacoma, Olympia, Portland, Oregon and hundreds of speakeasy joints in between were dependent on the rumrunners to supply their thirsty patrons. Prohibition had actually increased sales for brands such as Cutty Sark and others. Jill could see by her study of history, that rum running and bootlegging could be much more profitable than playing the stock market. Prohibition would probably assure the profitability of the illegal liquor trade into 1933, whereas the stock market would crash in less than a year.

"We need to stockpile enough money to weather the depression with some degree of comfort. Wow, I'm thinking 'we' now!" she laughed to herself. "The Three Musketeers of 1928. I wonder how they'd feel if they knew I wanted them to keep the boat when it's built and go into the distribution of adult beverages? And will Al go along if Don says okay?"

CHAPTER SEVEN

Christmas 1928 was the turning point in several ways for the future of Don, Al, Jill and their new partner, Ray. At the Brown and Haley Christmas party, the date that Jill had set Don up with turned out to be Goldie Moore, the youngest of Ray's daughters. They were getting acquainted on the improvised dance floor, almost needing to yell above the ragtime tunes from a quartet of young men.

"How do you happen to know my dad, Don? Does he work on your car for you? Or do you get your booze from him?" Goldie asked playfully.

"He's going to supply a special engine for a boat that my friend Al and I are going to build soon. I didn't know he was a ---. Well, anyway, I brew my own stuff at home. Kind of nasty junk really, or I would have offered you some. That is if you were old enough to drink," he kidded back.

"I'm old enough for whatever I want to do, big guy! And if you get tired of your nasty home brew, my dad usually has a bottle or two of good stuff available for his friends," Goldie replied saucily.

"Does he have a lot of thirsty friends?" Don asked, fishing a bit.

"More than he can supply, I think. Tell me about your boat and your friend. Is he the one dancing with Jill?"

"Yeah, that's Al Nelson. We work together at Foss Tug, but what we really want to do is build boats, especially the one that I've designed. It's going to be one of the fastest of it's type around," Don answered.

"Is my dad going to build you a Packard V-12 like in his car? It's the quickest car in Tacoma. He used to build engines for the Tacoma Speedway racers until they shut down the track a few years ago," Goldie informed him.

"That's why we went to him, but our boat engine is going to be a modified Duesenberg, about twice the power of his Packard, he says."

"I bet I know what kind of boat you want to build," Goldie guessed.

""What do you mean?"

"Something fast enough to outrun the Coast Guard, right?" she asked.

"Maybe. Say, why don't we take a break and get some food?

People are starting to get in line now. Let's beat the mad rush, okay?" Don said, steering his date toward a long table laden with sliced ham, several cheeses, all manner of condiments and every kind of candy that Brown and Haley manufactured. Two punchbowls, marked "His" and "Hers" were being attacked by thirsty guests, but the one marked "His" seemed to be draining fastest.

Al and Jill saw the other pair converging on the food and managed to move in just behind them. They took a few items and all moved away together.

"You two getting along okay?" Jill asked her friends.

"Don's a great dancer, Jill. Only stepped on my toes three times so far," Goldie giggled all the while giving Jill's partner the look over.

"I did not!" Don replied laughing. "It was only twice!"

"Sorry, Goldie, didn't know what I was letting you in for. Want to take a break and switch partners? Al dances so slow that he can't make a mistake," Jill offered. "But he does squeeze up close when he gets a chance, so watch him."

"Sounds like fun to me," Goldie quipped. "Are you ready for a good time fella?" she asked, rolling her eyes at Al.

He looked at Jill pleadingly, but surrendered as Goldie led him off to the dance floor as the quartet struck up a slower, more soothing number.

"Jill, I need to talk to you about her," Don started. "She talks..."

"While we're dancing," Jill cut him off. They joined several other couples and she continued, "I know. She talks way too much and she's a terrible flirt, but I thought you liked your dates lively."

"It's what she's talking about that worries me. As for dates, I'm now dancing with the only one that I want to be with," Don said seriously.

The party wound down about midnight. Don had borrowed his parent's Model T Ford, bringing Al and Jill along, while Goldie had been dropped off by her father. As Don opened the passenger side doors, Goldie drew Al into the back seat with her, surprising Don, who had finished the last dance with her. Jill slid into the front without a word. Don headed up to Pacific Ave, happy that the old car started without having to be cranked and, happier still, that Jill was close by his side rather than in back with Al.

As he started up Stadium Way, Goldie chimed in brashly,

"Oh, we're taking the scenic route are we? What do you have in mind for us big man?"

"Not what you expect, I think. It is a great view of the harbor from here, but these early Model T's can't climb up a street as steep as 11th without running out of gas or backing up the hill. So, rather than look foolish, I take the more gradual route and we all get home without problems," Don explained.

"Why would the car run out of gas on a steep hill?" Jill asked suspiciously.

"Because the gas tank is under the seat and feeds the carburetor by gravity. Only the last three years had the tank up on the cowl. This is a 1920 model, only the second year with electric starting as standard. The folks really need a newer car, but they've got all their money tied up in the market and our boat building deal."

"Well, I'll see to it that they have enough to get a new car in a couple of years when the prices go down," Jill said firmly.

"How do you know that prices are going down?" Goldie piped up. "All I see is higher prices every month."

"Uh, --I study economics in my spare time. Just an educated guess," Jill replied carefully.

"Is that how you've been doing so well in the market?" Goldie asked.

"That, really good luck and help from that nice stock broker fellow she's been cozying up to," Al joined in, perhaps saying more than he intended.

"Which one is your house?" Don broke in, trying to change the subject.

"Thanks," Jill muttered just loud enough for Don to hear over the engine.

"Second one from the corner on the right," Goldie answered.

Since Goldie seemed to have switched dates, Al was obliged to be the one to see her to the door. "Want to come in for awhile?" she asked, seductively.

"Better not,--tonight that is. Maybe another time when we start out together, okay?" Al suggested.

"Call me," Goldie said, giving him a firm kiss on the cheek before opening the door and sliding slowly inside while Al stared transfixed at her golden hair.

"Looks like strike three for your buddy. She acts like a silent movie queen, don't you think, Don?" Jill said.

"She's pretty forward for a girl her age. Yeah, maybe she watches too many flicks, but what worries me is how she talks about her dad being a bootlegger. Loose lips can cause trouble where we don't need it," Don replied.

"I think her lips were pretty firm on our friend's cheek just now. And you haven't done anything illegal to worry about." Yet, Jill thought to herself.

Al opened the car door and said, "We're only a couple of blocks from home. I'll hoof it and see you guys tomorrow. Good party, Jill."

Don took the cue, pushed in the low pedal allowing the old Ford to wheeze its way, somewhat quietly, the short distance home. As they climbed the stairs to Jill's front porch he asked, "Are you sorry how the evening turned out, the switch, I mean?"

She squeezed his hand, turned her face up to him inviting the inevitable. Don didn't need any further encouragement. He dropped his lips to hers and they kissed long and deeply. Saying not a word, she smiled, turned and disappeared through the door. Don's knees shook as he descended to the sidewalk.

"I'm in love with the most wonderful girl in the world," he sang to the star filled Christmas night.

CHAPTER EIGHT: JANUARY, 1929

Though the weather was plain lousy, even by January standards, raining steadily with wind blowing small whitecaps in the waterway near the boat building shed, inside, the steam box had all hands sweating. Long planks were being softened by steam to yield to the form of the framework of the "Ghost" as she was already being called. With the keel, transom and frames completed and the garboard planks fitted, the Ghost was beginning to look like a real boat, albeit upside down.

Ray Moore was effusive as he admired the skill of his young partners and Erik Nelson, a cousin of Al's, not too long removed from his native Sweden. "Boys, it's hard to believe what you've accomplished in just three weeks. You may have it all planked before I finish the engine!"

"With Erik's help it's going faster than we expected. Erik getting laid off from the school district cabinetry shop might have been bad luck for him, but it sure is helping us," Al replied as he firmly pressed the Yankee screwdriver down driving the fasteners through the planks into the frame.

"Yah, it's more fun building boats than fixing schoolhouses, you betcha," the wiry little Swede admitted. "Dose darn kids up dere at Stadium 'bout drove me nuts!"

"It was worth selling the Packard to get you guys started," Ray assured them. "I'll miss that baby, but I made good money on her and young Tommy Carstens is sure to break something on her the way he sports around. He'll be back to spend more money to keep her the quickest car in Tacoma."

Tom Carstens was the son of the city's largest meat processor, a member of the Tacoma Country Club and quite a ladies' man, tall, heavily built and with a penchant for all things expensive, beautiful or fast. He knew Ray had previously built engines for cars racing at the old Tacoma board speedway and had come to him for advice on gleaning more from his Stutz Bearcat. Moore had convinced him, over a few drinks of excellent Scotch, that the Packard had much more potential than the outdated Stutz. The rest was now history. Carstens had parked the Stutz, paid an outrageous sum for the modified Packard and gone his way with a new connection for his country club friend's whiskey appetite. Ray had plowed the money into the young men's boat project, prompting them to plunge into a full time building schedule. In the back of his mind he had big plans for 'The Ghost' and her builders.

"Our friend Jill Gardiner thinks that we'll have enough earned in the market to buy the engine by March. How long will it take you to get the engine ready after that?" Don asked as he began pulling another plank from the steam box.

"It's already on its way! I had a bit of extra money come my way from some of my other endeavors, which allowed me to buy the engine before we thought possible," Ray replied. "I'll have it ready when you turn the boat over to build the deck and cabin. While you're doing that, I'll install the running gear, wiring and controls. We'll be in the water and ready for sea trials the day after the paint dries!"

"I'm thinking we'll be painting her by May then, but if the weather doesn't get better the paint may never dry," Al complained.

"Five months? I thought it would take us at least a year to finish her! Of course, we still need a buyer after that, so money may be tight for awhile," Don reminded them, trying to be realistic about their finances.

"Leave that to me, boys," Ray said confidently. "It's all going to come together much faster than you think."

"The sooner the better," Al said thoughtfully. "Jill is certain that Prohibition won't last more than three more years and this won't make much of a fishing boat."

After Ray had left, Don asked, "Where do you think Ray is coming up with all the money Al? And how is he going to find a buyer as quick as he says?"

"I pretty sure, from what Goldie lets out, that he's already doing some bootlegging and that means he's got some connections to somebody already in the business," Al answered.

"You and Goldie are getting close then?" Don asked.

"I don't know if anyone gets real close to Goldie. Yeah, we've gone to a couple of movies and she's had me over to her folks place, but she's seeing other guys too. In fact, I think she's the one that brought Tommy Carstens to her dad's shop. She may seem to talk a lot, but she keeps quiet about her own affairs."

"What about our boat. She knows what it's being built for. Is she blabbing that around?" Don queried.

"No, she hasn't said a word about booze or boats since the Christmas party. Maybe her dad told her to shut up about private matters," Al mused.

"More likely that Jill warned her off. They work at the same place, but their friendship seems a bit distant the last few weeks. Jill can be quite outspoken when she wants to make a point, you know," Don said.

"She can also be real private as well. You've gotten to know her better. Has she confided anymore about what she does at night to out smart the stock market?"

"Not a word. Sometimes I feel she wants to say more, then she clams up. She's affectionate and she knows I'm crazy about her, but she holds back anything about her personal life. I hope you aren't put out with me for falling for her. I know that you ---"

"Forget it partner. She's your girl now. I gave it a try and she picked you, simple as that. She's told me that she cares a lot for both of us, but it's you that she seems most attracted to and I'm glad for you," Al finished.

"Hey, you two. Quit jawing around and get me anuder plank over here, Yah?" Erik yelled good-naturedly. "Dis bottom got more twists than a licorice stick, so be sure dat plank is good and soft, so I can bend her into place, Yah?"

"You betcha, Erik!" Don exclaimed. "You'll appreciate this funny bottom shape when she's slicing through the water on a day like today."

"Hey, I yust build her. I had all da boat ride I ever want coming over from da ole country. Tank you all da same," Erik called back.

CHAPTER NINE

Chief McGaw spit out the stub of his cigar and swore for the thirteenth time as he once again swung the crank of the old Mac crane truck. This time the big T-Head engine caught and began to bellow and shake, black smoke billowing from its open exhaust before McGaw could adjust the choke to lean out the fuel mixture. As the engine settled into a staccato bark, he mounted the open cab and released the long brake lever on the outside with his powerful left hand. McGaw was a small man with a wiry build and the temperament of a bulldog. A teamster all his life, he faced each day and task as a personal, never ending challenge; a tough little man battling with huge horses in his early days and now with raw, unsophisticated machinery in his middle years. Everybody called him chief, not because of his heritage, but because of his perennial role as head of a volunteer fire department in University Place, a growing suburb of Tacoma.

"What a way to spend my day off," he growled to himself as he eased the heavy vehicle toward the pale gray 30 foot boat that he was about to pick up and deposit in the equally gray waters of Foss waterway. Inside, he was grateful to be paying back a favor to an old friend and his son who had designed and help build this unusual craft. It was good to not be beholden to the man who had helped him overcome depression when his first wife had died so early in their marriage. Ralph Grant had even introduced him to Ruby, who was the most precious thing in his life now. Year by year Ruby was softening him, making him more approachable. Whether that was such a good thing, McGaw wasn't sure, but Ruby thought so.

"Get those slings under her and take care get the balance right!" he yelled at Don and Al. "I don't want to have to drop this thing before it gets wet the first time," he growled.

"Tough old bird, eh?" Al muttered to Don as they struggled to guide the lifting straps into place.

"Yeah, but he's got a heart of gold. He saved a child from burning in a fire last year and almost lost his life doing it. Dad says he's the most solid man he knows," Don replied quietly.

"He's solid all right. I wouldn't want to be on his bad side," Al agreed.

"Okay, Chief! Take her up slow and we'll see if we guessed right on balance," Don said.

McGaw set the hand throttle up a bit and engaged the winch drum on the crane. The Ghost came off its wheeled dolly evenly and was soon swinging over the edge of the dock. The tide was high and the wind light, although the overcast sky promised that would soon change. As McGaw began letting the winch line pay out, lowering the boat, Al and Don jumped down to the float, each with a mooring line in hand. As the Ghost touched water for the first time and settled into a somewhat bow heavy stance, Don breathed a sigh of relief. She rode as he had planned, knowing, that with cargo loaded, the attitude would be correct.

"Looks a little bow heavy," McGaw growled as the young men loosed the slings and made the mooring lines fast. "That big engine up there must weigh more than you figured."

"All is well, Chief! The gas tanks are only partly full and when it planes out the bow will come up okay," Don assured him.

"If you say so. Want me to hang around to see if she stays afloat?" he offered.

"I'll check the shaft and rudder boxes for leaks. Just be a minute," Al answered.

"We test ran her yesterday on a water hose and ran water in the bilges to test for hull leaks, so she should be fine as long as the stuffing boxes are adjusted correctly on the rudder and prop shafts," Don explained. "Unless you want to stay around for the christening. Our friend Jill is coming down with a bottle of non-champagne to do the honors and our folks are going to take some pictures of our first effort."

"No thanks. Ruby's waiting on me to help with decorating the fire hall for the May Day dance tonight," McGaw replied. He liked boats, but only if there was fishing involved and this craft certainly did not resemble a fishing boat to him.

"All okay Chief! Thanks a million for helping us out on such short notice. We didn't think we'd be ready this early in the spring; she just couldn't wait to hit the water," Al said brightly.

"Good luck boys," McGaw said as he stuck another cigar in his teeth and remounted the crane truck.

As the old Mac bellowed out of sight towards the motor freight yard on the next waterway, Al asked, "Does he ever light those cigars?"

"Not as long as I've known him which is almost all my life," Don replied. "Here come our folks and Jill. Let's get her cranked up and get some cabin heat going for them. It looks like the weather is deteriorating pretty fast."

They could see a front dropping rain as it moved across Commencement Bay toward them from the Olympic Mountains to the west. Their families arrived just before the squall hit. The Nelsons and Grants watched as Jill smashed the traditional bottle against the bow, announcing, "I christen thee 'The Ghost' and say be fruitful and multiply our fortunes!"

"Phew! Donald, what was in that bottle?" Mrs. Grant asked her son.

The last of the home brew, Mom. No more stinking up your attic with that awful stuff. Aren't you happy now?" Don joked.

"We're all happy Don," his father assured him. "Now, are we going for a boat ride or sit here and let the rain soak us?"

It was only a mild shower, but in short order, all were aboard and Al was casting off the mooring lines as Don eased away from the dock and turned towards Commencement Bay. The wind freshened as they cleared the shelter of the harbor buildings and a small chop came up. With seven people in the cabin the bow was even lower causing the hull to splash spray and buck a little.

"Hang on, I'm going to give her a little gas and get the bow up a little," Don advised. The big straight eight took throttle smoothly and the ride improved.

"My, this is nice Donald. I've never been in a boat with a heater," his mother exclaimed as the heat exchanger blower began to warm the cabin.

"Yes, Mrs. Grant, and it has forced air vents to de-fog the windshields and electric wipers as well. Better than a lot of cars, isn't it?" Al said.

"A lot better than our Model T for certain," Mr. Grant agreed.

"Our Studebaker has a heater, but no defroster and the wipers are vacuum operated so every time you start up a hill they give up and stall," Mr. Nelson added.

"Will we be going by Pt. Defiance Don?" Jill asked. "I've haven't seen it from the water before," she lied. She was curious to see if the old Fort Nisqually had been moved to the park by May of 1929.

"Sure, we're going to go right by there on the way to Gig

Harbor for lunch at the Tides," he replied.

"Wow!" Jill thought, "The Tides Tavern started this long ago?" The Tides had been a favorite watering hole for locals, boaters and college kids since her folks were in school, but she couldn't believe it had existed this long.

"I'm going to speed up to get her to plane out now folks, so you'd better sit down and hold on while Al and I make sure if everything is working at speed," Don advised.

Don pulled the cut-out release to allow the spent exhaust to flow freely through the transom rather than under the water for silent running at slower speed. The exhaust began to bellow as he increased throttle. The bellow was soon joined by the scream of the supercharger as its impeller rammed the fuel mixture into the big Duesenberg. The hull shuddered a little as it began to break free from the water. The bow rose and then settled as the single step hydroplane bottom lifted the whole boat several inches.

"My goodness," Mrs. Nelson shouted to Mrs. Grant. "I feel like we're flying, but the noise is frightful!"

"How fast are we going, son?" Mr. Grant asked.

"Knot meter shows 28. That's almost 32 miles per hour," Don replied.

"We're going to have to insulate the motor box better Don, or the noise level will deter anybody but a deaf person from buying her," Al warned "I'm going to check the stuffing boxes again, so hold her steady as you can, okay?"

"Right on both counts, partner. I didn't figure on the high pitch of the supercharger being so intrusive," Don replied.

"Are we wide open?" Jill asked, forgetting about Fort Nisqually entirely as they rounded Pt. Defiance and headed across the Narrows.

"Nowhere near, Jill. We only ran her for an hour on the hose yesterday, so we need to let the rings seat in before we hold her open for an extended period. On the way back we'll give her a couple of minutes at full throttle just to see if we have any problems. Are you impressed so far?" he asked, begging for her approval.

"Very, my Captain. You are a genius," she gushed quite honestly.

Within a few minutes Don throttled back and they crept through the narrow opening to Gig Harbor leaving no wake and with the exhaust once again muffled underwater. "Al, I'll swing her in to the fuel dock on the port side and you can make her fast, okay? Dad will you and Mr. Nelson get the fenders set to protect our fresh paint before Al tightens down the lines?"

The men quickly had the boat secured and everyone started up the gangplank except Al who had re-boarded and was now head down, peeking under the floor boards. "I'll be up as soon as I check the stuffing boxes and engine for leaks," was his muffled explanation.

As Jill reached the main dock she noticed that, though the Tides building was somewhat as she remembered it from a later time, the entrance now faced a ferry slip where later would reside the Stutz fuel dock. The dock that they were tied to was 40 yards or so to the west and large enough to service several of the fishing fleet at once. She also saw that the preponderance of boats moored in the harbor were commercial fishing rigs and sailboats rather than the cruisers that she was accustomed to seeing on her trips over the Narrows Bridge. Of course, even the ill fated and short lived first bridge was not to be completed until 1940. All visitors to Gig Harbor in 1929 came by ferry or a primitive road from distant Shelton. As they walked up to the Tides they almost ran into Ray Moore, who immediately extended his hand to Don who looked somewhat startled and confused.

"Hello, Don. Good to see you Jill. Looks like your shake down cruise was successful. Are these your parents?"

"I should have told you that Ray was going to meet us here Don," Jill said smoothly. "Yes, Ray. This is Mr. and Mrs. Nelson and these are Don's parents. Folks, this is Ray Moore, our silent partner in this boat project."

Everyone shook hands and made a bit of small talk as they crossed the ferry terminal to the Tides. It wasn't exactly the Tides Tavern that Jill remembered, but the smell of clam chowder, frying fish and chips was still familiar and welcoming.

The group ordered their lunch and enough for Al, who was taking his time inspecting the boat for potential problems. As they took a long table in the steamy restaurant, Ray explained that he had come over on the early ferry to take care of some business and had told Jill that he would meet them for lunch and take a look at the boat's engine if they had any problems or questions with its workings.

Al arrived just as the food was served, looked questioningly at Ray, who nodded pleasantly, and took his place. The conversation lagged for a time as everyone's appetite seemed piqued by their outing on the salt water. When the last plate was empty, Ray remarked, "Looks like it's blowing up a bit out there now, doesn't it. The ride back won't be as comfortable, but it will certainly give you a chance to see how she handles rough whether. By the way, I told the dock attendant to top up both tanks so you can see how extra weight might affect your speed." Al looked up sharply, realizing that they didn't have the cash to pay for the large amount of fuel required for a fill up. "Don't worry boys, the lunch and the gasoline are on me! I made a nice piece of change from my business here this morning, but I expect a free ride home, of course," Ray laughed.

As the group left the Tides, the ferry was just coming into the slip, its decks wet with salt spray. As the trucks and cars labored up the steep ramp to Harborview Drive, Mrs. Nelson remarked, "The cars in front are soaked with spray. Do you think we ought to wait until it calms down to leave, Al?"

"It does look like we're in for a rough trip back mom, but I'm sure the boat is up to it. We'll just take our time, okay?"

"You know folks," Ray started, "It might be more pleasant if you took the ferry back and the boys and I will come along in the boat. You can use my Packard that's parked at Pt. Defiance to get back to your cars down at the waterway and just leave the key under the floor mat for me."

"I thought you sold your Packard to Tommy Carstens, Ray," Don said.

"Yes, that's right. The one I'm using is a senior sedan model that I'm modifying for a friend of his from the Country Club. A very nice car to be seen in, I might add," Ray answered.

"Sounds like a good idea to me. What do you say Ralph?" Mr. Nelson asked Don's father.

"Yes, I'm sure the ladies will be more comfortable and feel safer on the ferry. Thank you for your offer, Mr. Moore," Mr. Grant replied.

"Please, just call me Ray and you're most welcome," Ray said handing Al's father the car keys. "Nice to have met all of you. You have talented sons. I'm very fond of them and pleased to help in their business efforts."

"If you don't mind fellows, I'd like to go back with you. I've got an investment in the boat too and I'd like to see how she handles her first challenge," Jill said. Her tone made it clear that she expected to be included in whatever adventure might be in store for them.

When Ray paid the dock attendant, Don asked, "How much did she take, Ray? I want to monitor the fuel consumption to know what range she will have with full tanks."

"110 gallons, $22.00 worth. How much does she hold with both tanks full?" Ray asked.

"An even 200 gallons. I'm hoping that will give her 10 hours running time at average throttle settings. What do you think?" Don wondered.

"I think it might do a little better than that. We'll have to see how hard you have to push her to stay on plane with a load. And speaking of that, my business here included bringing 50 cases of canned fish to Walt and Mabel's bistro over on Hylebos waterway. My clients are waiting for us up at the head of the harbor on their trawler. They've just come in from Alaska with fresh product and found it more convenient for us to deliver the goods for them than to take their big boat all the way into Hylebos. It will give us a good chance to evaluate the boat and it paid for our lunch and fuel as well," Ray asserted.

"A paying job on her first day out! Not bad, fellows. Ray, you certainly know a variety of people, don't you. From the Country Club crowd to the fish docks, who would have thought of it?" Jill said, smiling, but prying just a little.

Ray smiled back, saying, "You meet all kinds in my business and if you treat them well they'll usually refer you to others and the business burgeons as people find that you serve them well and honestly."

Al took his turn at the wheel, maneuvering the Ghost carefully up to the Black Duck, an 80 foot trawler that looked tough enough to have weathered the trip from Alaska to Gig Harbor without worry. Her jet black hull was topped with a low pale gray cabin that almost matched the Ghost's vague color. As Al nudged up to her massive rope bumpers he could just see a 50mm cannon peeking from a canvas cover on her bow.

"What's with the big gun up there Ray," he asked, pointing to the foredeck.

"I believe they use that to fire a harpoon if they have a chance at a whale," Ray said. "Native Alaskans are quite fond of whale meat, I hear."

Al and Don exchanged concerned glances. This was an odd situation that only might get more odd as the day wore on. Two heavy set, bearded men made the Ghost's mooring lines fast, but greeted the group silently and suspiciously until Ray introduced them as his business partners. They each then grunted an assent and began handing down tall cases marked simply 'King Salmon'. They worked quickly despite the weight of the unusual cases, easily keeping all three on the Ghost hustling to keep up. In less than a quarter hour the aft deck of the Ghost was half covered with the wooden cases and a tarp provided by the Black Duck crew was secured over the cargo. With only a curt salute, the two bearded men disappeared into their cabin and the Ghost set off for Tacoma several inches lower in the water.

Huddling in front of the welcome heater in the cabin, Don addressed Ray, "Those guys looked more like pirates than fishermen Ray. Who are they?"

"Nicholas and Marco Makovich, Slovakians by heritage. They don't say much because their English isn't too good and because they're used to being alone for long periods of time when they are at sea. But their money is always good and they don't cheat their customers with bad quality stuff," he replied casually.

"You say 'always' like you deal with them regularly. Do they come back from Alaska often?" Al asked, taking his eyes from the wheel for a moment.

"Let's just say that sometimes they only get as far as Canada before they get their limit, okay?" Ray answered.

"That salmon back there is really whiskey, isn't it Ray? You need to level with the guys, so they know the score, partner," Jill said firmly. "I was sure that's why you wanted to meet us here, but I think they were a bit more trusting."

"Are we carrying whiskey, Ray? And in broad daylight to boot!" Al yelled. "This is nuts! I just wanted to build this thing for someone else to take the chances, not to spend time on McNeil Island like Olmstead and his cronies!"

"Jeez, Ray," Don moaned, "Why didn't you tell us what you were doing? If you absolutely needed to make this delivery we would have done it at night to help pay back what we owe you, but we don't know anything about bootlegging except how to build a boat to haul the stuff."

"And a fine job you've done so far, fellows. Think of it like this: what better cover for our first operation than a family outing on the new boat? Who would think that you would be picking up a few cases of Canada's finest along the way, and, like you say, in broad daylight? It seemed a good opportunity to break you into the business and a new boat would be more safely shaken down in the daylight, don't you agree?" Ray said soothingly.

"Well, we're about to be shaken, all right," Al said as they passed the harbor lighthouse and entered the sound. "The wind's come up from the north and it's putting some rough seas between us and Hylebos Waterway. Guess we'll see how good your design is Don."

"Go for it, partner. I want this over as soon as possible. Try her at 1200 RPM. That should give us 15 knots or so," Don replied.

Al eased the throttle forward, the bow came up and the Ghost surged forward, splaying the waves to the sides with ease.

"A little hard to see with the bow so high," Al said shortly. "Shall we try to plane? She's not pounding badly at 15 knots."

"Are you all right, Jill? The jouncing isn't bothering you yet?" Don asked, concerned for her comfort.

"No problem, give her the gun, Al!" Jill said, feeling exhilarated.

Al brought the Ghost onto plane, the knot meter reading 20 or almost 23 miles per hour. The ride actually felt better as they flew over the top of the chop.

"You don't have to baby her boys. I built this engine loose enough to run at full speed from the get go. Just watch the water and oil temperature gauges. The only thing I'm not entirely certain of is whether the fresh water heat exchanger is large enough to cool properly at maximum RPM. I want to see what she'll do with full tanks, a decent load and bucking some weather, don't you?" Ray asked.

As mad as he was for having been taken in so easily, Al restrained himself from slamming the throttle forward, instead gradually bringing the boat to full speed. In the smoother water of the outbound leg the boat had merely felt fast, now, in the two foot chop at an indicated 37 knots it was literally flying. Don watched the gauges carefully while Al steered at an angle to the direction of the seas to avoid nosing into the occasional rogue roller.

"Are you sure we're okay running the engine this hard?" Don asked Ray.

"As long as the oil temperature stays below 200 degrees and the water temperature no higher than 180, she'll be just fine. Although I think the propeller is slipping or cavitating a bit. I'd like to limit the

RPM to 3800 and it might edge over that now. Maybe you can pull her out on a ways or grid somewhere tomorrow and I'll put some cup into the wheel for a better bite."

"What in the world are you talking about?" Jill asked.

"It may be possible to make the propeller work more efficiently if he changes the outer edge, the part that really grips the water and screws it away from the boat. It's called cupping because the blades are formed in somewhat of a cup shape," Don explained. "If it works, we could pick up another couple of miles and hour. We're doing over 42 now in statute miles."

"She's every bit what you thought she'd be Don," Al said, "but we've got to cut down the noise level. We'll be across the bay in less than 15 minutes at this rate, but the scream of the blower would drive me nuts if we ran at this speed any longer."

"I can work on that tomorrow while you're pulling the wheel off and taking it to Ray's garage," Don agreed.

"That's fine with me," Al said. Glancing at Ray, he added, "Because we need to spend some time talking about what we're getting into Ray. This stunt you've got us involved in today is not what we bargained for."

"This stunt, as you call it, is just a hint of the potential for using this boat for what it was built. Selling it would bring a one time profit. Using it can be an ongoing business venture with a payoff much larger than a tank of fuel and a good meal. I welcome the chance to show you a real business plan and what it could mean to your future," Ray responded.

"Besides jail time, you mean?" Don said sarcastically.

They ran on without speaking until they approached the Hylebos Waterway . Al throttled back, switched the exhaust to exit underwater in silent mode and asked, "Where are we supposed to unload this stuff?"

"The dock just beyond the bridge at 11th Street on the right side of the waterway," Ray replied. "I'll go up and get Walt to bring along a couple of helpers to unload."

"We're going to unload while it's still daylight?" Don asked incredulously.

"Relax, it's just a load of salmon as far as anybody else is concerned. The boys in blue are scarce down here on weekends and most of them enjoy a 'King Salmon' anyway. Walt has friends uptown as well as down here on the tide flats," Ray assured.

Jill, who had been unusually quiet for some time, piped up, "You mean the fix is in, right Ray?"

"Jill, you are just as sharp as I thought you might be. Boys, this girl is a keeper; she knows her way around!"

Jill winced at his remark, knowing that she knew way more than she was supposed to and probably enough to have put the young men close to her now into a situation that could change their lives in a frightening way.

CHAPTER TEN

The Ghost was once again moored at her home dock and Ray had driven off in his customer's Packard which the boys' parents had returned. As Don and Al were checking for leaks, Jill decided to openly ask her young partners to evaluate their situation.

"Look, fellows, Ray is right about the money. We need to take advantage of the times. Easy money in the stock market is going to be short lived. Prohibition will come and go as well. If you want to set yourselves up for the rest of your lives, now is the time to act." Taking their silence as a cue, she rushed on with her explanation. "Ray has some contacts now and we can develop more shortly. If we go directly to the suppliers in Vancouver and Victoria and sell directly to the retailers in Tacoma, Seattle and Olympia, we could maximize the profit on every transaction. This boat is phenomenal! Why don't we put it to use instead of selling it and letting someone else reap the benefits of your hard work?"

"You've been leaning this way all the time haven't you, Jill?" Al asked, deeply disturbed. "Aren't you aware of how many dangers there are to be considered?"

"Yeah," Don agreed, "It's not just the cops and Treasury guys to avoid. There could be some bad characters waiting to waylay us and grab the cargo in any number of places along the way plus having to run at night in unpredictable weather. The rewards might be good, but the risks are huge!"

"Jeez, I thought I was dealing with a couple of real men up to now. You guys sound like old ladies," Jill said, with mock disdain, watching closely for their reaction.

"Hey! That's not fair, Jill. We just got caught unaware by Ray not leveling with us today. We would have hauled the stuff for him, like Don said before, but I wish he would have been up front about it," Al exclaimed.

"Whoever told you life was fair, Al? That's a puny excuse. The winners in life are the ones who grab the bull by the horns and twist!" she retorted, her face reddening.

"Calm down, both of you. We're partners, we're friends and I want us to stay that way," Don urged. "Let's see what Ray has in mind tomorrow and weigh our options after that. Meantime, let's pull off the engine box so I can take it up to the shop to build some noise suppression into it." Turning to Al, he asked, "Would you go up and phone around to see where we can get the boat on a grid on the morning high tide to pull off the prop?"

"I want to help too guys! But first can we kiss and make up, 'cuz I'm sorry that I blew off like that?" Needing their approval and not waiting for an answer, Jill grabbed them, hugged them tight and planted a firm kiss right on their lips, each in turn.

"Jill, you are shameless!" Al declared, grinning.

"You think so?" she bantered coyly.

Al and Don looked at each other and said in unison, "We know so!"

Al took off to phone. Don broke out a toolbox and soon he and Jill were struggling up the gangplank with the heavy motor box.

"Maybe we should have waited for Al to come back from calling boatyards," she panted as they finally reached the shop building and were able to set the box down.

By the time Al returned, Don was cutting the last of the insulation blocks for the motor box and Jill had already glued and stapled several blocks to its underside.

"Any luck on finding a grid open?" Don asked.

"Yes and no," Al replied. "Nothing around here, but we can get on at Cummings place on Day Island and he even has a permanent mooring spot if we want it. Three bucks for using the grid and six bucks a month for the dock space."

"A bit out of the way, but if we decide to become crooks it might be the best place to operate from, cheap enough too," Don said thoughtfully.

"Do you really think of us as crooks?" Jill asked.

"How would you describe smugglers and bootleggers, Jill? I mean, realistically," Don replied.

"Entrepreneurs would be my description," Jill said.

"How about businessmen who see a need and hope to fill it profitably," Al joked, but without too much vigor.

"Less crooks than some politicians I've seen in Olympia," Jill said.

"Okay, not really crooks, better than politicians, entrepreneurs it would be, filling the need of the thirsty," Don agreed, with more enthusiasm.

"If we had held out a bottle of today's cargo, we could toast our new entrepreneurship," Jill laughed.

"Not I! If we're going to be in the liquor distribution business,

I'm going on the wagon for the duration," Don declared.

"No sense in wasting the profits," Al agreed, "If we do become whiskey runners, I would take the pledge as well. How about you, thou older and wiser matron?"

"A penny saved is a penny earned, they say. I'm agreeable to all except the matron term. I am a 22 year old, single woman, not an old married matron!" she retorted.

"What's wrong with marriage?" Al asked pointedly.

"Nothing at all when the timing is right. That and finding the right man, one who you really care about and who'll stick by you forever. I've seen too many marriages where neither of those criteria seemed to exist."

"I think we all want the kind of relationship you describe, Jill. And I hope that's what we all end up with. Meantime, shall we refit this motor box to the Ghost and head for Day Island?" Don suggested.

"Through the Narrows in the dark?" Jill asked.

"That's what we built her to do, silly!" Al replied. "Don and I made lots of night trips in the little tender we built last year. It was a much smaller, open boat with an unreliable two cycle outboard strapped to its transom, but we always reached our destination," Al declared.

"Yeah, although usually very late and with hair raising tales to tell. But he's right. The Ghost was built to run at night in tough circumstances. It'll be a good test tonight with the wind still up, tide running strong and black as pitch. I'm sure you'll get the picture of what a typical night of rum running might be like. Unless you'd rather we walk you up to the streetcar, of course. That would be the sensible thing for a girl to do," Don said salaciously.

"Bring it on bad boys!" she retorted.

Twenty minutes later the Ghost rounded Pt. Defiance and began beating into a nasty chop, the wind coming from the north and a strong outgoing tide piling the waves against it from the south. Don slowed some to allow the bow to rise, but spray still drenched the cabin.

"Your fancy windshield wipers can't keep up with the spray gentlemen," Jill noted, bracing herself with the grab bars affixed to the cabin side and the dashboard.

"Can't see a darn thing anyway, so it doesn't make much difference," Don replied.

"Maybe we could add some spray rails to the forward gunwale

to keep it down in conditions like this," Al said.

"That would work, but if we added them in the sheer area it might help even more, especially in a following sea at speed where the bow might need more lift. It'll be more difficult to do, but probably it's the best solution. I should have anticipated that in the plan," Don said, disgustedly.

"Hey partner, its working better than anybody else's design. I'd like to see the Coast Guard trying to make this much speed in this weather!" Al asserted. "You did fine."

"I wouldn't," Jill remarked.

"Wouldn't what?" Al asked.

"Like to see the Coast Guard try to catch us," Jill answered. "Could we really outrun them? Safely, I mean?"

"There's nothing safe about running at night to begin with, Jill. Even with a double planked bottom like the Ghost has, you could hit a dead head anytime. You just can't see that well unless the moon is out and the water is calm," Don said. "With the prop protected by the shape of the bottom we have less likelihood of damaging the running gear by hitting something, but a dead head or a rock could still puncture the bottom," he explained.

"As for outrunning them, Jill, I'm sure they wouldn't have the capability to get close with the speed we've recorded today. Even most of the boats running whiskey now are too heavy to attain the speed we can. The Ghost is in a class of her own. Light, fast and able to cut through all but the biggest seas with some degree of comfort," Al assured her.

"Is that Salmon Beach we're passing," Jill asked a few minutes later, looking at dim lights to the east.

"Yes and I'll bet they're getting their bottoms wet if they use the johns there tonight," Don laughed.

"Don, you are bad! What he is trying to say, not too delicately Jill, is that the waves bounce up under those houses built on pilings and, because the toilets open directly down onto the beach, the salt water can splash your backside when you flush on a night like this with the tide high and wind strong."

"How gross!' Jill shuddered. "It sounds like you have first hand knowledge though. How is that?" she asked.

"We have a couple of friends from high school who live down there," Don said nonchalantly.

"We dropped in on a party there with our little boat last

summer. It's a lot easier than walking down a quarter of a mile on the path than tripping over everything in their so called backyards to get to the party house. Boy, was that some kind of wild bash, too," Al said and remembering how the booze flowed and the girls danced, he added, "They don't believe in prohibition of any kind at Salmon Beach it seems."

"And here I thought you were just nice, neighborhood boys," Jill said, searching their faces for truth in the dark cabin.

"We are, Jill. We were really there to sell the boat to a neighbor of our friend. And we did. He uses it for fishing at the point. He paid us $200 for it, including the old motor and it has more than paid for itself with the salmon he's caught. Real salmon, not like our cargo today," Don added.

"Yeah, the party was just a bonus to make up for the hike back up the hill and the long walk to catch a trolley home from Ruston," Al agreed.

The boat caught a rogue wave just then. Jill lost her handhold and tumbled back against the motor box.

"Are you hurt?" Don yelled, momentarily loosening his grip on the steering wheel.

"Watch where we're going, I'll help her," Al yelled back. "I'm sorry Jill. That almost got me, too."

"I'm all right," she said, rubbing her lower back. "Nothing bruised but my dignity. Guess there can't be too much of that in a speedboat, right?"

A few minutes later they rounded Rocky Point, the waves moderated and Don accelerated the last mile to the Day Island lagoon, then slowed as they entered Cummings Marina. It was a small rather shabby place, with only a couple dozen berths that consisted merely of wide fir planks nailed to the tops of large cedar logs that were held in place by a smattering of piling driven into the mucky bottom.

"Definitely second cabin," Jill muttered to herself as she tried to make out the layout in the light of a single lamp near the head of the gangway that led to the narrow dock. She remembered the area as a first class array of wide docks planked with treated two by sixes resting on Styrofoam floats. Classic wooden Chris Craft cruisers from the late forties and fifties, with gleaming mahogany cabin sides, had peeked from their covered boathouses in the time frame she recalled. She shook her self back to the present and moved aft to fend off the rough dock as Don idled the Ghost in with the exhaust in quiet mode.

"Good grief, you startled me!" yelped old man Cummings when Al knocked on the door. The Cummings family lived right on the upper dock that formed the marina parking area. Their home was their office and the walk to work was minimal.

"Sorry, sir," Al replied. "I'm Al Nelson, called you about an hour ago about using the grid and getting a mooring spot for our boat, remember?"

"Of course I remember lad, but I thought you said you were coming from the tide flats. Tide and wind are running terrible out there tonight. How could you possibly have made it so fast? And how did you sneak up on us? Our dog usually barks the minute a boat comes past the point of the island," the marina owner demanded warily.

"Well, sir, she's fast, but she's quiet. Can we put her on the grid now so we can pull the prop off tomorrow at low tide? We want to add some spray rails as well. We took quite a bit of water coming here in that slop tonight," Al reported.

"I'll bet you did for sure. Yes, you can set her on the first grid just north of the inner dock if she doesn't draw too much water. Tides going out fast, so you'll have to hurry. The blocks are set up to handle from 25 to 32 footers. You said yours was about 30, so it should fit without too much worry. Just make sure she's secured well. I can't take responsibility for damage, you know."

"Thank you, sir. Can we settle up for the grid charge and the first month's moorage in the morning?" Al asked.

"That'll be fine. Your boat's not going anywhere when the tide's out," Cummings laughed.

Setting the Ghost on the grid to safely go aground as the tide receded was not an easy task in the dark.

"I've decided to stay aboard tonight and make sure she sets down without a problem. I'll knock the prop off in the morning and grab the first bus to town and get Ray to do his magic on it. You two better make a run for that last bus. It's coming across the bridge now!" Don exclaimed.

Al and Jill ran up the dock and barely caught the bus. At the late hour they found themselves the only passengers headed to town. They took a seat near the heater and Jill soon was asleep, her head resting on Al's shoulder. She awoke as the bus pulled up to 6th and Proctor.

"Come on, sleepy head. We've got to transfer to the 6th

Avenue trolley here. This guy's headed for the bus barn," Al said, hugging her like a child waking from a nap.

"Sorry, Al. It's been a long day. I guess I just drifted off for awhile. It was kind of nice to relax like that."

Taking her hand as they went down the steps of the bus, Al spoke huskily, "I wish we could be that close all the time Jill. I'm very fond of you, you know."

She held his hand warmly as they crossed to the trolley stop, saying nothing, confused as to how she might respond. She continued to hold his hand on the trolley and all the way on the walk home.

As they mounted her steps, Al said, "You've been awfully quiet coming home. I hope I didn't offend you by expressing my feelings."

She took his hand that she was still holding and pressed it to her lips softly. "I don't think you'll ever offend me, Al. But just right now, I can't express my own feelings very well. All I can say is that I'm glad that you're my friend and I feel good when I'm with you. Can we leave it at that for now?"

"Sure, Jill. Can we walk over to the garage together in the morning to meet with Ray and Don?"

"I'll look forward to it if the weather cooperates," she said. Then she surprised him with a warm kiss on the cheek before entering her door.

Al crossed to his home a happy but confused young man. "How is this ever going to play out?" he muttered to himself as he climbed the stairs to the porch.

CHAPTER ELEVEN

"I hope you don't mind me working while we're talking," Ray said as he lit the torch to warm the propeller that Don had removed from the Ghost early Sunday morning. "I've got to get this finished and run Don back to Day Island to beat the tide coming back in or we'll lose a day."

"I was up half the night getting the boat to set evenly on the grid and then had to slop around in that slimy mud to get to the prop. Luckily it came off easily, but the bus driver sure wrinkled up his nose at how I smelled when I got on," Don griped. "I'm going to need a real hosing down before the day's over."

"I can go back with Ray and put her back together," Al volunteered.

"No, I'll finish what I started," Don said matter-of-factly. "Now, have we decided to be rum runners or are we going to find a buyer for the boat and start a new project?"

"Maybe you could do a little of both," Ray suggested. "You said you think operating the Ghost from Cummings place might work well because it's not likely to be heavily scrutinized by anyone and I agree. I know Mr. Hallen that has the machine shop half way across the Day Island bridge. He does some specialty work for me every now and then. He also builds his own complete marine engines, small one and two cylinder affairs that are perfect for sailboats and economical fishing launches maybe a little larger than the one you boys built last year in school. There's a good market for such items and if you set up shop on the island you would be close to the machine shop and the Ghost. The nice part is that people on the island would be used to seeing you coming and going as legitimate workers. What do you think?"

"Is there anyplace available to work in?" Don asked. "If so, it might make more sense."

"I think there's an empty spot next to Willett's canoe factory on the south end of the island. It would be noisy that close to the railroad tracks, but that would probably mean low rent for your boat building business. It might take some time before I can make some contacts to get a direct supply of goods from Canada instead of being middlemen."

"I have some ideas on that," Jill offered.

"You?" Don asked, dumbfounded.

"Have I let you down in our stock market investments?" she asked. Seeing no dissent, she continued, "I'll find who the direct suppliers are in Vancouver and Victoria and contact them, then let Ray set up the details and method of delivery, okay?"

"If you say so, but how would you pay for the first load?" Al, always the most practical, asked.

"After I get a firm buying price and Ray negotiates the sale price, I'll sell just enough stocks to cover the bill and boat expenses. The market is about to peak anyway, so we won't be missing much profit," Jill explained.

"How can you be so sure, Jill?" Don asked.

"Just trust me, I really know what I'm doing when it comes to the market," she replied.

"Yes, let's let Jill do the research and I'll handle the sale connections to keep the three of you in the clear of any possible investigations," Ray agreed. "Meanwhile, I have a small delivery that you fellows can make tomorrow night, so let's get this prop back on today and let you get some rest for your night's boat ride."

Al, who had remained quiet for the most part of the discussion to this point, asked, "So we're really going to do it? We are committed to being law breakers?"

"It's an insane law that will be changed before long, I'm sure, Al. If you're really uncomfortable, we could buy you out --- when we get a bit ahead," Jill offered.

"I'd be stupid not to be uncomfortable, Jill, but I started this with my ideas of building the perfect rum runner boat and Don designed a beauty, so I'll stay in to the finish," he answered, thinking, "For better or worse, I guess."

"Plug your ears! I'm going to hammer some bite into this propeller now," Ray yelled as he began forming the edges into a definite cup. "We'll be out of here before church starts," he laughed over the racket of his blows.

"Yeah, just us hypocrites standing in line to take communion," Al said to himself without humor.

Ray soon finished the prop and he and Don left in the Packard sedan used the day before. Walking home, Al took Jill's hand as he had the previous night, but felt little response. As they neared her house, he said, "You seem distracted Jill. Is anything wrong? Are you feeling okay?"

"Just wondering if I'm getting you guys into something that

might backfire," she replied.

"Hey, we were headed right into this thing from the start. You and Ray just made it a reality instead of a schoolboy's dream. I mean, what red blooded American guy wouldn't want to be in our shoes right now. It's pretty exciting stuff, racing the Feds across the raging seas in the fastest boat in the northwest. Taking tons of money from shady characters on the slippery docks of darkened cities. Risking life and limb for the love of a beautiful woman. Pretty heady stuff for a guy not long out of short pants!" he gushed.

"This is serious, Al. Exciting maybe, but darned dangerous. And if it's about a competition over me, I'm not sure we ---" she trailed off.

"Not sure what? That you want either one of us? I thought we were getting pretty close Jill. Is it just wishful thinking on my part? Or what?" he repeated, turning serious.

"I'm not what you think I am, Al. Yes, I'm very fond of you -- and Don, too, but I might not always be here for you. There's some things in my life that I don't seem to have control over and I'm sorry that I can't explain it better. I just don't know is all. I don't want to lead you on, but I do need you to be my friend, to love me for whatever I am, for now." She stopped, tears streaming down her face.

"Oh, Jill, I'm sorry. I'll love you however you want me to. I know I'm probably just a dumb moonstruck kid to you, but I promise to be the best friend I can until you know who you want for more than a friend," he said, choking up a little himself

"Thank you, Al," she said simply and put his hand to her lips as she had the night before. "I need to be alone now. I'll talk to you tomorrow after work."

Jill stoked up her furnace and filled the old bath tub to the brim when the water got hot. She poured in some bubble bath and relaxed so well that she woke only because the water had cooled. After a snack of peanut butter and crackers she booted the computer to life and began a long search for history of liquor distribution in British Columbia. Fortunately, whiskey makers and distributors were quite proud of their trade which led to many informative web sites. She found that a couple of companies had been extant for over a century. She would have no trouble in contacting possible suppliers. She also found a plethora of articles of clashes where the United States Treasury agents had been successful in catching smugglers and bootleggers operating out of Canada. She recorded all the known locations of arrests and confiscations to help map out alternative drop points that Ray might deem safe for use in the future. Knowing that printed information might cause questions from her compatriots, she made notes in pencil until her fingers were callused.

"A good day's work," she said to herself finally.

As she turned off her light, ready to crawl in bed, she glanced across the street at Don's room. She could make out Don and Al standing close talking with great animation.

"I hope that's not about me. I couldn't stand those boys losing their friendship because of me," she said to herself. For the first time since September 13, 1928, Jill uttered a prayer; not for herself this time, but for the two young men that had become the closest thing to family that she might ever have.

CHAPTER TWELVE

Don and Al once again found themselves in Gig Harbor approaching the Makovich's trawler, this time well after sundown. They had entered the harbor without running lights and with the exhaust muffled underwater. Now they used a common flashlight to make the agreed upon signal, one short blink followed by two longer flashes. Immediately they received the same reply and moved into position to accept fifty cases of 'King Salmon'. The Slovakian brothers said not one word, but worked very quickly to make the transfer, took their money, counted it briefly and pushed the Ghost away from the Black Duck abruptly.

"Pretty cool customers," Al said quietly as he started the engine and headed for the harbor entrance.

"I guess we're the customers, but they are real scary guys for sure. Ray says that this is the last deal we do with them. Not much profit just being delivery boys. He thinks with Jill's help he'll have us headed for Victoria before the end of the week," Don replied.

"We'll have to study the charts real carefully until then, Don. I know the lower sound like my own body, but it would be easy to get off course up in the San Juans if we don't really memorize as much as possible."

"Even then, at night anyway, we could get fouled up," Don agreed. "Best to go up in the daylight at a slow pace, maybe dragging some fishing lines to get a feel for the area. We need to remember to attach the number boards during the day, then stow them whenever we have a load aboard. Watch yourself! There's a boat coming through the entrance with no lights on," he yelled to Al.

Looking closely, Al said, "They're not moving Don, just sitting there blocking most of the channel. Do you think it's the Coast Guard?"

"Doesn't look like any of theirs I've seen around the sound. Oh crap!! Hit it fast! I'll open the exhaust," Don yelled.

Al had already acted as he, too, saw four men with rifles and stocking masks move onto the foredeck of the boat that blocked their path. The Ghost leapt onto plane, the supercharger screaming and the exhaust bellowing. Al swerved impossibly close to the beach and cut across the bow of the other boat before their assailants could get off an accurate shot. The knot meter read 40 as they tore south toward the Narrows.

"Who were those guys?" Al shouted over the screaming engine.

"They looked like pirates and they probably were. If we hadn't had a boat that could accelerate as fast and skim the beach that way I think they probably would have taken our boat, whiskey and all and tossed us to the fishes," Don declared.

"So what do we do now partner?" Al asked. "Deliver the goods or take cover?"

"They may know who we are, somehow, but I don't think they have a clue where we're going, so let's throttle back and get this load to Mud Bay on the incoming tide. Mike Webster won't be expecting us for another three hours so there's no reason to try to beat the tide," Don answered.

Mike Webster was a friend of Ray's son-in-law Palmer, a guy that would have normally thought twice about trucking whiskey over to Ray's client in Olympia if he hadn't lost his job as a crane operator a while back. Webster had a nice piece of waterfront with a cottage not quite big enough for his growing family. But waterfront on Mud Bay was only waterfront when the tide was high. At low tide the area lived up to its descriptive name.

The rest of the trip the young men were so jumpy that they swerved from every shadow on the water. By the time they reached Mud Bay, they had agreed to unload, find a secluded cove and anchor the rest of the night to get enough rest to make the return trip a lot less harrowing.

Mike met them about 1 AM on his tiny two plank dock. He was a burly man for his early age, strong enough to carry one of the heavy cases on each shoulder at a trot, but well balanced enough not to miss a step that would have imperiled their cargo. In a quarter hour the boat was lightened and Mike's old truck was lumbering up the dirt road headed for Olympia and the payoff. He was to pass the money to Palmer who worked in a local saw mill where Mike had previously been employed as a log crane operator and Palmer would take it to Ray next weekend when he and Violet, Ray's second oldest daughter, came to Tacoma to visit.

By 2 AM the Ghost was anchored behind a log raft near Olympia, her number boards back in place. Her exhausted crew had opened the engine box to allow its heat to radiate into the cabin where they were soon lulled to sleep on the vee-bunk under the short foredeck. About 8 AM a tug pulled up to the log raft and tooted its horn twice. Don jumped out of his sleeping bag and moved to a side window to see what the commotion was about.

"Al, you won't believe who's out here hooking up to tow the logs away!"

Al joined his companion and rubbing sleep from his eyes, asked, "Is that Harold?"

"Yeah! Do you think it's coincidence that he shows up right where we're moored after taking a load of booze to a friend of his future brother-in-law? And that he also works for the company that we quit a few months ago?"

"That is such a convoluted question that I'd have to say yes, it is coincidence. At least I think so. Foss tugs are all over the sound and Harold is just one of a hundred or more employees. It's pure chance," Don assured him.

"Well, he's probably heard that we quit to build this boat, if not from other guys at Foss, then from his girlfriend Birdie."

Birdie was the oldest of Ray's three daughters and like Goldie, unmarried. The likeness stopped there; while Goldie was blonde, saucy, flirtatious and wild as a March hare, Birdie had dark hair and a serious, almost brooding nature. She was studying to become a social worker while working at California Florist. Violet, the middle girl, was a gorgeous redhead and devoted to Palmer, whom she had only recently married. Harold had intended to be a professional forester, but also loved boating. He had taken the job as mate for Foss to be near his second love, Birdie, who he was dating at every chance. She was a little older than he and not his parents' choice for a mate, coming from a family that, they, as educators, felt beneath their station. Being very much his own man, Harold was spurning his mother's wishes and courting Birdie earnestly.

Harold knew boats well. As he scrutinized the Ghost, he guessed what it was, or might be used for. When Don and Al emerged on the long back deck he immediately recognized them from Foss's repair facility and hollered a greeting. They waved back but didn't initiate conversation, instead started the engine, hauled up the anchor and moved off at a leisurely pace. Harold watched curiously as Al dropped a fish line with a shiny spinner on it into their calm wake and settled into the mode of a patient fisherman.

"That's not a fishing boat," Harold muttered to himself. "It idles way too fast for trolling. Those guys are faking it for our benefit!"

"Harold, shake a leg! Get that tow line in place. We need to get these logs to the mill before we're working against the tide," the skipper of Foss 29 yelled, not paying the least attention to the fisherman that Harold was staring after.

As the Ghost headed north toward Day Island at a lazy pace, Don joined Al in the cockpit and steered with the tiller that they had installed on the rear cockpit deck. "I have an idea about those guys that tried to stop us last night."

Al had almost fallen asleep again, fish pole in hand, as the mild May sunshine bathed the cockpit.

"Oh, what's that?" he asked, yawning.

"I think the Makovich brothers tipped off some acquaintances to our cargo and wanted to get it back to sell over again," Don said.

"Why would they do that? We paid them cash for two loads in three days' time," Al wondered aloud.

"Ray may have let on that this was the last he would buy from them. They may have figured how to cut out a future competitor and double their money on the stuff they had already sold. They have an ideal cover as fishermen to smuggle large amounts of liquor into the states and they didn't look to me like guys that would hesitate to do whatever they needed to keep an edge over any competition," Don explained.

"I don't know whether you're right, but we better keep a close watch in the future. They know what our boat looks like and they might just try to waylay us again if they think we're carrying goods they could sell," Al warned.

"It sure didn't take us long to jump into the thick of things did it? How do you suppose Ray will react when we tell him what happened and our concerns for future problems?" Don prompted.

"He'll probably take it in stride and just tell us to watch our backs. He's not the one out here on the line after all. His part is to make the connections, with Jill's help of course," Al said.

"Until he makes those connections, I'd like to set up shop on Day Island and start building another boat. It'll be good to take our minds off what happened last night," Don said optimistically.

"It will also give us some cover like Ray suggested as well. Are we going to expand the plan of the one we built last year or design a new one?"

"I think we'll just scale up the original design, add a heavier keel and engine stringers. Maybe make a provision for a canopy or hard top for some weather protection. I'm anxious to see Mr. Hallen's engines. I think about a ten horsepower twin would work nice, don't you?" Don asked.

"Sounds good to me. It seems amazing, doesn't it," Al mused, "That last night we almost got killed and today we're trolling along talking about our next boat building project like it was the most important thing in our future!"

"Maybe building boats will end up being our future. If we make enough money running whiskey we might end up being the Hacker Craft or Dodge Boat Company of the Northwest!" Don said with enthusiasm.

"You never can tell what the future will hold, can you?" Al said just as his pole jerked down violently.

"Well, if you play that line right, I think the future for tonight will be baked salmon!" Don yelled.

CHAPTER THIRTEEN

Using the information that Jill had researched on the computer, it took Ray only a week to secure a wholesaler in Victoria that would provide Cutty Sark whiskey for their operation. In another two weeks he had obtained enough orders from retailers for more than the 100 case capacity of the Ghost. He also had a commitment from another wholesaler in Vancouver for other brands and types of liquor when he could put together another 100 case order.

In the meantime Al and Don had rented the vacant Day Island shop and moved their equipment from Tacoma. They also moved their personal things from home into a small living quarters attached to the rear of the building and took up residence. Don laid out an 18 foot version of his previous design and they had begun its framework.

Jill had cashed in just enough stock to buy materials to get them started. She knew that the market crash was now less than four months away, but was playing their investment for all that she dared, all the while trying to maintain her position at the candy company as cover for her more nefarious work in making connections for the partnership.

At their Friday evening meeting at Ray's garage, Al noticed the fatigue and strained expression on Jill's face and asked, "Would you like to go out tomorrow night for some dinner, some dancing or a movie? You look like you need a break from the routine."

"Maybe dinner and a movie. I don't think I'm up to dancing these days," Jill admitted, wondering why Don never noticed things like her fatigue.

Breaking into their conversation, Ray said, "Sorry to spoil your plans partners, but we're ready to pick up our first order from Vancouver Island." He outlined the details and explained that they would be meeting the supplier's truck at his private dock in Oak Bay at 11 PM the following night. "If you gas up in Port Townsend on the way up at dusk tomorrow and don't run too hard, you should be able to make it to Seattle before dawn with fuel to spare. Our buyer is a restaurateur in uptown Seattle with good connections. He will personally meet you at Anchor Marina under the Spokane Street bridge. I had The Stationers Company in Tacoma make a large scale drawing of both locations and sketched in where the correct docks are located so you won't waste time milling around in the dark attracting attention. Jill has the money in a waterproof bag with flotation inside in case something unforeseen should take place," Ray stated.

"You mean like last time?" Don asked, sardonically.

"Yes, that was unforeseen, but you handled it well and it probably taught you to be much more vigilant for the future," Ray said smoothly. "Any other questions?"

"How do we know what our supplier and our buyer are supposed to look like? We don't want to be bamboozled at either end," Don asked.

"At Oak Bay the supplier's name will be clearly marked on their truck, 'Island Beverages, LTD. The bills of lading you'll receive are for a supposed inter-city delivery for a resort on Salt Spring Island, British Columbia. No need for anyone to worry over where you actually deliver the goods," Ray responded.

"How about in Seattle? How do we know if we're handing the goods over to the restaurant owner or Treasury Agents?" Don persisted.

"He's a tall, very natty looking black man," Ray answered, smiling.

"A what?" Al piped up.

"A black man. A Negro and a very wealthy one, I might add," Ray explained as if to a child. "He was one of Olmstead's most consistent customers. Now he's ours. He only expects prompt service and the finest liquor. His clientele are the cream of Seattle society."

"Olmstead was caught and he's still in prison at McNeil Island. Are we sure his customers didn't inform on him to keep themselves from the same fate?" Don asked warily.

Jill jumped into the conversation now. "Why are you so pessimistic all of a sudden Don? It's common knowledge that Al Hubbard, Olmstead's right hand man, sold him out to get a job with the Feds. Olmstead thought he was so well connected that he kept operating even after they caught his men three times. Ray's plan is to use different drop points every time and stay small enough to keep under the radar by dealing with the most legitimate people at either end from now on. Not like the Makovich bunch."

"Sorry, I guess I've gotten comfortable building boats in the last few weeks and need to get pepped up for running the boat rather than just thinking about it," Don explained, lamely. "I guess we better get some rest to be up early enough to get our gear and some food aboard the boat. It's going to be a long two days before we're back in town."

Al was wondering what Jill meant by the term 'under the radar', but only asked, "A rain check for dinner and the movie?"

"Sure," she said simply, trying not to show concern.

"Soon, I hope?" Al asked.

"I hope so, too, Al. I need to stay and iron out some details on the money with Ray, so check in with me when you get back, okay?"

"Wouldn't miss the chance, partner!" Al said as he gave her a peck on the cheek before leaving.

Outside the young men walked in silence for a block before Al remarked, "You were kind of hard on them tonight, don't you think?"

"Sorry, I get that way when somebody thinks they have all the answers and I know that's impossible," Don answered.

"They do seem to be pretty sure of themselves. I think Jill is feeding Ray more information than he has ever managed on his own. An odd pair for certain," Al mused.

"Jill is a mystery all right. I thought you might be getting some secrets out of her by now. What's happening to your charm, partner?"

"You're the one that's always charmed the girls. I can't believe you're sitting back and letting me ----" Al trailed off.

"Letting you what? Get a kiss once in a while? I promised always to be her friend and to be a gentleman. That's what I'm going to do and I'm sure you'll do the same. She'll choose someone someday and maybe it'll be one of us or maybe not. I think she's a person that needs a lot more security than either of us can provide for a long time," Don said seriously.

CHAPTER FOURTEEN: JUNE, 1929

June was always a month of weather changes around Puget Sound and 1929 was no exception. The Ghost was plowing at displacement speed in following seas with the wind at her stern. The new spray rails were throwing water to the sides on each swell, but the motion inside was making each of the young men feel queasy. A light but consistent drizzle limited visibility to a half mile, so they were running by dead reckoning with charts spread over the motor box, dividers and ruler at the ready.

"I hope the rain lets up tonight or crossing the straits is going to be darn tricky," Al said.

"I think it will be tough no matter what, but at least we probably won't have any unwanted company to worry about. The fish boats will be working close to shore and all we have to do is get the compass heading correct, avoid the rocky little islands to the east of Oak Bay and find our way back against the wind."

"Glad to hear how easy it will be, because it will be your turn at the wheel then," Al joked.

"How much money do you figure this trip is worth?" Don asked.

"What it's worth is a probably a heck of a lot less than we'll earn from it, but undoubtedly a lot more than we would be earning painting the bottom of Foss's tugs and barges," Al laughed.

"I think we can afford to celebrate with a cup of cocoa then. Want some?" Don asked.

"I'm not sure my stomach will handle it, but I'll try if you can light the alcohol stove without catching us on fire," Al warned.

"Not going to," Don grinned, "I've got a little secret to show you. Ray built a little warming pan for us to eliminate just such problems when we're rocking around."

Don swung out a small brass box from under the cabin heater, turned a tiny valve in one of the hoses that connected it to the heater and waited a few minutes for the hot engine coolant to warm the metal. Then he lifted a floorboard, pulled a quart milk bottle from the cold bilge water and poured half of it into a sauce pan. When it felt warm, he added cocoa powder, sugar and a dash of salt from the side cupboard.

"I'll be darned! What a neat trick," Al exclaimed.

"Watch where we're going Al," Don yelled when he realized

that Al was watching the cocoa production rather than the compass. "It'll be ready in just a couple of minutes."

By 6 PM they were tied to the fuel dock at Port Townsend eating canned chili that Don had heated on the little warming box while a grimy young gas attendant filled the gas tanks from a huge tank mounted on the main dock above. The fellow wore striped overalls, a greasy visor cap and had a dirty red rag stuck in his back pocket.

"This thing sure holds a lot for a boat this size," he remarked as the minutes wore by. "You staying over tonight? You're welcome to tie up at the far end. Don't expect anybody else in 'til morning the way the weather is."

"Thanks, we'll think it over," Don lied easily.

"Say, you don't have a stove goin' inside do you? 'Cuz I see you eatin' your dinner and it'd be dangerous with the gasoline fumes if you was to have a stove burning," he warned in a suspicious tone.

"No, we have a hot water heater that warms stuff for us. It was too rough to light the alcohol stove on the way up," Don explained.

"Well, don't that beat all! A boat with a heater and it heats food too. What'll they think of next? Say, what kind of boat is this, anyway. Never seen one quite like it afore," he asked.

"It's an Aldon, our own design," Al answered smugly. "Our factory is near Tacoma. Guess you'll see more of them in time when the word gets out how-- Whoa friend, she's full and overflowing there!"

Indeed, the attendant had lost attention and gas was streaming from the overflow vent into the bay, giving off an overpowering odor.

"Guess we better wait a while to start her up or we'll blow up the whole place," Don warned.

"Sorry guys! I hope it don't hurt your paint. I can get a water hose to wash it down if you like," he suggested lamely, wiping the deck with his red rag.

"The rain and spray will take care of it. If you'll figure what we owe you we'll settle up and let you get home to your own dinner," Don suggested.

The gas dock closed at dusk according to law and they headed out soon after the attendant locked up. Al took over the navigation while Don handled the controls.

"I think we better put on some speed and get across all this open water while we can still see a little. Then we can take it easy finding our way into the harbor among those rocks you mentioned Al."

Lamenting the lack of a dry run to get their bearings, Al agreed. "All we can do now is hope our compass is accurate and you can keep the speed steady enough that I can figure our position close enough to pick up the beacon on Gonzales Point. If we're off a bit maybe we could use the spotlight to try to pick up the first buoy, which should be a green one according to the chart."

"I don't think that's a good idea, Al. No use advertising our arrival to any boat that might be patrolling the area," Don warned

"I don't think the Canadian authorities are wasting their resources patrolling like our country is. There's probably not anywhere near as many people smuggling something into Canada as there is going out of it," Al argued.

"How about hijackers like at Gig Harbor? We don't know what kind of games are being played up here. Better to be safe than sorry. I'll keep her steady at 15 knots, you work the charts and we'll stay 'under the radar' as Jill calls it," Don advised.

"I kind of understand what she meant last night, but I wonder where her expression came from?"

"Another of her secrets?" Don asked.

"Maybe so, I sure don't know. I need to plot this course better. I figured it was 8:15 when we left Port Townsend. Did you notice?"

"Yeah, I made a mental note. It was actually 8:13, but I didn't kick it up to 15 knots until 8:20, so you'll have to interpolate the ground covered in the first 7 minutes," Don answered.

"Okay, I'll refigure the time from Pt .Wilson and plot the course from there."

Quickly consulting the chart, Al had Don turn to 130 degrees and mark the time. He figured that they should arrive opposite Brodie Rock in two and a quarter hours which was just one mile south of the first channel buoy. At that point he planned to slow and start picking their way through. As they entered the Strait of Juan de Fuca, the Ghost encountered the ground swell from the Pacific and her speed began to vary as she climbed each roller, then slid down the other side.

"It's going to be hard to keep an even speed quartering this swell," Don soon reported.

"Pick her up a few rpm and I think we'll be close enough. Just watch the compass, because it's easy to move off course riding the waves at this angle," Al suggested.

Two hours later Don's eyes were strained to the limit and he was visibly nervous. "Can you see any better than I can? I can't make a thing out in this rain. We haven't seen even one light since Pt. Wilson. Do you think we're okay or are we headed out to sea?"

"Give it a few more minutes. You're doing a great job. We still have plenty of time to find Oak Bay," Al assured him, "But I do hope the rain will slack off and give us a fighting chance to pick up the channel buoys."

Ten minutes later Don yelled, "Is that it ahead on the left, flashing red?" wondering if it was eye fatigue or really the beacon.

"Yes! Slow her down and bear hard to port. Quick, because I think we're closer to the rocks than we want to be! In fact, keep the beacon a little to our right and we should be in the channel. And douse the running lights while I switch the exhaust to underwater mode," Al advised.

"Aye, aye, skipper. Good job of navigating!"

"Good job of keeping her as steady as you did. We've got 35 minutes to make the next mile and a half, so let's just idle in and keep track of the position of the rocks in case we have to beat it out of here in a hurry," Al warned.

The bay was well protected by hills that surrounded it on three sides. The water was a smooth, glossy black, dimpled only slightly by the light rain. At the second beacon light they turned 90 degrees to the left and carefully approached the shore. There were only a few dim lights glowing feebly from homes overlooking the bay; nothing to indicate activity at the water's edge.

"Lets run parallel to the shore about fifty yards out and see if we can spot the dock," Al said softly.

He had no more gotten the words out when twin orange beams of a vehicle's headlights edged over the hill and descended slowly to the water. The lights briefly illuminated a small wharf, blinked off and on once and went dead.

"Hope that's our suppliers," Don said quietly.

"Me too. I guess it's show time. Move her on in. I'll throw out the fenders and handle the forward line if you can secure the aft one," Al said.

By the time Don had maneuvered the Ghost alongside the wharf, two men had emerged from the truck and were waiting to catch the mooring lines. As soon as he had secured the aft line, the older of the men stepped down onto the boat and looked it over closely.

"A tidy little craft," he remarked in a clipped Scottish accent.

"Thank you, sir," Don answered. "I think you must be a fellow countryman by your brogue."

"You're a Scot then?" the man asked keenly.

Feeling relieved and comforted, somehow, by the accents remembered from childhood, Don opened up. "Born there, sir. My father was killed in the war. My mom remarried, to a Scottish American and we came over when he recuperated from his own wounds. I was only ten at the time, so I don't remember much, but I plan to go back when I get rich enough to travel abroad."

"Good lad. Well, we best be getting about our business. You have the money with you, correct?"

"Yes, sir, $2400 US I believe is the agreed upon amount for 100 cases?" Al answered this time.

"Well, its worth $2600, but the young wench talked me down to $2400, telling me how difficult it was to--Uh--distribute it these days --and I gave in to her winning ways!" he laughed. "Is she a pretty one, lads? She certainly sounds like a bonnie lass!"

"We both think so, sir," Al said honestly.

"Ah, I see how that might be a problem, eh?" the Scotsman said, raising one of his heavy eyebrows.

"Not at all sir, we're partners and partners we'll stay," Don explained.

"Yes, yes! Well, let's get to our business. You have a long way to go before daylight I'm certain. And a bad night for it at that," he added, pulling up his coat collar to avoid the rising wind.

It took the four men almost forty-five minutes to move the liquor cases aboard and tarp them down securely. The money was exchanged and the truck groaned its way back over the hill as the Ghost slipped out from the shelter of the bay, moved slowly past the last of the rocks and light beacons and into the increasing swell of the Strait. As Al swung onto the opposite compass heading, back toward Port Townsend, they both began to realize how big the ocean was and how small their now heavily laden craft felt. With 3600 pounds of liquor and almost 1200 pounds of fuel in the rear section of the boat, the Ghost was well down by the stern.

The bow was riding too high and Al couldn't see much to begin with, but now with the rain and the wind whipped salt spray splattering the windshield, he could barely see beyond the anchor winch.

"This is bad, Don. I can't see a thing!"

"Much as I hate to run fast in such big water, I'm afraid we've got to get her up on plane and level her out. I'll watch for breaking waves so that we don't stuff the bow into something we can't rise over, okay?" Don asked with real concern in his voice.

"We're going to have to try, I guess. The only other alternative is to head with the wind across to Deception Pass and take the inside passage," Al admitted.

"It's about the same distance across that way as heading toward Port Townsend, but then we'd have a lot longer run to make Seattle. Unless it turned dead calm, we'd never make it before dawn," Don replied.

"Okay then, I'll bring her up to speed and hope you can tell me in time to back off if there's a big one in front of us. Hold on to your teeth!"

The Ghost leaped ahead as the supercharger pushed the fuel charge into her hungry cylinders. The attitude leveled, but Al had to steer at one angle up the swells and another angle as they rushed down the other side. Several times in the next hour and a half of terror Don had to yell for Al to cut the throttle to avoid broaching. They rounded Wilson Point at 2:45 AM and breathed sighs of relief as the swell dissipated into rough seas and a bit easier going.

"I'll take over for a while, Al. I know how tired you must be from concentrating that long."

"You don't sound so fresh yourself, partner," Al said, gladly turning the wheel over to Don.

"I'm beat all right, but we've got a long way to go, so I'm going to turn her up another notch and put some miles behind us. Check the next heading for me, will you? After we round Marrowstone Point, I mean. We should have a straight shot down to Point No Point and then from there to West Point. After that we'll back off and feel our way past Seattle and over to Duwamish Head."

At an indicated 17 knots the Ghost was taking a beating as they passed Point no Point. Although the rain had let up and the sky was beginning to lighten, the combination of a south wind and outgoing tide was stacking the waves directly against them, slowing their actual progress over the bottom.

"I figure another 20 nautical mile to the Duwamish," Al said.

"We're going to have to put on more speed to get this stuff unloaded before daylight. Do you think she can take any more?"

"We built her well. She'll have to. I want to be back out of Elliott Bay while it's still dark. I'll take her up to 25 knots, so hold on tight and keep your eyes peeled for anything in the way." Don gritted his teeth and braced himself more firmly in the pilot's chair as he advanced the throttle.

The Ghost was throwing spray 50 feet to the sides and 100 feet to the stern as she bucked off the nasty tide chop. Inside the cabin the considerable engine noise was almost drowned by the pounding of the hull.

"With all this spray she'd be a sight to see from land if it were daylight," Al yelled. "Nobody would believe a boat this size could make such speed in these conditions!"

"You're right, but I'm glad the visibility is still poor, because no one except a rum runner would be driving their boat so hard in water this rough to begin with. If anyone could see us, it would be pretty obvious that we're up to no good ---or insane!" Don yelled back.

It was after 4 AM when Don slacked off throttle, switched the exhaust to underwater and entered the Duwamish river. The passage was dark and narrow but they found comfort as they passed Harbor Island on the left and saw the big red barn, now famous as the birthplace of Bill Boeing's growing airplane company. The lights from Boeing's plant and the adjacent mills allowed the pair to see just well enough to avoid broken off pilings and log rafts that could have spelled disaster.

"Ray should have given us time to look this over in the daylight, Al. One of these old pilings could put us on the bottom in minutes if we hit at speed," Don grumbled quietly.

"Let's just hope that we can idle out the same way we're coming in," Al agreed. "I've had all the excitement I need in the last two days."

The sketches that Ray provided were accurate enough that the Ghost was tied to the main float at Anchor Marina by 4:20. They walked up the gangway to a dirt parking lot and found it empty.

"Not a good sign. I thought they would be waiting for us, not us waiting for them," Al whispered.

"Yeah, I expected that as well. If they don't show in the next half hour, we better high tail it," Don said. After a few minutes, he added, "I don't like this setup at all. Navigating the river in the dark is creepy enough, let alone waiting around this dump for God knows who will show."

Another 15 minutes passed before they heard the whine of a truck changing gears coming toward them. They ducked behind a small boat that was sitting on the dock waiting for much needed repair to its bottom planking. Peeking around its stern, Don watched three black men alight from the cab. While two of them wore overalls and stocking caps, the other matched the description Ray had provided. As he moved closer it was obvious even in the dim light of the awakening day, that he was dressed like a dandy, pin striped suit, patent leather shoes topped by white spats and a bowler hat adorning his head.

"I believe we have your delivery, sir," Don said quietly as he and Al emerged carefully from concealment, not wishing to provoke surprise.

Contrary to Don's guess that the man might be startled, he merely smiled, showing a gleaming gold front tooth and said, "Glad to see you are on time gentlemen. Considering the weather, I thought you might have been delayed."

"We'd like to unload and be out of here before daybreak, sir," Al said, stating the obvious.

"By all means," the dapper man said, motioning his helpers towards the gangway. "If you don't mind helping my men, we'll all be in our beds by sunrise."

With the help of hand trucks the two husky black men moved the cases up the ramp into the truck as fast as Don and Al could unload them from the boat. By 5:30 the agreed upon money had been exchanged, the truck had rumbled off toward Spokane Street and the Ghost was creeping back down the river to Elliott Bay.

"It's been a long day partner. How about crossing over to Eagle Harbor and getting some sleep before we head home?" Don asked.

"Sounds good to me if you include a trip to the bakery in Winslow after we get a couple of hours shut eye!" Al exclaimed. "I think we can afford it with $6000 in our bag."

"Yeah, we'll need to spend some for gas as well. We used more than I figured running so hard last night," Don replied.

A half hour later Al was paying out anchor rope in the well protected harbor, but paying more attention to the beautiful scene to the west. The lights of Seattle were fading as the robust city awoke to another day. Ships, airplanes and buildings were being built over there, just a few miles distant. Log rafts were being turned into those buildings, aluminum and steel from the east being hammered into shape for those ships and airplanes. And in uptown Seattle, a sharp looking black man was toasting his last client of the night with Canadian whiskey procured from two daring boys, now become men, who were nestling down for a nap in their marvelous creation.

CHAPTER FIFTEEN: JULY, 1929

The Ghost made another run to Oak Bay in early July. The weather was far more cooperative which allowed them to make better time and was easier on the boat and its operators than the previous trip. It was decided, by all parties, to make the drop farther south of Seattle at Fauntleroy just in case anyone might have been wise to the Anchor Marina drop point. The dock at Fauntleroy was only used on weekly stops by the Virginia V, a 50 foot steam vessel that moved small amounts of cargo and passengers between Tacoma, Vashon Island and a few other minor destinations.

It was just after 3 AM as the Ghost approached the small floating dock with Al at the wheel. The current caught the bow and swung it away from the dock just as Don was jumping onto it with the bow line. Al was heading aft to throw him the stern line and didn't see Don fall, but he heard the splash followed by a muffled curse. He dropped the line in his hand and ran forward around the side deck, peering into the dark water.

"Over here! Throw me the line and get me back aboard before I drift any farther," Don yelped.

Al coiled the bow line back in and threw it, but it was too short to reach Don. "Sorry partner! Swim around to the transom step and I'll help you out from there."

The Ghost was quickly drifting clear of the dock and towards the rocky shore. By the time Don reached the swim step the stern of the heavy laden boat was almost on the rocks. Don was shaking from the forty-five degree water and hardly able to grip the stern line with which Al was pulling him over the transom.

"Get down in the cabin where its warm and fire her back up. But don't put it in gear until I get the pike pole and shove us clear. We can't afford to ding the prop if we have to get out of here fast," Al warned.

"Hurry," was all that Don could manage through chattering teeth.

The stern hung up and commenced grating on a barnacle crusted rock as small waves rocked the boat. Try as he might, Al could not get the boat dislodged.

"Don, give me a hand, I can't get it to move!"

Don shed the blanket he had wrapped over his dripping body and ran aft. Immediately, he realized the dilemma and knew the only escape from the quickly lowering tide was to either lighten their load or jump in the shallow water and lift the stern clear.

"We've got to get in the water and lift her off, let's go!" He scrambled over the stern and slid into the waist deep water.

Al followed his lead, joining him in seconds. "Oh man, that's cold!" he moaned through gritted teeth.

With the load lessened by their own weight and through determination fired by absolute necessity, they lifted the stern enough to pivot it toward deeper water. Al cupped his hands to allow Don a leg up on the transom step and Don then pulled his partner aboard before running forward to throw the boat into reverse gear and move them away from shore once more.

"Let's try it again, Al. You can fall in this time," Don said as Al joined him, both dripping all over the cabin floor.

"Okay, but why not just run straight in this time. Put the bow right against the dock and I'll step off before the darn current grabs us again."

It worked well the second time, but before they could change from their wet clothes, a vaguely familiar figure emerged on the gangway.

"Quite a show boys! Have you thought of joining the 'Three Stooges'? Lots of money in the movies, I understand." His deep bass laugh and the glint of gold from his smile assured them that it was their buyer and that he had witnessed the aborted landing.

"Nice of you to think so sir, but how could you see us?" Don asked. "Its almost pitch black out here."

"Night glasses, binoculars like the Navy uses. I saw the phosphorescence of your wake a half mile out. You're not as invisible as you think when your wake glows like that. I think we'd better conclude our business quickly now. Your docking procedure was not exactly silent." He gave a low whistle, that resembled a bird's call and his two huge, black body guards emerged from the head of the gangway with their hand trucks. Don and Al pitched in with gusto, trying to warm their drenched bodies with activity. The 100 case load was on the dock faster than the men could truck it away. Money was exchanged, Al and Don both thanked their client for his business and boarded the Ghost.

"I've told your friend that I'll be in touch when I need more merchandise, but business is slowing a little, so if I don't see you for a while, play it safe --- and stay out of the water, unless it's in the bath tub!" With another flash of his golden smile, and a tip of his bowler hat, the black bootlegger disappeared into the dark.

They idled the Ghost out about a half mile before stopping to change into dry clothing. Neither said anything until they were almost back to Day Island over an hour later.

Al broke the silence, "You know he's right. About the phosphorescence, I mean. On calm, clear nights in the summer, like this, a boat that stirs up a wake like this one could be spotted pretty easily."

"Well, there's not much we can do about nature. The little devils like to show their lights when stirred up and we do stir up a lot of water, like you say," Don agreed. "Only thing we can do is stay as far away from land and other boats as possible."

"Or stay home on calm nights and only run in bad weather," Al said thoughtfully.

"I prefer nights like this. All but the falling in part, of course. It was a lot less hard on our bodies, our nerves and the boat this time than the last one. The money is good, the boat worked fine and we'll both be feeling great after a good night's rest," Don said, trying to allay Al's fears.

"You're right, I guess. It's been a good night's work. Wonder if the next trip will be as successful," Al said thoughtfully as they got ready to dock at Cummings Marina.

CHAPTER SIXTEEN

By the third week in July, Jill had negotiated a deal to buy 200 cases of mixed varieties of alcoholic beverages from a distributor in Vancouver, B.C. and Ray had made arrangements with a buyer from Everett to take delivery of the first load in La Conner, a small village on the Swinomish Slough, which both considered to be safe from prying eyes. The second load was coming to Tacoma, with a portion destined for Olympia, but they hadn't decided how to make the split yet. Al and Don wanted to make a daylight run to be more confident of making the trip safely when they would be heavily laden and running at night. However, Ray was concerned that patrol boats from either nation might be curious enough to stop and board the Ghost because it did not look like a pleasure cruiser and wasn't licensed as a commercial fishing vessel either. It was at a muggy, Friday night meeting at Ray's garage that the matter came to a head.

"Ray, the open water in the Strait of Georgia will be tough enough to handle if the wind comes up, let alone half a dozen rocky islands we need to miss," Al argued.

"Yeah, we have to stay off the shallows of Sturgeon Bank and Roberts Bank, which puts us in well into the strait," Don agreed. "Then we have to find the channel into Swinomish Slough, which might be impossible if it's foggy. We really need to know our way around better, Ray."

"Maybe so, but you don't need to advertise your presence to the Coast Guard or the Canadian Patrol. So far, the only problems you've had was with whoever was in cahoots with our former friends in Gig Harbor. Let's keep it that way," Ray admonished.

The room was silent for a while, tension exaggerating the muggy evening. Jill was trying to balance her concern for putting her young friends in jeopardy with the desire to make their operations successful. She spoke first. "You don't make the pickup until Tuesday night. Could you rent or borrow another boat to make a dry run this weekend? Maybe Ray could loan you a car to get up to Mt. Vernon or La Conner. I think it would be worth the added expense to look things over, don't you, Ray," she said, imploring him to finally nod his head in agreement, "Good, it's settled. We'll leave early in the morning."

"We?" Don asked. "We'll probably end up renting some old fishing scow that will take us all day and night to make Vancouver and back, Jill. Why would you want to go waste a weekend of discomfort with us?"

"Because I want to see what you guys do, where you go and how you plan things out. And --- because I want be with you for a change; not lying around home, worrying," she finished, with a wan smile.

"Are you sure, Jill? I mean, we'd both love to have you for company, but --," Al stammered.

"I'm certain. I'll pack us a lunch for tomorrow, some snacks for the boat ride and you can treat me to dinner in the port of your choice tomorrow night," she answered brightly.

"You can take my Dodge home tonight. I'm not going anywhere this weekend. Lena is on my case to mow the lawn and whitewash the back fence. That's the trouble with having all daughters, good for nothing but cooking and sewing and Birdie's not even much good for either of those," Ray complained. "Just don't overheat my engine. I hate fixing my own stuff!"

The trio left early Saturday morning and reached La Conner by 9 AM after a brief stop for gasoline and a Danish pastry in Everett. A search of the waterfront proved Al to be correct. Fishing boats were the only type currently for rent. With their approval Jill picked the most expensive one, but it did have a small cabin with berths forward, one stacked tightly on top of the other. Additionally it had a tiny wood fired cook stove and a short couch just aft of the pilot's wheel. Though the rental price was high the boys heartily approved of the power plant, a converted Star automobile engine of fairly recent vintage making 35 HP, enough to push the 28 foot boat to 8 knots. Within the hour they were motoring north through the narrow channel under blue skies.

"What a great day!" Jill exclaimed as she joined Don on the aft deck. "How lucky you guys are to spend days like this on the water, while I'm slaving away over accounts receivable at Brown and Haley."

"Yeah, but you get all the candy you can eat!" laughed Al. "And, remember, we're still building boats a lot of the time. Most of our time on the water has been at nights, wondering if we're going to get shot at again," he added more seriously.

"When I think of that, I get awfully sorry that I talked you into this business, Al. I'd never forgive myself if either of you were hurt."

"Hey, Jill, we made our own decisions and we'll live or die by them. I'm just as greedy as the next guy about making a buck from the stupid, unenforceable law of Prohibition," Al responded warmly. "Let's forget all that and just enjoy the boat ride, okay," he said putting an arm around her shoulder.

She snuggled close to him, enjoying the warmth of his embrace and the feeling of security he gave her. "Thanks, Al," she said simply.

"For what?" he asked.

"For just being there when I need you."

They stood there, close together, for the half hour it took to clear the slough and enter the channel dredged through the mud flats toward Anacortes. Jill knew that in later days, oil tankers would anchor near here to feed the refineries that supplied gasoline and fuel oil to the Pacific Northwest. In the summer of 1929, they passed only tugs towing log rafts to nearby mills and a few small fishing boats.

Much as he hated to break away from Jill, Al knew they had work to do. "Let's go chart the compass heading for Don. We need to plot a course past Guemes Island, just ahead there, and on through several smaller islands before we head into the Georgia Strait proper."

"Sounds good. The wind is getting a little brisk out here now anyway," Jill agreed, entering the cabin behind Al.

Don glanced back, "Enjoying the ride Jill? Kind of fun motor boating through cow pastures and tulip fields wasn't it? The slough was dredged out quite a few years ago for a short cut to avoid the terrific tide rips of Deception Pass, I think. It's not very deep but sure is a nice haven from the outer sound. Indian fishermen probably used it long before it was dredged. The San Juan Islands coming up are pretty spectacular, too. You can take a boat right up next to some of them on one side, while the sand bars and rocks extend for a hundred yards on the other side of the same island. Weird, huh?"

Al was poring over the chart, checking compass headings and distances. "If the weather stays this good, the Ghost should make the run from Vancouver to La Conner in three hours. If it's not, it could take all night. In this boat its going to take us the rest of the day. I think we should make the False Creek area before dusk though."

"Anyplace to stop along the way for lunch?" Jill asked. "I made some goodies last night that I'm sure you'll want to take time to enjoy."

"How about it, navigator? Anyplace with some shelter? It's a nice day, but the wind is starting to pick up from the north and it would be nice to eat in a calm situation, like she says," Don inquired of Al, who was still studying the chart.

"Looks like Echo Bay on Sucia Island should make good shelter from the north. We'll just have to watch the rocks closely when we head back around it to the northeast towards Pt. Roberts," Al replied.

It turned out that Sucia Island had several interesting bays to explore before they selected an anchoring spot for lunch. They all agreed it would be wonderful to have the time to go ashore to comb the smooth, sandy beaches and climb the rock formations that jutted so abruptly towards the sky. This was a place to be preserved in memory and for future generations of young explorers.

Reluctantly Don said, "Sorry to break up the party, partners, but we need to move out into the cold, cruel world and head for Vancouver."

It was, indeed, a rougher situation they faced that afternoon; the seas were building and soon began to crest as they beat their way north. Al had taken the wheel and soon found that the small fishing boat made the most comfortable progress at the very deliberate pace of about 5 knots. Its narrow bow cut through the crests, allowing the hull to avoid either pounding over them as the Ghost would have done or plunge into the troughs as a shorter boat might have.

"She rides pretty well if you don't push her," Don observed, "But she sure is slow compared to the Ghost!"

"What will it be like in the Ghost if it's this rough, Don?" Jill asked.

"Like trotting fast on a horse," he explained. "It rattles your teeth and can give you a headache that won't stop, but she flies over most of it better than could be expected."

"Unless we broach," Al added thoughtfully.

"What do mean by broach?" Jill asked. "What happens then?"

"The bow shears off the wave ahead of it and veers one way or the other," Don answered.

"Real fast!" Al added, "And then the whole boat can slam sideways and almost roll over."

"Al kept us from broaching several times on our first trip down from Victoria. I'd yell to him that I thought there was a big wave ahead and he would throttle back before we hit it and then accelerate back over it. It wasn't much fun and awfully hard on the boat. We put her on the grid later and spent a whole day making sure the bottom plank fasteners were still holding. Luckily, we built her well and only replaced a half-dozen or so," Don explained.

"Isn't that a lot of loose screws?" Jill asked.

"Not considering that there are several hundred in the bottom alone," Al replied. "My arms get sore just thinking of how many screws are in that boat and how fast we rushed to put her together!"

The afternoon went quickly as Al and Don in turn tried to outdo each other, reiterating details of their adventures in whiskey running to date and how marvelously their creation performed when called upon. Don even laughed at himself over his falling overboard incident, though recalling the cold water closing over his head brought shivers down his spine.

As expected, they entered the small harbor of False Creek at dusk being very careful to avoid the kelp beds that threatened to foul the propeller. They found the dock that would be their pickup point in a few days on the south side of the harbor and tied up for the night behind a row of other similar size fishing boats.

"Well, my lady, are you up to hiking a ways for your dinner? I don't see much commercial activity around here," Don observed.

"Probably why our supplier chose the spot for the delivery," Jill remarked quietly.

"Let's go," Al urged, "I'm starving!"

"You're always starving!" Don and Jill said in unison.

They found a cafe much like those in every seacoast town, serving fresh fish and chips, steaming clam chowder and mugs of black coffee strong enough to keep the fishermen awake through their long nights of hauling in gill nets. Jill was still picking bones from her fish when Al was already eyeing her chips.

"Go ahead Al. I don't know where you put it in your little body," she kidded. Al was only little compared to Don, who stood a lean 6 feet. While Al topped out at 5 feet 9 inches and 160 pounds, he was only 10 pounds lighter than Don. Evidently his metabolism uses up more than the rest of us, Jill thought, laughing to herself how different these two young men were, yet how much she cared for both of them. They left arm in arm, three abreast to look for an ice cream shop, but found none nearby.

"Don't despair fellows. I brought enough chocolate cake to get you through another day. Let's head for the boat. I need my beauty sleep and I'm sure you two will have me up before dawn, just like today."

Back aboard Don built a fire in the little stove to keep the chill off long enough to get into their sleeping bags, Jill on the little couch and the men forward in the height impaired bunks. The lack of a toilet was solved, somewhat crudely, by placing a number 10 can on the dark aft deck and hoping none of the night's fishermen would be interested in anything other than their own business. All were soon lulled to sleep by the gentle rocking of the round bottom boat.

The trip back was smoother. Jill took a long turn at the wheel as her partners worked out the exact courses they would follow in the dark on Tuesday night. They made no stops and arrived at the La Conner dock by 5 PM. The boat's owner was pleased to see his craft returned in good condition and earlier than expected. When he asked how the fishing went, they said only that the fish were delicious and left him scratching his bald head as they motored away.

"We've got to get one of these," Al said to Don as he poured the power to Ray's year old Dodge. "This 6 cylinder is so much stronger and smoother than the old four banger. And it's got hydraulic, four wheel brakes. She'd stop on a dime if you had to!"

"I'm holding out for a Model A Roadster, you know that, Al. It may not be as fast as a Dodge or stop as well, but I'll bet the girls would go for it . What do you think, Jill?"

"This girl would, but I'm not your average gal, pal."

"You sure aren't," Al muttered to himself. "And I want you to be more than my pal," he thought. He found that, since he was driving, it seemed to be Don's turn to have an arm around Jill and that she was sitting just as close as she had been standing with him yesterday. He frowned and put on more speed.

CHAPTER SEVENTEEN

The weather held nicely into Tuesday, allowing the boys to make Everett by late afternoon where they put in to top up on fuel. The run to Vancouver was far longer than their previous trips to Victoria, but they had the advantage of more protected waters [until they got north of Sucia Island] which meant they could travel faster. However, the big, dual overhead cam Duesenberg power plant sucked up gasoline at an enormous rate when they chose to push it as hard as they were doing that day. Rather than taking the shorter route via Rosario Strait, they chose to continue through the inside passage to the Swinomish channel, hoping to become even more familiar with the course they would be traveling in reverse later that night.

As they entered the narrow channel behind Goat Island that led to the Swinomish Slough, Al said, "This is not going to be fun in the dark. There's nothing but rocks on either side and a 90 degree with a sand bank at the end if you miss the turn!"

"Yeah, it could be nasty, but we will have unloaded and in no hurry then, so we'll just feel our way out to deep water. After that, I thought we might run down to Oak Harbor, anchor and get some rest," Don suggested.

"Then run back home in the daylight tomorrow?"

"If we're as tired as I think we'll be, it would be a lot safer than running all night to get back. We can phone Ray from Oak Harbor and tell him that the run went okay so they're not wondering if we made it or not," Don said.

"Sounds like a good plan. It's going to be a nerve racking night, I'm sure," Al agreed.

They motored slowly through the slough in the gathering dark, emerging at the north end to find the wind still calm. Consulting the compass headings they had made on Saturday, Don kept Al headed properly from point to point. As they neared Pt. Roberts, two hours later, he warned Al to stay well to the west to avoid the shallows created by the Fraser River outlet to the ocean. A half hour later they passed the bell buoy marking the river's channel and were twisted by the current .

"Feels weird, doesn't it," Don remarked. "Like we're going sideways half the time."

"Yeah, I can feel it tugging at the rudder more than on the boat we rented. Of course, that was going at less than half our speed, so that might be the difference," Al replied.

As they approached the Pt. Gray bell buoy, Al slowed down and asked, "Think we should go in without running lights from here?"

"No, there's too many fishing boats out here tonight. We better just move through them slowly with the lights on, like we're one of them. We've got plenty of time and there's no use making anyone suspicious," Don cautioned. "If everything goes well, we can do the same coming out and make up time running fast once we're clear of the fishermen."

The Ghost slid into the harbor at False Creek with no apparent notice and was soon tied to a private dock not far from the fish boat dock they had used on Saturday night.

After an hour's wait, Al began to fidget. "Do you think something's gone haywire?"

"No, they said the delivery would be made between 11 and midnight. Its just midnight now," Don replied.

"I just don't like hanging around this long. I always feel safer once we're under way," Al complained.

Another 15 minutes went by before a delivery van backed up to the dock and three men emerged from the cab.
The smaller of the trio walked briskly down the steep ramp to greet the young men who met him on the dock.

"Good evening mates, I'm McFarland, Mac for short," he said shaking their hands firmly. He was a wiry man of less than forty with a strong English accent.

"Glad to meet you! I'm Al Nelson and this is my partner Don Grant.

"A Scot, eh. Well, I won't hold that against you, lad. With the tide this low we'll need a big fellow like you to keep us from dumping our goods in the bay off this bloody ramp!"

McFarland's two helpers were wrestling a hand truck bearing the first four cases of liquor down the ramp. Don ran up to relieve one of the men, who had another hand truck already loaded with four more cases. While McFarland helped hold the second hand truck from descending too fast, Al began loading the cases aboard. They were irregular in size because this load included champagne and other premium wines as well as both Scotch and bourbon whiskeys. Despite having to deal with the awkward ramp, the 100 cases were aboard and tarped down, the money exchanged, farewells made and the Ghost was idling, quietly from the dock by 1:15 AM. They took as direct a course as possible, but still needed to weave around several gill net boats, trying to stay well enough away that they might not be identified as anything but another fish boat.

"We're getting a little behind schedule," Don warned as they reached open water. "Better get her up on plane and make some time, because we'll have to slow again in the Swinomish channel. It's too dangerous to run fast in there."

Al opened the exhaust outlet, pushed the throttle forward and the Ghost perked up. As she leveled out on plane, Al said, "That feels better, doesn't it girl? This is what you were meant to do. Run fast, run far and howl at the moon!"

Don laughed at his friend's description, but it did feel good to be tearing across the smooth sea in his creation. Even though it had taken three people to actually build the boat and two more to obtain the finances to do so, Don considered himself the father of the Ghost; his idea, his design and his handiwork come to fruition. She was his first love, though Jill might be a close second if she wanted to be.

They had passed Sucia and Matia Islands and were almost abreast of Orcas when Al roused Don from his reverie about Jill, yelling, "What's that to the right, cutting west from Orcas? Can you see the moon glinting off the windows of her superstructure?"

"What ever it is, it's stirring up a huge wake," Don replied, grabbing the big night binoculars they had purchased after their black customer from Seattle had shown them his pair. "I think there's a paint slash on the side--, yeah, it's a Coast Guard cutter and it looks like they're heading just where we are pointed. Kill the engine, now! Let's see what they do."

Al pulled the throttle back. The Ghost glided only a few seconds before the heavy load overcame her momentum.

She had barely settled into the water when Don warned, "It's changing course, but not slowing. They've spotted us. Turn west and give her all she's got. We'll duck behind Lummi Island and run its length."

The big engine backfired a few times before catching and sputtering irregularly to life. Al jammed the gear lever forward, but eased the throttle up, afraid that the he had flooded the cylinders by cutting the engine so rapidly. After more heart wrenching misfires, the boat began to move.

"They're changing course again. They see that we're moving and they're compensating to cut us off. Get us going Al, we're in trouble!" Don yelled.

Al continued to ease the power on, unsure whether he had caused anymore than a temporary problem by stopping so suddenly. He knew that superchargers were known to blowup completely if treated to unusual circumstances and without the supercharger the Ghost might still run, but not be able to plane with the load they carried. "Come on baby, come on," he coaxed. "You can do it, please!"

The big engine smoothed out and the Ghost surged ahead, but the Coast Guard cutter was now within a half mile of them. As the Ghost came to full speed, Don yelled, "There are two guys on the foredeck. I think they're going to shoot at us!"

Al headed inside the buoy at Pt. Migley and turned sharply to the right, putting the headland between them and the cutter before the Coast Guardsmen could get off a shot.

He yelled back at Don, "Give me a heading quick! I know this place is full of rocks."

Don grabbed the chart and a flashlight. "Cut left, right now! If that cutter tries to cut the point like you did they'll be on the rocks for sure. We must have just skinned over them ourselves!"

"And if they don't pile up on the rocks, they're going to follow us. If they catch up to us in the slough, we'll be trapped," Al warned.

"We're making almost 40 knots; they're making 18 at best. We'll be in the slough before they can tell if we headed there, to Anacortes, behind Guemes Island or one of the smaller ones. Odds are that we can be unloaded and out the south end of the slough even if they guess right. We just need to not make any more mistakes," Don replied.

"What mistakes? We were on time, on course and doing fine. They just showed up out of nowhere. How could we have avoided or prevented that?" Al asked, bewildered.

"It was my fault. You were watching where we were going, I was daydreaming instead of watching for trouble. On a moonlit night like this, with us throwing such a visible wake, they had the advantage of surprise. If I had been thinking clearly, and watching with the binoculars, I could have spotted them before they spotted us and we would have had a bigger lead," Don answered.

"I don't know which is worse, battling bad weather and getting beaten up, or being easily spotted in perfect weather," Al grumbled.

Don went aft, standing outside the cabin with binoculars

sweeping from their stern to the west side where he guessed the Coast Guard might be trying to head them off if they turned that way after rounding the south end of Lummi Island. He returned to the cabin when he felt the boat slowing.

"No sign of them. What's happening?" he asked Al.

"We're coming up on March Pt. and I need to know how close we can get to shore," Al replied.

"Not close at a tide this low. Look up there beyond it and head for the flashing red. That's the opening to Swinomish channel. But don't slack off; we need all the lead we can gain," Don said.

"Are we going to try to run the slough at this speed," Al asked, incredulously.

"Yes!" Don insisted. "If you want, I'll take the wheel. I remember the bad spots pretty well from this weekend."

"You got it. I'll go astern and watch for trouble."

Don did not slack off power until the Ghost was within a few hundred yards of their destination, although he did switch the exhaust to underwater mode as they pulled up to the dock. Al leaped onto it with the stern mooring line, took a turn on the bit, ran to the bow and tied it off before Don got out of the cabin. Immediately, they were joined by two men about their own age running down the gangway.

"Are you guys crazy? We could hear you coming a mile away and you've left the engine running now. This is a small town. We don't need to advertise what we're up to!"

"We're in a jam here guys. The Coast Guard spotted us and may only be a few miles behind, so if you want your booze, let's get cracking," Don advised.

"Right, sorry! I'm Tony and this is Lou. Our dad is the boss and he's got this stuff sold, so if you'll help, we'll get it off onto the dock, cover it up with your tarp for now and move it when the heat's off," Tony said hurriedly.

With no more said, all four men hustled the whole load onto the dock in 10 minutes. While Don counted the cash, Al threw off the lines and pushed the Ghost away from the dock. Lou and Tony hastily covered the pile of cases and ran up the gangway just as a spotlight began sweeping the docks a quarter mile to the north. Don ran to the wheel, pushed the idling boat into gear and yelled for Al to brace himself. The Ghost, now considerably lighter, leapt onto plane and disappeared beyond a turn in the channel before the searchlight caught them in its beam.

They roared under the old railroad bridge and soon were approaching the south end of the channel. Al turned on their searchlight to illuminate the danger coming up. At the last possible moment Don whipped the Ghost onto her starboard side and slid around the corner.

At that very second, Al yelled, "Watch out!!"

But it was too late. The Ghost ran up onto a raft of logs that was waiting a change of tide to be hauled north. The engine screamed in distress as the prop came out of the water. The whole boat seemed airborne for an instant, then crashed into the water on the other side of the log raft. As the prop caught water again, the engine bogged for an instant, then spun up to speed and the boat lurched back onto plane.

"Check the bilge, Al! See if we broke anything," Don yelled. "It'll be a miracle if we didn't." He slowed to 25 knots and steadied the ride as best possible while Al pulled up floorboards from the forepeak to the aft cockpit looking for trouble. Lastly he opened the motor box and went over the engine and drive shaft carefully with his flashlight.

"No leaks, --yet anyway. The shaft is running true and the stuffing box isn't dripping any more than it should. I think we got real lucky, partner," he declared.

"I hope so, but we're not home yet and that's where we're headed, tired or not. I want to pull this baby out on the grid and look her over real close before we try any more of this foolishness," Don asserted.

"Fine by me. I'll take over when you get tired of staring into the dark. Do you think we can make it by dawn?"

"Sure, if we don't run out of gas," Don replied.

"Are we cutting it that close?" Al asked, beginning to worry once again.

"Yeah, but I stashed two 5 gallon tins under the back deck, so if we start sputtering, they'll give us another 30 to 45 minutes running time."

The Ghost hurried on through the night, now at 30 knots, with four very tired eyes constantly sweeping the horizon for more trouble. George Harris, who lived on the north point of Day Island noted their arrival at 5 am.

CHAPTER EIGHTEEN

"Larry Tucci, whose boys you met the other night, wants another load with about the same mix as you brought down before," Ray told the group at their Friday night meeting. "Seems he's a bigger player than I thought he was. Evidently he's got clients from Anacortes to Seattle, all of them wanting to replenish their wine cellars, according to him."

"We don't dare go back to La Conner," Al asserted. "Has he got a better place in mind to land the goods?"

"No, he's leaving that up to us. He says he'll meet us anyplace north of Seattle that we feel safe with. I have to let him know by Monday when and where we can make delivery," Ray replied.

"Here goes another weekend," Don said glumly.

"I thought the last one was kind of fun myself," Jill chimed in. "Or was I such bad company?"

"If you are searching for compliments, I'm sure the boys will be forthcoming, dear, but I think after what they went through Tuesday night, that I'll have a look around for myself. We're in this game to make money, not go to jail, as one of you stated not too long ago," Ray said.

"Okay, but forget Edmonds, Ray. That's where Olmstead got caught the first time," Jill warned.

"And the bays and sloughs around Everett are too full of sandbars and old pilings to be safe to run at night," Don advised. "You might checkout Mukilteo, it would be easy to get in and out from."

"If the authorities aren't watching and the tide isn't running 90 miles an hour," Al thought out loud.

"I'll check the whole area tomorrow and if I find a spot that looks good, I'll hang around to see if it quiets down at night. Okay?" Ray said, looking for agreement. They all nodded and the meeting broke up much earlier than usual.

On their walk home Jill asked Al and Don to come in for a conference over cookies and milk.

"Mmm, these are really good," Al said, as he reached for his third one. "All that beauty, all those brains and she can cook, too. What a girl, huh, Don?"

"Absolutely the best. No argument there," he replied.

"Okay guys, flattery will get you nowhere, as they say, but I'm grateful that you've trusted me with our profits so far. Recently, I've been converting them into gold rather than plowing money back into the market," she explained.

"Are you afraid the markets going to bust soon, Jill? I mean gold is pegged at $16 an ounce here in the states. What's the future in that?" Al asked.

"Again, I ask for your trust. Yes, I'm not only afraid the market is going to bust, I know it is. I also know that gold will double in the not too distant future and will grow much more valuable in the long run if you can hold it. That is, if you don't need it for your other operations."

"Is that a crystal ball you have up stairs," Don joked.

"All I'll say is that it is a lot better than any crystal ball I've heard of. I can't predict everything guys, but there are some things that I remember--- that is, that I am sure of and I'm pulling my money out of the market soon and investing in gold. Double Eagles, to be exact, if I can lay hands on them. All I need to know is: do you want me to continue to work with your shares as well as my own?"

"You're really serious about this aren't you?" Don said, adding, "If you're that sure of what's going to happen, then of course I trust you to do what's best."

"I'm serious, yes, but its your decision. How about you, Al?" Jill asked.

"We're partners Jill, for better or worse, for richer or poorer, 'till death do us part," he said, smiling, but very serious in his heart.

"Let's not go that far, please, Al," Jill said, giving him a light punch in the ribs. "Okay, I guess it's settled then. I'll keep giving Ray his split, but plowing all the profits except what you need for spending money into investments that we'll divide three ways when the time is right ---to retire or whatever," she finished lamely.

"I'd like to buy a roadster pretty soon. Are you still thinking the price will be less next year Jill?" Don asked.

"I know you're tired of taking the bus or borrowing your folk's car, but you'll be able to buy a Model A for about $450 next year and I'll bet next year's model will be even sharper looking," Jill affirmed.

"If you're right, Harold will really be sore! He paid $550 for his a couple of months ago," Al said.

"Who's Harold?" Jill asked.

"He's a guy that works for Foss on old number 29 and he's dating Ray's oldest girl, Birdie. He was two years ahead of us at

Stadium High" Al explained. "Don's been lusting after his roadster ever since Harold got it."

"Speaking of transportation, partner, we better hightail it for the trolley before we have to hitchhike back to Day Island," Don warned.

"I was thinking of staying over at the folk's house tonight, unless you need me for work on the boat tomorrow," Al said.

The Ghost had been on the grid since Wednesday afternoon to repair damage from their encounter with the log raft. They had patched and painted the scrapes on the bottom, but found the rudder post bent. After removing it, they took it to Hallen's machine shop for straightening and reinstalled it late Friday morning when the tide was low.

"No, she should be afloat by the time I get back, so I'll just move her back into the slip. I believe we're all set for the next trip when Ray finds the best delivery spot. I think we both deserve a couple of days off," Don said as he moved for the door. "Goodnight, Jill. Don't keep him up too late!"

"Soon as he finishes the cookies, I'm heading for bed and he's heading for home," she assured him.

As Don waved good-bye he was thinking, "I hope it's in the order you described, Jill."

Al took his time consuming the last cookie, finally screwing up the nerve to ask, "Jill, when are you going to give me a clue as to how you are so sure of what's going to happen economically in the next year?"

"Actually, Al, I'd rather talk about almost anything but that subject," she said with an edge to her voice.

"I'm sorry, Jill. My curiosity gets the best of me when I think of how absolutely correct your financial decisions have been. But, okay, set that aside then. How about your feelings about us, and by that, I mean you and I?"

"I don't know what to say Al," she said simply.

He got up and kneeled by her chair. "All I'm asking is, do I have a chance with you? Will you ever feel the love for me that I feel for you?"

She pulled his face to hers and kissed him lightly. He put his arms around her neck and kissed her back. She began to tremble and before he could kiss her again, tears started rolling down her cheeks. He held her close, not understanding what was happening. They remained in that awkward position for several minutes before she spoke.

"I'm, sorry, Al. There's so much about me that I can't explain, so much that doesn't make sense. All we can do is live our future, or lack of it, one day at a time. I do love you and I'm always happy when we're together, but what I can't predict is if that can last. Can you understand?"

"I understand that these days hardly anybody knows what's going to last, but as far as I'm concerned, my feelings are never going to change. I want to be with you forever!" he choked out.

She replied, "Then let's start fresh tomorrow, Al. Take me someplace where we've never been before and nobody knows us. I promise I'll be better company than I am tonight, okay?" she begged.

Al was so overcome with emotion that he could only nod, squeeze her hand, kiss her forehead and back toward the door. Finally, he found enough voice to say, "Good night, my love, until tomorrow."

Jill closed the door slowly behind him feeling almost in a dream. "Am I going to stay here in the past? Can I say yes to a man from whom I might be snatched away by some weird warp in the time of our existences?"

She lay awake for hours, but no answers came into her mind. When she thought ahead to tomorrow, she finally relaxed and fell into a warm, comfortable rest.

CHAPTER NINETEEN

"Watch that she don't overheat climbing the pass, Al," his father was lecturing on the already warm Saturday morning. "And use only high test, we don't want to be burning no valves either," he worried. Mr. Nelson was very proud of his Studebaker Standard Six. Even though it was now four years old, he kept its Navajo Gray lacquer finish clean and waxed regularly. It had cost him three times what a Model T Ford might have in 1925, but he felt it was a good investment and treated it as such. It had taken a great deal of convincing on Al's part to allow him to take it for the whole weekend, especially so when he learned his son was heading over Snoqualmie Pass to the rodeo in Ellensburg and taking his friend Jill with him. Mrs. Nelson was much more concerned about the propriety of such a plan than her husband's precious automobile.

"Jill is a nice girl, mama. We'll get separate hotel rooms and I promise to be a gentlemen," Al had argued.

"Yah, you better be, for sure," she replied and stomped off, still unconvinced.

Jill arrived with a picnic basket in one hand and a small valise in the other. She listened to the last of Mr. Nelson's instructions to his son with a smile on her face, thinking of how much more dangerous and complicated Al's recent vocational missions were than a trip across the low mountain pass to Ellensburg. Of course, the Nelsons and the Grants thought their sons were manufacturing boats at Day Island, not running contraband liquor!

"Sorry Jill," Al said, suddenly realizing she was still holding her burdens while he listened to his father. He loaded her bag into the back seat with his and put the food basket in front. "Looks like we're ready to go, pop. I'll take good care of your Studie and we'll see you Sunday evening by dark, okay?" Not waiting for an answer, he ushered Jill into the car, ran around to the driver's side and backed carefully out of the narrow driveway.

"Isn't it a great day, Al?" Jill said as they headed down 11th Street toward the water.

"Absolutely perfect, with you beside me and the open road beckoning us!" Al pontificated.

"Oh boy, are you full of it today!" she giggled.

"Well, I'm really happy and excited is all. Hey, what have you got in the basket?" he asked, trying to look under the napkin that covered it's contents.

"Never mind! Just keep your mind on the road and I'll mind the food," she warned, moving the basket to the right side of the seat and moving closer to Al.

"Say, that's more like it," he exclaimed, putting his right arm around her shoulder.

"I don't think this car has power steering, does it? Maybe you better steer with both hands and snuggle later, okay?" Jill said, prodding him in the ribs lightly.

"What's power steering?" he asked, actually thinking more of the snuggling for later at which she had hinted.

"Never mind," she said, quickly hurrying on, "This is really a nice, old car, Al. I can see why your father is so particular about how you treat it. It's comfortable and you can sit high enough to really see the country side."

"Yeah, it's got a 50 horsepower, six cylinder motor , nice upholstery and silk curtains, but it only has two wheel brakes, so you have to be careful on these steep hills here in Tacoma. I'm still thinking about a Dodge when you say we've got enough saved up," Al said as they turned onto Highway 99 and headed north toward Seattle.

Jill had never been to the Ellensburg rodeo and had previously only crossed Snoqualmie Pass on the modern Interstate 90 multi-lane freeway. As they wound their way though the small villages of Issaquah and North Bend she thought of how much beauty that the modern roads had robbed from the motor touring experience. The mountains of Washington State in the summer had to be one of the most spectacular visions in the United States. They had rolled down their windows as the day warmed and the scent of the fir trees that closely lined their route permeated the air. She remarked at how lovely it smelled.

"Wait until we get over the pass into the pines. It smells even better," Al said enthusiastically.

"I thought you said that you'd never been here before," Jill exclaimed, feeling a little disappointed.

"I haven't been to Ellensburg, but I went to Boy Scout camp near Cle Elum in 1922 and it's in the pines. That was the year before the first rodeo in Ellensburg, so this is a first for me, just like I promised," he said defensively.

Jill snuggled closer, patted his arm reassuringly as they exchanged looks of mutual pleasure. They stopped at the top of the pass to stretch their legs. Jill was acutely aware of how different the summit looked than when she had seen it previously. Although the snow conditions were frequently wet and heavy compared to Utah or Idaho, by the 1990s, Snoqualmie had become the most highly developed, low altitude ski area in the world, serving both western and eastern Washington residents with easy access to winter sports. In 1929, it was barely a wide enough spot in the road to pull over and cool your radiator as they were doing. Continuing down the pass, they found a small lake to the left of the road and stopped to wander down and eat lunch beside its cool waters.

"This would be a fun place to camp out," Al thought aloud. "I'll bet the fishing wouldn't be half bad either. Do you like fresh trout Jill?"

"I don't think I've ever had any except from the market and those were probably not all that fresh," she replied. "I'd love to try catching some. Maybe next time we could bring some fishing gear and you could show me how to cook it outdoors. That's what you Boy Scouts do , isn't it?" she kidded.

"Some Boy Scout I am now," he said quietly.

"What do you mean? You haven't forgot to fish have you? Don said you caught a big salmon when you were coming back from Olympia a while back."

"Yeah, I did, but I was coming back from running whiskey, not exactly something I learned to do in the Boy Scouts," Al explained, glumly.

"Are you sorry that I got you into this, Al?"

"I guess not, and like I said before, I made my own choice and that choice was to make enough money to get set up in something better. I don't plan to be looking over my shoulder for someone chasing me all my life. When we get a big enough stake to set ourselves up, we'll quit!" Al asserted. Changing the subject abruptly, he continued, "We better get going if we want to get some rooms and catch the preliminary events this evening."

Jill packed up the almost empty picnic basket and led the way back to the car, sorry that she had inadvertently brought up the subject that seemed to have upset Al.

Although they arrived in Ellensburg in what normally would have been time to secure rooms, the rodeo fans had already filled the few good hotels. After an hour's search, Al found that the only accommodations were in a tourist camp.

"I don't know what to say, Jill. They don't have any singles left, just doubles or one with two beds," Don said, discouraged that he hadn't had time to plan better.

Noticing his discomfort, she patted his arm and said, "Two beds will work just fine. It was a last minute decision; we're probably lucky not to have to camp in the car with this big a crowd in town."

"You're a good sport Jill," was all Al could think to say as he headed back to the office. He signed the register as Mr. and Mrs. Allen Nelson with more than a little guilt, but a sincere wish that it was really true.

An hour later they were perched high in the wooden grandstand cheering the ropers with hot dogs in one hand and sodas in the other. The crowd around them was equally excited, despite the heat and dust of the summer evening. This was the seventh year of the rodeo and it was now drawing first caliber contestants from all over the West. It was well after dark before all the "wanna-bes" were weeded out from the true professionals that would compete in Sunday's main events. The arena had been equipped with more electric lights than Al figured there were in the rest of the small town, while Jill marveled at how well the cowboys worked their skills in such primitive conditions.

Walking back to the tourist cabin, which Jill had found quaint and cute compared to motels of her previous time, they found a soda fountain catering to the crowd too young to hit the more serious watering holes. Elbowing his way to the counter through a crowd of children, Al ordered two enormous chocolate ice cream cones.

"Wow!" Jill exclaimed, "That's the biggest hard ice cream cone I've ever had."

"Hard? Well, it better be, or it wouldn't be ice cream would it?" Al remarked, a little confused.

"Right," Jill said, wishing she could keep her mind in the present time frame better. "It's absolutely delicious. Thank you!"

It's just an ice cream cone, Al thought. Maybe she's nervous about having to share a room with me. I hope she doesn't mention it to Mom--or Don. But he didn't say a word, just kept licking his ice cream cone and leading Jill back to their cabin hideaway, wondering what was coming next in his crazy young existence.

CHAPTER TWENTY

"Allen!" Mrs. Nelson called upstairs to her son. "Don is on the phone for you."

Al had awoken only a few minutes earlier, had looked out the window of his second story room to see a gloomy, overcast day more typical of February than July and returned to bed. "What a way to start a week," he grumbled, then brightened up, remembering how marvelous the weekend had been with Jill. They had returned later than expected last night, so he had stayed another night at his parents' home.

Wondering what his partner was going to say about his weekend, if the subject came up, and he certainly hoped it wouldn't, he pulled on his trousers and headed downstairs.

"Hi, partner. What's up?" Al asked, taking the phone.

"Ray called at the crack of dawn. I don't know if he ever sleeps. Anyway he wants us to head for --uh, north as soon as possible. Everything is set up for tonight, so we need to hustle. I'll get the rig ready if you can bring some food and the money with you when you come, okay?"

Don's voice sounded tense to Al. Maybe it's that I'm feeling guilty for having left him to work while I was cavorting with Jill, he thought. Hopefully, it's because of the chance of being overheard on the party line. Speaking as positively as possible, he answered, "Sure, I'll catch the next trolley to 6th and Proctor, pick up supplies at the market, get the cash from the bank and catch the 10:30 bus to the shop. Anything particular you want me to get?"

"No, whatever is easy to fix. It looks like we've got a blow coming in, so it might not be much fun cooking while we're under way. Meet me at the dock, not the shop and bring your rain gear." He hung up without a good-bye.

"Is everything all right Allen?" his mother asked.

She only called him Allen when she was concerned or unhappy, so he put on a pleasant face and said, lightly, "Yeah, no problem, Momma. Don just wanted me to be sure to bring food and stuff when I came to work. Sounds like he missed my cooking over the weekend."

"Speaking of weekends, did you and Jill have a nice time? You got home awfully late last night, didn't you?" She knew very well that they had rolled in by 10 PM, but was fishing for more than that, of course.

"Jill loved the rodeo. They had some really unbelievable riders, top rate! The town was really crowded but everybody was friendly and the weather was perfect, not like here. The events didn't get over until after four, so we made good time getting home by ten."

"Did you get a good place to stay for Jill?" she pried.

"Not too bad. She didn't complain. Well, I'd better hustle. Don sounds like he needs my help. Thanks for putting me up and thank Pop again for using the Studie. It sure beat riding the bus!" He kissed her cheek, grabbed his gear bag and headed for the door.

"Aren't you going to have some breakfast?" she called, but he was already down the porch steps and just waved back.

"What's going on with him?" Mrs. Nelson mumbled, "And why didn't he say more about Jill? That boy is up to something and I'm afraid it's not good!"

Al felt relieved when he reached the trolley stop just a minute before it appeared, creaking its way up the hill on 6th Avenue. His relief was not so much for having caught the trolley as for having escaped his mother's questions, which he was sure were only in the beginning stage when he left.

Don heard the bus coming across the bridge just as he paid Mr. Cummings for topping off the Ghost's fuel tank. As Al climbed down from the bus trying to balance a heavy box of groceries and his bag of personal gear, Don crossed the street and took the box.

"Thanks Don, I appreciate the help," Al said, watching closely for further sign of irritation that he had noted from their earlier phone conversation.

"Just want to get going as soon as we can before the weather gets any worse. That way we might be able to run slow when it gets dark and still make Vancouver in time for the pickup," Don explained.

"I wonder what all the rush is about. We're going to have to run awfully hard, regardless of the weather. Doesn't Ray realize how hard it is to make time in the dark?" Al complained as they stowed the supplies aboard. He made ready to cast off as Don just shook his head unhappily and fired up the engine.

Not bothering to quiet the exhaust through the underwater outlet, Don mashed the throttle forward even before they had cleared the spit that acted as a breakwater and the Ghost leaped onto plane headed north. George Harris heard the roar as they sped by his house and noted the time.

The Ghost beat into a rising chop, windshield wipers working hard to keep the rain and salt spray clear of the glass. They had passed Gig Harbor and were well into the west passage separating Vashon Island from the mainland before either spoke.

"You don't look very happy Don. Did you have a bad weekend or are you not feeling well?" Al asked cautiously.

"Both, I guess. Saturday I worked on the new boat until I was too tired to make dinner. Then Sunday morning Goldie Moore got me out of bed when all I wanted to do was sleep," Don replied sourly.

"She came to the shop? What did she want?"

"Seems Ray hadn't told his wife what he was up to and since she doesn't drive, she sent Goldie to see if he was with us or if we knew where he was. Goldie says her mom, Lena, is real suspicious that Ray is seeing another woman!" Don replied.

"I don't know where he'd find time to chase women when he's running his garage five days a week and spending nights and weekends finding people to buy large quantities of booze," Al exclaimed.

"That's what I thought, but Goldie thinks differently. She knows about his bootlegging efforts, at least part of what's going on, but Lena doesn't and has Goldie convinced her dad is cheating on Lena," Don explained.

"What did you tell Goldie then?" Al asked.

"I told her the truth, but as little as I could to satisfy her; that Ray was up north setting up a deal to sell some liquor and that I was sure he'd be home soon," Don said.

"Did that satisfy her then?" Al asked.

"For a while. I told her that Ray was going to call us and that I would call her after that. Ray didn't call by evening and, lo and behold, Goldie shows up again at the shop just before dark." Al looked at him quizzically and Don continued. "Seems she had gone by your folk's place and found that you and Jill were away for the weekend. She's more than curious, so she comes back to pick my brain. Anyway, she ends up getting me to go with her to Salmon Beach, supposedly to see if Ray is down there sporting with the wild bunch and it turns into a very late party."

"And you got drunk." Al said, not as a question.

"And I got drunk," Don said darkly.

"Anything else worth mentioning?" Al asked lightly.

"Nothing else to mention at all, except I'm still hung over, mad at myself for breaking my word about drinking, mad at Ray for sending us out in miserable weather on short notice and just plain mad!" he finished.

Al said nothing for sometime, letting the pounding of the rain and waves against the hull fill the silence of words. Finally, he asked, "Mad at me too, for not helping with work on the boat? For spending the weekend with Jill?"

Don replied with a simple, "Yes."

"I don't blame you, Don, but nothing happened between Jill and I except a weekend of clean fun. Yes, we did sleep in the same room, but in totally separate beds. Yes, we were close to one another in the car, at the rodeo and in our room. Yes, we did kiss a few times, but as much as I care for her, she is not committed to me, you, or anyone. There's something that is holding her back from anything but a platonic relationship and she won't say anything more about what it is," Al said with emotion choking his voice.

The rain had quit and again they drove on with only the howl of the hard working engine and the pounding of water against the hull for a time.

At length, Don spoke, "I agree that Jill is holding back something very personal, maybe even secret and I can't begin to think clearly enough today to try to figure her out. So let's forget about the weekend and concentrate on getting ourselves safely to Vancouver before midnight, okay?"

"Fine with me," Al said, very happy to change the subject. "Let's have a bite to eat and then I'll take the wheel and you can rest. How does a donut from Hoyt's sound?"

"Sounds great and if you can heat it on the warming plate it sounds perfect," Don said, sounding a lot happier.

After polishing off a brunch of cocoa and a dozen donuts between them, Don lay down to relax and Al took over as pilot. The wind slacked off enough to allow him to push their speed up to 30 knots. As they rounded Snatelum Point, keeping well off its treacherous rocks, the low overcast had caused dusk to come early. They arrived at the Coupeville dock, which looked like an old wooden fortress, just in time to be the last gasoline customer.

Al returned to the Ghost shaking his head after paying the fuel bill. "At the rate we're burning gasoline today, we'll be lucky not to run dry tonight."

"To make it to False Creek by midnight, we're going to have to keep running hard and we'll have to go through Deception Pass, rather than Swinomish Slough," Don said.

"That's fine by me! We don't need the kind of trouble we ran into there last trip," Al agreed.

With Don at the wheel again, they pushed on north along Whidbey Island, west through Deception Pass and entered Rosario Strait as full darkness enveloped the myriad of small islands. Don slowed to 20 knots, the lowest speed that the boat would plane efficiently, and headed due north into increasing swells. Al watched closely to point out each flashing beacon that warned of danger, ticking off their progress at each point of land. As they bore more to the west, entering the Strait of Georgia, the swells became more pronounced and their progress slowed and the Ghost encountered resistance as she dipped her bow into each wave.

The wind had switched, coming now from the north, gradually clearing away the overcast and increasing the swells. It wasn't long before Don was throttling the power on to keep the bow up while climbing the waves and powering off to avoid burying the bow when sliding down the other side. Both men strained to see what was happening in front of them, growing more fatigued as the miles passed. They rounded Grey Point inside the bell buoy marking a huge rock, slowed to displacement speed and switched to silent exhaust mode for the first time that day. It was almost 1 AM when they slid up to the private dock. McFarland and his two men had half their load already on the small dock and were heading up the gangway for the rest.

"Sorry we're late," Don said, reaching to shake Mac's outstretched hand. "We got a late start and the weather has been mixed all the way. Glad to see you trusted us enough to start unloading your truck."

"My office took a call from your salesman concerning the timing. I must say you did every bit as well in getting here as was promised. That craft of yours must be very fast indeed!" McFarland said admiringly. "Must get a proper ride in it some day. Well, we won't hold you a minute longer than necessary. I know you must have a long way to go yet."

"A lot farther than the last time, but I hope with less problems," Al said, stopping himself before saying more than he should have.

McFarland only smiled and started handing cases to Al who was still in the boat. By 1:45 the load was in place, tarped down and the money exchanged. Don shook hands with McFarland as the latter pushed them away from the dock and Al started the engine. They moved slowly through the fish boats as they had previously with their running lights on. Back in the strait there was no moon to help visibility as on the last trip and the swells had not subsided, although running with them, even heavily laden, seemed easier to Al than going against them. He wasn't throttling up and down as Don had, instead plowing along at 15 knots, hoping to increase their speed when they moved into more protected water.

Don was rubbing his eyes, struggling to make out the next beacon to point Al toward. "I'm never going to do that again," he muttered, just loud enough for Al to hear.

"Do what?" Al asked.

"Get drunk, stay out that late or listen to Goldie!"

"Is she really that bad?" Al wondered aloud.

"No, but she loves to party. I was lucky to get a ride home. She dumped me for some tall, skinny, slick looking older guy and danced with him until I had to beg her to take me home, after I barfed over the railing twice," Don admitted.

"Sorry to hear that, but I'm glad you've sworn off again. Too much temptation riding back there." Al motioned with his thumb toward their cargo. "Was this guy taller and skinnier than you?"

"Maybe only a little I guess, but he had to be close to 30 and she's only 19 or so, isn't she? Anyway, this guy could sure put down the wine without looking drunk."

Still curious, Al asked, "Who is he, somebody she already knew?"

"Customer of Ray's, name of Oz Holmes, she said. Divorced, I think," Don replied, staring into the darkness. Changing the subject abruptly, he said, "I hope the Tucci brothers are patient because I don't see how we're going to make it to Mukilteo on time."

"Ray didn't give us any lee way for bad weather or anything else that might go wrong," Al agreed. "I don't think he could possibly understand how different and difficult it is running at night."

"Or maybe Mr. Tucci dictated the time element and Ray had to go along with it to make the deal. We should get him to let us in on that end of things. Jill is pretty straight forward about setting up the buying end, but Ray never tells us more than a bare minimum about the delivery side," Don mused, adding, "Of course, maybe that's for our own good."

The swells abated enough when they had rounded Pt. Lawrence on Orcas Island that Al could increase speed to 23 knots. The Ghost was throwing a good deal of spray from bouncing off the waves and making a large wake, but there was no moon to show up the phosphorescence this night. They both hoped that would make them less visible than on the previous trip through much of the same area. Backtracking through Deception Pass they encountered much stronger tide conditions than a few hours before. Al wrestled to keep the Ghost pointed safely through the narrow passage. Once headed south again he poured on the power through the smoother water of Skagit Bay and down Saratoga Passage. At 32 knots the Ghost was making up time, truly flying over most of the waves, the hull being beaten like a mad drummer.

"Oh--- I'll feel a lot better when this night is over," Don moaned. The incessant jarring had given him a throbbing headache and his equilibrium was failing.

"Sorry, partner, but we're over an hour late now even at this speed," Al said through teeth clenched against the vibration and noise.

The flashing beacon of Elliott Point ahead guided them toward Mukilteo which lay just to the north of the point. The Ghost sank deep in the water as Al pulled the throttle back to minimum and Don switched to silent running. Neither had docked here previously and were surprised by a twisting current that wanted to sweep them away from the dock despite applying more power to get steerage. Fortunately, Tony and Lou were on the dock available to catch the mooring lines that Don threw to them. As stocky as the Tucci brothers were, it took all their strength to secure the Ghost to the dock.

"Thanks fellows," Don said as he jumped to the dock. "Really sorry we're late. It's been a long hard run tonight."

"Hey, we're glad to see you at all after the last episode. That Coast Guard boat looked like it wasn't gonna give up very easy!" Tony laughed.

"Only more speed and plain dumb luck got us out of that one. We ran over a log raft coming out of the Hole in the Rock and they would have caught us if we hadn't flown clear over it," Don admitted, sheepishly.

"I'd like to have seen that part," Lou said, "But we were too busy loading the stuff off the dock. The ruckus woke up half the town and we barely got the goods loaded when a sheriff's car showed up."

Al jumped to the dock now and asked, "What did you do? Didn't he stop you?"

"Yeah, but we told him we was loading our catch from the night's fishing, when we heard this loud boat go by followed by a Coast Guard boat with lights flashing and then we heard a crash to the south, so he should go check it out, 'cuz it sounded real bad!" Tony explained.

"Well, it's a good thing he didn't want to see what you caught, eh?" Don joked. "Best we better get this night's catch into the truck and all get out of here. Too many lights around here to suit me."

"Too much current to land without help either," Al grumbled. "She doesn't handle all that well at slow speed with her prop tucked way up under the hull. Must be a design defect," he laughed, waiting to see how Don might retort.

"Inexperienced help, more likely," Don shot back. "Let's help these guys load and get going before the sun comes up."

The unloading went smoothly and quickly. The Tucci boys handed over the tarp the Ghost's crew had left them previously along with $7200 in cash and said good-bye. It would be the last time that Don and Al would see them.

CHAPTER TWENTY-ONE

George Harris was finishing his lunch as he observed the Ghost ease past his home at the north end of Day Island and slip easily into her berth at Cummings Marina. "A lot quieter than their departure at lunch time yesterday," he noted in his journal.

Ray Moore stepped out of a gorgeous Biddle and Smart bodied Hudson phaeton and walked quickly toward the Ghost. The north wind had cleared the skies and the wire wheels of the new Hudson sparkled in the warm sun.

"We need to talk, in the boat, now!" Ray barked as he approached Don, who was looping the mooring lines to their bits.

"What's up?" Don challenged, in no mood for trouble after only a few hours rest in Eagle Harbor.

"In the boat," Ray repeated, more softly, seeing the look on Don's face. "We've got trouble."

Al rose from checking the bilges and closed the engine box. "Surprised to see you here, Ray---"

"Listen to me," Ray broke in, "Tucci called me four hours ago wanting to know where his delivery was. He sent his boys out at four O'clock and they hadn't returned by eight. I told him I'd call back as soon as I heard from you. Now what happened?"

"Nothing!" Don exclaimed, "Everything went fine except we were late getting there because of the weather. They were loaded up and leaving Mukilteo before dawn. We ran down to Eagle Harbor, slept a couple of hours, took on some fuel and headed here."

Al produced a bank bag full of cash and said, "They wouldn't have given us this if they weren't happy with the delivery!"

"Okay, go back to the shop and stay put until I call you. I'll call Tucci from a phone that's not tied to any of us and tell him they took delivery only a couple of hours before he called me," Ray said.

"What's the big deal, Ray? They might have had trouble with their truck or any number of things," Al said.

"They might have even been stopped by cops or Federal agents, but that's not our problem, is it?" Don asked.

Ray looked thoughtful for a moment before answering. "I don't know. Tucci is connected and those kind of guys take everything real personally. I need to calm him down and let him know we kept our end of the deal and that whatever delayed his boys was out of our control."

"What do you mean connected?" Al asked.

"I think he means that Tucci is a mobster, one of the Italian families or something close. Right, Ray?" Don asked.

"Who do you think has the kind of money he paid us in the last week?" Ray exploded. "These guys don't like screw ups!"

Don rose to his full six feet and faced down the older man, "WE didn't screw up, Ray. We delivered, they paid and we parted company as friends. You tell that to your friend Tucci and make it clear we don't expect any trouble!"

Ray was red in the face, his fists clenched at the ready, when Al moved between the two and said, quietly, "Don and I have had a long, difficult, dangerous day and night. I think you should get off the boat Ray before this gets out of hand. We'll go back to the shop and wait for your call."

Al was frying some pork shops for dinner the following day before Ray's call came. Don dropped the metal plates that he was setting onto the table with a considerable crash and went to the phone on the back wall.

"The police found Tucci's truck this afternoon parked in a church yard in Everett. It has his restaurant's name and phone number on it of all things. They asked him why he had left it there for almost two days. He told them that his boys had gone to Seattle to pick up supplies for the business yesterday and never returned. The police told him the boys weren't with the truck; it was empty and asked if he thought they had been robbed."

"How could he answer that without involving lies that would lead to more trouble?" Don asked.

"He just said he didn't know, but he would handle it and thanked them for finding the truck," Ray said.

"You don't think this is the end of it then? With us, I mean?" Don asked nervously.

"I don't know. All I could tell him was that you said the boys were fine when they left with the goods. We'll just have to wait it out and see what really happened and how Tucci handles it if somebody double-crossed him."

"You think that Tony and Lou would double-cross their own father, Ray?" Don's tone indicated that he really didn't think that was the case.

"No chance! Family loyalty is essential to those guys. It could have been anybody that thought they could get away with it. Maybe even the cops themselves. There's more then one crooked cop out there you know. Like I said, we'll just have to wait and see. Meantime, it might be awhile before I find another buyer as good as Tucci. We'll also have to hope that word doesn't get out that one of our shipments didn't reach its destination. Trust, or lack of it, is real important to people in our business. I'll see you Friday night at the garage, okay?"

"Yeah, sure. Friday night." Don hung up and explained all that he had heard to Al as they finished preparing dinner.

"Maybe we should get back to building and selling boats," Al said thoughtfully. "There's even more down side to running liquor than I thought there might be."

"For now, I guess that's all we can do. I'm not looking for any more trouble than you are," Don agreed.

However, he was soon to find that trouble sometimes comes without looking for it.

CHAPTER TWENTY-TWO

Ray Moore was not a happy man and he was taking it out on the new Hudson as he raced back to Tacoma. $7600 worth of liquor and the sons of his best client to date had gone missing just after his young partners had delivered the load. Although Ray didn't really believe that Don and Al had anything to do with the disappearance, he wasn't so sure of Jill. Something about her just never seemed right to him. She was smart and ambitious, not to mention very nice to look at, but he couldn't get over her uncanny predictions in the stock market and the ease with which she had connected their little partnership with major liquor suppliers in both Victoria and Vancouver. Would she have had the nerve to have the shipment hijacked in order to resell it? Ray believed that was what the Makovich brothers had tried to do a few months ago. Could Jill have thought she could succeed where Makovich's cronies had failed?

The front tires of the big car howled in protest as Ray wheeled around the sharp bend entering Fircrest, the wide white side walls nearing scraping the pavement. His mind left the mysterious Jill and raced onto other possibilities. Who else could have known where and when the Tucci's would pick up the liquor? It had been a last minute decision on his part to use Mukilteo. The leak must have been on the Tucci's end. They must have---his thoughts were interrupted by the wail of a police siren. He didn't have to look back to know he was in even more trouble. He pulled to the side of the wide avenue and stopped the car.

"Guess you know why I stopped you," the stout Fircrest police officer said, citation book already in hand.

"Sorry, my mind was elsewhere," Ray replied truthfully, but beginning to sweat noticeably.

"I need to see your license and registration."

Ray noticed that the cop didn't say please. Not a good sign. Probably better not try to bribe my way out this time, he thought as he reached for his wallet. He handed his license to the cop, who took it and then stood waiting. Reluctantly Ray pulled down the sun visor and removed the registration from a built in pocket.

"License says you're Ray Moore. Registration says this car belongs to Joy Barlow. You want to explain that?"

"Yes, sir, Miss Barlow is a --a customer of mine," Ray was really sweating now as began to lie, "You see I own the Tacoma

Avenue Garage and she wanted me to test the car out for her before she leaves on a long trip next week."

"Looks like a brand new car to me. Why would she need a new car tested for anything?"

The cop was getting more belligerent by the second. Thinking fast Ray came up with another lie. "That's exactly it, you see; it's new and untested. Not like a car that you've had long enough to know well. They all have their foibles and idiosyncrasies, you can be sure. She wants me to make certain that its well sorted out and I'm putting it through its paces."

"Sounds to me like she's the one with idiot scyncracies or whatever and as for putting it through its paces, you were going at way too fast a pace for our town, mister. You're lucky I don't run you in for reckless driving!" With his stubby, sweaty fingers, the cop scrawled the charges onto the citation book, made Ray sign it and told him, "If I catch you speeding through our town again it's gonna cost ya a lot more than the twenty bucks for this time."

Ray cursed his luck as he drove slowly through the remainder of the hamlet of Fircrest. Twenty dollars was more than half a week's wages for most workers and even though Ray could well afford it, it just added to the day's problems. He knew Tucci would probably not buy more liquor from them and he might blame him for whatever happened to his sons. The only way out was to find out who had grabbed the boys and expose whatever the plot was to Tucci. He also had to get this borrowed car back to its owner without his snoopy daughter Birdie spotting him and digging into his affairs any further. He wished Birdie would marry that nice fellow Harold and get out of his house before she entirely spoiled what little relationship he had left with Lena. Ray suspected that Birdie was the one that suggested to her mother that his Friday night meetings were not all business. Truthfully, they sometimes were not, but this weekend had been all about business and when Birdie got Lena asking questions about where he had been all night Saturday, there weren't any answers that wouldn't compromise everyone in the business. The late night calls from their clients were also impossible to explain away. To top it off, Goldie had come home tipsy with that tin horn, second rate bootlegger Oz early Sunday morning. Lena, with Birdie's encouragement, had blamed Ray for Goldie's behavior when he had very little to do with the girl. Well, he had taught her to drive a few years back and she had gotten rather wild since then, but was that his fault?

He drove the Hudson into his lady friend's garage, put the keys in the door pocket, bolted the garage door and decided to walk back to his shop and call her later when he was in a better frame of mind. Or not at all, if he chose. There were plenty of other fish in the sea, weren't there? No use in tying himself down too long with anyone in particular. Safer and less complicated that way, too. Maybe my best decision of the day, he thought, as he began the long walk that he hoped would clear his head for more important matters.

*****

Larry Tucci, meantime, paced his Everett office, plotting exactly how he would rub out whoever might have taken his boys and stolen his liquor shipment. He alternated between rage and the grief he knew that he would feel if his boys didn't show up at all. How would he ever be able to explain such a tragedy to his wife Rose? Ray Moore had called him with the details of the supposedly, smooth delivery at Mukilteo, explaining that the only problem had been that it had arrived an hour later than planned. Moore had also promised to personally investigate who might have leaked any information about the shipment, but had assured him that no one on their end was at fault. Easy to say, not easy to prove, Tucci thought, bitterly, and what resources did Moore have to find the culprits? "Not as many as I have," Tucci swore out loud. He went back to the phone and started down his list of connections.

Jill was surprised and a bit startled to find Ray waiting for her when she exited the employee entrance on the side of the Brown and Haley Candy building. He motioned her to a shabby car that she didn't recognize and said nothing until they were moving toward Pacific Avenue.

"We've got problems, Jill," he started.

"Are the boys okay? What's happened?" she broke in.

"Al and Don are fine. The boat is fine, but we have a very unhappy client. His two sons and their load of liquor have gone missing," Ray stated flatly.

"Do you think they took it, the sons, I mean?"

"No, the truck was found by the Everett Police in a church yard, empty, of course. Tucci is so mad that it scares me. I assured him that no one on our end had anything to do with the disappearance, but I don't think he's convinced."

"What can we do to convince him, Ray? You know that the

boys wouldn't steal the load back or hurt anybody. Did anybody else know about when and where the delivery was going to be made?" Jill asked, frustrated.

"Don and Al didn't have time to say anything to anybody before they left. That leaves you, Jill. If there's anything you've got to say about who else might have had a hand in stealing that load, now is the time to spill it, because Tucci is not a guy to fool with," Ray said pointedly.

"Are you nuts? I would never jeopardize anyone by talking about our business! I know a lot more about guys like Tucci and the Mafia than you'll ever know Ray. When you told me that you had hooked up with somebody that was connected to the families, I almost choked. You may think you made a smart connection, but I know you may have made the biggest mistake of your life if something bad happened to Tucci's kids," Jill shouted at him.

"Listen, missy, I don't know who you think you're talking to here. I've been on this earth twice as long as you have and I'm a pretty good judge of who to deal with and who to leave alone," Ray snarled back.

"You don't know jack shit about me, Ray! Nobody knows where I've come from and nobody knows as much about what's going to happen to them as I do. You haven't got a clue! So back off me and start saying your prayers that Tucci doesn't really blame this mess on you."

Ray was appalled that Jill would speak to him so coarsely. He had stopped for a traffic light and stalled the car. Jill opened the door, got out and stomped away without looking back. She tore up the steep hill as if it were flat ground, so hot was her rage. Back at home, she didn't bother to get her wind back before booting up the computer and starting a search for the history of the Tucci family. What she found made her wish she had never seen the name.

CHAPTER TWENTY-THREE

Jill called Don and Al later that night to warn them of the danger of doing any further business with Tucci. She also told them of her confrontation with Ray. Don took the call and repeated what she was saying to Al, but, at a certain point, she asked to speak to Al directly.

"Al, I won't be able to spend much time with you for a while, and it's not because I don't want to. I need to use all my spare time working the stock market from now until October to maximize and protect our investment. Ray is undoubtedly so mad at me that he won't care if I'm part of your other business anyway."

"Well, Don and I have talked about things a little and have decided to keep our noses to the grindstone to finish this boat as fast as possible. So we'll just wait out what Ray might cook up next and hope that Tucci finds his sons soon. In the meantime, can I call you?"

"Why don't I call you, if you don't mind?"

Al squirmed a little, thinking he was getting dropped for some unknown reason, but said, "Sure, I'll look forward to it. Not too long, I hope?"

"I'll be in touch soon, don't worry. Good-bye."

Don guessed just enough of what was happening in their conversation to whet his curiosity even more. "What is she up to Al? Are we getting dumped or what?"

"I don't know, partner; she's acting like she knows more about the future than it seems possible to me. Has she ever given you a clue of how she does it? I mean outguesses the market so consistently?" Al asked.

"No, but you've spent more time with her than I have lately, so if she didn't confide in you, she sure hasn't given me any clues. Just now she warned us about the Tucci bunch, but didn't give any indication of how she knew they were mobsters," Don said.

"Is that how she described them?" Al asked.

"The very words. Not bootleggers, mobsters!"

"Of course, people might call us that if they knew what we have been doing," Al said thoughtfully.

"They might call us rum runners or whiskey merchants, but I don't consider myself a mobster, do you?"

"No, not really. I was just trying to look at it from a different perspective. Anyway, for right now, I guess we're back to being boat builders. And if we're going to be good boat builders, we better get some shut eye," Al concluded.

Later, Al lay staring at the ceiling, wondering what had happened to the romance he thought had been blossoming between Jill and himself. In the lower bunk, Don stared up at his partner's sagging mattress, wondering the same thing for awhile and then switched to wondering how Jill could possibly know the things she knew if she were not some kind of medium or----he drifted off dreaming of a witch gazing into a crystal ball. A witch with the beautiful face of Jill Gardiner.

By noon three days later, Don could contain his thoughts no longer. "Al, I think we should take a look in Jill's bedroom, you and me together!"

Al dropped the chisel he had been using to cut the excess from the plugs covering the screws fastening the bottom planking to the ribs of the inverted boat hull which they were finishing. "What the heck are you talking about?"

"Jill has something secret up in her room that has to do with how she gets information. I can't get it out of my head and I think its important to find out what really goes on with her. I know that may sound weird to you, but --"

"May sound weird? I guess so! You want to break in her house and raid her bedroom? Good grief, Don, that would end whatever relationship we have with her for good!"

"Look, Al, ever since we first spotted her that night last year, it's been driving me nuts on what she does up there. Now, we're supposed to be partners in two different enterprises with her, we're both greatly attracted to her and we still don't know what her story really is. You spent a night sleeping in the same room and don't know anymore than I do, right?"

"Yeah, but---sneaking into her bedroom, is that really the way to find out what her secrets are? Can't we just come out and ask her to level with us" Al asked, but doubtfully.

"I think we both already gave her that chance. Look, if we don't hear from her by Monday, we go to town while she's at work and check out that room for some answers. Agreed?" Don asked, firmly.

Al reluctantly agreed and went back to cutting off protruding screw hole plugs. Neither discussed the impending raid any further that day, but worked intensely to finish the boat's bottom so that they might turn it over to begin decking the topside. By six o'clock they had slings secured around the hull and easily somersaulted its round bilge to the bottom side.

"Looks more like a proper boat now, eh?" Don said.

Admiring their handiwork, Al agreed, "She's going to be a little beauty all right. I can't wait to get the engine stringers in and start rigging her."

"Sounds good to me. I'll work on the front deck carlings tomorrow and that'll leave you room to work inside. If we had Erik back with us, we'd have her in the water in two weeks. Too bad the school district put him back to work."

"He was a first class finish worker for certain, but I think they pay him more regularly than we could, so he's probably better off with them," Al stated.

They were interrupted by the phone ringing. As before, Don took the call. "It's Jill," he said to Al, his hand over the mouthpiece. He motioned Al to come and try to listen at the same time. "Go ahead, Jill. Al has his ear to the receiver, too."

Jill explained that she was selling the last of their stock holdings as buyers were available and would convert the proceeds to gold if they wished. She also said that she had contacted Ray and that he wanted his portion in cash. Taking a breath, she said cautiously, "He wants to use his money to buy another load of, uh--goods and to contract you guys, separate from me, to bring it down to a place near here to stash until he can sell it. I told him that I would have you call him."

"Why separate from you? And why contract us rather than go partners four ways?" Don asked, confused.

"Because he doesn't trust us after the--Uh--problems of the last trip, I guess," she said.

"Or could it be that he just wants to keep more profit for himself?" Don queried.

"Maybe some of both. I'm not a mind reader, but I think he doesn't trust me and I know he doesn't like me after I blew up at him. Goldie told me that her mother knows Ray is fooling around on her and he's probably trying to stash some money aside in case Lena kicks him out," Jill confided.

"When does he want us to make this run?" Al asked, taking the phone from his friend.

"Not until he gets all his money together. I'll probably have it for him by the middle of next week. The market is hard to judge just now, but it'll be real soon, because I've planned all along to have us out by September."

Al took the opportunity to pry. "Is that when you expect it will begin losing ground?"

"A bit maybe, but I'm sure that we'll see a big down turn by mid-October, so it'll pay to be out well before that."

"How can you be so sure?" Al wheedled.

"That's my job," was all she said before changing the subject entirely. "How's the new project coming? Beginning to look like a boat yet?"

"Yes, it is. We just turned it right side up and we'll start working on the topside tomorrow. Why don't you come out and see it Saturday? We're lonesome for some company besides seagulls and our own grubby selves," Al suggested.

"Maybe I will. I'll let you know. Got to get back to work now, bye!"

"She sure hung up in a hurry," Don said. "You think she's got a candy man friend down there at the candy factory?"

That wasn't what Al wanted to hear and said nothing to his partner, but headed to their little kitchen and made himself a peanut butter sandwich and washed it down with some homemade root beer that Hallen, the old engine maker, had given him a few days before. Jill should have been off work and home by now, so why had she said she had to go back to work? He climbed into the boat and started measuring for the engine stringers while Don busied himself with opening a can of soup, knowing that it was best to allow Al to stew in his own dark thoughts rather than plague him with unanswerable questions.

CHAPTER TWENTY-FOUR

Jill didn't show up that weekend, but she did call to say that she felt it best to rest up for what she expected to be a very hectic week trying to sell their stocks, replace them with gold and still carry on her duties at Brown and Haley. Don had no difficulty sensing how poorly his partner took this news, but he appreciated how much Al was contributing to completing the new boat, barely stopping work to sleep or eat. By Wednesday Al had the engine in place and Thursday he was mounting the drive shaft and propeller skeg when they were interrupted by a phone call from Ray.

"I've got the money for another load of goods. I'd like to drive out and discuss the details tonight, if you'll be there. Would seven o'clock work for you?" Ray asked.

"We're not going anywhere," Al replied, quite subdued. Actually, he was apprehensive of what Ray might have planned for them.

Ray rang off, noting the lack of enthusiasm in Al's tone. He hoped to talk them into bringing this load in for $500, plus expenses, but sensed it might cost him more to get the job done. Going it entirely with his own money was making him think about net profit a lot more. Just this weekend his philandering had finally caused Lena to pack his bags and tell him to find a new home. Jill had sold his stocks for enough to buy a load of whiskey, but he had only small buyers yet and needed to find a house or apartment. Money was going to be tight for a while and sleeping at the garage for four nights had not improved his disposition. He closed the business at six, drove a customer's car down to Pacific Avenue to a greasy spoon diner, then drove to Day Island by seven.

"Where's that gorgeous Hudson?" Don asked, when Ray arrived in a dingy Willys Knight touring car.

"It belonged to a friend. She's taken up with another fellow, so I'm back to driving customer's rigs until we sell another load of stuff," Ray explained frankly. He walked around the new boat, surprised at how complete it looked. "You boys sure have a knack when it comes to boat building. Looks like it won't be too long before its ready to launch."

"We've got a lot of finish work to do yet, but Al's really been putting in the hours and I've been trying to keep up or stay out of his way," Don admitted.

"How about taking a break long enough to bring a load down from Victoria for me. I don't have it sold, so I can only pay you for the transport. But rather than having to risk your own money, I'll pay you a flat fee, plus fuel expense and you'll deliver it to a place just a mile or so from here. Nobody but us three will know when and where it's going, so there shouldn't be any complications. Does that sound fair to you fellows?"

"How much are we talking about, Ray" Al asked.

"Five hundred dollars, plus your gasoline."

"That's about a third of what we've been netting!" Don fumed. "Why should we work so cheap?"

"Because the risk is all mine. It's my money, not yours. No third parties to worry about. No chance of anyone trying to shoot you to get the goods, because not even your friend Jill knows when you're going to make the trip!"

"No risk?" Al broke in. "Do you have any idea of how tough it is to run at high speed at night out there? And how do we know who is looking for us at the pickup point? It may not be our money, but it's sure as heck our necks!"

"Look, how much profit are you going to make on this boat here" Ray asked quietly, trying to calm the situation.

"Maybe five or six hundred bucks," Don answered.

"And how long will it take to build? And how much of your own money and time will you spend building it?" Ray argued. "Probably another thousand dollars and almost two months time, right? All I'm asking is for you to make a run that should be far easier than previous ones. With minimum risk and no investment in two days time you'll make as much as you will for the two months of hard work you've expended on building this boat. How about it?"

"Six hundred," Al said, turning back as if to work on the boat. "Plus the fuel, as you said."

Ray shook his head negatively, but stuck out his hand to Don and the deal was made. "Okay, $600. Get the Ghost ready. I'll call you when the time is set for the pickup. The drop off location and the signal for all clear will be found on a piece of paper hidden in the warming tray I built you on the boat. Remember, tell absolutely no one about this trip. I'll call you sometime tomorrow and pay you on delivery."

With that he walked out the shop door and drove away, the side curtains of the scrubby car flapping.

"Nicely done, Al! I didn't think he was going to budge from his $500 offer. What do you say we treat ourselves to an almost new car with that $600? I'm tired of riding the bus or the trolley and I bet you are too. We need to have a little fun in life. What do you say?"

"Yeah, good idea, if we don't get caught, shot at, break the boat or drown first," Al replied gloomily.

"Boy, you need some kissing or something in your life. Why don't you call up Jill and I'll call Goldie and see if we can get together tomorrow night for dinner and a movie after they get off work?" Don begged.

"Whatever you say," Al muttered.

"Okay, then I'll call Jill and you call Goldie. She'd get your heart or something pumping again, I bet!" Don laughed.

That roused Al enough to say, "With those two you never know who you might end up with. Remember the Christmas party last year?"

Don remembered well and wondered how things had changed so much. At one point Al had told him that Jill was his girl. Somehow, she had become Al's girl and now she seemed to be staying away from both of them. He went back to fastening deck planking, but his mind was really on Jill and all the questions that surrounded her. Why was she staying clear of them just now? Did she think that the Feds were on to them and didn't want to get caught ? Would they have to raid her house to find out how what magic she had used to do so well in the stock market? Why did Ray distrust her now, when she had done so much to establish the liquor suppliers?

Al interrupted his thought, asking, "Are we going to call or not? It's eight o'clock already."

"Go ahead. I'll try Goldie if Jill is good to go."

Jill agreed to meet them downtown Friday evening and said, when asked, that she had talked at length with Goldie on the trolley ride home from work. Goldie had told her that her mother had thrown Ray out the previous Sunday evening and things were in chaos in the Moore home. Goldie had planned on staying away for the weekend, but if Don called now, that she might consider going out with him instead of partying with her other friends. Al relayed the message to his partner, who, in turn secured a date with Goldie. They all went to bed in a better mood, anticipation of new experiences always able to lift one's appreciation of life.

The phone rang just after lunch Friday. Don lay down the rag with which he was rubbing stain into the deck planking to answer it.

Ray said simply, "The Scotsman will meet you at 10:30 PM tomorrow night at the same place you previously saw him. I'll expect you at the destination I spoke of before dawn unless the weather kicks up, in which case, make it after dark Sunday. Keep your fuel tank full and your lips sealed. Understood?"

Don replied affirmatively and Ray hung up.

"That was short and sweet," Al said. "What's up?"

Don repeated what Ray had directed, then said, "He's playing this run real close to his vest, isn't he?"

"Sounds paranoid to me, but that's better than being caught up in a scenario we have no control over. Let's not say anything to the girls tonight about our weekend, okay?"

"Agreed, we'll just tell them we have to get home early to get some varnish work done on the boat," Al said.

"Not too much choice about coming home early. Until we get a car, the last bus to Day Island is our only ticket home except hoofing it!" Don quipped.

"Maybe that will change next week partner. Your idea of buying a car sounds better every day," Al returned.

Goldie and Jill greeted them very warmly when they met them at the Olympic for a quick dinner of sandwiches and milkshakes. The girls wanted to see a big double feature that consisted of the longest movie, to date, filmed outdoors: "In Old Arizona" and an unusual film using all black actors called "Halleluia". They took the trolley up Stadium Way to the Temple Theater which was larger than the Pantages if not as grand in its decor. Relaxing with two big containers of popcorn, the two couples snuggled close. Worries and absence faded away as they were caught up in the magic displayed on the large screen.

With great reluctance Al removed his arm from around Jill's shoulder as the lights came up. "We've got to run to catch the last bus back to the island. Let's stay in touch more Jill. The last two weeks I've felt lost without seeing you. Did you miss me at all?" He begged for a positive reply.

"Of course I did, silly! I'll have more time now that the stocks are sold. Why don't you call me tomorrow?"

Don answered for him, "We're right in the middle of finishing the boat, but we'll be available next week if you girls are. If the weather stays nice, maybe we could take a boat ride. Are you game?"

"Sure," Jill replied. "How about you, Goldie?"

"Anything to get out of the house. Ma is driving me nuts since she kicked Pa out," Goldie answered ruefully.

They hugged each other all around and ran for their respective trolley stops, the boys to Division Street and the girls to Stadium Way. It had been a nice evening, not exciting, but certainly relaxing for each of them.

On the ride home Al and Don agreed that they needed to leave shortly after daylight to make the long run north without having to run hard both going and returning. They would try to catch a weather report in the morning if the local radio station came on before they left, but knew that might not be an actuality in these pioneer days of the airways.

"We're going to need extra fuel because we'll have to run her fast to make it back this far before daylight," Don warned.

"I hate carrying gasoline in cans. So many boats get blown up every year. It scares the heck out of me," Al said.

"Not much choice this time. We'll just have to secure them well and hope it's calm when we have to stop to top up the tanks. She's a great boat, but she sure drinks fuel!" Don replied. "Wish I could have found room for another tank, but it would have fouled the balance I'm afraid."

CHAPTER TWENTY-FIVE

George Harris heard the Ghost's exhaust burbling softly as it glided past his home on the north end of Day Island, but so little daylight was filtering through the morning fog that he could not see its hull just a few yards away. A couple of minutes later he heard the exhaust note change to a sharp staccato bellow accompanied by a lesser, but higher pitched noise that he recognized as coming from a gear driven supercharger usually found only on race cars.

"Those boys are hell bent on destruction running that fast in the fog," he muttered to himself. "They leave early and don't come back until almost dawn the next day or sometimes even later. They tear up the bay in the dark, rain or fog like mad men and for what? Money is the only logical answer! They're running booze when they don't even look old enough to drink the stuff, but they sure know how to build and run a fast boat. Too bad they didn't stick to just building them," Harris reasoned out loud.

The day after the Ghost first arrived at Cummings Marina he had walked over when no one was around and looked the boat over very carefully. Although he had been around Puget Sound and boats all his life, George had never seen a hull design like this one. Its cockpit was large enough to use as a salmon charter boat, but there were no pole holders fixed and a peek under the open motor box revealed an engine far larger and more complex than a 30 foot fishing boat required. He had decided right then to keep an eye on its comings and goings because someone was sure to wonder why such an unusual new boat was in a backwater moorage like Cummings. Information had always been George Harris's stock and trade, so all he needed to profit from his snooping was someone who needed good liquor cheap and there were plenty of those guys around these days. He noted the time he heard the boat leave in his journal again, lit a Lucky Strike and settled into his dining nook with a fresh cup of coffee and the morning Tacoma Times. An item at the bottom of the front page caught his eye. "Tony and Lou Tucci, sons of prominent Everett restaurant owner Lawrence Tucci, were found dead in an abandoned shed on a mill property near Snohomish. They were reported missing two weeks ago and local police say that they appear to be victims of foul play. A Seattle Post Intelligencer reporter says that Federal officials were also at the crime scene, but they would not comment on why they were interested in the case. Some might speculate that the G-Men suspect a link to Prohibition violations."

"No doubt in my mind. Sometimes things drop right in your lap," Harris chuckled to himself and made a note in his journal to follow up on the connection to the boys building boats at the other end of the island.

******

Even with the windshield wipers and defroster on full speed Al could see only a few yards past the bow as they skimmed north at 20 knots. He sounded the fog horn several times a minute, but felt little comfort that it would prevent a collision should any other craft be foolish enough to be running at more than idle speed in such conditions.

"How much longer before we change course?" he asked Don, who was plotting their position every five minutes on the chart.

"We're passing West Point on the Seattle side and should be able to hold this course almost to the south end of Whidbey Island. If we don't break out of this soup by then, we'll have to slow down and try to locate the Point No Point light and set a fresh course to Marrowstone Point from there," Don yelled over the blare of the fog horn.

"I'd rather run in wind, rain or even the dark, than in fog as thick as this," Al complained.

"I'm sure we'll get some of that, too," laughed his partner. "As they say around Puget Sound, if you don't like the weather, just wait a few minutes---"

"Yeah, and it'll get worse!" finished Al.

A quarter of an hour later they broke out of the fog as the wind began to rise pushing it toward the west. Al advanced the throttle to take advantage of the better visibility and calm water that would probably soon be churned up by the rising wind. He wanted to make Port Townsend for their fuel stop much earlier than on previous trips to leave a margin of time should the crossing toward Victoria become nasty again. "If only we could get accurate weather forecasts, smuggling would be so much easier to plan," he muttered.

They reached the fuel dock at Port Townsend several hours earlier than their first trip and found a different fuel attendant on duty. He had much less curiosity than the previous man and was only interested in getting the job done and returning to the protection of the warm office since the   temperature was dropping rapidly as the wind rose.

While Don secured four five gallon tins of extra fuel beneath the aft deck, Al prepared soup and sandwiches that was to be their combination lunch and dinner.

"It doesn't look good out there," Don warned as he came down into the cabin. "I'm glad we allowed plenty of time to cross the strait this afternoon."

Indeed, the water color was turning from deep green to a dark shade of gray and a few white caps were already apparent. The young men knew that it would only get worse as they headed north across the unprotected portion of their trip. The uncertainty of a long morning spent running in the fog was replaced by the certainty of a long night spent in discomfort from the hammering they would soon be subjected to.

"Yeah, it's going to be a rough trip," Al agreed. "Do you think it's worth it? I mean $600 is a nice piece of money, but is it really worth risking our boat, our necks and even jail time for, Don?"

"Just keep thinking of what it will buy, Al. Our own car! No more bus and trolley rides, or borrowing transportation from our parents. I don't think there is any thing that allows more freedom than having an automobile."

"Except a boat, especially one like this," Al said.

"True, but this boat is more a tool of business than something we could ever afford to enjoy otherwise," Don argued. "Anyway, I'm going to spend my time thinking about the car we're going to buy. It's a healthier way for me to deal with all the negative issues."

"That's what I like about you, partner. Sometimes I wish I could think as positive as you do," Al admitted.

"Okay then, damn the torpedoes and full speed ahead!" Don laughed.

"Yeah, and damn the Coast Guard, the Federal agents the weather and the pirates, too," Al rejoined, but with a scowl as he turned on the bilge blower in preparation to start the big hungry Duesenberg.

A half hour into the crossing, Don, who was now at the wheel, had reduced their speed to 8 knots. The Ghost was quartering the waves on her port bow, the motion tedious as she threw off the smaller waves and rose over the swells.

"I hope this dies down this evening, because it won't be much fun when we have to meet a deadline at the other end running with a full load through stuff like this," Don said.

"Well, Ray said that if we have trouble, we could make it Sunday instead of tomorrow morning," Al replied.

"Right, but where would we hole up all day that wouldn't cause attention?" Don argued. "I think it's best to stick to the agreed schedule if at all possible."

"Probably so," Al agreed, reluctantly. "Say, what do you think of his idea of stashing the stuff in the Chinese tunnel until he gets buyers? Seems pretty risky to me."

"It probably is, but not many people remember the tunnels these days and there are several ways to get the stuff out without drawing suspicion. They were made for smuggling almost fifty years ago and I suppose it should still work. Do you remember sneaking in there when we were kids?" Don ruminated.

"How could I ever forget! It was the scariest thing I ever did---until we got shot at last summer anyway," Al said.

"Yeah, it was scary all right and we only got part way through before we chickened out. You remember that guy Jack who went clear from Fircrest down to Day Island?"

"He's the guy who found that six foot sword wasn't he?" Al asked.

"You bet! It was supposed to be for chopping the heads off people who betrayed their secrets. Did you know he sold it to a curio shop down on the waterfront in Seattle? They keep it right in their front window to draw people in," Don expounded.

"I never got to see it, but I did hear that he found one room in there that was 30 feet long and full of bunks. Can you imagine how they whittled something that big out and actually lived underground?" Al shuddered at his own thought. "Did he tell you how many entrances there were?"

"Well, there's the one we went into in Fircrest, near the swamp the Chinese used as a rice paddy. There's the one south of Salmon Beach where we're taking the liquor, the one that Jack came through east of Day Island, I don't know exactly where and one that originally came out in down town Tacoma about Ninth and Pacific. In back of that printing shop I think."

"I know where another one is that I bet you don't know about," Al teased.

"I'll guess it has something to do with our old high school when it was still the Tacoma Hotel," Don laughed.

"Right! Do you know who found it and told me about it?" Al

asked, a twinkle in his eye.

"Not really, unless it was---"

"My cousin, Erik! I knew you would figure that one out. Actually, he found one blocked off place in the sub-basement of Stadium High near the janitor's supply room that he believes was an entrance to the tunnels and one under the bleachers that is still open. It's so well hidden that even high school kids never found it, at least as far as I know."

"Erik must be a lot snoopier than I imagined to find stuff like that," Don thought out loud.

"He's just a very curious guy. He wants to know how things are put together and he pokes around at foundations and junk like that and comes up with interesting stories all the time," Al explained.

They spent the rest of the ponderous trip across the Strait of Juan de Fuca talking about the marvel of the tunnels that the Chinese had built to smuggle in railroad workers during the prohibition of their immigration. The boys also speculated on the tales of Chinese women being smuggled in for white slavery purposes and of the relics that tunnel explorers had brought out. They decided that the huge quantity of dirt must have been hauled to the site on the Narrows and dumped into the bay and wondered how the massive project could possibly have been accomplished, let alone not have been discovered until its major usage was discontinued. Yet, though few people knew of the extent of the tunnel complex, it was still there, a mysterious wonder, existing just a few yards beneath the feet of thousands of Tacoma area residents.

Darkness overtook them as they approached Gonzales Point and the maze of islets and rocks that littered Oak Bay. Since they were early, they anchored in the lee of one of the islands and spent some time filling the fuel tank from the four spare tins of gasoline. Al warmed another can of soup while Don kept binoculars trained toward the mainland for signs of their supplier. A little after 10 O'clock he spied the truck coming over the hill, pulled up the anchor and Al guided the Ghost to the dock.

"How was your voyage over?" the Scotsman queried as they shook hands. "It looked a bit wild out there this afternoon for such a wee craft."

"Not too bad. We took our time to conserve fuel and our bodies," Don replied easily.

"Good thinking, lads. I've brought extra help to get you loaded and on your way more quickly tonight. I wish the weather was as good as your last trip, but it is better than the first time, I believe. The wind is dropping now, though I heard it is due to rain before morning," he said thoughtfully.

"Thank you, sir. We've a longer way to go tonight so we appreciate the extra time," Al said, remembering their terrifying first trip and hoping the Scot was correct about the wind. Within half an hour the whiskey was stowed, the money exchanged and good-byes said. The Ghost slipped out of the harbor quietly and back into the sea. The two young men set off into a night that they new would be long and difficult, but unaware of all the dangers it was to hold.

CHAPTER TWENTY-SIX

George Harris decided not to procrastinate using the knowledge of the movements of the suspicious boat that docked just a hundred yards from his home. If Harris had been a model citizen, he could have called federal agents in to have a look, but where was the profit in that? As a private investigator for much of his life he knew the authorities gave little credit to the citizens that helped them solve crimes and no monetary reward whatsoever. No, he would use what he suspected as bait for someone with substance and reason to pay him for his trouble. By 10 AM he had gotten the number of Lawrence Tucci's restaurant and by noon had an appointment with the man himself.

As agreed, they met at the Blockhouse, a restaurant and watering hole half way between Seattle and Tacoma. As Harris approached the table of a stocky, swarthy man in his fifties, wearing a white carnation in his navy blue blazer, he observed two equally swarthy, well built men sitting at the table adjacent to his future client. "Body guards, no doubt," he mused. "Well, he doesn't know who he's dealing with yet, so why not be careful."

"Harris, personal investigator," he said, extending a hand to the individual he believed to be Tucci.

"What's a personal investigator, Mr. Harris?" Tucci asked, not releasing George's hand until he received a reply.

"A private investigator with a more, discreet, shall we say, manner of business operation," Harris said, keeping his gaze straight into the other's eyes and waiting, patiently for the release of his grip.

"I'm glad to hear that description Mr. Harris--"

"George, please," Harris said with a sincere smile.

"All right,--George--, what do you have for me that brings us both to this wretched place?"

"First, I'm very sorry to read of the loss of your sons, a terrible thing. I lost my own son in the war a dozen years ago and I know it leaves an emptiness in your life."

"Thank you," Tucci almost whispered, then gathering himself, "Does the information you mentioned on the phone have something to do with my sons?"

"Possibly, I'm not certain," Harris admitted frankly, "But if they had a connection with two young men who transport beverages, I may be able to point you in the right direction. Might this be the case?"

Tucci stiffened somewhat. The men at the next table moved their hands toward the inside pockets of their double breasted, pin stripe suits. Harris kept his hands folded on the table in front of him, the picture of composure.

"You're implying more than I think our short acquaintance allows, Mr. Harris. I don't think we shall pursue this conversation further," Tucci said, but he didn't move to leave yet.

"I believe you're a fair man, Mr. Tucci," began Harris. "I'll tell you a story and you can tell me if it is worth a thousand dollars or it is not. If it is, here is my card; you may send me a check or have cash dropped by my home at your discretion. Here's what I know."

He flipped open the note pad that was his daily journal and began to describe two young men, their unusual boat, the exact time of their departure and arrivals over the period of the last three months, concluding with the supposition that they were bringing in a load of whiskey this very night and would probably be back at Cummings boathouse by dawn on Saturday.

"Make of it what you will and enjoy your lunch, gentlemen," Harris said, including with his eyes the two henchmen at the nearby table. "I have an appointment that I must see to." He rose to leave and added, "Good hunting!"

Tucci coolly watched the ordinary looking individual who called himself George push through the gathering lunch crowd and leave without looking back. "Pretty damn sure of himself, that guy," he muttered to himself as he motioned his compatriots to join him.

George Harris wondered just how well that little episode had gone as he motored north to Seattle. He had told the truth about everything, including the fact that he was seeing another prospective client. Without more specifics his plan consisted of planting seeds and watching what might grow into something that would benefit him. He arrived at the upscale restaurant just after the midday gathering of Seattle's elite had peaked, but still he was asked if he had a reservation. He announced that, rather than a lunch reservation, he had a 1:30 appointment with the owner. The maitre d' made George cool his heels for 45 minutes before pointing him upstairs to the business office. Surprisingly, he was greeted at once by the tall, very dark skinned owner who was dressed as if it were an evening at the opera, rather than a Saturday afternoon. A gold tooth glinted as he smiled at his guest, shaking his hand as an old friend might and, indeed, that was the case.

"George, you old son of a gun. Where have you been keeping yourself, man?"

"On my island hideaway, Jack. Staying out of the limelight and out of trouble; at least until now, anyway. How's business?" Harris asked, truly interested.

"It was down for a while, but doing very nicely again, thanks to a few competitors dropping out, you know."

George did know, because he was the one who had furnished his client here, with the information that was leaked to authorities who helped close down some of those rat infested kitchens, houses of ill repute or speak easy establishments. Harris was a thorough investigator and an ordinary enough looking individual to infiltrate almost any business. He almost always obtained sufficient dirt on whomever he was sent out to destroy to be successful.

"I'm happy to know circumstances are improving, my friend," George said sincerely. "There may be a situation developing that could be to your advantage and, if so, I know you'll make it right by me for knowing ahead of time."

"Tell me about it, George," the tall black man invited.

Harris outlined his suspicions that Lawrence Tucci was about to take revenge on two young liquor smugglers for what they may or may not have done to his sons to whom they were probably supplying whiskey. He suggested that some type of intervention might make Tucci look bad in the eyes of the law and remove him from the active bootlegging and restaurant business permanently. The operation might very well take place tonight somewhere in Puget Sound.

"I can see that you've thought this scenario through very well except for the location and Puget Sound covers a whole lot of acreage, my friend," the restaurateur remarked.

"If a person knew where they were coming from, wouldn't it be possible to follow them, at a distance, to the destination where they unload the booze?"

"Theoretically, I suppose, but if the boat is very fast and running without lights, it would be practically impossible to find them, let alone catch whoever might interfere with them," Jack said, knowing full well who Harris was speaking of and their capabilities. Still, he thought, he had spotted their wake before with his big binoculars and one of them had been careless enough to fall in the bay and almost gotten their boat damaged on the rocks at Fauntleroy. The two young men did make mistakes. Someone like Tucci, with his mob connection resources, might just get lucky enough to find them. But none of this was George's business, so Jack thanked him for the update, assured him that he would continue to use him when needed, made a little more small talk and bid him a pleasant week on his island hideaway.

Harris headed home really wondering if he had put some wheels into motion or if the black restaurateur was as disinterested as he appeared to be. Behind the gold toothed smile and flashy facade, George knew there was an intellect as sharp as the clothing. Jack may very well know more about this particular booze smuggling operation than he let on, Harris thought. Only time would tell what he had started today. How much or how little time he had no idea. Later, when he again reached Day Island, Harris decided to try to bring in another player, who might speed up the time table; a very major player who might spend freely to gain hold of the business in this growing corner of the country.

CHAPTER TWENTY-SEVEN

It was still too rough to put the Ghost up on plane without beating the bottom to death as they had on their first trip, so they mushed along at 8 to 10 knots hoping to make up time when they got into water more protected by islands. It started raining lightly before midnight, making it more difficult to see, but at least it washed away some of the salt spray. By one o'clock they had passed Pt. Wilson and were able to boost the boat onto plane making 20 knots but pounding a good deal.

Don was figuring their course and estimated arrival time while Al strained to keep on course. "It looks like we can reach the tunnel entrance before dawn if we keep it at this pace, but that leaves us short of time to unload. With only you, Ray and I, it will probably take at least an hour to get the stuff ashore and a lot longer if he hasn't rigged some kind of gang plank to shore."

"I'm afraid to push her much harder, Don. Our mile per gallon fuel consumption was terrible when we weren't planing and it'll be worse if we run harder now. We're going to come in with very little to spare," Al said worriedly.

"Caught between a rock and a hard place, as usual. Carrying the load so much farther south than on other trips kind of screwed us up, didn't it?" Don remarked.

"No doubt. If we repeat this trip, we'll have to install another tank somewhere. You've got your work cut out for you, Mr. Designer," Al said.

Don didn't reply. He was beginning to doubt his infallibility as a designer and curse their rather consistent run of unanticipated challenges.

By 3:30 the rain had ceased and the wind abated enough that Al eased the throttle up and watched the knot meter rise to 23. He felt the boat lighten up as it planed further out of the water and hoped their miles per gallon would increase. They were past Seattle now, heading down the west side of Vashon Island when the hull hit an object hard enough to jar them both from the temporary complacency that set in when in familiar territory.

"What was it?" Don yelled.

"No clue. I didn't see a thing," Al yelled back.

"Do you think it hit the prop?" Don asked.

"No, it feels okay, no vibration, but that was a hell of a hit."

You better pull up the floor boards and check for leaks. We could have punctured the bottom if it was something sharp," Al suggested.

Don climbed under the foredeck and started pulling up the floor boards, but saw no sign that they were taking water. "I think we got lucky. The bilge looks dry so far," he said.

They looked at each other, knowing that running at night without eventually hitting something was, for certain, strictly a matter of luck, because they were running almost totally blind on nights such as this one. Don broke the silence.

"Wouldn't it be nice to have a metal bottom for this kind of work?"

"Except for the weight, I think it would make a lot more sense," Al speculated, adding," That is, if any of this makes sense."

"It makes as much sense as prohibiting a whole nation to have a beer legally, I guess," Don retorted. "How about an aluminum bottom? That would be light enough. With the right mix of alloy it could be almost as strong as steel and it wouldn't rust."

"Sounds good if they come up with an easy way of welding the stuff," Al admitted. "Why don't you design an aluminum boat and see if we could sell the idea to some big company?"

"Maybe I will." Someday, Don thought. "The Point Defiance light is coming up. We're almost there. Let's slow down and switch to the underwater exhaust before we get abreast of Salmon Beach and make sure we're clear of any bogey men waiting for us."

Al nodded agreement and five minutes later they were idling toward the dark rip rapping rocks that protected the railroad tracks from the eroding current of the Narrows. Don surveyed a circle around the Ghost with a pair of large binoculars similar to those of their client, the black man from Seattle. Nothing was immediately apparent as they nosed nearer the shore.

"Hit the spotlight just above the tracks for a just half a second," Al whispered.

Don did so and was answered immediately by two quick flashes from a spot on the shore just north of them. Al turned the bow in that direction and nudged the throttle up just enough to make headway against the incoming tide. In a moment Ray appeared on the edge of the rock shore swinging a rope and launching it to Don who had moved to the rear cockpit. He caught the end, made it fast to the starboard stern bit and ran to the foredeck to throw a second line to Ray. In a minute the Ghost was held fast to stakes that Ray had planted in the rip rapping and the boys had lowered bumpers of old car tires over the starboard side to keep the chine from grating on the rough rocks. Ray dragged a long aluminum ramp from the other side of the tracks and motioned for the boys to start unloading. It was tricky work as small waves and the ever present current tugged the Ghost this way and that.

"Nice ramp Ray. I bet you built that at the garage, right?" Don asked, as he passed the fiftieth case up to Ray.

Ray only grunted agreement, hefted the case and carried it up to Al, who in turn carried it across the railroad tracks and through the doors that normally locked off the tunnel from trespassers. Ray had supplied wooden pallets to raise the cases from the floor which was running with an inch of water. Al was stacking the cases by the light of a kerosene lamp turned down as low as it would burn. He shivered at the thought of being locked into this hell hole like Tom Sawyer in the story he had read as a boy. He shook off the ghastly thought and rushed out for another case. They were only half unloaded when it began to rain lightly. All three men were already soaked from the exertion and the rain obliterated the dawn, so it was more a blessing than a problem. It took an hour and a half of back breaking labor to move the 100 cases. When they finished, Ray thanked them for their efforts, passed over $600 and told them he would be in touch in a week or so. He pulled out the stakes holding the boat, threw them into the tunnel, locked the doors with a huge, rusty padlock and disappeared up the hill into the woods as the Ghost idled quietly away, carried on the current to the south. Fifteen minutes later she was tied in her berth and the boys were walking toward their shop in the drizzle.

George Harris noted the arrival in his journal despite their stealthy entrance and was surprised that they had arrived at all. Five minutes later he saw the gleaming varnish of a Hacker Craft double cockpit speedboat entering the marina. Three stocky men in hooded rain gear scrambled onto the Ghost, poked around briefly, reentered the Hacker Craft and disappeared back into the mist heading north.

"I wonder what they waited for," Harris said to himself. "They undoubtedly caught up with those boys somewhere to have followed them back here. Why didn't they grab their whiskey or the boat itself?"

A few minutes later Lawrence Tucci's two henchmen were trying to hold the big speedboat off the rip rapping while Tucci was pounding unsuccessfully on the rusty padlock with a rock.

"If you want whiskey, I'd appreciate you ordering it from me instead of stealing it," shouted a voice from behind the tunnel door. "We have a delivery service you know."

Tucci dropped the rock and reached for the pistol in his shoulder holster. Before he could begin to draw it out, the voice said, "Not a good idea Mr. Tucci. There are two double barreled 12 gauge shot guns pointing directly at your chest. You are out gunned and outwitted. I didn't steal from you and I don't expect you'll be stealing from me. I also had nothing to do with the murder of your two sons. You are barking up the wrong tree entirely."

"Why should I believe you, Moore? I know that's you in there!" Tucci sputtered.

"Of course it's me and you should believe me because it's the truth. I only lie to pretty women, never to fellow businessmen. You've followed my delivery boys' boat, just as I thought you might. Now, if you need whiskey, I'll sell it to you as I said. If you don't want it, then get back in your boat and don't come back to steal what's not yours because it won't be here to steal anyway!"

"We'll see about that!" Tucci yelled, but he ran back to the boat and it disappeared in a cloud of steam and spray.

Ray chuckled as he loaded the train of ancient ore carts he had stashed in the gloom of the tunnel. By the time it was totally light in the outside world, Ray was half way to Fircrest towing his creaky little train with an electric cart he had built from an old, cut down Baker electric car chassis. By lunch time he was asleep in his new apartment on the top of the Ansonia just a few hundred yards from another outlet to the almost forgotten Chinese tunnels.

CHAPTER TWENTY-EIGHT

Don was jolted awake by the phone ringing out in the shop. He looked at his watch and found that they had only been asleep a bit over three hours. He dragged himself from the warm bed and tiptoed through the wood shavings and sawdust to the phone, which had almost rung itself off the wall. His mumbled greeting was cut off by the excited voice of Mrs. Cummings.

"Your boat is sinking! Mr. Cummings is trying to pull it to shore, but he needs your help right now! Hurry!" She hung up before Don could assure her they were coming.

"Al! The boat is sinking! Grab your pants and let's go!" Don yelled, as he pulled on his own pants and shoes.

It took them almost ten minutes to run the length of the island to the marina. They found Mr. Cummings in a skiff struggling to pull the low riding Ghost to the haul out grid.

Without thinking twice, Don dove into the frigid water fully clothed and swam to the stern step of the Ghost. With the boat already very low in the water, he easily scrambled into the rear cockpit and immediately threw a line to Al who had moved to the rear scaffolding of the haul out grid. With Cummings pulling from one side and Al from the other, they quickly got the boat in position to settle on the grid when the tide went out. But they quickly realized that the tide was still high enough that the Ghost would be submerged before the water lowered it onto the grid.

"Don, you've got to get the engine started and engage the big bilge pump or we're going to lose her right here," Al yelled.

Don was already climbing down into the cabin to do just that, praying that the batteries would still crank the big engine to life because they were already under salt water. He threw the battery switch to "Both", retarded the spark advance, moved the throttle to half speed and hit the start button. The starter engaged and the engine grunted twice then fired up. He pulled a lever to engage the auxiliary bilge pump and was rewarded by the belt spraying salt water all over the cabin, but water began pouring from the two inch fitting on the starboard side of the boat. He moved the throttle up to 2000 RPM and the outpouring had the force of a fire hose.

Al breathed a sigh of relief and yelled his thanks to Mr. Cummings who was maneuvering his skiff away from the blast of salt water and the blaring exhaust. Coming aboard himself, Al realized that they would have a lot of repair work to accomplish before they could trust the Ghost on another business run. Every electrical device and connection would have to be replaced to avoid the eventual corrosion that always claimed boats submerged in saltwater. The two big batteries were probably history and, of course, the cause of the leak had to be found and repaired as soon as the tide went out. There would be no more sleep today. Al started removing floorboards, all of them this time. He found the hole in the most forward section that was removable.

Don was leaning over him and said, "It was so far up here in the bow that it didn't leak until we unloaded and stopped. Then the bow dipped back in! No wonder we didn't see it earlier."

"If we hadn't been so darn tired when we got back, one of us would have thought to check the bilge again. It was a stupid mistake and now we've got a heck of a lot of repairs to make before we can put her back in business," Al groaned.

"For now, we can plug off this hole from the inside. Then as soon as we get her pumped dry we'll remove the batteries, wash them out with fresh water and refill them with acid. That won't cost much at all and I'm sure they'll be okay if we get them clean in the next few hours. Meantime, we can get a fresh water hose over here and wash down everything while the pump is running. When the tide goes out you can patch the bottom properly while I get to town and get the battery acid and other stuff we need to make repairs," Don said, trying to put as good a face on things as he could.

"I guess we ought to consider ourselves really lucky that you could get the engine started to pump her out," Al said. "It could have been a lot worse."

"It sure could have. Thank goodness Mr. Cummings saw what was happening and started trying to save her. Thank goodness, also, that the engine was still warm and started before the batteries went flat," Don commented.

Al was thinking that goodness had little to do with their luck, good or bad. Temporarily plugging the hole and hosing down the inside of the boat didn't take heavy mental activity, so his thoughts wandered to the idea that they weren't pursuing any noble venture as smugglers and God probably wasn't pleased with their vocation, but He didn't necessarily cause them calamities either. Bad stuff happened to good people and bad people as well. You just took things in stride and tried to learn from your mistakes. He sat down to rest while the tide lowered and continued his thoughts. Fatigue had caused their inattention, but how could one avoid fatigue when you were in the business of running contraband liquor by boat through the night? Maybe they should quit, but the money was good and it had boosted his ego at becoming a fairly successful smuggler. Could building boats ever be as lucrative or as much of a thrill? Not at the age of twenty he decided as he drifted off into slumber.

    Don had walked back to the shop, changed into clean, dry clothes and caught the bus to town. He got off at 6th and Proctor and went to the hardware store for electrical connectors and other pieces he knew they must replace. He was headed to the bank to deposit the cash from Ray, when he spotted a 'for sale' sign on a Model A pickup truck on the Big 6 Service Station lot. Since he was next going to buy a large jug of battery acid from Big 6 he decided to check out the truck first. It was less than a year old, dark green with shiny black fenders, a fabric top and had just 2657 miles showing on the speedometer. The sign said $475 or best cash offer, inquire within. Don's mind was in a whirl; wouldn't a pickup be very practical for their boat business? They could rig a trailer hitch and tow their latest creation to prospective customers, couldn't they? It was a roadster style pickup, so wouldn't it be a fun rig as well? What would Al say if he showed up with this car, not having had a vote on how his share of the money had been spent? "It's perfect, no matter what Al might think," he said to himself as he walked into the office.

    It turned out that the owner of the little Ford needed money immediately to meet a call on stocks that he had bought on margin and that were falling in value. Don walked out with the keys and the title for $425 and almost forgot to buy the battery acid. He spent $1.90 to fill the almost empty tank, lowered the top and headed back to Day Island on cloud nine, praying that his partner would feel the same way. He found Al asleep on the bunk, the Ghost settled evenly on the grid and the batteries cleaned and waiting to be filled at the head of the dock. Not bothering to wake Al, Don carefully refilled the batteries and carried them over to Mr. Cummings' charging station in the marina shop. Then he drove to their own shop, made some sandwiches and loaded tools and patching material to repair the puncture wound on the Ghost's bottom.

    Al awoke when Don came aboard with sandwiches and a Coca Cola in hand. Glancing at his watch he said, "You've been gone a long time. Did you have trouble making bus connections?"

Don handed him the soda and a sandwich and sat down to eat on the other bunk. "Not at all. I've been back long enough to refill the batteries, put them on the charger and bring some stuff from the shop to fix the bottom and quell our hunger for a while. I knew you needed the rest, so I didn't bother to wake you."

"Thanks, I believe I'll feel almost human after I finish the Coca Cola," Al said between bites and swigs.

"Actually, we have our own bus now. Want to see it?" Don said laughing nervously.

"What do you mean?" Al said, still thinking slowly.

"Look out the window partner. She's half yours!"

Al saw an almost new Ford roadster-pickup with the top down, despite the threatening weather.

"You bought that?" he gasped.

Don pulled out the signed off title and put in on the chart table. "Its ours. Soon to be the property of Aldon Boat Company, builders of fine launches!"

"Wow!" Al exclaimed, then squinted his eyes and asked, "How much?"

"$425, plus $1.90 to fill the tank. He wanted more, but--"

"Let's go for a ride! The tide won't be out far enough to work on the boat for more than an hour. I want to see Jill anyway. What do you say?" Al was on a caffeine high!

Don was so relieved that he threw his arms around his friend and beat him hard on the back to show how happy he was. They drove off leaving the Ghost to dry herself out.

George Harris put down his notepad and scratched his head. "Those two are the strangest pair of smugglers imaginable," he muttered to himself. "They barely avoid Mafia goons, they almost sink their boat, one jumps in the bay to save it then goes out and buys a car and they drive away leaving the boat wide open for anyone to make mischief on. How did they possibly live this long?" He took a long drink of fine Scotch and picked up the phone to do some business.

CHAPTER TWENTY-NINE

Jill was pleasantly surprised to see Al and Don coming up her front walk. When they asked her to come out and see their new car she was dumbfounded, because, as far as she knew, she had put every spare penny they had into their investment schemes.

"How do you like it?" Al asked enthusiastically.

"It's real cute and looks like new," she replied.

"It'll be fun to run around in, handy for the boat business and it's only got 2600 miles on it!" Don said excitedly. "Besides, I darn near stole it from a guy who was in trouble in the stock market."

"I'm thinking that you guys made some quick money this weekend or you really did steal it," Jill said, searching their faces for a clue.

"We'll tell you all about that later," Al said. "Don bought it while I was sleeping on the boat, but I'm glad he did. We're going have some good times now that we have decent transportation. Want to take a spin?"

"Sure, let me get a jacket. It looks like rain again and I see you showoffs have the top down!" she replied.

Al drove while Don explained that it only took a few minutes to put up the top and insert the side curtains on the doors if it rained. He slid open a small trap door in the right side floor panel and hot air shot onto their legs.

"It's a manifold heater, not sophisticated, but it works pretty well for the passenger side, doesn't it?" Don said.

"I guess so, but you could put a real heater in like your boat couldn't you?" Jill said, thinking how crude this little car really was compared to those of her former world.

"Sure," Al answered, "Soon as we get more cash. We had a little setback with the boat that's going to tap our resources just now, but we'll make this little hummer cozy for you before winter, girl friend!"

"You are happy campers today, aren't you?" Jill said giving Al a quick kiss on the cheek and putting her arms around each of them. "I think it's real cozy in here now!"

Indeed, the Model A seat was a squeeze for three adults, but seemed no problem for this trio as they drove down to their favorite ice cream shop in Old Tacoma. As they sat on the deck overlooking the deep green water of Commencement Bay, Don elaborated on their setback from having struck something and not realizing that the hull was punctured until the marina owner had found the Ghost sinking at its slip. He explained that they could easily repair the hull damage this evening, but the saltwater had done a good deal of harm to the interior and perhaps even some of the mechanical components.

"So, we hate to eat and run, but duty calls," Al summed up. "Maybe we can get together middle of the week, if you like?"

"Sure, but call me so I can fix my hair and put some lipstick on. I look a mess today," she said, pouting.

"You look fine to me," Don said, smiling charmingly.

"Simply gorgeous," Al said, trying to one up his partner, realizing Jill was playing them a little.

Just as they dropped Jill off it started to sprinkle. They took time to raise the top and pop in the side curtains before heading back to work on the boat. It was messy working in the rain and slime beneath the boat grid, but they finished the repair and reinstalled the batteries before dark and decided to stay aboard for the night to make sure the hull was water tight. Al warmed a can of pork and beans on the stove for a brief dinner and they both fell asleep by eight o'clock. A couple of hours before dawn the Ghost began rocking a bit as it once again came afloat. Neither of the young men stirred from their exhaustion until Al was prodded awake by a stocky figure wielding a pistol.

"Rise and shine, pretty boy! We've got things to talk about," the intruder growled.

"What do you want?" Al stammered, sitting up to face his assailant.

"I want to know what happened to my sons and my load of liquor and you're going t---" He was cut off by a choke hold from behind by Don, who had leapt from his bed and throttled the shorter man before he realized the threat.

"Drop your weapon immediately or I'll break your neck before your next breath," Don yelled directly into the older man's ear.

Tucci dropped the pistol into Al's lap and Don relaxed his choke hold just enough for the uninvited guest to speak.

"My men are just outside and they won't hesitate to drown your asses if I just say go!" Tucci threatened.

Al pushed the gun into Tucci's ample belly and whispered to him, "My partner there is a wrestling champion. He can easily break your neck if you call out and I'll finish the job by blowing your guts all over our boat before I shoot your henchmen and drag their bodies out in the bay for fish bait. You see, mister, we face the prospect of death every time we take this boat on a night run and you can't scare us more than that, so speak your piece and live to fight another day!"

Don was grateful for his friend's sudden fortitude and tightened his choke hold enough to emphasize their solidity.

"Okay, tough guys," Tucci sputtered, "You delivered a load to my sons, the load was hijacked immediately and they were found murdered two weeks later. I think you and your partner, Moore, stiffed us or put someone else up to it to double your profit. Any reason I shouldn't be looking at you for the hit, since you seem to be ready to finish me right now?"

"We also delivered the first load to your sons under the guns of the Coast Guard and all of us lived through that one. We were prepared to keep delivering to you in the future. Your money was good, your boys were efficient guys to work with and we figured you as a man that would never rat us out to the authorities. Why would we jeopardize a sweet working business deal by hurting your sons just to sell a load of booze twice?" Al argued.

"Ray told us enough about you to know that you were not a man that could be double crossed and neither he or us had any intention of doing anything but delivering what you need for your business," Don stated, releasing his grip enough for Tucci to feel less threatened.

"Who else knew about that particular delivery then," Tucci asked, half believing their version of the events.

Al moved the pistol away from Tucci's stomach and answered. "Only our other partner who made the order and the suppliers themselves. Only us four partners knew where it was to be delivered and we were very careful to be sure we weren't followed or observed that night."

"Like last night, you mean?" Tucci said, sarcastically.

"What are you talking about?" Don asked.

"My boys and I picked up your trail just south of Seattle and know you unloaded into some kind of hole in the west bank of the Narrows. After you left, we talked to Moore, who somehow had locked himself behind the doors and told us off totally! You see what I'm driving at now?" Tucci said, angrily.

"You must have a darn fast boat and some special information to have found us on a night like last night," Al ventured.

"Faster than yours. It's sitting at the next dock now, a 28 foot Hacker Craft with a 300 horsepower Scripps-Booth engine," Tucci bragged. "We didn't have any trouble keeping your wake in sight."

"We were low on fuel and taking it easy," Don argued, "Your speedboat could never catch us in rough water if we went all out!"

"What he says is true, Mr. Tucci," Al reasoned, "But I still think you must have some inside information of your own to have found us last night, because even we didn't know where we were unloading until the night we left. Ray bought this last load himself, told us he didn't have customers for it yet and to not tell even our other partner we were making the run. If I was you, I would be looking at whoever has been feeding you details of our movements and only you know who that is."

Tucci stared at Al for a full minute, digesting the last thought before replying. "I think we're through here, unless you're looking for more trouble."

Don released him, saying, "We're not looking for any trouble. You came to us remember? We were extremely upset when your sons disappeared and we're sorry for your loss, but we're delivery boys, not hijackers and not plotters of killings. Our actions tonight were purely defensive, no more than you would have done under like circumstances, right?"

"It was a process of elimination. Our family name won't be worth spit if we don't find who did this to us. You've given me an idea where to look. Thanks," Tucci said roughly as he turned to leave.

"I think this belongs to you. Hope you don't have to use it," Al said, handing over the pistol. Tucci took it with a surprised look. "And this." Al tossed him the empty clip that he had silently removed during their discussion.

"Good night, wise guys," Tucci said with just the slightest smile as he jumped onto the grid scaffolding and quickly disappeared into the dark.

CHAPTER THIRTY

After Tucci left there was no thought of returning to sleep for either Don or Al. Al started a Presto-Log fire in the main stove and cooked oatmeal and cocoa while Don inspected the bilges to make sure their repairs were holding.

"Everything looks okay," Don reported, "but I'd like to take her out and run at full speed to make certain we don't have any other problems."

"We'll have to take on some fuel first, we're practically sucking the bottom of the tank now," Al warned.

While they were eating they discussed options for their future, whether they should try to sell the boat, rather than risk further involvement with characters like Tucci or be found out by the authorities.

"Tucci had to be tipped off that we were bringing in another load or he couldn't possibly have found us delivering it to such a weird place as the Chinese tunnels," Al reasoned, "How do you think that was possible?"

After thinking for a moment, Don said, "My best guess is that somebody is watching us. Somebody that doesn't care to report our activities to any authority, but might profit from telling someone else their suspicions."

"Do you think it's Mr. Cummings?" Al asked.

"No, he doesn't give a rip what we're up to. He's got enough on his hands raising those daughters and keeping these docks floating. Besides, he enjoys a drink himself and thinks the whole Prohibition thing is a joke," Don replied.

"I didn't think you had talked to him that much."

"When I came back with the car yesterday, May, the girl that's near our age came out to admire it and we got to talking. I asked where she thought her dad would like us to park it when we're out on the boat. She said her dad left things around here up to her a lot of the time because he went to town a good many evenings to drink with his VFW buddies," Don explained.

"What else did she say?" Al was very curious now.

"I thought it might be nice to get to know her better, so I let her ramble on a for a while, but it was mostly about their family life here at the marina. She doesn't get out much it seems," Don said, "And I think she just wanted company from someone other than the older boat owners that she usually has to deal with."

"So you're going to help by asking her out, right?"

"Well, we don't want to let our new car go to waste, do we?" Don joked.

"Not much chance of that with Don Juan Grant on the job," Al declared, glad that their mood had been lightened for the moment.

By eight O'clock they had cleaned up the boat and moved it to the gas dock, where Mr. Cummings had just turned the fuel pump on.

"Your repairs work out okay, boys?" he asked.

"Everything looks okay, but we're going to take her out for a run to make sure," Al replied.

"I'm sure you got it right," Cummings remarked, "You two do good work. I peeked in at your new launch the other day and she's a beauty. You must be about ready to sell her it looks like."

"It won't be long. Know anybody that might be looking for a good fishing or day boat?" Don asked.

"Nothing comes to mind, but I'll spread the word if you'd like," Cummings volunteered. "How much are you going to ask for it?"

"We think it's worth $1250 with the 10 horsepower inboard and the hard top. That would include side curtains to close in the hard top and a steering wheel forward besides the tiller at the stern," Don said.

"That might sound expensive for an 18 footer, but we built her to last with first class fittings, paint and varnish. It'll be a boat that the owner will be proud of twenty years from now," Al added.

"Not like this one, huh," Cummings said, looking down at the Ghost.

"Why do you say that?" Don said, astonished that someone would feel that way about his marvelous creation.

"With that big engine, it's likely to come to no good end long before twenty years," Cummings opined.

"Maybe so," Al agreed, "But she's put together right and Don's design is far ahead of anything being built now. She may last longer than you think!"

"Glad you're the ones buying the fuel!" laughed Cummings. "Forty bucks worth today, boys," he said as he put away the fuel hose.

As the Ghost accelerated away from the marina the exhaust bellowing under full power, George Harris followed its progress northward toward the Narrows, wondering if this was another working day for the young men so soon after their last adventure. When they returned just twenty minutes later, he relaxed and poured another cup of coffee. His clients would have to wait a while before he could promise them meaningful action.

Back at the boat shop after taking the Ghost through the test run, the boys turned to putting finishing touches on the launch. Six uprights, fluted like balustrades, held up a hardtop that was suggestive of an earlier era of day boats. Each chose a side to apply the third and last coat of varnish to the mahogany uprights and trim of the hardtop. They resumed their discussion as whether to sell the Ghost or continue running contraband liquor, but could come to no final decision. By mid afternoon they had completed the varnish work and also had applied a coat of green over the white primer coat on the hull.

"One more coat of green and we'll be done," Don said as he cleaned their brushes with mineral spirits.

"Maybe you can put the finish coat on tomorrow while I rig the steering rope," Al suggested.

"As long as you can stay out of my paint," Don said. "I'm beat, why don't we try to catch up on the sleep we haven't had for the last three days."

Al agreed and they were both soon dead to the world in the back bedroom, so tired that they had no idea of the figure that quietly inserted a skeleton key in the front door and slipped silently inside the shop just after dusk.

CHAPTER THIRTY-ONE

Ray Moore was feeling justifiably pleased with his recent efforts. For a very modest sum, he had learned well enough ahead of time that the Ghost might be followed and had managed to surprise Tucci and company by having secreted himself inside the tunnel entrance when they had come to find his liquor. Subsequently, he had encountered little difficulty in moving the load to the remote Fircrest outlet of the tunnel, from whence he could remove it with little chance of being detected. Later that morning, by another phone call, he had been made aware of Tucci's visit to his partners on the Ghost and been appraised that, perhaps, the boys had gotten the upper hand in the situation, since Tucci's speedboat had left without hostages. In fact, the boys had taken the Ghost out for a short run later in the morning and put her back in the slip directly thereafter. By late afternoon, Ray had made contact with Tucci, asked for a meeting in a very public place and gotten it. By dinner time, he had managed to convince Tucci that he and his partners had nothing to do with the murder of Tucci's son and had negotiated the sale of the load that was just brought in. A lot of progress in 15 hours, Ray told himself. Of course, he had made a promise that he might not be able to keep: that he would find the murderers and allow Tucci the first chance to take care of business, as they said in mob circles. Ray knew the chances were slim that he would actually stumble on such information, but one never knew when something got dumped in your lap. Such as the totally unexpected calls from a certain "personal investigator" that identified himself as Jeff Harrison. Ray was sure of one thing, though, after meeting and paying off Jeff Harrison, or whoever he really was, that Jeff was selling information about his partners' comings and goings to any party who would pay him for it. Ray was here to see the boys and plug that leak if at all possible.

"You really should get a better lock, fellows," Ray said as he snapped on the light switch. "You never know what kind of person you are going to wake up to find, eh?"

"Son of a----, Ray what are you doing here?" Don yelled, jumping out of bed in only his underpants.

"This getting to be a bad habit," Al said sourly.

"That's exactly why I'm here," replied Ray. "Let's go get some dinner and talk over what we can do to remedy it."

They took Ray's car over to the Titlow Beach Cafe, formerly

the Titlow Beach Tavern before Prohibition. It was less than a mile from Day Island and sparsely frequented now that it didn't serve beer or wine. Which made Ray think that maybe he could improve their business if the owners might be interested. But that wasn't the discussion that needed to take place this night. All three ordered the daily special of pork chops, cabbage and mashed potatoes. It was dished out in what seemed record time, since there were no other patrons at this late hour.

"Not too bad," Al muttered.
"At least I didn't have to cook it."

"Not too good either," remarked Ray, "But the quality of food is not our concern tonight. Finding the party that's watching you is!"

"Who's watching us?" Don blurted out, louder than he wished he had.

"A man who calls himself Jeff Harrison. What we need to know is how he's been doing it and how we can change that, short of killing him, of course," Ray replied.

"How do you know this guy has been watching us and what his name is?" Al wondered aloud.

"He sold me information that someone was going to be following you the other night and today he told me that Tucci had paid you a visit last night and left in a hurry, luckily without you being dragged by a rope behind his boat. He also told me that you had taken the Ghost for a run and returned to the slip a short time later without being followed."

"Wow!" Don exclaimed. "He must live on another boat at our dock or almost as close to know all that about us."

"Tucci did come aboard our boat and threatened us with a gun. Don got a choke hold on him and I took his gun. We persuaded him, at least in that circumstance, that we didn't have anything to do with what happened to his sons or the load of liquor," Al explained.

"Yes, I gathered as much," Ray said. "I had a meeting with him today and I think he believes us now. In fact he's buying the load you just brought in. I've got it hidden in a room in the tunnel near the Fircrest outlet and I'll deliver it in a borrowed truck tomorrow night. Nobody knows this except us three. Before I make the delivery, we need to find this Harrison guy and take him out of the surveillance picture some way so that we have eliminated further interference from whomever else he may be selling information on our movements. Tucci might not be the only party."

"He might be the key," Al said quietly.

"To who did in Tony and Lou Tucci?" Don asked.

"I'm thinking that, as well," Ray said. "Let's go back to the island and take a good look at where this guy might be hanging out, because we've only got one day to deal with the problem."

"Ray, Don and I have been thinking about whether we should continue this business or sell the Ghost as we originally planned and stick to boat building," Al stated.

"If the economy goes to hell like your friend Jill thinks it's going to, I don't think there's going to be much of a market for high priced boats, fellows. But that's your decision to make. I'm in no position, with my personal life as messed up as it is, to be telling anyone else how to run their lives. Meantime, let's try to solve the problem we have with our mysterious informant, Harrison."

The trio drove back over the bridge to the island, parking the car in a vacant lot a block away from the marina. They conferred quietly, deciding to split up. Don would go down to the boat and act as bait to attract the attention of anyone who might be watching. Ray would walk out the north spit to get an idea of where one could set up to see the boat while Al canvassed the dock to look for anyone staying aboard their own boat that might be attracted by Don's visit to the Ghost. They agreed to return to the car in one hour.

When they came together again, Don asked," Did you catch anyone watching me?"

"I think someone in the house clear at the end of the spit could watch everything in the marina, but there weren't any lights on to indicate anybody is home," Ray said.

"There's nobody hanging out on their boat that I could tell," Al said, "but I agree that someone in that house over there could spot anything going on in the marina."

"When I turned off the light in the cabin, I looked up there with our big binoculars and I'm almost certain there was a person sitting by the window looking back at me. With the light out, I don't think he could see me, but I think that's the place to look for whoever is watching us," Don agreed.

"Let's pay him a visit then," Ray said and started the car's engine.

"What are we going to say?" Al said, momentarily panicked by the thought of accusing a total stranger in his own home.

"If he's the guy I paid $200 to yesterday, we tell him he's out of business or we feed him to the fishes when he least expects it," Ray growled.

"You said we weren't going to do anything--like killing him, I mean," Al stammered.

"We're not, Al. Ray is saying that we intimidate him like Tucci and his kind do," Don replied. "I don't think Tucci was ready to kill us last night, but if I hadn't got the drop on him he sure could have made us think he was going to."

"Don's right," Ray said, "The threat of force can be just as useful as the actual use of it. I don't intend to go to jail or be hung for killing somebody, but this guy doesn't know that! We're not going to give him the chance to think otherwise, though. We'll bust in there like we mean to take him out permanently and then let him talk us out of doing so. When he promises to say nothing to nobody, ever, we let him off easy with just a slap in the face or a good punch to the belly to make him think we know our business."

That's exactly how it went down. Mr. George Harris, AKA Jeff Harrison, agreed to close his eyes to all activity of the Ghost and her owners in exchange for keeping what he had extracted from Tucci and Ray. He got away with only the punch to the belly by Don while Ray and Al had him pinioned. What the three partners didn't learn was who else Harris had told of their operation and Harris didn't bother to tell them of what might be their greatest danger.

CHAPTER THIRTY-TWO: OCTOBER, 1929

Don and Al worked continuously on repairs to the Ghost for two weeks, replacing anything that might have been affected by her partial submergence. Don tore up enough of the aft deck to allow the installation of a 20 gallon fuel tank that Mr. Hallen had fabricated for them. It was a very tight fit, but it assured an increased range of at least 35 miles. The weather had cooled into the low fifties and most days they had to contend with rain showers which slowed progress and definitely dampened their spirits. September became October before the young men were satisfied that the Ghost was truly seaworthy for the use which it was intended. To add to the dreariness of the situation, Jill was certain that the economy was going to suffer terribly after September's market losses became worse in October. Since they had not yet found a buyer for the completed launch, it appeared that their boat building career might be finished before it got a good start.

Meanwhile, Ray had been making excuses for not being able make deliveries to several small customers that he had intended to sell some of the last load. He had also secured enough additional orders to make up a 75 case load, but he was short of cash to buy that much. He had spent a fortune on a lawyer that was smart [and slimy] enough to keep his garage from falling into Lena's hands in their ongoing divorce battle. She was to get the house and a small bank account; he was to get the garage and whatever cash he could hide. Thus it was that he swallowed his pride and called a meeting of his three former partners on the first Friday in October.

"I've got enough orders to fill a 75 case load right now, but there's a problem," Ray started.

"Let me guess," Jill interrupted, not too kindly. "You don't have the money."

"Yes, that's part of it," Ray began again. "Also, the delivery will have to be made in three stops rather than one. The good news is that we'll be making a bigger share of the profit with no middle man and because the nights are longer now, there is more time to get the deliveries made."

Don and Al didn't look like they were going to say anything yet, so Jill plunged ahead. "You want us to finance and deliver the load and collect the money, while you sit back and collect a share, right?" she said caustically.

"Not totally," Ray replied quietly. "If the boys wish, I'll go along and help with loading, unloading and making sure we're delivering the stuff to the customers who paid for it rather than somebody trying---"

"To rip us off!" Jill completed his thought.

"Do we have the cash to make the buy?" Al asked.

"It would take a couple of days to sell some of our--" Jill cut herself off, not trusting anymore information to Ray at this point of their relationship. She had been bombarded at work for weeks with negative comments about Ray from Goldie, who in turn, had been bombarded by her mother. Lena was never going to forgive or forget Ray's infidelity and was making her daughters feel the same way.

"What about the three stops, Ray? Aren't we going to triple our chances of exposure?" Don asked.

"Hopefully not. Two of them we've already used safely, Walt and Mabel's on Hylebos Waterway and Webster's place on Mud Bay," Ray replied.

"You didn't mention the third," Jill muttered.

"A quick stop at Salmon Beach. Just 15 cases, which shouldn't take more than ten minutes to unload. I'll get the money before we deliver, so the customer will be taking the biggest chance," Ray assured them.

"There are people at Salmon Beach that know Al and me," Don objected. "I don't want to show my face there in connection with smuggled liquor and this boat!"

"Those people you know are probably the same ones who'll be drinking the stuff!" Ray shot back. "But if it will make you feel easier, I'll get my buyer to row his fishing skiff out a ways to make the pickup."

"The tide runs really fast by there. Do you think he can make it with 15 cases aboard?" Al wondered.

"As thirsty as his patrons are, he'll make the effort," Ray said. "Besides, it's his problem, right?"

"Do you want me to make the order then?" Jill asked.

"Yes, from the Scotsman in Victoria, for Thursday evening at eight o'clock, if you can have the money for us by Wednesday," Ray replied.

"What's your cut, Ray?" Al asked.

"Seventy-five cents a bottle. Yours will be $2.25 per bottle. Nice profit, eh?" Ray grinned.

"Yes, it is, Ray," Jill said, figuring in her head. "$675 apiece, and your investment is only your time, not your money and not your boat!"

"And yours is---?" Ray asked smoothly.

"My money and my time, but not my neck, like these guys," she said, indicating the young men.

"It's okay Jill," Al said, "If it's okay with Don, I'm fine with the split."

"Let's do it," Don agreed. "I'm tired of working on the boat. Let's make it work for us."

"Thank you all. I'm glad we're back in business. I hope we can stick together as partners better than I've handled my private life," Ray said contritely. "I'll see you Thursday morning."

As the other three left, Ray shook each of their hands in turn.

Jill was last to the door. Looking him square in the eye, she said, "I hope you meant what you said just now. You damn well better be straight with us, Ray."

"You three are my only family now. I don't intend to mess up with you guys," he replied softly.

Jill thought that she saw a tear in his eye as he closed the door behind her.

The three partners crowded into the little Ford and headed back to Jill's house for snacks. Over a leisurely card game of rummy they discussed the merits of the deal they had just struck with Ray.

"You were pretty hard on him, Jill," Don remarked, "Any particular reason?"

"Plenty, aren't they obvious?" she asked, wondering how Don could be so dense at times.

"From a woman's perspective, I guess Ray looks like a real bad character," Al reasoned, "But I think he was sincere about his relationship with us and I also think he has a good grasp on what it takes to survive in the business we've embarked on."

"I'll grant you that," Jill agreed, "And I hope he sticks to business for our sakes. Are you comfortable with having to make three drops to move off one undersized load?"

"For the profit margin that he's talking about, I'm willing to give it a try," Don responded.

"The boat will use a little less fuel and be more responsive running with less weight," Al noted, "As long as we don't have any trouble with the transfer at Salmon Beach it should work out all right.

Will you have any trouble getting the money on time?"

"No, I can handle that," Jill answered, adding, with a triumphant laugh as she laid down her cards, "Rummy!"

"Licked again by a girl!" Don moaned in mock grief.

"Smarter than the average bear," Jill grinned.

"Whatever that means," Al groused. "Do you cheat, or are we just so pitifully dumb that you always win?"

"I won't answer that on the grounds that it would tend to incriminate me either way! I'll make it up to you with ice cream sundaes, okay?" she teased.

After the boys bought the pickup, Jill had decided to splurge on a refrigerator, something most people did not yet have as a common kitchen appliance in 1929. Don had hauled it home from the Sears and Roebuck store in the truck and was very pleased that they could now enjoy ice cream when visiting. They consumed the whole quart before the boys departed, each with a kiss on the cheek from their favorite hostess.

They drove back to the island with the single windshield wiper grinding away at the rain and wind pushing through gaps in the side curtains.

"It looks like winter is starting early. What do you say we invest a little of our upcoming profit in a right side wiper and a hot water heater for this thing?" Al asked from the passenger's side seat.

"Fine by me," Don agreed, "And maybe we could build a nice looking covered box for the pickup bed, too."

"Good idea! It would keep our stuff dry and we could even put some advertising on the sides," Al suggested.

"With a picture of a whiskey bottle?" Don joked.

"I was thinking more of a boat," Al laughed.

CHAPTER THIRTY-THREE

George Harris watched the Ghost slip past his home and disappear into the Thursday morning fog a hundred yards to the north and noted that his former client, Ray Moore, was aboard this time. He wrote in his journal and went back to his perusal of the newspaper account of the failing stock market.

Don moved the throttle forward enough to put the Ghost onto plane and checked his compass heading closely.

"Do you feel safe running in the fog at this speed?" Ray asked, feeling very claustrophobic after only a few minutes, despite Al's repeated sounding of the horn.

"Not entirely, but it's what we're doing for a living," Don replied. "The wind is supposed to rise this morning, so it'll clear up pretty soon."

"Yeah, and by the time we leave Port Townsend the swells will be spitting foam from the crests," Al said, "And we'll be thinking how nice and calm our morning was!"

Ray realized that the boys were not going to coddle him. It's going to be a long day and night, he thought, so I may as well relax and let my expert young friends do what they've learned to do to survive. He lay back on the couch at the back of the cabin, closed his eyes and tried to rest.

Don gestured to Al who glanced at Ray and winked back. Both knew he wasn't really asleep. Don pushed the throttle ahead just enough to cause Ray to open his eyes again, wondering how they dared increase speed in such circumstances. When Ray scrunched his eyes closed once more, the boys exchanged grins.

The fog hung on until they cleared Blake Island and entered Elliott Bay, when, as Don predicted, the wind began to build and the waves with it. By the time they reached Port Townsend for their fuel stop and late lunch, it was obvious that crossing the Strait of Juan de Fuca was not going to be a walk in the park. The gas attendant from their first trip was back on duty and as talkative and curious as he was several months previous.

"Nice to see you guys again, but it sure doesn't look like a good day to be goin' boatin'. Where ya headed?"

"Port Angeles," Don lied. "Showing the boat to a prospect up there that might want us to build him a fast fishing boat."

"No kidding! Well it's sure gonna get rough goin' around

Dungeness, I'll bet. Weather report says the wind is gonna drop tomorrow. Maybe you oughta stay in port here tonight," he suggested, wiping his dripping nose with a dirty red handkerchief that hung from the back pocket of his striped overalls. "They's a great seafood cafe' just over two blocks yonder if you was to want a good dinner. Cheap too!"

The banter went on for another half hour before all the tanks were topped off, the bill paid and they had managed to escape the harbor. Al took over the wheel, allowing the Ghost to plow along slowly as the three consumed sandwiches and warm soup that Ray had concocted during the refueling.

"Does that happen every time?" Ray asked.

"You mean the comments about the boat, bad weather, how much fuel we buy and where we're headed?" Al asked. "Yeah, pretty much. This guy was even worse the first time we stopped here. You can't blame him, though. Its got to be a lousy, boring job waiting on other people who are doing fun or exciting things, while you just hang around fueling boats and cleaning up the mess."

"Puget Sound is an amazing place for boating and if you have to see everyone else's activities and can't even drop in a fishing line, it would be hard to deal with," Don agreed.

"In the part of Wisconsin that I came from, boating was confined to a skiff or a canoe on the local lakes. I guess I never got the fever for fishing, sailing or speeding on the water that you boys have. I'll bet you'll always be hooked on boating," Ray observed, feeling a little nauseous as the Ghost slowly pitched and rolled its way into deep water.

"But you like fast cars. Didn't you used to build race engines for the board track racers on the old Tacoma track?" Al asked as he accelerated to get the bow to raise enough to throw off the increasing swells.

"Yes, I still like improving performance for my customers. It pays better than repair work and it's a lot more fun, but I'm sure I'll always feel safer gong fast on land than on the water, despite how much I enjoyed putting the engine for this boat together," Ray said, doing a bit of self analysis.

After an hour of quartering into huge swells, topped by a nasty chop and wind blown spray, Ray was regretting that he volunteered for this part of the operation.

"Is it usually this bad crossing the Strait?" he asked.

"Sometimes it's better, but this will be our slowest crossing so far. I'm not pushing it since we have plenty of time before dark. Coming back we'll have to run a lot faster, but we'll have more of a following sea then, so it'll be easier," Don explained.

"If we don't broach in the dark," Al added, wickedly.

"Thanks for making me feel better," Ray said, feeling totally miserable by this point and knowing the trip was far from completion.

The Ghost passed Brodie Rock, weaved cautiously through the other obstacles and slipped into the protection of Oak Bay at 7:45. By the time they were secured to the pickup dock, their supplier's truck was almost down the hill.

"Perfect timing, Don, nice navigating," Al said.

"We're both getting better with practice," Don replied.

Ray greeted the Scotsman warmly, explaining that he was the salesman for the four partners and how pleased he was to have such quality products to sell. In actuality, he was even more pleased to be on dry land, if only for the short time it took to load the 75 cases. A few more pleasantries and the payment were exchanged before the Ghost headed south just after 9 o'clock. Once past Brodie Rock, Al, who was still piloting, accelerated to planing speed and Ray began to experience a little of what his partners had been enduring over the past several months.

"I need both of you to yell out if you see anything I need to avoid," Al warned. "I've got my hands full watching our compass heading with this cross slop and the swells moving us all over the ocean!"

"I can't see much of anything," Ray complained.

"Look ahead as far as you can," Don instructed. "After a while your eyes will adjust and you'll begin to notice any change in the wave pattern, like foam or shadows or dark spots. If and when you see anything that looks out of place, sing out, okay?"

"I'll do my best," Ray muttered, in great discomfort.

Six very tedious hours later the Ghost rounded Point Dalco on Vashon Island and picked up the glitter of Tacoma's waterfront lighting through a lowering mist. They reached Hylebos waterway by 2:10 AM, five minutes ahead of their scheduled meeting. Walt and Mabel's closed at 2 AM, leaving Walt and his helper plenty of time to cross the few yards to the adjacent dock, armed with hand trucks to move their twenty-five cases to Walt's store room. With five men working, the Ghost was under way again in 20 minutes with Don now at the wheel. By 3 AM they were off Salmon Beach in quiet mode, calm water and gathering fog, looking for Ray's mystery buyer.

After several minutes of waiting, Ray whispered, "Maybe we should use the spotlight."

"No way," Al hissed. "There are still people up. We don't need any nosy neighbors seeing us making a drop!"

"Al's right, Ray. Let's just wait it out. We've got plenty of time to get to Mud Bay before daylight," Don muttered.

Another ten minutes went by as the Ghost idled quietly against the incoming tide, managing to stay almost in the same spot. They were about a hundred yards offshore of the house the buyer was supposed to be using. Like all the buildings on Salmon Beach it was built mostly over the water on pilings, with a narrow launching ramp of wood for a small boat on one side. Most of the houses had hand winches to skid their skiffs or launches back up to the deck level when not in use. Barely visible, the three partners saw movement from the base of a slimy launch ramp. Al turned the Ghost toward shore to make ready to transfer the 15 cases.

As a large skiff approached very slowly, Ray exclaimed, "Something's wrong! That boat came from the wrong house!"

"Maybe he borrowed somebody else's skiff," Don suggested. "Can you tell if it's your buyer or not?"

"No, but I think we should get out of---" Ray was interrupted by the flash of a spotlight from above and behind them to the west.

Turning, they saw only the faint outline of a much larger boat, its spotlight turned directly on the aft cockpit where they stood. It had evidently slipped within a quarter mile of them while their attention was toward shore, but now was accelerating for them.

Don ran to the throttle and jammed it forward and wrenched the wheel to the right, away from the shore. Ray dropped to the deck as a torrent of bullets shattered the starboard cabin window just ahead of him.

Al was thrown off the port side of the rear deck where he had been ready to unload the whiskey cases. The frigid water enveloped his body before he could get a breath and he could not tell, in the utter blackness, which way was up to the surface.

"God help me to please find the way and forgive me for the greed that brought me to this hellish watery grave if I can't make it to shore," he shouted in his mind. He let his body relax and in a few seconds a swirl of rip tide threw him half clear of the surface. He caught the glimpse of a light from a cabin at the south end of Salmon Beach and got his bearings. Striking out towards the light and shore, it was soon apparent that he was being swept south faster than he was heading east to safety. Above the pounding of his heart he could hear the bellow of the Ghost's exhaust disappearing toward Rocky Point. Had Don left him to drown or didn't he realize what had happened? Further thought was cut off as the beam of a searchlight illuminated the rip rapping of rock that held the shore intact bordering the railroad track. His destination was under surveillance, probably by whoever had shot up their boat. Can it get any worse, Al thought as he ducked under to avoid the lowering searchlight.

On the Ghost, Ray had crawled forward into the cabin. "Al went overboard!" he yelled to Don.

Don reached to pull back the throttle, but Ray gripped his arm tightly. "They'll kill us with that machine gun, we've got to as far as we can away from here."

"We can't let him drown!!" Don screamed back, turning the wheel away from his heading toward Day Island.

"He's either going to get to shore and get away or he's going to be shot in the process!" Ray retorted. "We don't have any way to stop what's happening now."

"There's got to be a way," Don argued. "We're faster than they are. We could cut between them and Al or even ram them to divert their attention."

"We're outgunned and outplayed by somebody who wants to finish us once and for all, Don. It would be suicide to go against that machine gun and whatever else they have in the way of weapons," Ray said with finality.

"Okay, then what do we do, report them to the Coast Guard?" Don asked, sarcastically.

"We go deliver this whiskey, find a place to hide this boat where no one can possibly find it, get ourselves back to Tacoma and search for Al," Ray said grimly. "With our own set of guns, if you're with me."

Don took his time before answering. "You've got an idea where to start, don't you, Ray?"

"I have a couple of ideas, yes, but first we need to empty the boat and hide it. Have you any idea where?"

"Take the wheel and keep the compass on 210 degrees for 8 more minutes than bear right to 225 degrees for 2 minutes. By that time I will have found a place to hide her later and I'll head us between McNeil and Anderson Island. And for God's sake don't hit anything!" Don yelled over the screaming engine.

Ten minutes later Don took over the wheel as promised and guided the flying boat through several course changes that brought them to Mike Webster's little dock on Mud Bay a half hour before they were expected.

"I'll start unloading while you go up to the house and get Mike down here to help. We've got to beat the tide to the place I have in mind or it's not going to work," Don urged.

Mike took it all in stride until Ray told them that they had lost Al overboard and that somebody had shot out their window. He volunteered to go hunting with them, but Ray asked him to stick with the delivery plan and stash the extra 15 cases in a safe place until they could get together again.

The tide had been receding for over an hour before they arrived at the spot Don planned to hide the Ghost. There was enough daylight to just pick out the darker area of water that indicated a very narrow channel into Dutcher Cove off Case Inlet. He approached going north almost parallel with the shore line and just a few feet from its edge.

"We're going to ground!" Ray warned. "I think we've missed the tide."

"Hold your horses," Don said between gritted teeth. "The water's deep enough ahead if we can make the point of the spit."

Just then the front starboard chine touched the beach. Don gunned the Ghost forward, stirring mud as the prop, protected by the unique bottom shape, pushed the boat past the shallow and around the corner into an absolutely hidden lagoon. Murky water was quickly emptying from the T shaped estuary. Don idled the Ghost to the southern end where fir boughs hung well over the water's edge. He turned left and, with a final burst of throttle, drove the bow aground in a soft bank of mud.

"We're here, partner," Don said. "If we throw a few fir branches over her, no one could see her from an airplane!"

CHAPTER THIRTY-FOUR

When Al surfaced for the third time the searchlight was scanning the area where he had gone overboard, but the incoming tide had swept him over a quarter mile to the south. He struck out as fast as he could for shore and with the help of an eddy made land just as the searchers realized where the tide might have carried him and moved their pattern to the south. Al made it up the rock embankment and almost over the two sets of railroad tracks before the light found him. He heard the bark of a single rifle shot and, simultaneously, the whine of a bullet passing considerably over his head.

"Bad shot, thank God," he muttered, running for the cover of small trees clinging to the clay bank inside the twin railroad tracks. The spotlight found him once more and again a shot whizzed over his head.

A small power boat had been launched from the stern of his assailant's craft and was almost to shore when Al reached the doors to the Chinese Tunnel. They were locked again, this time with a heavy, new padlock. Another shot clanked its way into the door, just a foot over his head, as once again the searchlight found him.

"Damn," Al swore, "They're going to get me one way or another, but why?"

He heard the whine of the reverse gear of the launch as it nosed up to the rip rapping and knew its occupants would soon be coming over the tracks to----what? Whatever it was, Al didn't want to find out. Remembering the trick that Ray had pulled on the Tucci gang, he realized that there had to be another entrance to the tunnel; one close enough that Ray was able to lock up the doors and get back inside before Tucci had gone to Day Island and returned, only 10 or 15 minutes with a boat as fast as Tucci claimed his was. Grabbing the branches and roots of the overhanging trees, Al scrambled up the clay bank to the side of the tunnel doors and began feeling for anything that might allow him into the tunnel below. The men from the launch had scaled the rocks and were within earshot when the tunnel found Al. Without warning he slipped into the darkness, headfirst and at a violent rate. The fall was short and the stop abrupt and wet. Al landed on his elbows in two inches of foul smelling water, bruised but not broken. He stood up, shivering more from fear than from his second dunking of the night. The dark night outside was like daylight compared with the utter blackness that pressed in on him now. He stumbled over one of Ray's pallets and sat down to consider what was happening to him. Though he knew he was 30 or 40 feet behind the locked doors he could hear the men outside them conversing in guttural tones, menacing tones, angry tones. It seemed that they had not shot to kill or he couldn't have gotten this far. One burst on full automatic and he would have been splattered all over those doors that his pursuers were now trying to enter.

"They want to take me alive," Al thought. "They want to know what I know!" And what did he know? He knew where the whiskey was going. He knew there was money on board and more money to be made when the liquor was sold. He knew who the sellers were and he knew some of the buyers. He knew how to build a boat that was faster and better than anybody else was running just now. He thought he knew who had betrayed them. He knew a lot of stuff, but what part of it did they want? He also knew it wouldn't take the awful sounding creatures outside too long to break through the tunnel doors and find him sitting here thinking if they thought that he had gotten inside. In fact, it sounded like they were starting to do just that.

Al stopped thinking and started walking, away from the doors, deeper into the gloom, slowly at first, then, keeping one hand against the wall to steady himself, more rapidly, until he was going at a normal pace. He tried very hard to remain without conscious thought, a very difficult thing to accomplish, but necessary to preserve his sanity, because every time he tried to plan ahead, he was overcome with the gravity of his situation and began to falter. He stopped momentarily, held his breath and listened. At first all he could hear was his own heart beating, but in a very few seconds it became obvious that someone else was now in the tunnel and moving toward him. No light was evident, so he knew, as he picked up his pace, that the pursuer or pursuers were still well behind.

"Unless the tunnel is curving," he said to himself and increased his speed again. "How far did Ray say it was to the Fircrest entrance? Maybe over two miles? Can I possibly stay ahead of them that long when they must have light and I don't?" Al asked himself under his breath.

His mind began working on the problem before he could disengage it again: If he didn't fall, lose his way or come to a cave in, he might reach the entrance in as little as an hour, but it could take as much as an hour and a half. He figured that he was making about two miles per hour and those following might make three miles per hour with illumination. If the tunnel was two miles in length, that meant that he would have had to have a twenty minute head start. If the tunnel was two and half miles he would need a twenty five minute lead. He had a fifteen minute start or less. They were going to catch him!

      Fear of the unknown natural danger of traversing the tunnel in total darkness gave way to desperation to elude captors, whom he had not doubt, would take his life after they obtained whatever they wanted from him. Al began running with long strides, dragging his hand against the wall for direction. He slowed only enough to wrap his shirt around his fingers, feeling the sticky warmth of his own blood as he did so.

      After what seemed like an eternity, his lungs about to burst, he stopped. It took a few seconds to be able to catch enough breath to be able to hold one in his lungs and listen. The echo of heavy footsteps was unmistakable, but how close they were was impossible to tell. Al began to run again.

CHAPTER THIRTY-FIVE

Leaving the Ghost securely grounded, anchored and tied off to trees, Don and Ray followed a creek bed up a steep canyon bordered with young Alder trees. The alder trees had not quite shed their leaves for the upcoming winter, so little of the early morning light filtered down to aid their progress as the two men labored to gain higher ground. It was an hour of climbing through huckleberry brush and huge ferns before they came across a gravel road that looked promising.

"Which way?" Ray asked, leaning over, his hands on his knees, trying to catch his breath.

"Left, I think. The chart showed a road to Vaughn."

"What's at Vaughn?" Ray asked, still breathing hard.

"A school, post office and a few homes around the bay. We might be able to catch a ride up to Key Center. The state put in a cement road from there to Gig Harbor, so chances of finding transportation are pretty good," Don replied.

After a half hour of walking, they saw a farm wagon full of pumpkins coming down a narrow side road on the right and ran to intercept it. The driver saw them waving and halted until they drew near.

"Could you give us a lift to Vaughn or Key Center," Don said, smiling up at the old fellow at the reins.

"You look like you could use a ride all right," the farmer said, showing a kind, but toothless mouth. "Hop up and take a load off!"

"Thank you, sir," Ray said, very grateful to rest his weary, bruised body.

"You look like you been trampin' through the woods. How did you happen to be on this road? It don't go no where but a couple of farms," the older man asked.

"Our fishing boat broke down and we had to go through the woods to access the road," Ray lied easily.

"Where did you have to leave it?" the man inquired.

"Not sure exactly. We're going to have to come back by the water and tow it home with another boat. I don't think we'd ever find our way back otherwise," Don explained with another lie. It surprised him how much easier lies were coming to him these days.

Ray turned the subject to the old man's pumpkins and farming in general. Ray had grown up on a farm and soon was entertaining the others with tales from his youth in Wisconsin. The team of horses trotted along well, soon bringing them to Vaughn where the farmer was meeting one of the Mosquito Fleet boats that called daily, taking produce and passengers to Tacoma. Rather than take a chance on a finding a ride to Gig Harbor and then taking the ferry to Tacoma, Ray and Don settled for traveling on the steamer with the pumpkins.

Several hours later, Don prodded the sleeping Ray back to life. "We'll be docking in Old Town in a few minutes."

Ray yawned, stretched and asked, "I really conked out, I guess. Did you get any sleep?"

"A little, but I started thinking about Al and how we're going to find him---if he made it, that is."

"First, we need to get a car. Whoever planned the attack on us probably will be looking for me at the garage and you at Cummings' place or your boat shop. Any ideas, Don?"

"Its almost 5:30, I could call Jill at work and ask her to take the bus out to Cummings and get the pickup. She knows where we keep the extra key," Don suggested.

"Someone might follow her if they see her taking your car," Ray warned. "We don't want to lose---"

"Right!" Don said cutting him off. "I'm too darned tired to think straight. How about calling your mechanic and have him meet us somewhere after normal closing hours?"

"Good idea! We can meet him at his apartment near Wright's Park and nobody will be the wiser," Ray agreed.

Ray made the call, telling Mitch, his mechanic, to bring the late model Dodge on which they had just installed a high compression head, exhaust cut-out and down draft carburetor. He also told him to put a double barrel shot gun, two Army issue .45 caliber pistols, a 100 feet of light rope and two flashlights in the trunk that was mounted above the extended rear bumper and not to be seen doing it.

"And make sure it's full of high test," Ray finished.

Overhearing the phone conversation, Don asked," Are we going hunting?"

"We certainly are. Let's get some chow before we walk up to Mitch's apartment. I think better on a full stomach," Ray replied.

They ate at a fish bar right on the Old Town dock where their disheveled appearance caused no curiosity. It was almost dark as they picked up the car and headed for Day Island.

"You still suspect George Harris? I thought we scared him off pretty well on our last visit," Don said.

"I think he was too easily convinced," Ray explained. "He may have told someone besides Tucci and me about our operation. Or, somebody else came into the picture and is leaning on him harder than we are. This time we are going to get serious, make him believe we are his biggest problem in life," Ray said, darkly.

As it shortly turned out, Mr. Harris had no more problems in this life. When Don and Al entered his unlocked side door, they found George in his favorite chair, upright, but with a large bullet hole in the middle of his forehead and a small dead, yellow canary stuck in his mouth.

Ray grabbed Don by the shoulder and backed him silently out of the house. They crept back to the Dodge, hidden in a thicket of rhododendrons and drove across the bridge with their lights off.

"Where do we go next?" Don asked, shakily.

"Into the bowels of hell, I'm afraid," Ray said as he headed for Fircrest.

CHAPTER THIRTY-SIX

Jill arrived home from work a little after 6 PM on Friday night, prepared dinner and made a dessert large enough to fill her two young partners whom she thought might be calling her soon. She figured that they would have needed to sleep most of the day after being up all day and night Thursday, but would wish to tell her something of how the trip went when they were rested. She called their shop at 7 with no answer. Becoming steadily more concerned, she called Ray's garage at 7:30 with the same result. By 8 o'clock she needed to take her mind off what might have become of her friends and went upstairs to work with the computer.

Having almost all of their assets in gold now, she had decided to try her hand at speculating in foreign currency fluctuations. The market was extremely volatile, which meant, that with concentration to detail, she should be able to enhance their investment greatly. Suddenly, the computer's speaker blared out, "You've got mail!" It had not done so over the 13 months since Jill had been transported to the 1920s. No matter how many times she had attempted to e-mail back to the future, nothing had transpired. Now, for no apparent reason, something had been mailed from the future! With trembling hands she moved the mouse to the icon that opened her e-mail and clicked twice.

It read simply, "Jill Gardiner, Move the gold to a safety deposit box at Puget Sound Bank. Add the name: Jack L. Johnson III, to yours on the authorized patron list and leave the second key in a container in the space beneath the trap door that is hidden under the bed of your dormer room. If you want to return to your former life, you will not deviate from these instructions. Simply click on "reply" with the two word message "mission completed" when you have finished the above task and are ready to return. JLJIII

Jill sat frozen, her thoughts spinning in overdrive, as she processed the message. Slowly, the memory of an evening in September, 2001 began to unreel in her mind. She had gone to a private club in Olympia with the son of one of her father's political cronies. He had insisted that she have a drink with the owner of the establishment who was also an associate of her father. The young man escorting her was a fellow economics major who had an odd fascination with hypnosis and time relativity. Jill had been only mildly interested in his outlandish theories, but went along as a political consideration for her father. The club owner was a light skinned African American with a gracious manner, a broad smile and sharp clothes. The decor of his office was gleaming dark mahogany from another era. A large portrait of a black man, wearing a pin stripe suit, a huge diamond stick pin and spats, hung behind the proprietor's gigantic, polished desk. Jill remembered remarking to her new acquaintance how the smile of the man in the picture resembled his own right down to the glint of a gold inlaid tooth.

"My grandfather!" he had said proudly. "A man with a vision of the future. He started with a nice restaurant in Seattle and, with help from a few well placed people, built a distribution empire that now stretches the length of the West coast. Your own father has been of assistance in the growth of our company and I believe you may have a place in our future growth as well."

"How might that be?" Jill remembered asking. "I'm studying to be an intern for a stock brokerage firm."

"So I've been told," the black man said, "Pull up a chair, have a drink with me and I'll tell you how you may be involved in the stock market in a very big way before long."

Jill searched her memory of what followed, but nothing came to the forefront. In fact, she didn't remember anything of the rest of the evening until her escort deposited her at her parent's home in Tacoma. The next morning she woke in this very room, but----it was 1928, not 2001! While everyone else in the country was reeling from the terrorist attacks against the United States just two days before, she had been whisked away to the past with no warning and no apparent reason, until now. In some unknown, and to Jill, farfetched manner, she had been sent to the past to bring a hoard of gold into the possession of men with tremendous wealth and power who wanted even more of the same.

"What can I do?" she cried to herself. "If I do what they say, I'll be abandoning the two closest friends I've ever known. They'll think I've stolen everything they've earned and left them holding an empty bag! But if I don't stash the gold for these others, I may never get back to my family."

She went on for an hour, alternating between fuming and crying, before the thought hit her, "My father may have an actual hand in this. Either he's in trouble with those guys over money or influence, or he's in league with them, using me as a pawn, to enrich them all. Maybe there's no future in the future for me. But if I don't respond, can they send someone to coerce me? If I say their mission is complete and they don't find the key to the safety deposit box in this room in the 21st century, will they be able to come after me?"

Jill knew it was time to confide in her partners, no matter how crazed they might think she was. She needed their input and the comfort of their love to sustain her. Or she might, indeed, go stark raving mad. If she wasn't already there now.

She went downstairs to the phone and began calling again.

CHAPTER THIRTY-SEVEN

Al awoke so thirsty that his tongue felt like it was stuck to the top of his mouth. How long he had slept, he had no idea, but knew it must have been several hours because he needed to empty his bladder. Before he had lain down he had scratched an arrow into the side of the tunnel with his pocket knife and he now felt for the tip of his mark to know which way to head. After making a small puddle on the floor he resumed walking, slow and steady, now that he knew he had eluded his pursuers.

His would be captors had reached the room where three of the tunnels converged just minutes after Al had felt his way around the room and chosen the farthest to left. He was then still close enough to hear them move away, presumably into one of the other two. Now, many hours later, Al was praying that they thought he had gotten out of the one that exited in Fircrest and had given up. He also was praying that he would eventually come out under the concrete bleachers of his former high school.

"It's a long shot," he thought, "but if I don't die of thirst or hunger, I can always backtrack and get out in Fircrest."

Too many 'ifs' he knew, as he stumbled on in the awful blackness, again trying to shut his mind off from everything except putting one foot in front of the other and repeating the process again and again.

****

Ray and Don reached the swampy area near the Fircrest opening of the Chinese Tunnels by 9 PM. Despite having had almost no sleep in two days, they were keyed up to the point of bursting as they approached the entrance. Each carried a loaded shotgun, a .45 pistol stuck in their belt, a flashlight and a spare set of batteries. Don had slung the loop of rope over his shoulder, not sure why he did so, but knowing it might be useful when heading into the depths that made up this mysterious maze.

"Somebody has been here since I moved the whiskey out," Ray said grimly.

"How can you tell," Don whispered.

"I stuffed the entrance full of brush and wiped away my tracks with fir boughs. Look! There are three or four sets of foot tracks and the mud hasn't dried yet. I think some of that bunch that was shooting at us found the tunnel and came all the way through it."

"Why would they do that, Ray? They know we didn't unload any whiskey into the tunnel this trip," Don argued

"They were looking for something more important, I think. And they know, now, that I used the tunnel to move whiskey to Fircrest, because I left the ore cars and the electric tow cart here to use again," Ray said thoughtfully.

Don's mind raced to grasp Ray's meaning. "You think that they were chasing Al in there, don't you?"

"I'm afraid so. The question is did they catch him?"

"Why do you think they would chase him this far, Ray?"

"Because he knows where the whiskey comes from and where it goes. Maybe even for ransom. We're dealing with guys who will do anything for profit, Don. Let's see if we can puzzle out what happened in there," Ray said as he squeezed into the exposed opening.

In a few minutes they entered the room where the tunnels converged. In the middle sat Ray's ore cars. To their left a tunnel slanted down to the southwest. Ahead another led off toward the northeast. To the right of that another led slightly more easterly.

"My electric buggy is gone!" Ray exploded. He followed the tracks to where they disappeared. "The dirty bastards must have taken it back down to the Narrows!"

"Doesn't look like we're going to be needing it for moving whiskey around," Don said glumly.

"No, but we could have used it to check out the other tunnel for Al. Now we'll have to do it on foot," Ray griped.

"You don't think he got out the way we just came in?"

"There's no way to know for sure, but he couldn't have had much lead on them. To get in to the tunnel he would have had to find the little side shaft that I made so that I could lock up the big doors to keep anyone from finding our little operation. That would have taken some thinking, because I didn't tell anyone how I managed that trick until now. He would have been trying to get away in the dark, soaking wet from swimming to shore, while his pursuers could have broken through the doors in a few minutes and brought lights with them. No, if he got away at all, he probably was barely ahead of them," Ray concluded.

"So, just in case, we're going to search the other tunnel, right? What if he doubled back after they left and went back to the Narrows," Don wondered aloud.

"We may have to check that out, too. There's another possibility too," Ray said soberly, as he led the way into the tunnel that headed toward old town.

"They may have found him and left him here dead," Don said, finishing what he knew Ray must be thinking.

****

There was still no answer at the boat shop, Ray's garage or his new apartment. At 10 o'clock, Jill called the marina and reached an unhappy Mrs. Cummings. When asked if Mr. Cummings was there, his wife demanded to know who the young tramp was that would dare call him at this late hour. Jill very carefully explained that she was a close friend of the young men who owned the blue-gray thirty foot boat that they called the Ghost. She told Mrs. Cummings that she had expected them back much earlier and wondered if the boat was back in its slip.

"Those boys come and go at all hours. The darn thing near sunk a while back! I ain't seen it come back in and wouldn't be surprised if they didn't sink it for good, the way they run it so fast at night or in the fog. Maybe you best call the Coast Guard if they don't show up by morning!" She hung up, leaving Jill to believe that the Ghost had worn out its welcome at Cummings Marina.

As a last resort, she called the Moore residence and was relieved to recognize Goldie's voice answer.

"What's up?" Goldie asked, when Jill identified herself. "No date tonight?"

"No, that's why I'm calling. I haven't heard from Al---or Don and I wondered if you might have heard from your dad or---anything," she faltered, not knowing what to say next that wouldn't compromise their operation.

"I think we need to talk. If it's okay with you, I'll just walk over for a cup of coffee," Goldie suggested quietly.

"Sure, I'd love the company. I'll warm up the pot."

"Hope you were serious about the coffee," Goldie said, upon arriving, while shaking the rain from the beautiful head of hair for which she was named.

"Of course," Jill said going for the steaming pot. "I'm sorry to get you out on a night that's turning bad."

"I'm happy you called. Ma's still ranting around, Birdie is upset because Harold has to work the weekend for Foss and Oz called to tell me our date to go dancing is off. That's what I need to talk to you about," Goldie confided.

"About Oz calling off your date?" Jill couldn't believe Goldie could be worried about that. She had a string of guys calling her all the time. Wonder if she---Jill cut off her own nasty thought and looked quizzically at her friend.

"No! It's WHY he called it off," Goldie retorted.

"Which was because---?" Jill took the bait.

"He was down at Salmon Beach late last night, to buy some hooch, you know, and this big boat comes out of the fog and shoots at a smaller boat. Rat -tat -tat! a machine gun, like in the movies, right? Anyway, the smaller boat takes off making a helluvalot of noise and the big one moves into shore, south of the beach, and a bunch of guys started bangin' around and cussin' and then it gets quiet again, but Oz beats it up the stairs and says he's not goin' back down there for booze or dancing or anything until he knows what the score is." Goldie stopped, lit up a Lucky Strike and sat back in her chair. She had watched Jill's face grow more and more pale as she reiterated her tale and knew her friend had guessed who had been involved. "So what do ya think?"

"You already know what I'm thinking. Yes, it was probably the boys. What you didn't know until now, is that your father was with them for the first time and they haven't showed up anywhere that I know of!" Jill cried, tears spilling down her cheeks.

"Oh jeez," Goldie blurted out, "They're smart guys, Jill. They'll figure a way out of----," but Goldie was beginning to spill some tears now as well.

Jill knew, though Goldie blamed her dad for much of the family turmoil, she really cared for him deep inside her tough little soul. "What a mess," Jill choked out, wishing she could confide more of her problems to her friend Goldie, but that would never be possible, she was certain.

CHAPTER THIRTY-EIGHT

Al was near exhaustion, stumbling often, falling occasionally, yet he kept moving on. Without being able to see his watch there was no way to judge how far he had come. He only knew that the tunnel had to end somewhere, "Even if it ends in a cave-in, I know it has to have an end," he moaned, deliriously.

He stumbled again, this time on a slick spot. That meant mud, which meant water! He felt along the roof and found a seep. It took a full minute for his cupped hand to fill up and when he drank, it tasted more foul than Don's home-brew had, but it was wet. He stood there until he had consumed 10 handfuls. It gave him time to think, something he had put aside for---how many hours? It didn't matter, he was thinking once more. There were water seeps in the clay banks near Commencement Bay. Maybe he was getting close to the outlet. He picked up his pace, a little hope displacing his despair. He fell over a piece of wood, picked it up and moved forward more cautiously. His shoes touched more wood fragments. He reached up and found that the tunnel was now shored with wood instead of being just tunneled through rock, clay or earth.

"I'm getting close, I can feel it," he said loud enough to cause a slight reverberation.

Not far ahead there seemed to be just the slightest hint of light. Not an opening, because it seemed to come and go as his head bobbed with each stride, but light, nevertheless.

"Maybe a crack from a door?" he thought. He didn't like that thought; he wanted the tunnel to end in a true opening under the stadium bleachers.

Al knew his eyes were totally dilated and that whatever light he was seeing must be minuscule and he was correct. He stopped just short of running face first into a door. The sliver of light was coming from a tiny crack at the top where its seal was not totally complete. He felt around all the edges with his pocket knife. The fit was almost perfect. He kicked one edge as hard as he could. Nothing happened. He kicked the other side, hoping to break loose whatever dead bolt or lock might hold it in place. Not a sign of movement, though he kicked again and again. This door had been fitted by someone that intended and knew how to make it stay in place for good.

"That would be cousin Erik!" Al laughed hysterically. He was just two inches from the sub-basement of Stadium High School and his own cousin had told him of closing off this gateway to the tunnel where he was now trapped!

Al was surprised that there was any light showing at all since Erik had made planking joints on the Ghost that were water tight without needing caulking. Erik was a master craftsman, but where was he now? Al figured that it must be Saturday and not likely anyone would be in the school, let alone in the sub-basement. Nevertheless, he pounded and yelled until his throat grew too tight and his fist too sore to continue. No one came to his rescue. He sat on the ground and wept. Later, he knew not how much later, he began to slowly whittle on the door where he hoped the dead bolt might be located. His energy dissipated, he made little progress before falling asleep, alone in the great darkness.

******

Don and Ray had been hiking steadily for two hours with only a few words uttered between them when Don yelled, "Look!"

Ray pulled up and shone his light back to where Don was pointing at a crude arrow shape carved in the left side of the tunnel's earth wall. He shone his light all around the area and stopped at a small damp spot on the floor. Bending down he scooped up a bit of the damp earth and smelled it.

"Urine!" Ray smiled and announced, "He's been here and he's headed the way we are!"

"AL, WE'RE COMING FOR YOU!!" Don yelled. The reverberation caused dirt to fall from the ceiling above.

"SHH!" Ray managed, "Let's not bring the whole mess down on us. This spot isn't that fresh. We've a ways to go before we find him, I think."

They picked up their pace for another hour before coming to a fork in the tunnel. Searching the hard floor, they could not tell which branch Al might have taken.

"You take that one and I'll head up this one," Ray suggested. "Give me a drink from the canteen and then take the rest with you."

"I think we should stick together, Ray."

"We can't be far from the end now. If I find a way out I'll backtrack to this point and you can do the same. We should be out of this place in a half hour, if there's still a way out. If there isn't, then we find Al, give him some food and water and head back the way we came, okay?"

"If you say so, but I hate to leave you alone," Don argued.

"I won't be any more alone than you are. The quicker we find out if Al's in here, the faster we can get out. This place is beginning to give me the creeps," Ray said, laughing nervously.

They separated and were soon lost to each other in the gloom. In the beam of his dimming flashlight, fifteen minutes later, Don picked out the form of his friend slumped against what appeared to be a solid wood end to the tunnel. He ran the remaining distance, crying out Al's name. There was no response and Al's left hand was wet with blood.

Ten minutes into the branched tunnel, Ray's light was so dim that it was of almost no use. He turned it off and felt his way forward, hoping to let the batteries rest long enough to function a while longer. He had been moving slowly for another few minutes when he noticed a hollow ring to his footsteps. Turning on the light, he found that he had almost run into a cement wall and that the ceiling was all cement as well. He was under the stadium bleachers and there seemed to be no way out.

"Like a giant cement tomb," he muttered, just as his flashlight failed completely. He sat down on the floor and very carefully unscrewed the butt of the light. He knew one mistake at this point and he might never find which way he had come from. Slowly he removed the dead batteries, reached into his pocket and fumbled for the new ones. His hands were shaking and his breath coming fast as his boyhood fear of the dark returned. The blackness seemed to be descending to crush the life out of him.

"I'm going to have a heart attack and croak right here," he thought in panic.

He caught just enough breath to stuff the new batteries in the canister and shakily screw the butt back on.

"It works! Thank God!" Ray exclaimed, something he rarely did, he was ashamed to think now.

He headed quickly out of his 'cement tomb' hoping to find Don at the fork with better news. Don was not there and Ray commenced to worry and curse his luck once again. He started running in the direction that Don and gone. He was totally out of breath when he came upon Don supporting the limp body of their partner.

"He's not---?" Ray stammered.

"No, but he's lost some blood, probably dehydrated and he won't come around totally. The only thing I got out of him was something about Erik that made no sense."

"What have we got here?" Ray asked looking at the wooden obstacle that barred them from freedom.

"I think we're in the sub-basement of Stadium High School. Al's cousin Erik told us--Oh, that's it! Erik may have been the one that walled the tunnel in; to keep the kids from getting in here," Don explained.

"So, all we have to do is get through there and we're home free," Ray said.

"It's solid Ray. I booted a few times and it looks like Al did the same, before he started to carve his way through," Don said, motioning to the small pocket knife still in Al's right hand. "Help me get some water into him before we try anything here."

It took both of them to hold Al upright enough to allow him to swallow water from the canteen. Don splashed a little on his face and that seemed to bring his friend back to a semblance of reality.

"You found me, partners. I knew I could count on you not to let me drown or---oh man, I'm still in this damn cave. I tried to --- Hey, we don't have to go clear back to the beginning, do we? Those bad guys---are they---gone?"

"Yes, they are gone and no, we are not going back the way we came," Ray said, emphasizing his words carefully. "We don't have enough battery power to make it back and I, for one, can't make it in the dark like you did, Al."

"What have you got in mind, Ray?" Don asked, "Shooting our way out? That might bring the roof down before we got a hole big enough to get through."

"The roof of this section is shored up with wood. I think it will hold," Ray said, hoping that would be true.

"Shotguns or pistols?" Don asked.

"If it's not too thick, the shotgun will make a good sized hole," Ray replied. "I'll try it at close range, giving her both barrels. You both move back a few feet and turn your backs in case of splinters."

Don helped Al move away about 15 feet and Ray let the door have it with both barrels. Several pieces of the shoring material fell from the roof, but didn't hit anyone. Don turned his flashlight on Ray to find him peppered with wood splinters and bleeding from a dozen that had hit his bare skin. The door was still in place with no apparent hole.

"That wasn't much fun," Ray yelled. All three were

temporarily almost deaf from the shock of the two gun blasts.

Ray moved up to the door and kicked the portion the shotgun blasts had affected. The wood creaked but did not break through. He pulled out his .45 and told the other two to hold their hands over their ears. He ripped his handkerchief in two and used it to plug his own ears. Don held a light on the door while Ray shot the .45 through it in six places. Then he kicked the area again. It buckled slightly.

"Let me," Don yelled, still half deaf. He took aim and launched a long legged kick with all his might. The wood was a full two inches thick and it was screwed into a metal casing to permanently seal off would be trespassers; until now. The piece broke away and they all cheered.

Don wriggled through and with Ray pushing as he pulled, they squeezed Al through next. Ray had to strip down to his red union suit to get through, but would have given up that and some skin to reach clean air and the light from a single bulb that hung from the basement ceiling.

"We better get those splinters out of you before we hit the street, Ray. It's almost morning and we're a sorry sight to begin with, without you looking like a walking pin cushion. Sit down and we'll both work on you," Don suggested.

Al rallied enough to be of some help, but could only use his right hand, his other badly in need of attention. Ray shivered on the cold cement and shortly told the boys to forget helping him.

"Let's get out of here," Ray insisted. It's less than two blocks to my apartment in the Ansonia. We'll get patched up there and get some food and coffee into Al before he conks out again."

Getting out was not that easy. With the utility elevator turned off for the weekend, they had to find their way through a virtual labyrinth of cluttered storage items before they found a stairway leading up. At each of the doors, Ray had to shoot the dead bolts with his .45 before they could reach the ground level. Hoping the shots from below ground had not been heard, they exited from one of the rear main floor doors and headed across Stadium Way toward the Ansonia, the shot guns hidden in a coat they had purloined from a coat rack. They had accomplished one of the two blocks when the wail of multiple sirens assailed their sore ears. Don and Ray literally picked up the sagging Al and dragged him behind the hedge of a nearby apartment building. They waited until the third police car had passed before trying to cover the last half block. Another siren was approaching from Tacoma Avenue, but Ray motioned Don to keep moving.

"It's a fire engine from the Tacoma Avenue Company. I hear them all the time. Let's get around the back and take the elevator up from the parking garage. It should be empty on Saturday morning."

CHAPTER THIRTY-NINE

The phone jangled Goldie into semi-consciousness from the couch on which she had been sleeping. She looked up at the pendulum clock on the wall. It read 6:30, meaning she had gotten almost four hours sleep. Staggering to the wall phone in the kitchen, she wondered if Jill ever heard her phone calls from her third story bedroom, or just ignored them as Goldie would have preferred to do now.

"Hello," she muttered, groggily.

"Who's this?" a familiar but suspicious sounding male voice inquired.

"It's me, Goldie! Is that you, Don?"

"Yes, can I speak to Jill, quickly please?"

"She's asleep upstairs. Are you guys all right? We've been worried sick! Why didn't you call her before this?"

"Uh, ---it's a long story. I don't have time to talk now and you might not to want to hear it anyway. Can you get Jill down to the phone?" Don pleaded in exasperation.

"Not 'till you tell me what's going on," Goldie said stubbornly.

"Al's hurt. We need some first aid supplies right now and I don't want to argue about it, Goldie!" Don said emphatically.

"Where are you?" Goldie asked, a bit subdued now.

"Never mind, you don't want to get involved in this situation and I'm sure your dad doesn't want you involved, either. Just get Jill on the phone," Don insisted.

"What's my dad got to do with it?" Goldie asked. When Don didn't answer, she dropped the receiver cord and ran upstairs to get Jill. She was dumfounded to find Jill's door locked and began pounding on it. Jill came to the door shortly and opened it only far enough to slip through before facing her fellow worker.

"What's wrong?" Jill asked, only half awake yet.

"Don is on the phone and says Al is hurt and he needs first aid supplies. He clammed up when I wanted to know what happened and where he was calling from, but I think my dad is involved somehow," Goldie explained in a rush. As they started down the stairs, she added, "He's being a jerk, you know!"

"Your dad?" Jill was totally confused.

"No, silly! Don! He acts like I'm a child and can't be trusted," Goldie cried impatiently.

Jill took the phone and listened without comment as Don outlined their situation, told her where they were and asked her to bring a good supply of first aid necessities, some canned fruit juice and some fresh pastries or whatever she could gather that had plenty of sugar content.

"It's too far to walk in the rain and I may have to go to the pharmacy for some of the stuff--,"

Don interrupted, "I'll call my folks and ask them to loan you the Model T. Do you think you can drive it?"

"I'm not sure, but I'm willing to bet Goldie does," Jill suggested.

"I already told her to stay out of this," Don argued.

"Fat chance of that. We had a very long talk here last night. She knows some of what happened Thursday night and she's not going to sit still until she pries the rest out of us. You know her! Besides, she cares about you guys and she still cares about her dad. We'll be there within the hour," she said with finality and hung up.

Goldie gave Jill a huge hug. She had a friend that actually stuck up for her; what a change from the way she was treated at home by her mother and sisters! Goldie almost forgot about Jill's locked door as a feeling of new self worth washed over her.

Jill got dressed and put a few things she had on hand in a bag while Goldie, who had slept in her clothes, went over to the Grant's house to get the old Ford. Ralph Grant took her out to the little garage in back and went through the starting routine with Goldie.

"Are you sure you can drive one of these?" he asked, doubtfully. "It looks to me like you can barely reach the pedals."

"No problem, Mr. Grant. Pa taught me to drive a Model T before they had electric starters. I had to stand up to reach the pedals back then, but I'll get her back to you in one piece, don't worry!"

With that, she mashed in the middle pedal and the car jumped out into the alley. Before Ralph could say more, Goldie had pushed in the left pedal, pulled down the throttle lever and spurted down the alley toward 9th Street. He shook his head in wonder and retreated inside to his morning paper and coffee cup, hoping his wife wouldn't ask any more questions than she already had about what was going on, because Ralph didn't have any more answers to share.

The girls picked up some pastries just out of the oven at the bakery on 11th and K Street and the rest of the needed first aid supplies at Tacoma's only all night pharmacy just a block down on

12th and K. As promised, they arrived at Ray's top floor apartment by 7:30. Ray and Don had cleaned Al up fairly well and got him into a pair of Ray's pajamas, but they were still a mess themselves.

Goldie stared at her father's wounds for a moment, then went to him and hugged him a long time. When they parted, each had tears streaming from their faces.

Covering their mutual embarrassment over such a public display of affection, Jill took over tending to Al's damaged hand. Don handed out butterhorns and poured grape juice from a can for Al.

"You need to get some moisture back into you, partner," Don said. "You're still as white as a ghost!"

"You need a bath!" countered Al, after a long drink and a bite of butterhorn.

"Sit down Pa! I'm going to try to de-sliver you, if there's such a word," Goldie laughed. "You look like a dart board after a hard night at the VFW hall!"

"I feel like it, too," Ray laughed. "My customers will think I have the measles!"

"Wait until Erik sees what you did to his door!" Al joined in, trying to shake off the memory of being trapped.

"I hope you're not going to be dumb enough to tell him," Ray said, suddenly very sober.

"Never!" Don promised.

"Never," Al echoed.

"What are you going to tell US?" Goldie demanded.

"Just that some very nasty and determined people shot at the boat, chased Al for miles in an underground tunnel without catching him and probably killed a man that was feeding several people information about our operation," Ray said. "That and no more," he finished firmly.

"We had to ditch the boat for the time being," Don volunteered.

"Good idea," Jill said. "I called Cummings place last night to see if you had gotten back in. Unfortunately, I got Mrs. Cummings on the line instead of her husband and she wasn't very happy about your odd goings and comings. I think she actually hopes your boat would sink!"

"Bad news," Don said thoughtfully. "Cummings, himself, never indicated he had a problem with us."

"Women sometimes take an entirely different view," Jill

stated.

"Amen." Ray said wryly. "Ouch! Take it easy with those tweezers, Goldie."

Jill continued her thought, "Maybe she's just mad at her husband and decided to make you the butt of our conversation."

"Can we leave the Ghost where you hid it for awhile?" Al asked hopefully. "Will it be safe?"

"I think so. It's really off the beaten path," Don replied. "Do you have any plans for us soon, Ray?"

"Not until we find out who's behind the violence against us and why," Ray answered. "It's not like we're some real big eastern gang outfit or anything."

"I think the boat that shot at us was the same one that did it before, outside Gig Harbor," Al ventured.

"I barely caught a glimpse of it," Don said. "What makes you think it was the same guys?"

"I heard their voices in the tunnel. They sounded foreign, like they might be from the same place as the Makovich brothers."

"I looked into the Makovich boys," Ray said. "They work for someone big, using their trawler to bring in really large amounts of stuff. They're not pirates. They're just transporters for someone way bigger than us. Probably someone who ships the stuff to Oregon and California labeled as salmon. I'd guess whoever went after us these two times is somebody, maybe a fellow fisherman, who has been watching the Makovich boat and knows what they're doing," he speculated.

"Okay, if the Makovich guys are such innocent characters, why do they have that big gun mounted on their foredeck? And don't give me the harpoon story again, Ray," Don warned.

"To scare away pirates like went after us! They probably can carry five times what you can and that's a lot of potential profit for any pirate," Ray replied.

"There's got to be more to it than that, though," Don said. "To murder somebody gangland style--"

"Who and what are you talking about?" Goldie asked.

Ray was shaking his head negatively, but Don said, "She's going to read about it in the papers anyway, Ray." Turning to the two girls, he continued, "We found a man who lives near the marina, shot in the head with a canary stuffed in his mouth. It looked like a mob style hit."

Jill caught her breath and paled.

Ray took notice and asked, "Does that mean something to you, Jill? Because I think he was left like that to make the authorities think it was a mob murder when it may have been something else entirely."

"They're after the gold," she blurted out, before she could think to keep her thoughts to herself.

"What gold?"" Ray demanded. "We weren't carrying any gold!"

"After I paid you your share from the stock sales, I converted the rest to gold and have been working all our trades into gold since," she explained lamely.

"How much does that amount to?" Ray inquired.

"Almost $20,000 now," Jill stated.

"That's a lot of money, maybe enough to murder for, but what has that to do with whoever is chasing us all over hell's half acre?" Ray asked, exasperated.

"It's impossible to explain. I'm probably wrong anyway," Jill said, trying to close the line of inquiry.

Al was watching the woman he adored very carefully and realized that she was trying to tell them something, but was too frightened--- or something--- to be able to confide what she believed to be true. He wondered what she was holding back and whether he might be able to break through the barrier when they were alone together. Maybe he could prolong his 'recuperation' a bit and get closer to her.

"Until we figure things out, I'd like to borrow one of your shot guns and this .45," Don said to Ray. "If they knew how to find our boat, they know where our shop is and I intend to protect our new boat as well as our bodies."

"Good idea. When we get cleaned up, the girls can take us back to the car in Fircrest and I'll run you back to the island before I go back to the shop. I'm supposed to deliver the Dodge at noon, so we better get moving. Thanks for un-slivering me or whatever you said, Goldie." Ray ran his hand over his face, "Still feels pretty sore. Guess I'll skip shaving for a few days. How do you think I'll look with a beard?"

"Worse," Goldie said flatly. "You're not going to let me in on this any further, are you?"

"I think it's best that you stay clear of it--and the boys, for the time being, Goldie," Ray said seriously.

"Oz saw what happened Thursday night, Pa. He called to break our date and I think he knows who was getting shot at. I'm part of it now," Goldie stated firmly.

"I thought I warned you to stay clear of that tin horn bootlegger," Ray erupted.

"He's not a tin horn bootlegger! He's a shoe salesman who buys and sells a few bottles of hooch when he can get his hands on it and you were the one selling it to him this time. Besides, you're a smuggler, a bootlegger and a --a philanderer!" she yelled back. "Who are you to call the kettle black?"

Ray threw up his hands in resignation and shut up.

"You really like that guy, don't you?" Don asked.

"I'll probably marry him," Goldie replied tartly. "If he ever asks me," she added, pouting now.

"Oh Lord," Ray breathed, lowering his head into his hands. "What a mess I've created."

Goldie crossed the room to her father, patted his shoulder and said, "I'm sorry for what I said, Pa. I know I've got a terrible temper. Don't know where it came from, but-"

Ray took her hand and kissed it gently, but couldn't look up at her for the shame of the truths she had uttered.

CHAPTER FORTY

The boys were greatly relieved to find nothing out of place in the boat shop when they returned. They jury rigged a primitive alarm system with hay wire running from each window and door to a ship's bell that could be heard a half mile away if it were disturbed.

Talking as they worked, they agreed that Jill had not intended to speak openly of the gold she had accumulated for them, but somehow had linked it, in her mind, to the mad chase of Thursday night.

"Either I'm still too tired to think straight or there's just way more to the situation than I could comprehend even fully rested," Al decided.

"I think its the latter and Jill may have the key to why anyone but the authorities should be so interested in our small smuggling operation," Don agreed.

"I'll try to get her to confide in me tomorrow when I feel well enough to be persuasive," Al suggested. "Right now, I'm going to get some shut eye and try not to dream of that terrible tunnel."

"That was way more nightmare than dream! I think I'll do a little final touch up on the launch. Maybe it'll take my mind off all that junk so I can catch up on sleep as well."

Don worked on his new pride and joy until he couldn't see to paint anymore. He awoke wondering how the Ghost was handling going aground twice a day in Dutcher Cove. He smelled coffee brewing and bacon frying and realized that Al was already cooking breakfast.

"Good morning, sleepy head! You must have stayed up real late. The boat looks ready to launch," Al said cheerfully. "Looks like a better day today. Last night's drizzle has dried up pretty well and the sun is poking through a bit."

"That's good news. I was dreaming of the Ghost filling up with rain water and sinking into the mud."

"You never told me where you ditched her. Any place I'm familiar with?" Al asked.

"I don't think so. It's called Dutcher Cove on the chart, a couple of miles south of Vaughn Bay on Case Inlet. It probably goes completely dry on a low tide, so it's not a place that most people would even give a second look. The spit is high enough that you can't see behind it even at high tide," Don explained.

"Is there a road down to the beach?" Al asked, wondering if somebody could stumble on it that way.

"No! It was awful getting out of there. It took us an hour to climb up a stream bed in the bottom of the canyon that is the only access to the water. And there's no beach except the spit, just mud," Don elaborated.

"Sounds like a great place to hide out. If things get worse we can put the launch in the water, fill her full of food and live on the Ghost in Dutcher Cove!" Al laughed.

"I hope it doesn't come to that," Don rejoined, digging into the bacon and eggs that Al had served.

Al was shaving when the phone rang. Don answered it with a simple set of yes and no answers and a final 'okay'.

"What's happening?" Al asked, wiping shaving cream from behind his ears.

"Jill wants us to come over to talk," Don replied.

"Both of us?" Al asked, somewhat disappointed.

"Yes. She sounded very tense, but she asked both of us to come and to hurry before she changed her mind."

"I don't think anyone could get there that fast," Al joked, trying to strike a light note.

"I think she's real serious, Al. Let's get moving."

Twenty minutes later the roadster pickup was parked in the alley behind Jill's house. The two split up, one going around to the front and one watching the back door. Neither wanted to be ambushed by someone who might be playing games with them and using Jill as a pawn.

"Come in, Don," Jill said giving him a kiss on the cheek as he entered. "Where's Al?"

"Watching the back door to make sure no one's playing tricks on us," Don replied carefully.

"I don't blame you after the past few days. Let's go back to the kitchen and get him inside," Jill said quickly.

"Is there something wrong here, Jill? I'm getting odd feelings," Don said warily.

"We're alone if that's what you mean. But, yes, there's things that aren't right and I hope that, together, we can make them right," she said seriously.

Don gave Al the okay sign through the window. Jill greeted him with a kiss on the cheek and then hugged him so hard he had to beg her not to bruise his bruises.

"I'm just so happy to have you safe and looking so much better," she gushed. "Sit down at the table and I'll pour you a fresh cup of coffee. You're going to need it, I think."

Once all were seated, Jill took each of them by the hand and looked into their eyes with all the sincerity she could muster. "What I'm about to tell you is going to make you think I'm totally nuts, but it will be the absolute truth. Will you both try to believe me?" she began. "Because you guys are all that I've got in this world that means anything to me at this point. The money we've made, the experiences we've had, the affection we've shared--all that doesn't count for anything if you won't try to understand where I've come from and the situation I find myself in today."

"I thought you came from Olympia and you got yourself in this mess because you were greedy--and you loved us --and couldn't make up your mind which of us --" Don broke off his attempt to lighten the mood as he realized how sensitive and serious Jill seemed to be. "Sorry."

"What is it, Jill? Please go on!" Al urged.

She took a deep breath and commenced. "I'm from another time. I was born in 1979. I left my own time involuntarily in the year 2001. I don't yet know how that was accomplished, but just Friday night I discovered who managed it and why. If that sounds utterly preposterous to you, it seems that way to me as well, even after being here over 13 months. This house belonged to my grandparents and later my parents. It is the only thing familiar enough to me to allow me to grasp any reality sometimes. I went to bed here September 12, 2001 and woke up here on September 13, 1928. I went out the door cold and hungry and you guys jumped into my life and you know most of the rest of the story," she finished, out of breath and flushed.

"This is not a joke, Jill? Because our collective senses of humor are pretty much wiped out just now," Don said grimly. He looked at Al, who appeared totally stunned. "Are you going to say something or am I the only one that can't swallow this story?"

Al rubbed his head, deep in thought. No one said anything for several minutes until Al raised his head. "You have some proof of all that you've told us, don't you?"

"Yes," Jill breathed out. "It's what you both have been waiting all these months to see." She rose from her chair.

"It's in your room!" Don burst out. "You've got---?

"Something that's so common in my time that we take it totally for granted, but so far advanced from 1929 that you may be hard pressed to believe what you see. Please come up with me and try to keep your minds as receptive as possible."

Al extended his right hand to Jill and allowed himself to be guided where he had begun to doubt he would ever go. Don followed, more excited and curious than he had been doubtful just a few moments previous.

Opening her door, Jill asked them to come close enough to the computer screen to observe it, but not to disturb it or the keyboard. She began to explain how messages were sent via telephone line or radio antennae to other such computers all over the world in milliseconds.

"It's like a big radio tube and a telegraph merged into one," Al said staring at the screen in fascination.

"Or a totally improved version of the invention that guy, Philo Farnsworth demonstrated last year in San Francisco!" Don burst out. "He called it---tele-vision, I think."

"Yes," Jill agreed, "It uses a television screen of sorts, but it's more for communication than television, which is used for entertainment, like movies and other dramas or news programs. Both television and computers have a lot of advertising on them as well, to pay the expense of the programming or phone lines, I presume."

"Does this contraption have anything to do with your success in the stock market, Jill," Al asked, warily.

"Yes, I admit it has a lot to do with it. In some bizarre manner this computer is still hooked into to my time, but it has allowed me to research the past, -- your present you understand. I haven't been able to contact anyone from my own time, but I can find almost anything that has been recorded from the past through a program called the internet. Let me show you, because that's probably the only way you'll ever really believe me."

She opened the Google search engine and typed in "Stock Market crash of 1929". A plethora of titles concerning the market came up on the screen in seconds and she chose one of her favorite sites. Immediately both Don and Al were hovering over the statistics of what was to happen in just a few days, commentary on why it was happening and more details than they could possibly absorb at one viewing.

Before they could say anything, she closed the window and

typed in "Inventor of television". Again many titles came up and she chose one that gave a concise account of the amazing story of a 14 year old boy who came up with the idea of television while plowing a field and who had a working model patented by age 21. How the RCA company beat him out of any royalties and he died in obscurity, hating what his own invention had become by the late 1940s.

"RCA stock is one that we made a great deal of money on, by the way," Jill said. "And it's going to make a whole lot more in years to come!"

"So, in essence, you were cheating the market?" Al asked. "You knew which to buy and which to sell because it was already---history for you?"

"Yes, and more degrading, is that I knew smuggling whiskey was going to be real profitable until Prohibition is repealed in another three years. Do you hate me now, knowing that I'm almost a common thief?" she asked.

"Do you hate us for smuggling the whiskey that probably hurts more people than you ever could affect?" Al asked thoughtfully.

"You know I don't! I love you guys with all my heart. I wish I could marry you both and live happily ever after on a desert island!" she blurted out, then turned redder than the reddest beet.

"Maybe we should become Mormons and take her up on that offer," Don laughed.

"They haven't done that since 1890 and I can prove it to you right here on the computer if you like," Jill said, totally embarrassed. "It wasn't an offer either; it was just a silly wish. Oh, wow, I did it again!"

The two young men covered their mutual embarrassment by plying Jill with dozens of question about not only the computer, but her life before being dumped into their earlier time frame. She told them much of what was easy to explain and then paused.

"There's a reason why I chose this particular time to tell you the truth about myself. For the first time since I arrived here, in the twenties, I mean, ---I received an e-mail message from 2001---or maybe it's 2002 now, I don't know. Anyway, it's a directive for me to hide our cache of gold in a safety deposit box of a bank that exists now and in the latter time, add a coded name to the security card and hide a key to the box in this very room!"

"Are you saying that someone from the future, your time I mean, knows that you have gold and they intend to ---Uh-- steal it by having you stash it away for them" Don asked, incredulously. "How could that possibly be?"

"The answer is yes!" Jill cried. "And I think it was possible because they planned the whole scenario, or at least the part about playing the market and turning the profits into gold."

"How in the world could anyone have done that?" Al asked, as dumfounded as his partner.

"How did they send me here in the first place? I don't know! But I suspect the plan was put into my mind through hypnosis by a guy whose father is one of my dad's political cronies. I also think that it has something to do with one of the men we've been selling to, that black guy with the fancy restaurant in Seattle. What's his name?" Jill asked.

"The guy with the expensive suits and white spats," Don said thoughtfully, "Jack something or other."

"Jack Johnson," Al chimed in. "Ray dropped his name one time when we were talking about future sales."

"That's it!" Jill exclaimed. "The safety deposit box code is JLJIII for Jack L. Johnson III, the owner of the club in Olympia that I met the night before I arrived here in your time! He had a huge picture of his grandfather hanging in his office and it fits your description of our buyer perfectly. I was sent here to make them rich. Our $20,000 or so in gold at $16 per ounce will be worth half to three quarters of a million in 2002, but the coins themselves will be worth far more than the street price and there may be some rare coins in the bunch that would bring a fortune each."

"It's unbelievable that any individual or group could devise and pull off anything so bizarre," Don commented.

"It is! But here I am! And," Jill cried, going to her e-mail box, "here's the message from Jack Johnson. Read it for yourselves."

Don and Al crowded close to the computer where Don read the cryptic message aloud, still shaking his head. Finally he asked, "What are you going to do, Jill?"

"I-- don't-- know," she stammered, trying to control her emotions.

"Do you want to go back?" Al asked, softly. "I know you must miss your family and friends and all the luxury that must be available over 70 years in the future."

"If you stay, do you think they could send someone to get you? They probably only want the money, right? What if we put the money in the safety deposit box like they said and the key under the trap door? You could stay then couldn't you, -- if you wanted to, that is," Don suggested.

"I don't know, I just don't know," Jill cried.

"You don't know if you want to stay?" Al asked. "Because we sure want you to, right, Don?"

"More than anything, Jill. More than the money if that's your worst concern. We started with nothing and we can replace what we lose if you send it to them, but we can't replace you," Don said boldly.

Jill looked at the two of them, sat back in the computer chair and burst out in a literal flood of tears that she could no longer hold back. Don stood over her and stroked her hair softly while Al kneeled in front of her, wiped her tears with his handkerchief, then held her hands. They stayed in that position for several moments before Jill regained her composure. Eventually she stood and embraced them both in turn, lingering longer with Don then Al really thought necessary.

"I'm staying! To heck with whoever put this scenario together! We'll let it play out and meet them on our own turf if they actually come looking," she said defiantly.

"How about the money," Al asked.

"The money stays, too! Let's go spend some of it on lunch." She took each by the arm and marched downstairs.

Don looked around very carefully before leaving the alley. "Looks all clear," he said. "Where are we headed?"

"I have a very special place in Seattle in mind," Jill answered, a sly look on her face.

"Not into the lion's den surely?" Don asked, incredulous at what she might be intending.

"You guessed it, Buster! We'll hit 'em head-on."

"If you mean Jack Johnson's place, that's not exactly our own turf," Al said in a worried tone.

"Don's packing, isn't he? I don't think that bulge in his coat is just excess cash. We're going in the middle of the day for lunch in a high tone restaurant. There's no reason to think Mr. Johnson would do anything out of the ordinary, except give me an order for more liquor when I ask him, right?" Jill said saucily, her demeanor completely upbeat.

"This ought to be interesting!" Don groaned.

CHAPTER FORTY-ONE

Ray awoke Sunday morning aching all over. When he looked in the bathroom mirror he found that even three days' growth of whiskers did not hide the wounds on his face. When he bathed, his wrist and face stung from the damage of a hundred wood slivers.

"Somebody is going to pay for messing with us," he spit out in disgust.

He left his apartment with hate in his heart, revenge in his mind, bitter coffee eating at his stomach and a .45 pistol in his inner coat pocket. Walking a dozen blocks in the rain to his garage didn't improve his disposition one iota. By the time he had fired up the old Overland touring car and headed for the ferry to Gig Harbor, he was in an absolute rage. He was first on the ferry which put him near the bow where wind whipped salt spray on the already decrepit car. From the ferry landing he drove the few blocks to the Makovich's dock and marched down to their boat with murder in his eye. He caught the two brothers with their backs turned to him, mending nets on the aft deck.

Pulling out his .45, he barked, "Drop your knives and get down in the cabin with your hands up. No tricks or I'll splatter what little brains you've got all over your already slimy deck!"

To Ray's surprise and relief, the two big men did just as he had said. He jumped onto the boat and followed them, staying just out of arm's reach. The cabin was dank with the smell of cabbage, diesel oil and unwashed bodies.

"Sit down!" Ray yelled at them, his shrill voice bouncing off the cabin walls. "Tell me the truth and you'll live to fish another day. Anything less and you'll become bait. Understand?" A slight bob of both bearded faces was the only response. "Good! Now who do you transport whiskey for? The top man, not some middle man gopher!" Ray demanded.

"He would kill us," the older brother stated simply.

"Do you think I won't?" Ray yelled, cocking the .45. "You are going to tell me who you work for and who shot up our boat Thursday night. Was it you or your men chasing my partner through the Chinese tunnel?"

No response came, except both were shaking their heads negatively. Ray took aim at the younger man's crotch.

The man yelled, "It wasn't us. It was other guys hired by boss. Same guys tried to shoot you first time you come here last year. Not us!"

"Now we're getting somewhere," Ray said, with just the glimmer of a grim smile. "So who's the boss and why does he want to hurt us guys and our little operation?"

"Man nobody messes with, from the east coast. Sells whiskey all over the country," the older brother said.

"A name is what I want, mister. Nobody will know where it came from. Just a name!" Ray was yelling again.

"Kennedy," the younger Makovich said softly.

"You work for Kennedy? Don't make me laugh," Ray sneered. "He's got half the politicians on the east coast in his pocket. What would he be doing with guys like you way out here in the Northwest? Come on! Some truth here, now!"

"We get paid by his friend Gardiner from Olympia. We don't bother nobody, nobody bother us. We bring fish from Alaska and whiskey from Canada. Good clean business. No trouble 'til you guys come along--start selling to some of his competition---," the older brother broke off, knowing what he was saying could get him killed in a much worse manner than the madman that confronted him at the moment.

"You mean Tucci, right? Gardiner had somebody knock off the Tucci boys and probably the snitch Harris too. Then made Harris look like he'd been done in by a mob outfit like Tucci. That's it, isn't it?" Ray was waving the .45 madly now, but no matter how wild Ray became, neither Makovich would say another word. He stood glaring at them some time before giving them a parting warning.

"We're going to find that trawler that shot at us and we're going to sink them before they know what hit them! Tell that to your compatriots, if you dare! Stay the hell away from any of my partners or we'll finish this for good!"

He marched back to his car in fine spirits and decided to forgo the ferry for a Sunday drive around the peninsula through Shelton and Olympia since the sun had begun to shine again. It was turning out to be a fine day after all, Ray thought.

****

"It looks like it's clearing up," Don said as the interurban train neared the Seattle station. "We could have driven after all!"

"The train is a lot more comfortable and warmer than your little car," Jill jibed," and faster too."

"Yeah, it's kind of fun pretending to real travelers,"

Al remarked, "Even though it's only thirty miles."

"Well, we still have to walk to the restaurant," complained Don, who loved their roadster pickup.

The two young men worked up a good appetite in the ten minutes it took to reach Johnson's place. They were quickly ushered to a table overlooking Elliott Bay, which was turning from gray to a deep green as the sun broke through the earlier overcast. The steak and shrimp turned out to be top quality and prepared to perfection.

When they prepared to leave, Jill, their treasurer, peeled the bills off a large roll and gave them to the young Negro cashier, who looked at the two young men oddly. "She's our mom," Don explained with a sly grin, causing the cashier to smile as well.

When Jill asked to see the owner, the young woman's smile turned to concern. "Was our food or service not satisfactory ma'am?" she asked, apprehensively.

"Both were excellent!" Jill replied, sweetly. "We're business associates of Mr. Johnson and just wanted to say hello if he has a moment."

"Yes ma'am. I'll have your waiter take you to his office in just a moment," she said, relieved.

Their waiter, who had just pocketed a very generous tip from their table, whisked them up to a small office and whispered instructions to the voluptuous black secretary. She went into the inner office, returning in a moment to tell them that Mr. Johnson would be with them as soon as he finished a phone call. While they waited she gave Don a thorough look over which made him wish that he was holding Jill's hand instead of Al. A buzzer on her desk sounded and with a final wink at Don she ushered them into Johnson's presence.

Jill's first thought was "Deja vu!" Except for the large painting hanging behind Johnson's giant polished desk, the room was exactly as she remembered his grandson's place in Olympia, right down to the hue of its mahogany wall panels.

Noticing Jill staring at the portrait, Johnson said, "George Washington Carver, a brilliant man and a very generous one as well. He is a cousin of my late father. He has invented hundreds of uses for peanuts, potatoes and even won a prize two years ago for finding many ways to use the common soybean. He helped start my business when I left the South and came to the Northwest a few years ago. Well, enough about my illustrious relative. How can I help you today?" his gold tooth gleamed as he smiled at them warmly.

"I'm sorry, I should have introduced myself," Jill warmed to her task as her nerves settled. "We're one of your beverage suppliers, the best I hope. I'm Jill the buyer and I believe you've met Don and Al here, as well as our salesman, Ray, who ---obviously isn't here."

They shook hands all around, giggling a bit at Jill's awkward introduction. Johnson's laugh actually struck a deep bassoon like note as they recalled Don's falling overboard incident at Fauntleroy. He asked them to call him Jack and offered them a drink.

"It's the finest Scotch available, you know. I have friends that go to great lengths to provide me with the best." He laughed his marvelous laugh once again, but sobered as he saw a look of concern on Jill's countenance.

"No thank you, Jack, but that's part of the reason we've dropped by today," Jill began. "You see, we would like to continue to supply the finest beverages for you and your clientele, but we believe there is a conspiracy, to not only prevent that from happening, but to steal our boat, our money including our savings and our very lives!"

"I see," Jack said very soberly. "Or maybe I don't. That is, how might I be of help to avoid this --uh, conspiracy--to be successful?"

"We're not sure yet, Jack," Al said. "We just want you to know that we intend stay in the business and we're going to take whatever measures we must to protect ourselves to do so. We don't intend to pick any fight with the authorities because we could out run them in almost any situation, but if you hear any information that will help us to avoid them, it would be appreciated."

"That doesn't mean we're not going to be aggressive toward any would-be pirates, high-jackers or thieves," Don warned. "Someone leaked information about us to other parties and he's now dead."

The trio watched Johnson carefully for his reaction.
It didn't take long in coming.

"How do you know that?" he said quietly.

"We found him!" Don said, his hand in his inner pocket on the cold, hard .45.

"It was made to look like a mob job," Al picked up the explanation. "A yellow canary stuffed in his mouth, the way they do to show the guy was a snitch."

"That would be George Harris then. And you think I had him snuffed! Sorry folks, not my style, not at all. I've known Harris for years. He did private investigations for me whenever I needed the real story on anybody I might have an association with. It's the only way to stay clear of trouble and stay in business, legal or otherwise. Harris was meticulous in his work, a real snoop and accurate to the minute in his observances. He wrote everything down and if somebody has his journals, we're all in a lot of trouble!" Jack shook his head in frustration.

"What do you mean, we're all in trouble?" Jill demanded.

"He was watching you all right. For me and whoever else would pay him. In fact, he reported on your boat schedule almost free, because he admitted that somebody else was paying him, too. I told him that was crazy, but he said it might be ironic, but not crazy. The poor dumb sonofa--excuse me Jill, no offense please," Jack sighed.

"So you didn't try to set up Tucci for Harris's murder?" Don said bluntly.

"As I said, no! I didn't even know he was dead. The police must be keeping a lid on it or running down leads from his journal if they have it," Jack said with a scowl.

"We didn't see any journal lying around. Whoever did the deed probably took it to protect themselves and maybe blackmail somebody else, "Al suggested. "Isn't that what you really meant about trouble?"

"Exactly! So what makes you think Tucci didn't do it?" Johnson asked in exasperation.

The trio was not able to explain that satisfactorily even to themselves, although they kicked ideas around for another half hour with Johnson. When they left, it was with mixed feelings. As they walked back to the train station they argued about the genuineness of Jack Johnson's statements to them and how there might be a connection with his grandson's duplicity 72 years in the future. Again, it was impossible to come to a consensus. At Union Station in Tacoma, the rain began, as if on cue, as they ran for the little Ford. It was a wet ride home from the dripping side curtains, dimming their spirits further.

CHAPTER FORTY-TWO

The weather hadn't improved over night, neither had the news. Ray called the boat shop at 8 o'clock and asked the boys to join him at his garage as soon as possible. When they arrived he told them of his confrontation with the Makovich brothers and finding that their pursuers were being backed by the biggest whiskey tycoon in the country. He also made it clear that there was a local tie-in with a political boss in Olympia with the same last name as their partner Jill.

They, in turn, filled Ray in on their meeting with Jack Johnson, but left out the part about Jill believing that his future grandson had a part in setting up the whole scenario in which they were embroiled. Even though Don and Al believed that she was from a future time, they couldn't agree that she was a pawn in Jack Johnson III's scheme and, of course, they had promised not to reveal Jill's story to anyone else.

"We're going to have to be ready for anything from now on," Ray concluded. "Kennedy or Gardiner's henchmen may still have us in their sights or they might leak enough information to the authorities to put them on our tail. Somehow, we need to find that trawler and put it out of business without anyone knowing how it was done. That would eliminate a potential threat and open up more opportunities for sales."

"At least until it was replaced," Don added. "But before that we have to find a different place for our boat to work from, which may prove time consuming. Any ideas?"

"I'll work on that. It'll be hard to find anything as cheap and convenient as Cummings place, though," Al said.

"By the way, I picked up those 15 cases at Mike Webster's place yesterday and peddled them in Olympia, so here's another $405 to divide up," Ray said, handing Al a wad of bills. "It's a new customer that a friend in the car business put me on to. Young black guy with a nice, new restaurant, name of Johnson. Odd coincidence, isn't it?"

The two younger men exchanged glances and shook their heads, almost in disbelief.

"I don't think so, Ray," Don began, "What's the guy's first name?"

"I'm not sure. He calls his place Johnnie's, so it could be for John or Johnson. Why?" Ray asked.

"Is there any chance he could be Jack Johnson's son? Does he look like him, I mean?" Don asked, with eyes narrowed.

"Not at all. He's lighter skinned. Wasn't dressed flashy like Jack does. No spats or gold tooth either," Ray laughed. "Why, do you think there's a connection? There's lots of Negro boys getting into business these days. People like their music and their food's not bad, either."

"I think we'll let Jill figure out if there's a connection. She says she knows her way around Olympia," Al pronounced. "Meantime, I'm going looking for a mooring spot for the Ghost. Don's itching to get the new boat ready for the water and we'll let you get back to repairing cars and selling adult beverages."

Before dropping Don back at the boat shop, Al stopped at Brown and Haley just long enough to give Jill the money to bank and ask her if they could meet at her house that evening. He was rewarded with a kiss, a dinner invitation for both of them and half a box of Almond Roca.

"Nice job, partner," Don said to Al, as he plunged into the open candy box, "Dinner tonight and dessert now!"

"I'm going out to Chambers Creek and see if there's room to park the Ghost in that little moorage behind the saw mill," Al explained, when he left Don at the boat shop.

"Awful shallow down there, isn't it?" Don asked

"That's what you designed her for, partner, see you this afternoon," Al replied.

The road from Day Island took Al through the growing community of University Place before winding its way out toward Steilacoom. It wasn't a long drive, but much of the way was unpaved gravel and the descent to Chambers Creek make Al wish that the Model A had brakes as good as the Dodge he had hoped they would buy. He found the moorage between the saw mill and the railroad bridge full of small fishing boats, probably owned by the nearby residents of Steilacoom. The oldest town in Washington State, he remembered from history class. The little moorage had no full time attendant or gasoline dock, but on this drizzly day, Al was fortunate to find someone replacing rotted planks on the gangway.

"What can I do fer yuh, young feller," the white haired man asked.

"If you're the owner, I'd like to rent a slip for my boat," Al replied. "It's a thirty footer, nine feet wide."

"I got a slip that size all right, but she'd have to be a real shallow draft not to go aground on low tide here. Some of the flat bottom boats moored close to the bank have to sit on the bottom some days, as you can see there." The owner pointed with a finger bent from arthritis at a couple of good sized skiffs that appeared to be growing out of the muck.

"She draws about 18 to 24 inches, depending on how full the tanks are," Al explained. "Her light mast swings down on hinges, so we should clear the bridge with out a problem. Could I see the slip you have?"

"Sure. The tide's low now, so you can judge for yourself if it will do for your boat. Just be a minute while I finish pounding a couple more nails in this here board. This fir don't last like the cedar we used to get, you know," the old man complained. "Lucky to get five years out of it!"

Al paid for a month's slip fee and drove back through increasing rain, water dripping on his coat from the left side curtain, vowing to find a proper hot water heater to install before winter set in for real. He found Don bolting together pieces of steel and the new boat sitting out in the rain.

"What are you building, Don? I thought you were getting the boat ready to launch."

"It's all ready to go. I rolled it outside on the dolly to let it absorb some rain to swell the planks. That way it'll be water tight before we launch. As a little surprise, I had Mr. Hallen prefabricate some trailer rails. All we have to do is bolt them together, hang that old axle and wheel set that Ray gave us, mount this small winch on the bow stop and it'll be ready to paint. Mr. Hallen also made up a trailer hitch that you can bolt on the pickup while I finish assembling the trailer. If we paint it today and keep the fire going in here all night it should be dry enough to set the boat on it tomorrow."

"That sounds great!" Al responded. "I got us a slip at Chambers Creek, so if everything comes together, we could make a shake down cruise to retrieve the Ghost with the new boat tomorrow. I know you want to get her off the bottom at Dutcher Cove as soon as we can."

"Good thinking. I'll check out the tide table to see if it will be high enough by tomorrow evening to rescue her," Don agreed.

Both worked hard the rest of the afternoon to complete the trailer, paint it and install a hitch to the rear of the truck. By 5 o'clock they had cleaned up and were on their way to town to surprise Jill by picking her up from work. She was pleased to not have to walk in the continuing drizzle as she squeezed into the middle of the drafty car. Al apologized for the mediocre heat supplied only from the right side hole in the floorboard and explained that installing a real heater was next on their to do list, after they retrieved the Ghost and repaired the damage inflicted on her recently.

"You found a new moorage then?" Jill asked.

"Yes, at Chambers Creek. It's pretty shallow, but out of sight of snoopers and not all that far from our shop. I think it will work fine and it was dirt cheap," Al explained.

"We hope to launch the new boat tomorrow and use it to go after the Ghost at high tide tomorrow evening. It looks like we'll be making another night trip with the days getting shorter every day and the smaller boat being so much slower," Don sighed.

"You sound as if you don't like running at night any more," Jill said, raising an eyebrow in question.

"It's not like its going to be a summer evening outing or a money making trip," Don explained. "One of us is going to be chugging along at 7 or 8 miles and hour in a basically open boat in really crappy weather!"

"Why don't you just tow the small boat back and stay dry and warm in the Ghost?" Jill asked.

"Smarter than the average bear, as she says," laughed Al as Don pounded his head in mock frustration. "By the way, Jill, where the heck did you come up with that?"

"It's from a cartoon that was popular on television when I was a kid. Maybe I can find it on the internet and show it to you on the computer after dinner."

"You can do that?" Don sounded amazed.

"A lot easier than digging through old stock market reports probably," Jill replied as they arrived in the alley behind her house. "Let's get in where it's warm!"

Al stoked up Jill's furnace with coal while Don made a hot fire in the kitchen range and Jill set the table. While she was cooking, the boys brought her up to date on Ray's latest customer and their suspicions that he might be Jack Johnson's son and a link to her present predicament. They took turns relating Ray's bold confrontation with the Makovich brothers and then Don dropped the bombshell.

"Jill, the older Makovich told Ray that they were paid by a man named Gardiner from Olympia who works for Kennedy, the biggest whiskey importer in the country. Ray thinks that Gardiner had the Tucci brothers killed!"

Al picked up the line of thought, "Ray also thinks that Harris was killed by the same guys and his death made to look like a mob style murder to implicate Tucci and remove more of the competition. And the same could go for us!"

Stunned by the possible implications, Jill turned over the simmering pork chops and said nothing for a few moments. Finally she gasped, "You think that someone in my family is involved in a--, a conspiracy to control the liquor business and they order murders to accomplish that!!?"

"I don't know," Don began, "But there seems to be too many coincidences coming to light at once. Maybe we'll never learn the whole truth. All we can do is watch our backs every minute, and be vigilant for any scrap of truth in what we hear, so that we don't fall into another trap."

"Sometimes I wish I were never born," Jill whispered, her falling tears sizzling in the fry pan.

"Please, don't ever say that, Jill," Al pleaded, taking her hands from the spatula. "I couldn't bear that!"

Don, only a bit embarrassed, lifted the fry pan from the stove and began serving up the meat and boiled cabbage and apples. After a moment he said, with emotion, "We are going to see you through this to the end, Jill. Neither of us are fair weather friends. Whatever happens, we'll be here."

"And if my family is the cause of me being sent back to your time and of having people killed? How could you defend me then?" she cried, total despair in her voice.

"It's not you, Jill!" Al exclaimed. "You're basically a good person doing what you need to do to survive. It's someone else pulling the strings."

"How can you be so sure?" Jill moaned. "I'm not even sure myself what this is all about!"

"Because we love you, girl," Don said huskily. "I love you--- there I said it! And Al is totally nuts over you. Can't that be enough for now?"

She hugged them into a tiny circle and didn't let go until Don demanded that they sit down and eat.

CHAPTER FORTY-THREE

"What do you think about Ray's idea of sinking that trawler?" Don asked as they passed between McNeil and Anderson islands, their new boat slipping easily through the slight tide chop at seven knots. Mr. Cummings had been curious when they told them they intended to keep the new, smaller boat in the slip previously occupied by the Ghost. When he asked where the large boat was, Don had just replied that it was gone for good and continued rigging the slings from the dock mounted crane under the new boat. There had been no ceremony in its initial launching, just a wave good-bye from May as they motored quietly out of the marina and headed southwest. Last night's drizzle had subsided, although the overcast hung low and the temperature was only in the high forties. The new boat handled the conditions well.

"I can't imagine how we could sink a boat as large as that trawler without ramming it," Al replied from his place at the steering tiller.

"How about a torpedo?" Don ventured.

"Do you know how to make one?" Al laughed.

"I know how to find out and once I do I'll bet that between Ray's garage, Mr. Hallen's machine shop and our own place, we could build something pretty darn good."

"I don't think the Navy leaves plans for torpedoes lying around," Al argued. "So where's your source?"

"The internet! Jill says you can find anything on the internet, even how to blow up buildings. It seems that's a popular undertaking in the distant future!" Don explained.

"You're serious, aren't you?" Al was shaking his head. "Let's worry about fixing the damage they did to our boat before we go trying to sink them, okay?"

"Yeah, sure, but I'm going to check out the internet thing anyway. Jill says she'll teach us if we want to try it."

They had passed the McNeil Island Federal Penitentiary and changed course for Devils Head when Don spotted a familiar shape coming toward them

"My gosh, speak of the devil!" Don cried out.

"That isn't the guys that were chasing us is it?"

Don picked up the big binoculars to look more closely. "I'm almost positive its the same boat. What do think they're doing in the lower sound? There's not much fish down here this time of year."

"Probably hauling booze to Olympia for their crooked friends, or looking for a good place to dump the bodies of their competitors," Al replied dryly. "I think I'll head around Anderson for Amsterdam Bay."

"No! Stay on course. I want to get a close look at them and their boat," Don ordered. "

"I've been close enough to them when they were chasing me through the Chinese tunnels!" Al argued.

"You want to be sure we're sinking the right boat when the opportunity comes, don't you? They don't know who we are or what we look like. Just pass by them close enough for me to get a real good look," Don said with determination.

Al pulled the hood of his coat up over his head and slouched down as far as he could and still see where he was headed. It looked like they would pass the other boat no more than a hundred yards to starboard.

Don stared intently at the trawler from beneath the mid ship hard top of the launch, set to memorize every detail of the other vessel as it approached. When he saw an ill disguised cannon mounted on the foredeck, he was certain that he was correct in his identification. As they passed its stern he saw three stout, heavily bearded men smoking as they worked on their fish nets. They looked briefly at the smaller boat and returned to work.

"Whew!" Al breathed when they had passed and were rocking gently in the large boat's wake. "Those were bad looking guys, Don. I'm sure glad I gave them the slip!"

"So am I, partner and for what they put you through and did to our boat, they're going take a very cold swim as soon as I can make it happen!" Don agreed, grimly.

They reached Dutcher Cove at dusk and found just enough water depth to maneuver the launch into the small lagoon without grounding. Don climbed aboard to check the Ghost out well before starting the engine. Al stayed aboard the small boat to tighten up the propeller shaft and rudder stuffing boxes which were dripping a good deal. After Don had let the big Duesenberg warm up a few minutes he engaged reverse to back off the mud bank. Nothing happened. He advanced the throttle a bit and waggled the steering wheel to one side and then the other. It didn't move. Gunning the engine only produced a great boil of sooty mud at the stern. Al gave him the universal sign to shut down: a hand across the throat in cutting motion.

"She's stuck hard!" Al yelled above the idling engine. "I'll throw the tow line to you and give a pull sideways while you put her in reverse."

The little boat squatted as its two cylinder engine began to bark hard, trying to drag the heavier boat sideways. The Duesenberg roared once, quieted, then roared louder and the Ghost shot backwards out of the mud bank. Al led the way out through the opposing spits, fighting the incoming current, followed by the Ghost, now an eerie specter in the gathering gloom. Once they reached deep water, Al boarded the Ghost, made the tow line secure to its stern bit and they set off at 8 knots without further problems.

"That heat sure feels good," Al said between chattering teeth as he turned the cabin heater to full power.

"It would be a lot better if half our windows weren't shot out," Don retorted bitterly. "I can't wait to catch those birds with their pants down!"

"Hopefully we won't catch up to them tonight, because we're the ones with our pants down just now," Al reminded him.

"They're probably back in Gig Harbor by now, but I'll keep an eye out. Is the launch towing all right?"

"Yes, as long as we stay at this speed. Anything faster and I think it might veer to one side or the other. Pretty nice runner though, don't you think?" Al remarked.

"It's a sweet little boat. I hope we can sell it soon and start another project," Don agreed.

"Like a torpedo?" Al joked.

"That too, but I want to build another high performance boat if we can interest a potential buyer. I'll bet I could find some ideas from the future from Jill's computer that would put us ahead of anyone building right now."

"Your own ideas are real advanced already, Don. I don't think you need to steal anyone else's to be out front in design," Al chided him.

They passed the penitentiary about 8 o'clock and headed due west toward the lights of the saw mill at Chambers Creek. As they neared the ominous black railroad bridge, Al suggested that he lead the way into the shallow moorage with the launch. Don agreed, following him at a dead slow idle with only the glow from the mill's waste burner to help him avoid old pilings and stray wood pieces.

When the Ghost was securely moored and they were heading out in the launch, the wind began to raise a nasty chop. The boat rode well, but still, a little spray blew in on the young builders.

"How much do you think it might cost to rig a heater in this one?" Don asked his chief estimator.

"Quite a bit. We'd have to buy a generator, a belt, some fittings and the heater itself. Probably as much as $40."

"It'd be worth it on nights like this," Don said.

"This is supposed to be a day boat, but I agree. It would sure make a nicer ride. Maybe we could offer a heater as an option. Nobody else does! Hey, what's that to the left ahead?" Al cried in alarm.

"Probably the Toliva Shoal marker buoy. Bear a bit to starboard. There's some nasty rocks out here," Don said as he turned to look forward. A minute later he motioned Al to steer even farther to the right. "It's that damn trawler!" he whispered hoarsely. "They must have stopped to make a set off Fox Island and then drifted out farther in the channel."

"You don't want to ram them tonight then?" Al chuckled as he turned away from the dull gray form ahead on their left.

Don glared back at his partner through the darkness and pulled back the throttle to quiet the engine. The launch slipped well to the east of the fish boat and soon rounded the tip of Day Island and idled up to its new berth. The young men quickly secured a tarp over the cockpit to prevent it filling with rain water and left the marina parking area as quietly as their rattling home made trailer would allow.

Two encounters with their enemy within a few hours left them with much to think about as they bedded down at the boat shop. Sleep did not come soon to either.

CHAPTER FORTY-FOUR

Jill couldn't sleep that night, either. For a whole day and night she had been trying to piece together how or why any one in her family could have formulated or be involved in such a devious scheme as her young partners had suggested. Finally, when sleep failed, she resorted to the computer, making a search of the Gardiner name. She found her grandparents listed at her present address in old Tacoma City Directories; she found her parents listed in phone books in Olympia and later at this same address. She found no criminal records for her father or grandfather. When she brought up the Kennedy name there was so much data on different Kennedys that it was impossible to determine much truth or positive connection to the Pacific Northwest in the 1920s or 1930s, only that Robert Kennedy was a good friend of the mountain climbing Whitaker brothers from Tacoma during the 1960s until his murder on the campaign trail in California.

"Maybe no news is good news," Jill muttered to herself, "But who is this Gardiner that is paying the Makovich brothers? And what possible connection is there to Jack Johnson III in the year 2001? Or is there any?"

After some thought she decided to look at what might have happened with the Tucci family. From Seattle Post Intelligencer articles of the time it appeared that the murder of Lou and Tony went unsolved. Scanning farther ahead she found pay dirt. On the night of January 20, 1931, Lawrence Tucci was arrested for shooting a man who was leaving a movie theater in Olympia. The unidentified man died less than an hour later in a local hospital. Tucci was indicted for murder, but never came to trial because he was found dead from strangulation in his cell two weeks later. No one was charged with his death, despite a through investigation, supervised by police commissioner Arnold Gardiner.

"Great-uncle Arnold!" Jill exclaimed aloud. "He was the one that got dad his job as a lobbyist in 1965, just before he retired himself. I went to his funeral when I was still in kindergarten."

She remembered her father's uncle as a man of large stature, with an Errol Flynn mustache and long silver hair. He drove a long black Cadillac with huge fins right up to the day before he suddenly died, supposedly from some bad shell fish that he had eaten at a downtown Olympia restaurant. An investigation by the health department had not found any contaminated seafood and the restaurant got a clean bill of health and flourished despite the publicity.

"Or because of it?" Jill wondered. She went to bed still wondering and awoke twice from disturbing dreams.

A little before noon as Jill sat nodding at her work station, she was startled into awareness by Don's voice.

"How about a break for lunch?" he asked. "You look like you could use at least some coffee!"

"Oh, hi! Yes, I could use a lot more than that," Jill admitted. "What brings you down here?"

"I'm picking up some glass that we ordered this morning to repair the boat. Al's still getting the sills prepared to replace the windows properly and cleaning up the inside. She's really a mess after sitting under the trees for several days. The glass won't be ready for another hour, so I thought you might like company for lunch, okay?"

"More than okay!" Jill said, taking his arm and heading for the front door. In the pickup she snuggled close to Don at once. "When are you going to put in that heater you guys were talking about?"

"I kind of like this arrangement," Don quipped, "Using body heat, I mean."

She pressed even closer and said, "This is nice, but you said something about lunch, right?"

Don drove up Pacific Avenue to the cafe they had been to the first night the threesome had gone to a movie. It was steaming with the pleasing odors of fresh coffee, clam chowder, French fried potatoes and bustling with office workers on their lunch break. They arrived just early enough to get the last available booth. Jill asked that coffee be served before the meal was brought.

"Bad night?" Don asked. She nodded. "Neither Al or I slept well either. We saw the boat that shot at us last evening, both going and coming to rescue the Ghost. Pretty unnerving, to say the least. What about you?"

Making sure that no one could overhear their conversation, she explained her long search on the internet and what she thought it might mean to them.

"It left me with very little time to sleep and bad dreams to boot," she concluded.

Don spooned his chowder, looking thoughtful for a while before he spoke. "It still seems impossible that you can look into the future, your past I guess, and dig up what's going to happen. But you do believe that what you found shows a tie-in to your great uncle, Tucci and Kennedy?"

"Yes, and possibly Jack Johnson's yet unborn grandson. How am I involved? I can only guess that it's about the gold and its future value, although, unless there are some really rare coins involved, it doesn't make sense."

"You said it would be worth from half to three-quarters of a million dollars in your time. That's an awful lot of money and motive, Jill," Don argued.

"Not really. See this cup of coffee? A nickel these days with a free refill, right? In my day it takes a dollar for one cup of plain old coffee and an espresso or latte' could cost you $6.50 at a Starbucks in Seattle or more at an airport! There's more to the plot than I can fathom just now," she concluded firmly.

After dropping Jill back at work and picking up the new window glass for the boat, Don returned to helping Al with the repairs. As they worked, Don reiterated what Jill had found in her internet search and the theories that she had conjured from it. After a good deal of bantering back and forth, neither could come up with a solution of why Jill had been thrust into their lives, but did agree that they did not want to lose her back to the future.

It was near dark and starting to rain when Don finished scrubbing the parts of the bottom that he could reach with a stiff brush on a long handle. Al secured one of their cargo cover tarps over the freshly installed windows to allow the putty to dry properly before they set off for their shop.

"Jill wants us to put a real heater in this thing," Don said absently, as they drove to Day Island.

"First thing tomorrow then. You can make up the parts list and I'll call Ray to see if he can round them up for us. I want to ask him to spread the word to some of his wealthier clients that the launch is ready for sale. He knows several people that live in the lakes' district that might want such a boat to putt around the lake with. Kill two birds with one trip, right"?

"Sounds good. You might want to check in on Jill as well. She was in a pretty low mood today. Guess it's your turn to take her to lunch," Don said with a grin.

"I didn't know we were taking turns," Al replied a bit testily.

Don held up his hands in mock surrender. "Sorry, Al. I didn't mean to tread on your feelings."

Al drove on in silence until they reached the shop, where he asked Don to start dinner while he went down to Cummings to check the launch for leaks. He returned in a half hour to find soup warming on the stove and Don at his drafting table drawing something that looked suspiciously like a launching tube for a torpedo.

"Oh, oh!" Al said, shaking his head.

Don looked up and gave him a sly smile before going back to his work.

CHAPTER FORTY-FIVE

"I think she's getting close to what we're looking for sir," Jack Johnson III was reporting by phone to his 'benefactor'. "Our mutual friend is monitoring the search engines that she's using and it looks like she is already in possession of a St. Gaudens Double Eagle, which could easily bring several million dollars."

"Undoubtedly that's an important find, but I am still counting on our friend to push her toward the 1854 San Francisco Double Eagle Proof. It's out there in the Northwest somewhere and I don't want you to let her give up buying gold coins until that one is in my collection. It could be worth $12,000,000 and I don't intend for that coin to go lost, understand?" the caller stated firmly in his demanding, hoarse northeastern accent

"I understand, sir and I'll have our numismatologist and computer expert point the young lady in the correct direction. But we'll have to alter our initial message as to when her mission will be complete," Johnson reminded his distinguished caller.

"It's only been a short time since you sent the first e-mail, so she probably hasn't taken any action yet. The main object is to get her looking for that particular coin and to continue to hold out hope to her that she has a chance of returning to her normal existence if she does what we wish. Make it clear that any deviance from the path we dictate will cause her and her family incalculable harm. I'm trusting that you will proceed to accomplish our goal without fail." He hung up without saying good-bye.

Johnson turned to the swarthy young man who sat on the other side of his beautifully polished mahogany desk. "He's as greedy a bastard as his old man was Larry, but maybe that's good for us. If we can keep our hands on the money he's pointing us to, we can free ourselves of him and his family once and for all. They've pulled the strings in the liquor business for over seventy years and that's more than long enough, our turn is about to come!"

After Johnson had explained what the man from D. C. had ordered them to do, Larry smiled and said, "I like it! If Jill can fill that safety deposit box with enough rare coins, we'll have the means to unseat our family's nemesis with money made from his own insane scheme."

"Or if she doesn't come up with that much, there will surely be enough to accomplish his demise by the means your father and grandfather did," Johnson suggested as he breathed out a cloud of aromatic cigar smoke.

"It cost granddad his freedom and his life. My father was more successful taking out our friend's younger brothers over the years. He even got one of the old bastard's grandchildren in that so-called plane accident, but they finally figured it out and pop disappeared just like my uncles did. I intend to finish this business and live to celebrate it!" Larry announced, raising his glass in a toast joined by JLJIII.

****

The e-mail directive to Jill was staring at her from the computer screen when she arrived home from work. She sank onto her bed, forgetting her clothing that had become sodden during her run from the trolley in a downpour. It was clear that the time manipulator believed that he could coerce her into continue using the partnership's assets to buy unique gold coins and store them away for the benefit of Jack L. Johnson III and the son of her father's friend. "Larry, that was his name," she remembered, "Larry O'Brian!" Jill also remembered remarking to Larry that he didn't look like he matched the Irish name. O'Brian had told her that he had taken the name of his step father after his dad had mysteriously disappeared on a fishing trip and his mother had remarried. Jill had accepted a date with the brooding, but handsome O'Brian, only after a firm push by her father. Larry treated her with genuine respect but his odd preoccupation with computers and time relativity made for one sided conversations until Jill mentioned her dependence on computers for accurate, up to date information for her career training as a stock broker. On their second date, Larry had taken her to Johnson's restaurant and insisted that she meet the owner. "The rest is history," she thought, "How they figured this scheme out is beyond me!"

After changing clothes and a hurried dinner, she called Ray to see if he had secured any new orders.

"Yes, I have almost enough to make a full load, but it looks like we've lost our major customers," Ray replied.

"What happened? Did something leak out about the trouble you've had?" Jill asked with concern.

"I'm not sure, but I don't think that's it. Both Mr. Tucci and Jack Johnson said that despite our good service and first quality goods, that they are obliged to use another supplier. My only hunch is that they're being blackmailed by the people who got Harris's journal.

I'm certain that it's some big time operator who has filled the hole that was left for us small time guys when Roy Olmstead got put away a few years ago." Ray explained.

"They're being pushed by the same bunch that shot up our boat and chased Al in the tunnels!" Jill exclaimed.

"Did you know that Don wants me to help build a torpedo launcher to sink whoever might attack the Ghost again?" Ray said with a chuckle.

"You're kidding! When did he come up with that idea?" Jill asked with concern.

"Last night. He's already working on it while Al is putting a heater in the Model A, so he can keep you happy until summer comes again. Anyway, to answer your original question, I hope to give you an order to call in to McFarland within a few days. It's going to be a lot of this and that and we'll have to make several stops, but we won't be under the gun for time, so I think it will work out okay. Al tells me the boat is ready to go whenever you and I get the details set."

They said their good-byes and Jill went back upstairs to stare at the computer message and worry what she could do to accomplish the demands of those from far in the future who seemed to be controlling her life.

CHAPTER FORTY-SIX

The Ghost left Chambers Creek on an outgoing tide a few days later, headed for Vancouver. It was not yet fully light, rain was falling, the wind was calm and the temperature relatively mild.

"How does she feel?" Don asked as Al brought the boat up to planing speed.

"Not bad. She's making 20 knots without any effort, so I don't think we're growing any barnacles on the bottom."

"Any vibration in the wheel?" Don inquired.

"No, but you might want to check the stuffing box in a while to see if it's dripping enough to stay cool and not so much to fill the bilge. How about a cup of hot cocoa to settle my stomach?"

"If you hadn't let Jill talk us into eating her spicy Mexican food last night, our stomachs wouldn't be needing settling," Don grumbled.

"I didn't see you turning any down," Al retorted, swinging the wheel hard to avoid a drifting log that he had spied at the last moment in the dim early morning light.

"Whoa! Give me some warning next time, okay?"

"You're sure grumpy this morning, Don. Are you mad because you didn't get your torpedo launcher finished or because you think Jill's going to give our gold to whoever sent her back in time?"

"The torpedo launcher is ready. All we have to do is figure a place to mount it, build the torpedo or steal one or two from the Navy. No, what I'm really unhappy about is that I don't know what's happening next! I mean, are we up against some organization that we can't even see to fight? It's driving me nuts!" Don exclaimed in frustration.

"From our conversation at dinner last night, Jill figures that the Kennedy guys are moving some of their liquor operation from the east coast to the west because of the heat back there. They're going to knock out the smaller runners like ourselves, put pressure on the retailers to buy only from them--or else--and provide protection from the authorities and the mob by keeping corrupt politicians in power. She even hinted they would succeed!" Al groaned.

"Well, I'm not convinced that we can't control our own destiny. I'm not kidding about the torpedo. I'll make it work and we'll sink those crackers if they try for us again!"

"Let's get through today first, okay? How about calming down and heating up some cocoa?" Al pleaded.

"Yeah, yeah! Soon as I use the head. Those beans are going right through me," Don said disgustedly.

Not long after, Al handed over the pilot's wheel to Don while he visited the head himself, a chore they repeated several more times before stopping for fuel in Anacortes. With little wave activity they had been able to make good speed, taking the shorter outside passage around Whidbey Island.

"If it stays this calm in Georgia Strait, we'll be in Vancouver by supper time," Al remarked as they cleared Guemes Island headed toward Lummi. "Remember coming down here that night with the Coast Guard on one side of Lummi and us racing to take cover on the other?"

"Yeah; now I almost think of them as the good guys, compared to the ---. Speak of the devil! Look what's heading across our path! Have we got the number boards mounted?"

"Yeah, we're okay. You might set a couple of fishing rods out in the cockpit to make us look a little less like a rum runner, because---I think we're about to be boarded!" Al answered, as the larger vessel stopped directly in their path.

When they were about a hundred yards from the Coast Guard vessel, Al slowed to idle speed, Don threw the bumpers over the port side in anticipation of a boarding. As they drew along side, the skipper of the Coast Guard boat joined two of his crew at the rail.

"Where are you headed?" he yelled to Don.

"Vancouver, sir," Don yelled, truthfully.

"What's the purpose of your entering Canadian waters?"

"Pleasure, sir, and we hear the fishing is better," Don said as the two boats came together easily in the calm water.

"What kind of pleasure would that be?" the skipper asked. "Women or drinking?"

Don grinned, "Well, both sound about right to me, --if they're legal, of course."

"Yes, of course," the other said wryly. "You have your registration? Can't put ashore in Vancouver without it," he warned.

Al, who had come out, waved the registration and said, "Right here, sir. You need to see it?"

"No, but I do need to see life jackets and a fire extinguisher and I'd like you to turn on your running lights."

They complied at once; the Coast Guardsman gave them an

official looking salute and motioned his helmsman to get underway.

"We're going to have to watch out for them tonight," Al said in a concerned tone. "They know what we look like now and it appears that they hang out just inside the border to catch guys like us."

"Then I suggest that we plot a course inside Canadian waters, just in case we catch sight of them again tonight," Don said. "We can run south to Saturna Island and if there's trouble, we can head west, staying north of Prevost, then south past Sidney and straight across to Dungeness like we were coming from Victoria."

"That's the long way home, with a lot of open water. I hope it doesn't come to that," Al said wistfully.

"So do I, because, even with three tanks, we'll be pushing the limit of our fuel range," Don warned.

The seas remained calm, but light rain and early darkness made careful navigation a priority. They reached the dock at False Creek with time enough to spare to catch a quick bite of dinner just a few blocks from their moorage.

"Here comes McFarland," Don remarked as the two left the diner. "We better get moving."

The beverage distributor was already handing cases down to his driver when Don and Al arrived.

"Sorry Mac, we needed to get some real food in our bellies for the long trip home," Al said, laughing..

"Not a problem, lads. I'm glad to see you here early and able to take a full hundred cases," McFarland said.

"We're glad, too! Our sales partner had to do some scrambling to put together a good order. Its going to take us two days to make all the delivery stops, as a matter of fact," Don explained.

"Our business has slowed here as well," McFarland said thoughtfully. "At first I thought it was the failing stock markets, but I now believe that we have a competitor putting pressure on some of our accounts."

"We've apparently lost our two largest buyers to a bunch of tough guys from the East, but we're not going to knuckle under easily," Don said heatedly.

"They have actually attacked us, but we survived and we have an idea who they are and who they are using to do their dirty work," Al added with fervor.

"Just as I thought!" McFarland exclaimed. "If I can be of any help on this end, please allow me to do so. I am not without resources, you may be sure!"

The two young men thanked McFarland and set to work loading the boat. By eight thirty the Ghost was moving slowly out of English Bay through a fishing fleet somewhat diminished from their last visit.

Running barely on a plane at 17 knots to conserve fuel, they approached East Point on the southern end of Saturna Island, the closest point to the United States border.

"What do you think, partner," Don asked. "Are we going to chance meeting up with that patrol boat or are we going to head west toward Vancouver Island?"

"I'm afraid we'll run low on fuel if we go west. The visibility is getting worse, which might cause us some real problems navigating in an area we're not familiar with. Let's head for Sucia and stay well away from anything with running lights on," Al replied as he switched off their lights.

"Let's hope the Coast Guard doesn't bend their own rules and use the same trick," Don muttered in reply.

Two hours later they had managed to wend their way through the islands and were heading south in Rosario Strait with rapidly thickening fog. Al was at the wheel with Don at the chart, trying to pinpoint an exact course that would get them to their first stop in Port Townsend.

"We've got to stay far enough west to avoid Lawson Reef, but not so far that we hit Smith Island or Partridge Bank farther on. As soupy as it is, I think we'll have to stop soon and listen for the bell on Lawson Reef," Don declared.

"I don't know which is worse, big seas, being chased or trying to stay afloat while running in the dark and fog!" Al griped with good reason. "I'm depending on you, Don!" he added, knowing that, despite's Don's sometimes wild nature, he had already proved to be a superior navigator.

A few minutes later Don asked Al to shut down the engine. They both went out into the damp cockpit and stood as still as they could as the Ghost rocked from its own wake.

"Over there, I think," Al said, pointing to the east.

"Okay, let's idle over that way until we get close enough to know for sure," Don directed. He stayed outside straining to be sure they were closing in on the bell buoy. "Back her down, fast! We're almost on the rocks!"

Al brought the boat to an immediate stop almost pitching Don into the cabin's rear wall.

"Back off a little more and head south," Don ordered as he dove back onto the cabin. "I'll have a course for you in a minute."

He was as good as his word. In twenty minutes they stopped again and could hear a bell buoy on each side of them, which placed them safely between Partridge Bank and Point Partridge on Whidbey Island. Fifteen minutes on a new heading brought them even with the light on Point Wilson and in another six minutes they were poking behind the breakwater at Port Townsend. They tied up to a small float not far from the gas dock where they had filled previously.

"Doesn't look like our customer thought we'd make it here in this fog," Al whispered after a few minutes of waiting.

"I'll go up to the street level and see if I can spot him," Don said quietly. "If I'm not back in 15 minutes, take off and head for Tacoma."

Al didn't reply to Don's ominous warning. He was already spooked by delivering to a spot so near where they fueled their boat in a small town they might be recognized as rum runners. All Al wanted was to get moving, fog or no fog. He almost jumped out of his skin a couple of minutes later when a figure appeared from the gloom above him pushing a rubber tired hand truck.

"They're here. Ray told them to wait on the street and that we would bring the stuff up to them. Guess he was trying to keep them from seeing our boat," Don explained. "Hand the cases up to me and I'll truck it up to them."

It took three trips, carrying five cases each time, for Don to complete the delivery and return with the money. By one o'clock the Ghost was heading south in Admiralty Inlet, still in dense fog, bound for the sawmill town of Port Gamble on Hood Canal.

"A long way off the beaten path for only 15 cases," Al grumbled, straining to see even a boat length ahead..

"Ray thinks the sawmill workers will lap up this stuff pretty quick when they find how much better it is than the local rot-gut crud that they're probably drinking now. Besides, he says the G-Men caught the resident moonshiner two weeks ago, so it's a supply and demand situation," Don explained as he plotted the turn in their course as they rounded Marrowstone Point. "Due south now, Al."

They found a lone buyer waiting with a Model A panel truck

at a dock just beyond the rafts of logs waiting to be made into lumber. There was barely room to back the Ghost into place. The nervous bootlegger was dripping wet from the fog which was now turning to a drizzle.

"I didn't think you'd make it in this weather," he said between chattering teeth, "but I stuck it out 'cuz my friends around here are about to go nuts with no booze to drink!" He opened a bottle from a case as Al handed them out to Don on the dock. "Whoeee!" the skinny bootlegger whistled, "That is sure enough fine whiskey. Yes, sir!" he continued after another swallow, "I'll have no trouble selling this stuff. When will you have more?"

"We'll have Ray call you about that," Don replied. "Now, if you don't mind loading this yourself, we've got a long way to go yet tonight, so I'd be obliged if we could collect and get moving."

Their customer took another swallow, wiped his lips on his wet coat lapel and pulled out a wad of cash. He was still carrying the first case up the ramp as the Ghost slipped from behind the rafted logs and headed north.

"Two-bits says that fellow drinks all his profit up before his customers get their hands on a bottle," Al said.

"Wouldn't bet against you," Don agreed. He was studying the chart closely. "If this fog doesn't lift so we can run faster, we're not going to make Tacoma tonight."

Their course was back north around Foulweather Bluff, then south to Winslow in Eagle Harbor where they had spent a night on an earlier trip. They were to deliver 20 cases to a fellow who purportedly sold a lot of liquor to the workers at the big plant at Creosote, just across the harbor from Winslow. Ray had inferred that he also supplied most of the local Indian tribes as well, which put him in double jeopardy from the federal authorities.

The closer they got to Seattle the better the visibility became. A rising wind was blowing out the fog, but had not yet caused much wave action. Al advanced the throttle and the big Duesenberg began to bellow as the bow dropped onto a more level plane.

"Sounds good!," Don said, grinning.

Al grinned back, relaxing a bit for the first time in 18 hours. "I think we're going to make it on time."

CHAPTER FORTY-SEVEN

They were met by two totally silent gentlemen in dark suits at a private dock in Winslow. The 20 cases were quickly loaded into the back of an enormous Pierce Arrow hearse, the money handed over by one of the solemn pair and the boys were left shaking their heads over the brief, but odd transaction. They motored quietly out to the harbor's entrance where they could now see an array of light glittering from Seattle to the east. Once clear of the many rocks in the area and with reasonable visibility, Al brought the Ghost up to 25 knots. In a few minutes they entered Colvos Passage on the west side of twenty-five mile long Vashon Island.

"Oh, oh, I think there's trouble up ahead, Al!"

They were catching up with a large, but slim boat, traveling at a rate that produced a sizable wake.

"I think you're right. Only the Coast Guard would be running that fast in the dark," Al replied. "We'll have to slow down and hope they don't continue into Tacoma. Old Walt won't be happy if we mess up his delivery!"

"Better yet, swing her about and we'll go around Vashon on the east side. We'll have to hustle because it's further to go, but we won't risk the Coast Guard seeing us."

"Okay, but we might run into them later if they do go into Tacoma," Al countered.

"We'll be lighter on cargo and fuel by then. If we have to run for it, we'll be able to make twice their speed," Don assured him.

Al banked the boat in a 180 degree turn and advanced the throttle farther. The wind had increased enough to make a light chop which allowed more air under the hull and greater speed. They circled Vashon Island on the east and reached Hylebos waterway without problems, unloaded 20 cases to Walt and his helper and pulled back into Commencement Bay in lightening skies.

"Where are we going to park and sleep for the day? I'm about dead on my feet here," Al said, yawning. "I can't keep my eyes focused."

"How about behind that little spit in Lakebay. Its deep enough at low tide and not many nosy people out there," Don suggested.

"Sounds fine. Since you know the way, you can take the wheel. I'm going to sit out the rest of the trip." Al was asleep in his bunk long before Don rounded Point Defiance.

Al jolted out of his bunk onto the cabin floor as The Ghost banked hard over on her port side. He scrambled up to see why Don had taken the abrupt measure. Just then the engine backfired and died out, leaving the boat gliding for a few seconds before it settled into the water and slowed to a halt.

"Switch to the small tank quick!" Don yelled to his confused partner.

Out of the starboard side window, Al saw the familiar, but dreaded gray shape of a trawler getting up speed and heading directly for him. He rushed back to the stern tank valves, closed the mains and opened the auxiliary. Don was already attempting to start the engine. It cranked over and over --sputtered--died--cranked some more--and finally caught. Before Don could engage the gear lever, a shot rang out. Al dove through the cabin door, hitting the floor just beyond the couch.

"They missed!" Don yelped as he jammed the gear lever forward, followed by the throttle.

Al reached under the couch and brought out Ray's double barrel shotgun, cocked it and ran back out of the cabin. Don swung the Ghost away from the trawler's bow mounted gun, gained enough speed to circle the larger boat half way and aimed his bow toward the other's stern. Al balanced the shotgun on the rear of the cabin top and aimed at the trawler's crew, who were coming aft with hand guns. As Don climbed the trawler's wake and looked ready to ram it's stern, Al fired both barrels in quick sequence and threw himself to the floor in time to avoid being thrown overboard again when Don veered off at the last second. The trawler turned and fired again, catching the Ghost just above the waterline on the port side. A shot from another direction hit the water just in front of the trawler's bow. Al rose just enough to see a Coast Guard cutter bearing directly toward the trawler at a good 15 knots.

"Don!! Turn south and give it all she's got!!" Al screamed forward to his partner.

Don had only heard the second report, but he wheeled the Ghost south and jammed the throttle to its limits. The knot meter rose beyond 40 as the Ghost flew away from what now sounded like a full blown gun battle.

When he had recovered enough breath to speak, Al said, "I think one our largest problems has just been solved by the Coast Guard, of all people!"

"If they win," Don replied, only half joking. "But we still have a couple of big problems left."

Al smiled grimly, "Yeah, the Coast Guard saw <u>us</u> too, the second time in less than a day. We can only hope the two patrol boats don't talk to each other frequently."

"Jill says they'll soon have two-way radios, short wave things that can transmit over long distance. But we have the immediate problem that we're almost out of fuel and we still have two deliveries of liquor to make."

"Those are scheduled for tomorrow night. We can hide out today and---" Al stopped, unsure of how to solve the fuel problem. "Could we get fuel at Joe's Bay? There's a dock there that the Mosquito Fleet uses."

"Yeah, they probably have fuel, but we'd have to stash the remaining 30 cases somewhere and that's not only a lot of work, but likely to get us seen by somebody curious."

"Let's move them forward onto the vee-bunk, after we get some sleep, of course, and cover them up with the tarp," Al suggested.

By dawn the Ghost was anchored behind a steep, well protected spit in Mayo Cove, known locally as Lakebay. The few summer cottages were deserted now in late October allowing as peaceful a day's sleep as one might be able to enjoy after such a night's activities. In the late afternoon they were awakened by rain drumming on the cabin roof.

"Great!" Don grumbled as he rolled out of his sleeping bag and stretched his aching limbs. He built a fire to cook some oatmeal and opened a tin of condensed milk from the cupboard. "Rise and shine, partner. Looks like we'll have to move the booze inside in the rain."

Al rubbed his sore eyes and cursed the thought of working outside on a day as miserable as this one was starting out to be. "Maybe nobody will notice our cargo since it's all tarped down," he suggested, with a yawn.

"Best not to take the chance. If you want to take over the cooking, I'll start moving the stuff forward. Just keep that fire warm so I can dry out," Don offered.

An hour before dusk, they motored slowly up to the Shell Oil dock in Joe's Bay, far down by the bow with empty fuel tanks and cargo loaded under the Ghost's foredeck. It took some time before the dock attendant could free himself from his duty as store clerk and hand them down the gas hose. Al told him it would take a while because their tanks were empty and assured him they would keep accurate track of how much they pumped. They took turns pumping up the ancient 10 gallon glass dispenser and allowing it to drain into the boat tanks. After 15 such refills, the supply tank sucked bottom and they gave up. When they told the clerk that they had used up his supply of 150 gallons he was dumfounded.

"What am I going to tell my automobile customers tomorrow? The tank truck won't be here for two days!" he blubbered.

"Same thing as you're going to tell us," Don quipped. "Sorry! ---Because we wanted another 70 gallons and you ran out! We'll have to cut our fishing trip short now, but we don't blame you because you keep so little on hand, not at all. At 29 cents a gallon, though, I would keep my tank full to take advantage of all the trade I could get, if I were you."

After they had cruised slowly off into the gathering dark, Al turned to Don and asked, "Why were you so sarcastic with that guy at he store? It wasn't his fault the place only has a 500 gallon tank."

"Because I'm tired, dirty, wet and we had to pay him almost half again what it would cost to fill up in Tacoma or Olympia or any decent marina," Don growled.

"It's not that we can't afford it Don, and treating people that way forces them to remember you and that's one thing we really can't afford," Al argued.

"I suppose," Don muttered and went back to laying out the compass headings needed to weave their way through the islands and into Hammersly Inlet. They were headed for Shelton to drop 20 cases before they completed their delivery of the last 10 at Webster's on Mud Bay.

"The tide's low tonight, so we're going to have to be extra careful to stay off Wyckoff Shoal and the spit beyond Pitt Island on the right. After that there's another shallow before we get to Devil's Head. From there I'll give you the headings and which side to keep the lights from the points on. Once we get in Hammersly Inlet it'll be like running up a river seven miles with the tide helping us," Don summed up.

The rain had stopped, but Al still strained to stay on course as they mushed along at 17 knots, barely planing. It took 12 course changes in the 15 miles or so that brought them to the inlet. Here, Al slowed to 10 knots, trying to get the feel of running in such a narrow confine in the dark.

"This is spooky as heck," he remarked to Don.

"Agreed! Next time we'll bring Ray along to see what he's getting us into. Which, is a dead end, by the way. I mean, if we had to get away in here, there's no place to run!"

"Hmm, you're right," Al said slowly. "That makes it even more spooky."

In the 45 minutes it took to run the length of the inlet, they saw only a half dozen dim lights from shore, presumably lanterns in small farmhouses. It seemed an eternity before they pulled up to a deserted fuel dock just east of a large sawmill. They waited almost an hour before their new customer drove up to the dock in a Reo stake bed truck.

"Are you going to drive through Shelton with 20 cases of whiskey and wine exposed to the world?" Al asked the barrel of a man, dressed in a hickory shirt and stagged off trousers held up by dingy red suspenders.

"Would if I had to, but I'm takin' this out to the loggin' camps and no one out there is goin' bother me if they want a drop of this here liquor!" he guffawed and spat out a long stream of brown liquid. "Let's get to gettin' boys!"

In the time it took Don and Al to unload 20 cases onto the dock, their burly customer had managed to get 14 of them to his truck, carrying one on each shoulder with ease. He paid them the agreed amount, cranked up the Reo, gave them a cheerful wave and chugged off into the darkness.

"Happy guy, eh?" Don remarked as they reboarded the boat and prepared to cast off the mooring lines.

"Strong as a bull, too!" Al agreed, starting the engine. He idled well away from town before advancing the throttle. He was rewarded with a backfire, a sputter and finally a surge of power. "Doesn't sound very healthy."

Don joined him in the cabin. "Sounds like it's missing; give her more throttle and I'll go out and listen again." He returned in a moment shaking his head. "It's dropping at least one cylinder, maybe two. If it doesn't clear out pretty soon we better stop and check her out."

Fifteen minutes later it sputtered, backfired loudly and quit, leaving them drifting with the incoming tide at a bend in the channel.

Al tried to restart with no success. Don grabbed a flashlight and opened the motor box.

"The sediment bowls are full of water and crud! Shut off the fuel tank valves and get me something to dump this stuff in besides the bilge."

Al shut off the fuel supply, got an empty can from their garbage sack and started to unscrew one of the sediment bowls from the dual carburetors. He stopped, suddenly alert .

"What's that?" Don asked.

Al scrambled out to the cockpit to find a raft of logs closing slowly on them, a tow line extended back the way it had come. Don joined him, his eyes not yet adjusted well enough to see what was happening. Just then a tugboat rounded the bend, accelerating to catch up with their tow that had somehow passed them.

"Hit the horn and turn on our running lights!" Don yelled, reaching for a pike pole to fend off the impending disaster. "We're going to get caught between the raft and the tug by the tow line!"

Al fell over the upturned motor box and crashed into the dashboard. Confused, he blindly reached up and pulled what he hoped was the light switch. He staggered to his feet, found the horn button and sounded three long blasts before limping back to rejoin Don. The tugboat pilot swung his wheel to the left and accelerated to the maximum in an effort to take up the tow line slack and pull the log raft away from the boat that lay in its path. The line came taut and snapped with a loud "twang", then whipped past the bow of the Ghost like a gargantuan snake. The tugboat careened to one side, straightened up and raced off around the bend in the direction it had come dragging the severed line.

"What the hell is going on?" Don yelled in confusion.

"I don't know but we're about to----Crap!"

The leading log of the raft collided with the bow of the Ghost, which was riding high with almost full tanks and a partial load of liquor in the stern. The impact lifted the bow clear of the water and sent both young men sprawling.

"I hit my head Don; it fouled up my equilibrium. You've got to get the water out of the sediment bowls and the carbs and get us off the log raft before we end up in Shelton," Al cried, holding his bruised forehead.

Don scrambled to find his lost flashlight and returned to clearing the water and debris from the fuel system. He had cleaned one bowl and emptied one carburetor when Al yelled to him to come out again. The tugboat was approaching again, this time at a dead idle and with its searchlight playing on them. It swung around their stern and nudged up to the log raft directly beside them.

"You all right down there?" a somewhat familiar voice asked from the foredeck of the tug.

"More or less," Al answered. "We got a batch of bad gas and fouled our fuel system. What happened to you? I mean, why did you take off the other way instead of pushing the tow away from us?"

"I was sleeping and the deck hand who was piloting must have dozed off too, because the raft got going faster than we were with the strong tide. He was trying to get back ahead of it when he found your boat in the way and turned to avoid you. When the tow line parted, I woke up to find the tug healed over. Then, because it's a damn two cycle diesel, the crankcase oil must have sloshed up into the cylinders and the engine started running away with itself using its own lubricating oil. It took a good mile before it calmed down enough to turn around!"

"That's you, isn't it, Harold? It's us, Don Grant and Al Nelson. Can't believe running into you like this!"

"Yeah, it's me, still on old number 29, but I'm afraid that its us that ran into you! Do you think it damaged your boat?"

"We're probably okay. We built her pretty tough. I'm going to finish cleaning the second fuel bowl and carb while you guys figure out how to straighten out our mutual problem," Don suggested as he went back to work.

Harold told Al that he would keep a slight push against the raft to keep all of them from moving aground with the tide while his deck hand rigged and secured a new towline. Al asked Harold to put the searchlight beam on the bow so they could check for damage.

"Thanks, it looks all right!" Al yelled up to Harold.

"Hey, Al! You've got another problem; there's a hole in your port side near the waterline and with the bow raised it looks like you're probably taking water now."

"Yeah, something poked through there earlier today. I forgot about it. Thanks, I'll turn the bilge pump on," Al replied, mortified to think what a lame story he had just told.

Harold was correct; water poured from the bilge pump outlet. Al was afraid it might drain the batteries before Don could get the engine restarted and engage the big pump. He rummaged around, but could find nothing but their dish towel to plug the splintered side plank.

"Not pretty," Harold laughed from above, "But better than sinking, I guess!"

"Turn on the main valve and I'll give her a try," Don yelled from inside. The engine turned over a dozen times, but wouldn't fire. "The water may have fouled the plugs. Come in and pull some of them, while I find some alcohol to clean them with."

The big straight eight was equipped with two distributors and two sets of spark plugs due to its aircraft inherent history, where redundant systems were essential. Al removed every other plug while Don doused them with alcohol and blew each out with a sharp breath. When he engaged the starter 10 minutes later, they were rewarded by a bellow of water and exhaust from the stern that soon settled into a heavy rhythm.

"She's a loud one for sure!" Harold yelled down. "Back her down and see if she'll pull off the raft."

With one quick jab of the throttle from Don, the Ghost was once again in clear water. Al gave Harold a thumbs up and received a wave in return as Don gunned the throttle and brought the Ghost onto plane. He left the running lights on, deciding that, until they were out of Hammersly Inlet, it was safer to be seen than the alternative.

Before they arrived at Mud Bay they had repeated the process of cleaning the sediment bowls and draining the carbs three more times. There was barely enough time to reach Webster's dock. By the time they had awakened Mike, who had given up on their arrival hours earlier, the Ghost was settling in the mud for a day's rest.

"Oh well," Don rationalized, as they bedded down, "You and the boat both need some rest and recuperation. Before the next tide your head will probably feel better and we'll have our dish towel back after I patch that little reminder of what fun smuggling can actually be!"

Al gave him a grim look, rolled over against the hull and prayed that he wouldn't dream about any such fun.

CHAPTER FORTY-EIGHT

Jill was depressed with worry; Al and Don were over a day late and had not contacted either her or Ray. The only promising thought was that none of Ray's customers had called to ask why he hadn't received delivery. The only one Ray had been able to check directly with was Walt in Tacoma, who reported that they had taken delivery early in the morning two days previous. Jill knew her work at the candy factory was suffering from her inability to stay focused.

"I've got to quit trying to trace gold coins on the computer," she told herself, realizing that she was being led by subliminal thoughts that overrode even her concern for Don and Al at times. "I'm going nuts!" she said aloud.

"That's what we're all about here, candy with nuts!" a fellow office worker said as she passed Jill's desk.
"Anything I can do to help?"

"No, sorry. I was just thinking out loud," Jill replied nervously. She went back to posting invoices, vowing to clear her mind of all but her work until quitting time.

As she waited to transfer between the Pacific Avenue and 6th Avenue trolleys that evening, Jill heard a newspaper vendor calling out, "Get your Tacoma Tribune paper! Coast Guard sinks boat off Point Defiance!" Her heart almost stopped with trepidation. She ran to buy a paper and almost missed her trolley connection as she scanned the front page article. Grabbing the first available seat, she read:

"The Coast Guard Cutter Winslow, while on routine patrol early this morning, came upon an Alaskan registered fishing trawler firing on a smaller, unidentified cabin cruiser off Point Defiance. The smaller vessel exchanged gunfire with the trawler, but suffered at least two hits before disappearing south at high speed after the Coast Guard intervened. When Capt. James Rochester ordered the fishing vessel to cease fire and heave to, it then fired on the cutter and attempted to evade them. In a running gun battle, the faster Winslow ran down the trawler and pierced its hull with sufficient cannon shots that it sank in 20 minutes. As far as can be determined, the Coast Guard saved all the members of the errant trawler's crew, none of whom have given any reason for the attack on either the unidentified boat or the Winslow. In fact, they have not even produced their own identities under questioning by the Coast Guard and Pierce County

Sheriff's investigators. Little is known about the smaller boat except that, despite being damaged by the aforementioned gunfire, it was still able to flee at a surprisingly high speed. Capt. Rochester reported that it had no discernible name or registration numbers and was painted a light gray or blue. A preliminary search of moorages in south Puget Sound has produced no vessel of such description. Further investigation will continue. See related story on page three."

Jill ran all the way home from her trolley stop on 6th Avenue and immediately called Ray at the garage.

"Have you seen the evening paper?" she asked breathlessly.

"No, I've been trying to catch up customer work. That's why I'm still here," Ray replied. "What's the matter?"

Jill read him the article verbatim before beginning to cry. "It's all my fault Ray!" she sobbed. "I got them into this awful business and it's almost got them killed three times! Where can they be?"

"Probably licking their wounds somewhere safe. They're pretty resourceful guys, you know," he said, trying to put the best face on a potentially grim situation.

"Isn't there anything we can do to help?" Jill cried.

"Maybe so. Tell you what, why don't you rustle up enough dinner for both of us while I finish this car I'm working on. I'll drive over, to test it of course, we'll eat and then head down to Webster's place. His phone is temporarily disconnected so we'll just have to drive there and see if they showed up, okay?"

"Okay," she said, trying to calm herself, "But please hurry. I'll have something ready in a few minutes."

She had forgotten that there was no microwave to warm leftovers, so when Ray arrived half an hour later he had to settle for lukewarm chipped beef and toast, which was probably no worse than he would have made himself at his apartment, Jill figured.

It was a cool, crisp night for travel. The wind had changed to the north, clearing out the clouds and rain of the previous few days. A harvest moon was just rising as they dropped into the Nisqually River Valley, coating the pasture land with a tint of gold. It would have been a particularly splendid evening for driving if Jill were not consumed with worry for the two young men for whom she cared so much. She shivered, despite the lap robe that Ray had found in the rumble seat of the almost new DeSoto deluxe coupe. It was a flashy car with a smooth, rubber mounted 6 cylinder engine that pulled strongly as they climbed the long hill out of Nisqually. Ray had steered the conversation away from their partners, explaining the modifications he had made on the DeSoto and how pleased he was with building both his garage business and the lucrative smuggling trade that he believed would soon pull him out of debt and allow him to expand. Jill showed little interest in the latter and the one-sided conversation slowed as they left the lights of Olympia behind. Soon they were bumping down the half-mile tree lined path that Webster called his driveway. The effect was as if they were driving through a very long, unimproved tunnel, the moon blanked out by the barrier of trees.

Jill let out a pent-up breath when they finally emerged into a large clearing, lit dimly by lamp light from a modest cabin. The DeSoto's head lamps illuminated the grass path leading to the bay and reflected off the windshield of the Ghost.

"They're okay, the boat is here!" she cried, pounding Ray on the shoulder. "You were right, they made it okay."

"Let's go find out the whole story," Ray urged.

Mike Webster was already at the door, surprised to find visitors at his remote home after dark. He greeted them warmly and introduced them to his family before telling them that the boys had retired to the boat after dinner.

"I'll walk down with you," Mike said, wishing to draw any conversation concerning the liquor business away from his wife and children's ears.

Don and Al welcomed Jill with long hugs and Ray with firm handshakes, while Mike excused himself to get ready to head to Olympia with the remaining liquor order. While the two young men took turns relating the myriad of events that had taken place in the past three days, Jill heated some cocoa on the presto log stove, striving for composure.

"Jill, you've been unusually quiet tonight," Al observed. "Are you feeling all right?"

"I've been worried sick, to tell the truth, and I'm more than concerned about what comes next. The authorities are looking for this boat and we really don't know what story those bas---those guys from the trawler may have told them." She broke off, on the verge of tears.

Don put his arm around her and gently whispered, "We're big boys now and whatever we got ourselves into, we'll figure a way out."

"I think you need to alter the appearance of the boat," Ray offered. "As far as we know, the Coast Guard is looking for a high powered, light or blue gray cabin cruiser with possible damage. There was no name or registration number showing, so what else have they got?"

"Jill says that the authorities are searching marinas. It won't take them too long to get our description from either Cummings place or Chambers Creek," Al warned. "Even if we change the color boat, put the registration numbers back on and paint a name on the stern, there are still people who can tie Don and me to a boat of the description they have."

"Could we buy off Cummings and the owner of the Chambers Creek place?" Ray suggested.

"Probably," Don began, before being interrupted.

"Not Mrs. Cummings!" Jill exclaimed. "She told me on the phone that time, that she would be happy to see the Ghost sink! I don't know why, but she is one belligerent--"

"It was me," Don broke in. "She thinks I was going to lead their daughter May astray."

"Why was that?" Jill asked, her eyes narrowing with suspicion. "Did you have something going there?"

"No! May just liked to hang around sometimes when we were working on the boat. Nothing happened. May's a nice girl, she's attractive and, well, probably kind of lonely."

"Did you ask her out?" Jill demanded.

"Yes, but I think her mother told her not to take up with guys like us," Don said, truthfully.

"And what kind of guys are we?" Al asked disparagingly.

"I guess we're smugglers, wanted by the authorities. Guys that have shoot-outs with other bad guys in the middle of the night. Guys who will do most anything to make a fast buck!" Don spat out. "Is that what you wanted to hear, Al?"

"Hey, fellows!" Ray broke in. "Come on, let's put a lid on it, okay? What we're doing was perfectly legal a few years ago and will probably be legal in the future. We are distributing a commodity that a large segment of the public wants and has used for thousands of years. Don't be so hard on yourselves. We need to concentrate on changing the boat's appearance and finding a new home for it, preferably north of Tacoma, but as inconspicuous as possible, of course. Any ideas?"

No one spoke for a couple of minutes. Al finally shook his head and said, dispiritedly, "Yes, sell the boat and get out of the business while we still have our skins."

Don was scanning the charts for a better answer, but just kept shaking his head. At length he shrugged his shoulders negatively and rolled the charts up.

"How about up the Hylebos waterway?" Jill suggested. "In my time there were all kinds of old boats up there to hide among. If you disguised the Ghost to look more like a derelict than what she really is, would anyone give her a second glance?"

Ray looked at Jill very curiously, while Al shifted uneasily and Don rushed to cover her faux pas.

"That might be the best solution, Jill. Hide her in plain sight so to speak! We'd probably have to take her up to Canada to get a decent price with the publicity that's bound to get out about a missing high speed rum-runner. We could give her a real nasty, flat black paint job and throw a dirty, oily old tarp over the cockpit. What do you think, Al?"

"It might work for the time being," Al agreed.

"Good!" Ray said smiling. "It would be close to work from, too. Why don't I snoop around tomorrow to find just the right spot while you fellows get to work on making the Ghost fit in with the other denizens of the Hylebos boat graveyard."

CHAPTER FORTY-NINE

In the next two days the Ghost became the Sea Bird, its new dull black paint coarsely applied with dirt in the mix and streaked with runs. The name 'Sea Bird' showed only faintly on the stern. A boat cover was fashioned from two of their cargo covering tarps that had been dragged in Mike's dirt driveway after pouring used motor oil on them. The transformation was startling.

"What do think? Will she pass for an old, forgotten boat, just another victim of misuse?" Al asked his partner.

"It's horrible to think of her that way, but, yes!"

"Well, the fuel has been strained as best we can, the hole in the side is patched, our disguise looks convincing, Ray paid for a month's slip at Hylebos Creek, so I guess we're ready to head for Tacoma, okay?" Al suggested.

"I'm more than ready. I don't think I could ever get used to the stink of this place at low tide. I'll say good-bye to the Websters while you fire her up," Don replied.

An hour and a half later they were approaching Point Defiance near the site of their confrontation with the trawler.

"Seems odd to have the running lights and numbers on," Al commented. "Do you think we're driving right over the remains of the boat that shot us up twice?"

"I hope so! Serves those pirates right! I hope the cops can keep them in jail for a long time, because I don't want to think of them creeping up on us again some night."

Al thought for a while before he spoke again. "I think our luck has about run out, don't you?"

"I don't think luck has much to do with it, Al. The boat has handled rough weather as well as we expected. We haven't run over anything that would sink us on the spot. Our connections with our customers have been remarkably good, considering the obstacles of running at night in every kind of condition and they've paid us well. Somebody, --probably the Kennedy bunch, just wants us out of business, period! "

"How about the boat nearly sinking at Cummings, or crapping out when we most needed to get away?" Al argued.

"That wasn't bad luck! We were careless from not checking for leaks after we ran over something that night and we didn't install good enough water separators to prevent bad fuel from reaching the carburetors. Actually, that was a design fault on my part," Don admitted. "I'm not ready to give up on this business yet. I hope you aren't."

"I don't know if we're still in the liquor business or not. I guess we'll leave that up to Ray. For now, I'd like to concentrate on selling the launch," Al said as they slowed at the entrance to the Hylebos Creek waterway. "I hope we can find this place in the dark."

The waterway, actually a creek dredged out to accommodate good sized vessels, stretched back almost two miles. The makeshift marina that Ray had chosen was so close to where the dredging ended that some of the slips went dry at extreme low tides, just as those at Chambers Creek had. There was no electricity to the area, making it necessary for Al to use the searchlight to spot what they hoped was their slip. Don jumped down onto the dock, which amounted to nothing more than a large cedar log held in place by two pilings, and found the mooring cleats were pieces of two by four spiked to the log.

"We're going to have to secure some real mooring bitts into this so called dock to hold a boat as heavy as this," Don warned his partner. "I hate to leave her without being held in place better."

"If Jill or Ray doesn't show up to pick us up, you'll get your wish," Al chuckled.

"I'm here," came a voice from the darkness several yards away. "I've been waiting in your car for the last hour!"

"Jill?" Al cried.

"Who else would be dumb enough to sit out here in the dark, cold and mud, waiting for a couple of sailor boys?"

"Somebody who is really hard up for a free steak dinner!" Don yelled to the wraith advancing slowly on the slippery log dock.

"You guessed it, big boy," Jill laughed, trying to keep a dim flashlight focused near her feet. When she got close to the boat she stopped short. "My gosh! What have you done to the Ghost?"

"She's officially the Sea Bird now," Al answered, "Hopefully well enough disguised to fool at least casual observers. Sure glad to see you, how about a hug?"

"Not until I see that steak dinner your buddy mentioned. Let's get out of this creepy place," she urged.

With Don at the wheel of the Model A they were soon heading for the Poodle Dog Restaurant on Highway 99 at Fife only a few miles from the moorage. Over a dinner of the Poodle Dog's finest steak, a huge pile of French fries and ice cream sundae dessert, Don and Al filled in all the details of the past week that hadn't been discussed earlier. Al admitted to his fear of continuing to smuggle whiskey while Don argued the case for not giving up. Jill listened quietly, only picking at her steak and not touching the French fries.

"I thought you were starving," Don said. "Isn't your steak up to expectations?"

"Oh--yes, its delicious. I just keep thinking---"

"Thinking what?" Al inquired, sure that she might be having the same doubts that he was concerning the wisdom of continuing to try to overcome the weather, authorities and pirates that were definitely conspiring against them.

Jill started again, "I received another e-mail."

Al realized suddenly that Jill was on an entirely different wave length than he had believed. Don dropped his jocular manner and both young men lay down their dessert spoons to concentrate on Jill.

"It was a short directive to keep collecting gold coins until I find a certain Double Eagle. To do that, we need enough income above our normal needs to invest and trade in the coins. With the mess in the stock market right now a lot of people are afraid of paper money and are investing in gold and silver, so there's a lot of trading going on. The particular coin in question might actually get back in circulation, but the chance of me finding it is minuscule. I have no idea how to proceed or whether to even try!" She looked from one of them to the other, her brow furrowed in confusion.

"Oh, this is too crazy to believe, let alone understand!" Don exclaimed. "I thought you had made a decision to stay here with us-- in our time, I mean; that we would make all the money we could while Prohibition lasts and--and---"

"Live happily ever after?" Jill asked, softly.

"Something like that," Don replied, looking at Al for conformation. Al nodded agreement, but said nothing.

After a couple minutes of awkward silence Jill said, "Let's get out of here. We can talk at my place, okay?"

It was past midnight when Don and Al left Jill's house for Day Island. Decisions had been made that would alter futures for many generations to come.

CHAPTER FIFTY: NOV. 1929--JAN. 1930

Despite the gloom and doom attitude that prevailed in most circles after the devastating collapse of the stock market in late October, 1929, those with old money still continued to spend for premium goods. So it was, that the patriarch of Weyerhaeuser Timber bought the launch from the Aldon Boat Company of Day Island to putter about on family outings at their American Lake summer home.

"It's not what you know, it's who you know," Ray had admitted when he informed the young men of the deal he had brokered. Through his ongoing automobile performance modifications for Tommy Carstens and Carstens' country club friends, Ray had spread the word of his young partner's unique boat building talent. The senior Weyerhaeuser was pleased with the quality workmanship he observed when the boys brought the launch to the company headquarters for his perusal. He paid a premium to have his daughter's name painted on the stern in gold leaf before taking delivery. Ray had asked $200 more than the boys thought they could sell the launch for and kept $100 for his effort which still left Al and Don with sufficient to start a new project.

Don had designed a single cockpit, 16 foot, streamlined, mahogany speedboat that he thought might take the eye of the country club set they hoped to continue to cater to. Al thought its several compound curved shapes too difficult to build until they had more experience. Don set the design aside and went to work drafting a less complex small speedboat while Al constructed an oak framed pickup box covering which would become an advertising billboard for their boat business.

Since liquor reorders languished over the late fall and winter of 1929-30, Ray poured his time into his garage, improving his image as a luxury car performance enhancing specialist. He switched alliances from Packard and Pierce Arrow to Cadillac and its sibling, the flashy new LaSalle. By milling their cylinder heads for higher compression, fitting higher lift camshafts, dual exhausts and carburetors, Ray increased horsepower by 30 percent. He became so involved in courting young, wealthy customers, that he had no longer had time for courting female alliances. He felt satisfied despite the lifestyle change.

In mid December Jill gave notice to Cliff Haley that she would be leaving the company at the end of the month. Haley encouraged her to stay, citing the company's need for a competent collection worker to keep the firm's accounts current in the declining market. She thanked him for his confidence in her, but said she needed to move on. When he asked her in confidence if she was in "trouble" or was going to get married she only smiled and replied that she had other interests to attend to. She did not attend the company Christmas party despite Goldie's persistent requests.

"Are you becoming a nun?" Goldie asked one evening as they shared a trolley seat on the way home from work. "I never see you out with Al or Don anymore and Mr. Haley says you've given notice that you're quitting. What goes?"

"I'm trading in foreign currencies," Jill said frankly. "And it takes all my concentration to keep from losing the whole bundle."

"Wow! That sounds like a real gamble with the economy so upset just now. What made you take that up?"

"I've been trained for it, before I came here I mean. I'm good at it, Goldie and I can't get ahead working at the candy company. This is my way out," Jill said, not realizing how that might sound to her friend.

"Way out of what?" Goldie asked, puzzled. "Don't you like working with Al and Don and my dad? I thought you really liked those guys."

"Of course I do, but, for right now, I need to do my thing and they need to do theirs, that's all."

Goldie frowned, not swallowing such a simplistic answer, but she decided to keep that thought to her self.

In early January, Don had completed a full size layout of a double cockpit, 18 foot speedboat with a stepped bottom design. He was certain that it would provide superior performance over the Dodge, Chris Craft and Century models that were currently in use. It was to be powered by a marine converted Lycoming straight eight that was being used in several current automobile, truck and commercial uses. Two weeks into the new year the two partners had the keel laid and were assembling the first two frames on the jig when they were interrupted. The visitors drove a new black Ford sedan and wore three piece suits and wide brimmed hats.

"Looks like Elliott Ness's boys," Don joked when he saw them coming across the narrow street to the shop.

"Let's hope not," Al rejoined. "It's been nice and peaceful around here for almost 3 months now."

The two strangers entered without knocking, causing Don to glance to the nearby corner where Ray's borrowed shotgun was propped, judging if he had time to reach it before something went awry. One of the strangers observed his eye movements.

"I wouldn't do that if I were you," he said flatly, pulling out his identification. "I'm Goodman, my partner is Fielding. We're with the treasury department."

Don gave Al an 'I told you so' look and asked, "How can we help you agent Goodman?"

"We've been told that you built and operate a high speed cruiser, about a 30 footer, gray in color. Is that correct?"

Before either could answer, Fielding asked, "Where is it? We would like to look at it."

"In the market, are you?" Don said, avoiding the question. "I can show you pictures of it if you like."

The color rose in Goodman's face, "We want to see the actual boat, not pictures. We know you used to moor it at Cummings place at the other end of the island. Where is it now?"

"We moved it," Al said, "To Chambers Creek."

The agents nodded. They apparently knew that, too.

"Shortly before we sold it," Don completed Al's thought. "To a generous buyer in Canada."

"Really," Fielding sneered, "Where in Canada would that be? It's a large country I hear."

"I've heard that too," Don said. "Very large."

"Look, wise guy, we can --"

Al broke in, "You look, Mr. Fielding. You're the wise guy here. You come into our place of business with a badge and stupid questions on a fishing trip. You got your answers, now get out of here and let us build boats!"

Neither of treasury agents budged for a moment. Then they turned and carried on a whispered conversation. Abruptly, Goodman asked, "How much did you say you got for that boat?"

"I didn't say, but our profit was $2500, which is filed on the income tax form we mailed in last week. $1250 each to be exact," Don replied with a slight smile. "That's really what this is all about, right? You wanted to be sure we pay our federal taxes, right? You'll find that we also reported the profit on our second boat on the same form. So, if you'll let us get back to building our third boat, we'll be

236

able to report any profit to you on next year's form as well. Good day, gentlemen, don't let the door hit you on your way out."

"And don't come back again without a search warrant!" Al warned, his face flushed with frustration.

The phone rang just then. Don answered it.

"Don, have those G-men got to your place yet?"

"Yes, May. They just left. Why do you ask?"

"Oh, Don, I'm so sorry. I tried to warn you, but Ma wouldn't let me use the phone until she figured they had time to find you. Are you in trouble?" May asked.

"I don't think so. They were looking for the Ghost. I told them that we sold her to a Canadian, paid our taxes on the profit and they left. I appreciate you trying to tell us they were on their way, though. Is your mother still mad at us this long after we left?" Don said, soothingly.

"Oh she's mad most of the time I guess. Pa's been drinking and she blames everybody but herself for stuff that goes wrong. Maybe it would be better if we don't talk about it on the phone, though," May warned.

"Well, you know where I live, darlin'. Come by to talk whenever you like and thanks again," Don said coyly.

"Oh brother," Al said, rolling his eyes. "Aren't you the sweet talker. Two-bits says she'll be here before dinner!"

"She's a nice kid, Al."

"Kid's the key word. She's only 17, isn't she?"

"No, I'm, sure she's over 18 now. Shoot, my mom was married at that age! Anyway, we could use some female companionship around here with Goldie all but engaged to Oz and Jill avoiding both of us. Put some extra grub in the pan tonight, 'cuz its your turn to cook and you just might win that two-bit bet!" Don declared.

"What are we going to do about those Federal Agents?" Al asked, becoming serious again.

"Not a thing! Let them check us out. It'll probably take them months with all the bureaucracy and then they'll see we declared a fair income, like I said. As long as they can't find the boat, what can they nail us for?"

"I don't know! That's what bothers me, uncertainty," Al said wistfully.

Don shook his head and went back to screwing frame members together. "You know what the only certainties are in this life, don't you?"

"Yeah, death and taxes, and I'd like to avoid both as long as possible," Al muttered as he reached for his own screwdriver.

Al didn't win his two-bits that night, but May did show up the next morning and hung around for lunch, which Don talked her into preparing. After lunch she washed the dishes and tidied up the kitchen before starting to sweep the shop floor which was littered with wood debris.

"Hey!' Don yelled over the noise of the power saw, "You don't have to do that."

May looked a bit disappointed as she set the broom aside. "I thought you might like the help," she murmured.

"We'd love the help, May! But we don't want to get used to something that won't last," Don replied. "Oh, gee, that didn't come out right, did it?"

Tears welled in May's eyes and she turned away. Don crossed the room and patted her gently on the back. She turned and lifted her face toward him. Instinctively, Don dropped his lips to hers for a second before hugging her in a long embrace. Al turned off the power saw and went to the kitchen for a drink of water that lasted long enough for May to pull away from Don, return his kiss firmly and let herself out the door. When Al returned, Don was still at the window watching her walk up the street.

Al broke the spell. "Oh boy! Here we go again."

"What do mean?" Don said, still staring after May.

"You have fallen, hook, line and sinker. You just haven't been reeled in yet," Al laughed, a bit grimly.

"I think she needs a friend right now," Don said defensively. "She's a nice girl with nobody to confide in."

"Well, I take back what I said," Al stated.

"What's that?" Don asked, not really thinking.

"About her being a kid. She's a full blown woman, body and soul. And she knows what she wants!"

"Are you jealous?" Don asked, incredulous.

"You bet! Only not over May. I just wish Jill would look at me that way. I'd be married before the next weekend!" Al declared.

CHAPTER FIFTY-ONE: FEBRUARY, 1930

Al hung up the phone and turned to his partner who was adding fuel to the steam box in preparation for an afternoon of fitting planks to the speedboat's sides.

"Jill says she's found the coin she's been searching for. A collector in San Francisco wants $1500 for it."

"For a $20 gold piece? That's crazy!" Don exclaimed.

"She's going to get it; says she'll take it out of her share of the investment account. She claims it will be worth millions in ---"

"Her time? A heck of a lot of good that will do any of us! We'll all be six feet under before 2001 or whatever her time is by now," Don griped. "The whole idea of leaving gold coins to someone in a future time that wants to use them for some devious purpose is unbelievable. Can't you get her back on track?"

"Her track and ours seems to have split in different directions. We want to use the money to build boats; she wants to trade in currencies and collect gold coins. I don't think she's made up her mind to give anything to anybody yet, but I can't really be sure," Al said.

"Why do you say that?" Don asked.

"Remember, four months ago she was committed to sticking it out with us, continuing to try to increase our investment fund and give us moral support in battling whoever wanted to stop our running liquor. Just now she turned me down for a Valentine's Day date! The short answer to your question is no; I don't seem to have much influence with Jill anymore," Al concluded with a sigh.

He let the conversation drop as Don pulled a steam softened plank from the steam box and moved it into place. All four of their hands were needed to quickly clamp the plank to the rib before it cooled and became too stiff to bend into place. They inserted screws into the pre-drilled holes and fastened it firmly to the ribs. This was the first of the side planks, the bottom having been finished just the day before. With the weather too wet for outdoor activity and Ray not finding enough orders to warrant a boat trip north, Al and Don were making rapid progress on their third creation. Their only distraction was the occasional appearance of May Cummings, usually occurring in the early evening after her work at the family marina. Don had not yet asked her out on a formal date which puzzled Al, but he enjoyed May's visits, too, as she added variety to their games of rummy or poker and she often whipped up a batch of cookies while she brought them up to date on the comings and goings on Day Island. From her office window she could observe every car, bus or pedestrian that crossed the rickety wooden bridge to the mainland, as well as every boat that used the marina facilities. She made up stories concerning what the passersby might be involved in and related her ideas to the young men as she cooked or played cards with them. Don sometimes drove her back to the marina when it was raining, but always returned in less than ten minutes, which certainly surprised Al, because Don had never before been so slow in cozying up to a girl that showed any interest in him.

Don broke the silence as they waited for the next plank to soften sufficiently to work. "Do you think Jill would let us use her computer thing to see what boat designs might be popular in the next few years? I mean, maybe we could get a jump ahead of other builders and cash in by building something really outstanding."

"I've asked Jill about that already. Her family has had several boats, so she's quite familiar with what will be popular. But she says boat designs stay pretty much the same, except for more streamlined cabins and better power plants, mostly lightweight automobile engine conversions. That is until the 1950s, when glass fibers saturated with a polyester resin, whatever that is, allows building boats in molds with more intricately curved forms to revolutionize the industry. A few years later, boats will be mass produced like cars, with lots of synthetic materials and very little wood. She says that racing hydroplanes will exceed 200 miles per hour using turbine aircraft engines and shallow draft boats for rivers will have pumps like fire engines used to propel them."

"So until fiberglass is available, we keep building the same old thing?"

"I've never thought of your designs as the same old thing, Don. The Ghost is certainly proof of that. The launch may have been a tribute to nostalgia, but it brought a good price and this speedboat should be faster and ride better than the current competition," Al assured his partner.

"I'd still like to get Jill to show me what all that stuff you were talking about really looks like. As long as she has access to future information, she could share it with us."

"I'll try to talk her into it, but I haven't gotten more than five minute phone conversations lately," Al said.

"Maybe we should just pay her a surprise visit and talk the whole thing out with her. Try to get her more involved with day to day stuff and out of that house once in a while," Don suggested. "How about tonight, after dinner?"

Al agreed as he put on gloves to pull the second plank from the steam box. They worked steadily until six that evening and completed planking half of one side. They cleaned up, changed out of their overalls and drove to a diner in the 6th and Proctor shopping area, ordering the days' special of pork chops, mashed potatoes and blackberry pie. As they headed for Jill's place the drizzle turned to steady rain, whipped by a nasty wind. The irritating drone of the electric wipers added to the frustration of leaking side curtains, dim headlights and slippery streets. When they arrived, the only light from the house was a bluish hint from the dormer window. It was obvious what Jill was doing. They knocked three times before Jill came down the stairs and turned on the porch light.

"What are you doing here?" was her greeting.

"We're glad to see you, too," Don snapped back. "Can we come in out of the rain?"

"Sorry, you startled me. I was working on---'

"Right, we could see it glowing in the window," Don finished. Noticing that Jill looked distraught, he added, "We didn't mean to scare you, just wanted to talk, okay."

"Come in, but you'll have to excuse the mess. I've been really busy," she faltered and stood looking up at Don.

"Hey, I'm sorry I barked at you. Can I give you a hug and start all over?" Don said, tears coming to his eyes as he realized how vulnerable Jill seemed at the moment.

Al watched his best friend holding the love of his life and thought, "It's okay, it's true affection and they both need it right now. I'm lucky to have both of them in my life."

At length, Jill released Don, took both men by a hand and said, "I have something to share with you, a very important breakthrough. Come up and take a look at what I've found."

They followed her upstairs, both believing that she was about to display the rare gold coins for which she had searched so long. They were in no way prepared for what was to be revealed.

CHAPTER FIFTY-TWO: FEBRUARY, 2003

Larry O'Brian was frantic. He needed to confer with Jack and the restaurateur's secretary said he was tied up in an interview. She knew very well that Jack's interview was with a red headed waitress that was earning a little 'overtime' on her boss's couch in the back room of his office.

"You get him on the phone right now or you'll be out of a job in an hour!" Larry shouted.

The secretary was unaccustomed to anyone demanding such a thing from her or John L. Johnson III. She told O'Brian so and hung up on him. Ten minutes later the swarthy young man with the unlikely Irish name burst through the door, crossed the room, lifted the woman clear of her chair by her neck and threw her to the floor.

"You stupid bitch!" O'Brian raged. "Get out of here and don't come back or you'll be fish bait!"

Before she could catch a breath, he kicked the inner office door open and began swearing at the occupants. The redhead ran out barefooted, clutching her dress to her chest in a failed effort to cover her bare body. The secretary caught hold of her desk, raised up and staggered to the closet as a stream of oaths erupted from a second voice before a door slammed behind her and shut off the torrent. She put on her coat, grabbed her purse and closed the outer door, knowing she would never return.

The yelling had ceased, but the very incompatible pair still stood, glaring at one another. Johnson broke the silence.

"You got no right to---"

The other broke in, "She's figured it out, Jack!"

"Who figured what out, you crazy son of a--"

"Jill! She's back!"

"Back?" Johnson asked, bewildered.

"Back in our time. She figured out how we did it and she got herself back long enough to charge a digital camera to her credit card and disappear!" Larry blurted out. "Look, I'm sorry about blowing up, but this is a damn disaster!"

"You sure someone else couldn't have used her card? That happens all the time," Johnson argued.

"Of course, I'm sure! I've got everything monitored ten ways from Sunday. Every move she makes on that computer shows up on mine. The big deal is that she bought the 1854 Gold Rush coin and I doubt if she's left it or anything else in a safe deposit box for us if she knows how to return to her own time. The only thing I can't understand is where she went and why she bought the camera," Larry said, still breathing hard.

"Okay, sit down and let's go over all this," Jack began. "What else has she been doing with the computer that might give us a tie in?"

"Besides trading currencies, on which she's made a hell of a lot of money, by the way, she found three St. Gaudens Double Eagles and the 1854 S Double Eagle and accumulated around $10,000 in Double Eagles at the 1930 price. After that she started scanning portions of articles on boat design and pictures of boats from the thirties through the sixties."

"What kind of boats?" Johnson asked.

"All kinds, eastern built cruisers from the thirties, PT boats and landing craft from World War Two, Fairliners from right here in Tacoma after the war. Hot boats and jet boats in the later years, rigs built on the west coast. Probably stuff she thought might interest her boyfriends. But then she switched to scanning photos of her friends and that's when she must have figured out how she got where she was," Larry said.

"How did she do it?" Johnson asked.

"Same way I did. She scanned her own photo, then she somehow, I haven't figured where, found one of her house as it looks today, scanned it, put it in a file and moved her own picture into the same file. BANG! She's back!"

"And you don't know where? You've gone to the house, I presume?" Johnson was certain of the answer.

"In person. Her mother never met me and Kennedy made sure her father was taken care of the day we sent Jill back in time, so there was no reason to connect me with Jill. I showed her my badge and inquired if she had any further leads on Jill's disappearance that might help us locate her."

"She undoubtedly said no, but could you read her face for anything she might be hiding?" Jack pried.

"No, I think she's gone into the bottle. She looked really bad, nothing like when they lived in Olympia and worked the lobby circuit. Just an old woman waiting to die who lost hope long ago that her daughter would be found."

"Crap! You better get back to monitoring the computer. It's the only connection we have for now. We don't dare put out a new missing person alert, it's been too long. What you can do is start a search for trading on those coins. She's bound to try to sell them and we could easily grab her in the act when she does," Johnson directed.

"I've got traps set on the net now, the best the Japanese have built. If the coins come up for sale, I'll know in minutes," O'Brian agreed.

He left Johnson to get help for his broken door latch, a new secretary and a new whore. He was sure Jack would have no trouble filling the latter two openings.

****

Jill opened a computer file to show Al and Don how scanning was accomplished, not realizing that Larry O'Brian would soon have a record that she had returned to 1930.

****

Two days later, after calling ahead for an appointment, Larry O'Brian entered JLJIII's office in a much more subdued manner. Jack greeted him with a firm, if not overly friendly, handshake.

"You have news of our lost lady?" Johnson asked.

"Yes, good and bad," O'Brian said. "She's not trading the coins yet, but she's scanning miscellaneous contemporary items. Nothing to do with trading currency or searching for coins."

"Then her mother must have been lying! She's got to be in that house to use the computer; it won't work anywhere else will it?" Johnson thought he was sure of the answers.

"No, that computer won't work anyplace but where we rigged it and no, she's not in the house. I let myself in last night and she's not there in our time. She went back!"

"How!" Johnson said in disbelief.

"I'm not sure how and I can't imagine why. But she's in 1930 and we can't touch her until she decides to come back and God only knows when that might be!"

CHAPTER FIFTY-THREE: MARCH, 1930

Jill had sent Al and Don off into the miserable night with their minds in total disarray, but with assurances that she was going to find a way to make the bizarre situation work out safely for all three of them. She had told them that she thought she belonged in her own century, but she was sure that the men who had sent her back in time would not hesitate to kill her after they extracted the gold coins, whether she stayed in the 1930s or not. "Please give me time to find the best solution. Okay? This may take months. Be patient, build your boat and check on me when you're in town, but don't expect more than that," she had pleaded. Then, with hugs and kisses she had sent them back to stew it over, argue and wish they were able to change her mind about continuing to work the computer day and night.

"She looked awful, don't you think?" Don said.

"Worst I've ever seen her, but she's still beautiful to me," Al agreed, switching to high beams, trying to see the center line through the rain.

"She is a beautiful woman, Al, and she's darn smart, too, but she's too bull headed for me," Don said.

"Yeah, I wish she'd throw that blamed computer in the bay, fall in love with me and live happily ever after on a boat builder's earnings, but that's not likely, is it?"

"Oh, cut the sob story! She likes you just fine and there's nothing wrong with wanting security that you can't give her just now," Don replied. "Let's give her the time she needs and buckle down to work, okay?"

"Nothing much is okay, but work might help."

The following three weeks saw the planking completed, the new hull turned right side up and the foredeck installed but not stained and varnished. Don had asked Ray to order the engine, transmission, shaft and propeller. The distributor said his firm needed a large cash deposit because of tightening credit from the manufacturers. Ray called a meeting at his garage for the first time in several months. The boys picked up Jill early and treated her to sandwiches and ice cream at the Olympic, one of their earlier favorite haunts.

Ray got right to business when they arrived. "Guys, I've gathered orders for 120 cases of assorted liquor. The weather looks like it may give us a break later this week. You need money for mechanical parts for the new boat and that large a load would give you enough to buy it all without dipping into your reserves. It would mean going clear to Vancouver to get the variety we need and making five delivery stops, pretty much the ones that we've used before. Are you and the boat up to it?" He searched their faces, hoping for a positive answer.

"Even split, you front the payment to the supplier?" Don asked, thinking Ray would come up short to do so.

"I can handle the front money, but Jill, I need you to make all the arrangements for the timing of both the pickup and the deliveries. You'll have to work with Don and Al to figure a schedule. I've promised a mill up in Port Angeles some work that will take me out of the shop for two weeks and my helpers here at the garage are not to be involved in any of our private enterprises." Noticing Jill's pale appearance and obvious loss of weight, Ray asked, "You look a bit peaked. Can you handle all that in the next three days?"

"Sure, I need something different to concentrate on. If Don and Al can handle it, I can." She looked at them for affirmation. They nodded positively.

"We'll have to get right on it, though," Al stated, "The bottom of the boat will need scrubbing to remove the marine growth after sitting so long and we're bound to have condensation in the fuel with the cold weather. What do you think Don"?

"Why don't you work with Jill on the navigational schedule while I work on the boat?" Don suggested. "We've never carried that much before, so she's going to have to be in top running order. We'll have to allow time for a solid test run too."

"We'll also need to allow more time for loading and unloading, since we'll be stacking 20 cases inside to keep the balance right," Al said.

"With the nights getting shorter, you're going to have to use all the speed you can. And, of course, find a better place to buy fuel than last time," Ray added wryly. He gave Jill the details of the orders, phone numbers of customers, locations of deliveries and promised cash for the buy would be left with her the next day before he left for Port Angeles.

The three young people crowded into the Model A for the short trip back to Jill's house for a planning session.

"Thank goodness that you finally put a decent heater in this thing," Jill remarked. "I'm freezing!"

"Maybe we should move to a warmer climate," Al said.

"Maybe we should," she answered, snuggling closer.

Don grinned in the dark pleased to see his two best friends in concert with one another again.

A weak sun began to lift the fog as the Sea Bird passed under the Hylebos Bridge at 11th Street already on plane headed for Colvos Passage. She was making 25 knots with Al at the wheel and Don trying to catch some badly needed sleep in his bunk. The water of the sound almost matched the fog in color, flat and gray. Forty-five minutes later as they passed Southworth and entered less protected water a slight chop began drumming the bottom. Don slept on, exhausted by the effort it had taken to make his creation seaworthy after over four months in the dank slip on Hylebos Creek. He had cleaned the fuel tanks thoroughly, installed bigger fuel-water separators, had the boat hauled out on a marine railway where he scrubbed and repainted the bottom and checked every electrical component aboard. He changed the blocks of zinc attached to the rudder and prop shaft that had been eaten away by electrolysis from the action between metal boat parts and the log floats. Al had joined him, after the second day of plotting courses and fixing times with Jill, to clean all the surfaces inside and out with a Clorox solution to kill the mold that had turned from green to black. The Sea Bird was not as pretty as it had been as the Ghost, but it was again functioning well. With the weather looking reasonably calm, they planned to take Admiralty Inlet to Point Wilson, cross the Strait of Juan de Fuca to Cattle Point on San Juan Island and fuel up in Friday Harbor where they knew the needs of the fishing fleet kept fresh gasoline in plentiful supply. Don slept all the way to Point Wilson where the action of the ocean swells replaced the chop and stirred him back to life.

"How we doing, Al?" he asked.

"Good on time, fair on fuel, but I'm getting rum dumb. Can you take over now?"

"Sure, soon as I hit the head and get a sandwich. Are you hungry?" Don asked, moving towards the toilet.

"No, I'll wait until we're getting fuel. Hurry up though, because I've gone all day without a potty stop."

After filling the tanks and two spare tins in Friday Harbor they motored around to the north side of San Juan Island and took a good look at Roche Harbor where they were to drop 12 cases of whiskey and 3 cases of wine for the thirsty fishermen and lime miners of the island. The tide was low when they arrived, exposing several rock spires in Mosquito Pass which they might have otherwise used as a possible escape route should the Coast Guard show up.

"We'll have to be on our toes here tonight," Don warned. "All these islands are tricky, but it would be really easy to hit something and sink or get trapped in this one."

"Yeah, there are rocks everywhere and only a few of them marked. When we come back tonight, I think we better head east into Canadian waters again before turning south toward Point Wilson," Al suggested.

Don agreed and they set off on a zigzag course through the islands that eventually brought them out in Rosario Strait and rougher going. Don slowed to conserve fuel and allow greater comfort for Al who was trying to rest his eyes from the long day at the wheel. As darkness began to overtake them Al dozed for the last hour. When Don reversed to dock at False Creek on English Bay, Al rolled out of the bunk and jumped to the dock to secure the mooring lines.

McFarland's truck was waiting near the dock which surprised them because they were a half hour earlier than anticipated. He greeted them warmly and motioned his two helpers to begin hand trucking the boxes down to the dock.

"It's been quite a while since we've seen you, eh?" Mac stopped short as he got a good look at the boat. "What's happened to the fine little craft that you first came in?"

"She's been through hell and low water," Don said trying to make light of the ghastly appearance of their boat.

"We've had a few problems Mac, like getting shot up twice by pirates and chased by the Coast Guard more than once. She's been tucked away in a dreadful marina all winter, but she's up to the task," Al said.

"It's mostly a disguise," Don laughed.

"A good one at that, mates. Well, we better be loading now, my boys want to spend time at home tonight, that's why we're here early."

"We're going to put at least 20 cases inside, Mac, to even up the weight. We're heavy on fuel tonight as well as the extra liquor," Don explained.

As before, they motored slowly through the ever present night fishermen, lights on, to avoid appearing unusual and didn't come up on plane until well around Grey Point. Al was at the wheel powering over the swells as fast as he dared while Don called out the several course headings necessary to keep them in Canadian waters almost to Roche Harbor.

"She feels water logged coming off these swells," Al yelled to Don, who had lifted the motor box. "Are the bilges dry?"

"That's what I'm checking. I can feel it too," Don responded. He couldn't reach any floorboards because they were covered with cases of liquor, so he poked a flashlight past both ends of the engine. "It looks good! Guess it must be the extra weight." He hoped that was why the boat felt so sluggish, but he wasn't totally convinced.

They crept into Roche Harbor at 8:45, glad to eliminate a bit of their load with no Coast Guard in sight and find their new customer on time. He turned out to be an oriental strawberry farmer who needed more income to feed his large family. A very polite fellow with strength belying his small stature, he whisked the 15 cases into a battered Ford Model T farm truck and chugged over a rise long before the rum runner cleared the harbor.

Al pulled into the lee of Henry Island and stopped the engine so that Don could top up the tanks from the spare tins of fuel they had stored under the aft deck.

As they accelerated to planing speed, Al said, "I'm glad to have that extra fuel in the tanks where it belongs, because it looks like we're going to have some real swells to contend with crossing the strait tonight."

"Yeah," Don agreed, feeling the increased rolling of the boat, "It must be kicking up out in the ocean to the west and heading in toward us."

A half hour later the Sea Bird was running through the troughs with a wall of water on each side at times. Al kept as much speed on as he could without broaching, but the ride was uncomfortable and extremely dangerous. Don was having great difficulty judging their position because of the variation of speed as Al had to throttle up and down to keep any semblance of stability. Don caught a fleeting glimpse of a white flashing light to their right that he believed must mark Hein Bank and realized they were badly off course.

"Come right 5 degrees," he yelled to Al.

"Are you sure?" his partner asked, sweating despite the less than warm temperature.

"Not completely, but I think we're too far east. Start looking for two flashing lights ahead, one every 15 seconds and one every 5 seconds. We need to keep them well to our port side or we'll be on the rocks!"

As they topped a wave a few minutes later, Al swung more to the right. "You were right! We've been getting pushed way to the east of where I thought we were. Good call!"

Though they were still battling large swells, Al was soon able to spot the Point Wilson light and adjust course.

"I'll sure feel better when we get beyond Marrowstone and get a little protection," Al said, "This is wearing me out."

"Want me to take the wheel?" Don asked.

"No, your navigation is better than mine most days and that's the real key to staying afloat running at night."

Don appreciated the vote of confidence and smiled to himself in the darkened cabin. "These will be nights to remember in our old age, Al. Beating all odds and living to tell about it!"

"I hope so," Al replied, not really sure that they had beaten the odds yet.

The Sea Bird took a beating all the way to the entrance of Hood Canal where the swells abated enough for Al to increase speed for the last few miles to Port Gamble. Their skinny, nervous customer and his Modal A panel truck were waiting. By the time they had landed, he had brought a hand truck down to the side of the boat.

"I was getting worried that you wasn't goin' to make it," he said. "But I'm sure glad you did!"

"It was rough coming down tonight, sorry we're late," Don said. "At least you're not all wet tonight!"

"True, my friend and I got me a hand truck, too. Carryin' that stuff to my truck last trip nearly broke my shoulder blade."

Don felt sorry for the guy and went along to help him load the panel truck while Al unloaded cases to the dock.

"You better have a drink, big fella," the customer offered from a 'sample' he had just opened. "You done most of the, work after all!"

Don politely refused, collected the money and ran for the dock where Al had already fired up the big Duesenberg and cast off the lines. They accelerated north into the swells, the boat pounding hard until they rounded Foulweather Bluff and put the wind at the stern, heading south once more.

"I hope we don't break any bottles," Don remarked as they bucked into and over the backs of the waves.

"Me too," Al answered. "Twenty five cases was quite a load for that little Ford, wasn't it?"

"Yeah, filled it up completely. But it's a new rig with fatter tires than ours. 4.75x19s, I think, instead of the 4.50x21s that ours has. Probably rides better. He was drinking again, right off the bat. Sure hope he makes it okay," Don said thoughtfully.

Al was really glad to stop for unloading at Winslow, where they were met again by two silent men with the huge hearse. He brewed a pot of coffee on the stove and warmed some two day old pastry while Don unloaded and collected. When he came back, Don took the wheel as they idled out of the long harbor that faced the shimmering lights of Seattle.

Al handed him a butterhorn and a cup of coffee. "Did they say anything this time?"

"Not a word; what weird guys! I think they really are undertakers. We put 30 cases in that hearse without a peep from either of them, not even a grunt. But their money is good. They paid in gold!" Don exclaimed.

"Gold? That'll get Jill's attention," Al remarked as he finished his coffee and took over piloting again. Lighter now, the boat moved easier over the waves allowing them to make the run to Fauntleroy in 20 minutes.

"I'm going to try to make a better landing here, but the wind is going one way and the tide the other, so don't leap for the dock until I've got her really close," Al urged.

"I remember only too well and I don't want to make a fool of myself in front of Ray's new customer," Don said.

A tall, slim man with a Douglas Fairbanks's mustache caught the line from Don and quickly curbed the boat from being swung away by the tide. He greeted Don by name.

"Oz, is that you? What the heck are you doing up here?"

"Buying good liquor from my future father-in-law's partners, I hope!" he said in a low laugh.

"I thought your customers were down at Salmon Beach," Don said, looking up at the man he thought Ray would be the last to sell to.

"I'm staying well away from that place after what happened to you guys. I may have to travel a little farther to find customers now, but I'll never have to run up that quarter mile path in the dark wondering who's shooting who again!"

Al had come out to unload and was just as surprised to find Oz Holmes as Don was. Their greetings were cut short when running lights of a boat appeared coming around Alki Point from the north.

"We better get this stuff up to your rig and get going," Don said. "That boat is moving too fast to be a fishing vessel and that's the only guys that are out at this time of the night."

"Except the Coast Guard and fellows like you," Oz replied, grabbing a case and running to his five year old Hudson Super Six coach. He fumbled to release the seat pivot to stuff the cases into the rear where he had removed the seat cushion. By the time the three men had crammed 8 cases into the car the oncoming craft was less than a half mile away and appeared headed directly for Fauntleroy.

"Here's the money, get going! I'll be okay," Oz panted as he wrestled the last four onto the running board.

Don had released the mooring lines and allowed the boat to pivot out into the current before Al could get the engine to catch. It sputtered into life and ran unevenly when Al engaged the transmission. He eased the throttle forward ever so gently in an effort to bring it up to speed without backfiring or stalling. The oncoming craft turned its searchlight toward the tail light of Oz's Hudson as it labored up the hill away from the Fauntleroy dock. When the big Duesenberg bellowed into full chorus, shooting the Sea Bird onto plane, the searchlight caught the wake in its beam, but could not reach the hull. Al swung directly west at maximum throttle. For two minutes the following boat gained ground, then more and more rapidly, was left behind as the Sea Bird came to full speed.

"Deja vu!" Al yelled above scream of the engine and the machine gun like pounding of the water against the hull.

"Yeah, all over again," Don agreed. "We've got to beat them by long enough to drop Walt's order and hide back up the waterway. It's going to be light soon and we'd be sitting ducks if we tried to run south tonight."

"We'll have to cover her up good and get hold of Jill to tell the guy in Shelton to hold tight. He's going to be one pissed off logger!" Al exclaimed.

"How much gas have we got left?" Don asked.

"More than enough to get back to the moorage, but running this fast is going to leave us way short to get to Shelton and Mud Bay.

We'll have to take a chance of gassing someplace in the daylight tomorrow," Al replied, shaking his head negatively.

They continued at as near maximum speed as was possible in the nasty tide chop that prevailed in Colvos Passage, not throttling back until they had crossed Commencement Bay and neared Hylebos Waterway. Walt and his crew were waiting in a truck above the dock.

"We were about to give up on you tonight," Walt said to Don as he caught one of the mooring lines. "Did you have trouble?"

"Rough weather up north, too many stops and trouble right behind us since Fauntleroy. We're going to have to get your 25 cases on the dock and get out of here pronto, Walt. I'm pretty sure the Coast Guard is less than 5 miles behind us," Don explained.

Walt needed no further notice; he urged his two helpers into action as he joined Al and Don in transferring the boxes from the boat to the dock. Behind them the lights of the pursuing vessel appeared around the south end of Vashon Island and headed for the Tacoma waterfront. Al started the engine and backed away from the dock as the last hand truck was ascending the gangway. The Coast Guard boat was swinging its searchlight from side to side, but as powerful as the beam was it couldn't find the dull black boat that was disappearing up the waterway with its exhaust in silent, underwater mode. The Sea Bird was creating enough wake to rock boats in the several moorages it passed, but not enough to create a path of foam. They reached their slip in 10 minutes and turned the bow out in case a rapid escape might prove necessary.

"If they followed us in here, the chances of getting by them in this narrow channel are pretty darn slim," Al said in a hushed voice.

"We'll do what we have to if that happens, Al."

"Which one of us is going to make the call to Jill so that she can try and find the guy in Shelton?" Al asked.

"Go ahead, I'll stay here and guard our goods. Matter of fact, why don't you just drive up there and take the money we've already collected. I feel awfully funny carrying this bag of gold coins around in the boat," Don suggested.

"Why is that? Al asked as he helped drape the grimy boat cover over the cockpit.

"Paper money you can stash on you if you go overboard. Gold would take you straight to the bottom!" Don laughed, nervously.

"Okay, I'll head out. Try to get some sleep and I'll meet you about 4 o'clock and we'll head over to the public float at Point Defiance for some fuel before we start south."

"Yeah, you too, I mean get some sleep. Don't let Jill get you side tracked or anything," Don kidded

"Fat chance of that," Al muttered as he picked his way off the dark, slippery log dock.

Don slipped under the tarp covering, stumbled over a case of whiskey and cursed the blackness. "I'm tired of running at night, tired of being chased and just plain tired!"

He fumbled his way to his bunk and collapsed into a deep sleep that lasted until noon despite repetitive dreams of running, running in the night, always just a few steps from being caught by men without faces. The men wore black clothing with a big 'K' monogrammed on their ball caps. It took him an hour and several cups of coffee to dim the images from his dreams. The day outside the boat cabin was gray from a low overcast. He knew it was going to start raining and keep raining, he just knew it.

CHAPTER FIFTY-FOUR

Jill had been asleep only three hours when she heard something strike the dormer window. She peeked around the roller curtain and saw Al standing under the streetlight. After a wave of assurance, she hurried downstairs to let him in.

"We had some trouble, can you get hold of the guy in Shelton?" he asked, immediately upon entering.

"Good morning to you too!" she rejoined.

"I'm sorry! I'm so darn tired I've completely lost my manners. Can I have a hug and we'll start over?" Al asked, holding out his arms.

Jill melted into his embrace and didn't let go until he lifted her head and gave her a lingering kiss.

"I'm glad you're here, Al, I've been worried sick that something terrible was going to happen tonight. Tell me what's going on."

He sat down at the kitchen table and poured out the details of the last day and night while Jill made breakfast of cocoa, eggs and toast. When he had finished his tale he asked her again if she could contact the customer in Shelton.

"Sure, I'll call him on his cell," she joked. When Al cocked his head in wonder, she said, "Never mind, you'll understand soon. Yes, he gave me the number of the hotel he uses when he's in town and I can leave a message when to expect delivery or if you can't make it."

They conferred on what time frame would work best and Jill called the hotel. Since it was only 6:30 in the morning, it took several rings until she was answered by a groggy sounding clerk. He promised to put the message in the patron's key box and hung up.

"Thanks, that'll give us some breathing room in case we have more trouble, which is likely. For some reason that Coast Guard cutter seems to have had us almost in its sights several times now. With all the miles of water to patrol, I can't figure how they've spotted us more than once, but I know I'm getting tired of the whole game. I wish there was a way out," he sighed.

"There is, Al," Jill started, "If you are really ready to make a change, a big change, there's a way."

She was staring at him with such intensity that Al couldn't imagine what she had in mind. After a full minute of silence, he said,

"You must have something important to say the way you're looking at me. What is it?"

"Do you love me, Al? I mean not just caring about each other, but are you in love with me?" She held her breath for having been so bold.

"I'm absolutely crazy about you!" he said fervently. "I've told you that before and I thought you understood that my feelings have never changed. I've been waiting---and hoping---that you would feel the same way in time." He rose to embrace her, but she held him away, her hand on his chest.

"I do feel the same way. Al, but what I'm proposing is a commitment that goes far beyond anything normal. If you're serious about what you've just said then follow me upstairs and I'll show you what I'm driving at."

Al fumbled in his mind. Did she want to make love right now? He followed her up the two flights of stairs in bewilderment. When they reached her room, he saw the computer screen lit, some kind of camera plugged into it and pages of paper littering the desk.

"Pull up the other chair and let me show you what I have figured out," she directed in a firm manner. "When I'm finished, you can make a decision whether you really want to make the kind of commitment towards me that I need or not, because this will take more courage than your smuggling ventures have taken, regardless of what you've experienced in the last few months."

Al thought, "I doubt that!" But he held the thought as he watched her scan the paper on to the screen. They were newspaper clippings and magazine advertisements. The common theme seemed to be boats; several types and sizes of boats. The other commonalty was the name of the designer: Donald Grant!

Before Al could ask, Jill spoke. "These are pictures of Don's future, Al. He is going to design some of America's finest yachts, speedboats and cruisers as well as utilitarian boats for use in war. Don is going to survive this period of running whiskey and graduate into a first rate citizen."

"Okay, you've managed to look into his future and see success. What does that tell you about me? Am I his silent partner in all that? Because that would be fine with me, if it's meant to be." Al sounded nervous, even to himself.

"Your future is entirely up to you, Al. I haven't looked for you and I won't do it for you now. I want you to use your own free agency, just as I intend to myself."

"What it is it that you're driving at? Maybe I'm just too tired to understand, but what is it you intend to do, Jill?"

"I'm going back to my own time frame. I'm going to leave the country for New Zealand and I'm going to try to live as normal and complete a life there as God will allow."

Al was stunned into silence by the conviction in her tone and the message itself. His mind tried to assemble a response, but couldn't manage to bring words to his lips.

"I want you to come with me, Al. I want you to be my husband." She paused, took a deep breath and continued, "There's a chance that it won't work; that you'll be left behind here, or maybe worse. I don't know and I don't want to begin to think of not being with you, but it's possible. If it works we'll both be leaving our friends and family forever. We will disappear from their lives without a trace. They'll probably think we're dead and to them we are! Are you understanding what I'm saying?"

"I'm beginning to. You think you can transport us into the future, right? I thought you had no idea how you were sent back in time!" Al exclaimed.

"I figured it out, Al. That was what I was doing all winter; why I was so worn out and depressed. I've been back, to the year 2003, to be exact. I bought this digital camera and brought it back to 1930 to prove to myself and you that it was possible. But I'm sure that the guys that sent me here know what I've done. They are undoubtedly connected, somehow, to everything I've used this computer for. Their goal seems to be to gain enough resources to put the Kennedy group totally out of business and has probably also been to take revenge by eliminating the whole Kennedy clan over the years for what they did to the Tucci family and others. It has worked to this point, but if we arrive back in the twenty-first century with the gold and leave the country before they can find us, we'll have a life again and they'll have to settle for what they have already have done."

"If you went back to your own time already, why didn't you stay there?" Al asked, hoping he already knew the answer.

"I'm greedy, Al. I wanted you and I wanted what we've worked for the last year and a half. We'll leave Ray his share. We'll leave Don his share, the boats and these hints of what he'll be doing for the rest of his life," she said, holding up the sheaf of clippings and advertisements. "I care about Don a lot and this was the least I could do for him. That and steer him toward May, who is crazy in love with him."

"How are you going to accomplish that if you're leaving?" Al asked. The idea of his friend settling down with a fine girl like May was beginning to make the decision to abandon Don easier to deal with in Al's mind.

"He's going to find her here, waiting for him, when he comes looking for us. She'll have his share of the investment account, this folder of his future accomplishments to present to him and---well, I think nature will take its course from there. What do you think?" Jill wanted more than a single answer at this point.

"I think you're about the smartest girl in the universe and I want to be part of wherever you want to be in that universe. If you promise to marry me as soon as we ---"

"That would be next week, thank you very much, if all goes right," she finished for him.

Al smothered her with kisses before she could begin to tell him the process she had worked out to implement her plan.

"I showed you and Don how a scanner works, remember?" Jill had turned very serious. "What I didn't show you was how a person can scan pictures directly from a digital camera. What I'm going to do is take pictures of you and I, dressed in appropriate clothing and when we're ready to leave, I'll scan them and a picture of this house taken in modern time, into the computer. Then I move our pictures into the folder with the house picture, we'll hold hands, I'll type in a certain code and we'll be in 2003. The house will look a little different then, of course. We'll sneak out the back, avoiding my mother who, incidentally, has become a hopeless alcoholic, I'm sorry to report."

"Don't you want to see her, to tell her you're alive, at least?" Al asked.

"Yes, but she's so far gone, now, it probably wouldn't even register and might complicate our disappearance even more."

"So, what's your plan to leave the country?"

"When I went back I bought a used car and hid it in the old garage. It's still registered to the previous owner so the bad guys won't have a record of it. We'll drive to the bank and get our share of the money and the rare coins from the safe deposit box and drive to Reno. We'll need to get new driver's licenses and passports, which will take a few days and probably cost plenty, but there are people in Reno who can make anything you want at the right price. After that, if you still want me, we can get married, catch a plane to Los Angeles and another to New Zealand."

"Why New Zealand, Jill?" Al asked, his head in a whirl from her rapid fire description.

"They speak English, or their version. They're very friendly people who love to have fun. The climate is mild, but with a tremendous variety, from fantastic ocean beaches to skiing as good as the Alps of Europe. And it's a long way from the people who will likely want to kill us," she summarized.

"Sounds a lot more civilized than what I learned of it in school as a kid. Wasn't it a British Penal Colony to begin with?" Al asked, trying to imagine living on the other side of the world.

"Quite civilized now, except for driving on the wrong side of the road, too many sheep and the odd kangaroo hopping in front of your car. I visited there on one of my dad's political junkets when I was seventeen and fell in love with the whole country, especially the Maori people. We visited all the tourists spots, took a jet boat ride on a river so shallow you wouldn't believe it was possible and on luge sleds with wheels down a mountain on the south island. You'll love it, Al. We'll be happy there. It's a great place to raise a family."

"I'll be happy anywhere with you, Jill and I can't wait to start a family--or at least practice at it for a while," he said, giving her a playful pinch on her buttocks.

She gave him a love tap on his head, saying, "Right after the judge pronounces us man and wife. Come on, we've got lots to do!"

CHAPTER FIFTY-FIVE

Don waited as long as he dared before leaving the marina without Al. He figured that whatever had gone wrong wouldn't get any better if he was caught with 43 cases of liquor aboard. He moved the 20 cases that were in the cabin to the rear cockpit with the remaining 23 there and tarped them down securely. He reached the public float fuel dock in the Tacoma Yacht Club moorage basin just before the 6 PM closing time. Fortunately, the dock attendant was more intent on closing up then on inspecting the contents of Don's cockpit. Don idled all the way past Point Defiance, trolling a fishing line and steering from the cockpit with the outside tiller. The mild disguise served him well enough to clear all the other boat traffic in Commencement Bay. As darkness began to fall, he accelerated to planing speed, glad to be passing Salmon Beach and the Chinese tunnel entrance without problems this evening. Still, a shudder ran through his body as he thought of how close he and Al had come to losing their lives there previously.

The outgoing tide made it necessary for him to stop at Mud Bay first while there was still enough water to reach Mike Webster's dock. It was a long run over familiar territory, but Don knew that running at night was no time to let down his vigilance, especially without a second set of eyes to keep watch. He passed Fox Island, bucking the nasty little tide chop that was usually present during ebb tides. As he approached McNeil Island, running lights of a fast, medium sized vessel caught his attention. It appeared to be about the size of the Coast Guard cutters that had pursued them several times. He cut the throttle to idle speed and waited to see if he had been spotted. The larger boat continued its course, heading across his vision toward Steilacoom.

"It's the prison boat, going to pick up guards for the next shift," he said to himself. "Better to be safe than sorry though," he muttered as he brought the Sea Bird up to speed.

Halfway between McNeil and Anderson Islands he hit something. The propeller began to cavitate, losing enough bite that the hull fell off plane and slowed to 10 miles an hour. Don shut the engine down and came back to the stern with a flashlight. Long trails of kelp trailed from the rudder post, shimmering in the green water.

"Damn, I cut too close to the marker buoy," he cursed to himself.

He went back into the cabin and started the engine, being sure that the exhaust was switched to the underwater, silent mode. Pulling the gear lever into reverse, he gunned the engine twice then tried it in forward. It cavitated, unable to push the boat onto plane. He reversed again, this time turning the wheel hard to one side to swing the stern violently. Before he could put the lever in forward, the cabin was lit by two searchlight beams from the McNeil Island Prison ferry dock. Don was totally blinded. By sheer instinct he jammed the gear lever forward, followed by full throttle and opening the exhaust. The hull shuddered, the propeller cavitating wildly, then biting in and bouncing the boat forward and on to plane. The searchlights followed, but were soon showing only the foaming, white wake as the Sea Bird attained top speed. In ten minutes he rounded Devils Head and was out of sight of anyone on McNeil Island.

He slowed to 25 knots and promised himself not to cut any more corners during the several course changes required to reach Mud Bay. It paid off; the remainder of the trip was uneventful. He pulled into Webster's dock at 9 PM.

Mike Webster was relaxing in the living room, reading with his wife when he was surprised by a knock at the door.

"Don! You scared the daylights out of us!" Mike exclaimed. "Where you been? I thought you'd be in about 4 or 5 this morning." He stepped outside and closed the door before expecting an answer.

"Too long a story to tell Mike. I've got 23 cases for you, but no partner to help unload tonight," Don replied.

"Don't tell me Al is in trouble again," Mike said with genuine concern.

"I hope not. We got into Tacoma and had to put the boat away for the night to avoid the Coast Guard. Al went to Jill's place to have her try and get a message to our customer in Shelton. I'm headed there next and have no idea whether I'll find him or not. If I don't make contact, I'll have to run the other 20 cases back here for you to stash until we can sell it. Al never came back today, so I figured it was up to me to get the stuff off the boat," Don explained.

They got to work wheeling the liquor up to Webster's truck, hurrying to beat the tide. Don left a streak of mud in his wake as he carefully left Mud Bay a half hour later. He continued at low speed weaving his way between Hope and Squaxin Islands. When he found the opening to Hammersly Inlet he increased speed to 20 knots to overcome the out rushing current and arrived at the rendezvous spot in Shelton at 10:45. To his surprise and relief their grizzled customer was waiting in his stake bed truck, smoking an obnoxious smelling cigar.

As he approached, Don said, "I'm sorry about not getting here last night, or early this morning, I guess. Our partner got a message to you, I hope."

"Yeah, I waited until daylight and found the message when I got back to the hotel. What kind of trouble did you run into this time?" The burly man asked, reaching for the case Don was holding above the gunwale.

"Bad weather, Coast Guard, nothing real terrible," Don replied with a smile.

"You didn't lose your partner again, did you?"

"Not overboard or worse. He drove up to get the message to you and didn't come back. But there's a pretty woman involved, so I'm not too worried," Don joked.

"Maybe you should be! Has he got your money with him?" the big logger inquired.

"As a matter of fact, yes! But I'd trust them both with my life," Don added a bit more seriously.

The other man just kept laughing as he began loading cases, leaving Don to ponder if the situation was humorous or not. He had to admit the guy was being pretty nice about having to wait an extra day to take delivery of his booze. He let the conversation lag and concentrated on keeping up with his customer, unloading the last 20 cases in record time. When the job was done and the money collected, the logger waved good-bye and wished him good luck on finding his other two partners and the rest of his money.

Don was still thinking about that a half hour later as he exited the narrow mouth of Hammersly and almost broad sided his nemesis: the Coast Guard cutter. It seemed there was nothing to do but turn hard right and apply full throttle. It didn't occur to him to continue at a slower pace with the running lights on. There was no liquor aboard. The hull had registration numbers, they just weren't posted right now. All his safety equipment was in order. He would think about all this later, when his mind was rested and clear; but now all that mattered was running. Running fast and far, letting the dark hide the presence of him and his creation. It was working. By the time he rounded Briscoe Point on Hartstene Island the cutter was a mile behind. He was sure he would be out of sight when he reached Johnson Point. In between was the treacherous Itsami ledge, which he kept well to his right, keeping his eyes directed toward the warning beacon to be sure he was well beyond the rocks before changing course. A loud thump followed by the bow rising clear of the water and veering to the left brought Don's vision back ahead where it should have been to avoid the impact. He pulled back the throttle to take stock of what had happened. Turning the searchlight to the stern revealed the head of an almost submerged log. He was living the night runner's worst nightmare: hitting a dead head at full speed. Yanking up the forward floorboard confirmed his fears. The bilge was filling too rapidly for the electric pump to keep up. Don engaged the larger engine driven pump and brought the boat back on plane, hoping the bow would clear the water enough to avoid scooping it in. Glancing quickly astern, he found the cutter had closed to within a half mile. He made a decision and turned to the left. Water gushed into the hole and pulled the boat down flat on the water. He compensated with more throttle and brought it onto an even keel. The cutter was losing ground again. It was nine miles to Dutcher cove and safety; just 18 minutes at his present speed, if he didn't sink first!

CHAPTER FIFTY-SIX: LATE MARCH, 1930

May sat in the house on J Street looking out the front window. It had been four days since Al had brought her here after an urgent call from Jill asking her if she loved Don enough to pack a suitcase and leave her parent's marina. Nothing had seemed more desirable just four days ago, but now, alone and confused, she wondered if it had all been a dreadful mistake.

Jill had given her a typed list of instructions and begged her not to vary from them. She was to stay here, no matter how long it might be, until Don returned. She was to give him a pouch containing several thousand dollars in cash and ask him to read the sheaf of clippings and advertisements in an envelope that May was not to inspect herself. She was to tell Don that Jill and Al were going abroad as man and wife and not to expect them to return. That the computer, whatever that was, was no longer available; that it had served its purpose and would be gone. Then May was to present Don with two train tickets to Reno, Nevada and ask him if he understood what that meant.

Jill had promised her that she was certain that Don would return, understand and fill the rest of their lives with more peace, happiness and success than May could imagine. Then she and Al had embraced her, said their farewells, had gone upstairs and, oddly, never come back down.

Tears formed in May's eyes as they had each day since her friends had disappeared. A faint ray of hope came to her face as a taxi pulled up to the curb and a familiar form exited. She opened the front door and ran out with arms outstretched and tears flowing freely now.

***   APRIL 2003   ***

"Here it is, Al!" Jill exclaimed. They were in the records department of the Washoe County Courthouse in Carson City, Nevada. "They were married April 6, 1930 in the Wedding Bell Chapel in Reno. If you're satisfied, we can still make the evening flight to Auckland if we hustle back to Reno and get the noon flight to Los Angeles."

"I just wanted to be sure your plan worked," Al assured her, "But if Auckland is as nice as you say, why are we going on to Hamilton."

"Hamilton Jet Company, the world's best boat propulsion system. You're going to love owning that place!"

EPILOGUE

Monday, Oct. 10, 2005

Dear Rebecca,

Its 3:20 in the morning, my leg is killing me and I can't sleep. As you may have heard from your sister, I got t-boned at the motocross race Saturday at Woodland. I had the best hole shot I've had since winning high points 6 years ago and I was in the middle of turn one when this dufus guy on a Matchless 500 runs right through the corner and nails me. The doctor says I'll be laid up for a while and that guys over 70 shouldn't be on old racing motorcycles anyway. Looking on the brighter side, it'll give me more time to read and that made me think of reading and telling stories to you when you were a child. One story that I never told you came to mind; it had to do with the old boat you and your cousin used to play in at our beach house and a place called Dutcher Cove where we used to explore in the smaller boat that replaced the wrecked one that you played in. It's a story of remarkable coincidences.

Christmas of 1975, your sister, Bonnie and John came up from Las Vegas to spend the holidays with us. You may remember from the pictures we took, all bundled up for a winter boat ride on the sound. Christmas morning a north wind came up and the boat dragged anchor and disappeared. John and I searched all the roads that were near the beach and found it over two miles away outside Dutcher Cove. We levered it off the beach and I got one of the outboard motors running, but it was taking on so much water that I was in danger of sinking. I ran it into the cove and beached it in front of an old, almost hidden cabin. The owner, a small gentleman about 80 years old, came out to help me. The tide went out and left me stranded before I could repair the damage well enough to try to get the boat to a launching ramp. Mr. Best, the property owner, walked me back to his cabin. On the way around the spit we passed half dozen derelict boats of various sizes. When we reached the cabin they insisted that I sit in front of their wood stove until I could dry out. Mrs. Best served me hot cocoa and sweet rolls and we began to talk about the old boat hulls that I had observed and how they came to be there.

Mr. Best was out of work in the spring of 1930. Somehow they had managed to buy a 27 acre parcel that comprised the cove, a lot of tide lands at low tide and the back land, consisting of a steep canyon that led out to a primitive road. It was an out of the way place with almost no value then, whereas now it's probably worth a fortune. They arrived at the site with only the clothes on their back and some home canned food. They waited through a long night and half the next day for their meager furnishings and a pile of lumber to arrive on a small barge towed by a launch which could barely move with the tide and not at all against it. They constructed the cabin during the next few days but found themselves short of enough nails to finish the siding. Mr. Best walked several miles to Key Center and traded some postage stamps for 10 cents worth of nails, but they were still short and had to lean the boards against two sides and hope the wind didn't blow through the gaps.

 Early one morning in late March they were awakened by the tremendous roar of an un-muffled boat engine. Looking out, they saw a black apparition slide around the point of the spit, tear toward their cabin, veering just beyond it and run almost half out of the water on the muddy bank. Their dog, an Australian Blue Heeler, ran out and severely bit the right leg of the young man who was climbing from the beached boat. The man climbed back over the gunwale and remained there until Mr. Best came out and tethered the dog with a rope. The boat driver introduced himself, apologized for the intrusion and explained that his boat had been badly damaged when he hit a dead head just a few minutes previously. The Bests took him in, fed and warmed him, just as they had done for me, and tended to his bitten ankle. He ended up staying with them three days, providing them with more than enough money for Mr. Best to buy not only plenty of nails, but a good supply of food. Before he left he helped Mr. Best finish siding the cabin and built a kitchen table and two dining chairs which they were still using when I arrived as unannounced as their visitor 45 years before.

 When the young fellow [Mr. Best guessed him to be in his early twenties] left, he said that the Bests were welcome to use the boat, if they could patch the bottom well enough to stay afloat, and that he might not return for a long time. Indeed, they had raised three children and sent them off on their own before this man returned. Mrs. Best thought it was about 1960 or 61 when he showed up one day in a nice Ford truck. He introduced himself as Donald Grant and this is where the story really caught my attention, because my dad had a second cousin by that name. Mr. Grant wanted to see if his old boat had, by any chance, survived his long absence. The Bests walked him out past their flourishing garden area to the opposite side of the spit. There lay the Sea Bird, which Grant called the Ghost, high and dry, pretty much in one piece, but no longer usable. Mr. Best said he had repaired the holed bottom and they used the boat for fishing until the war when gasoline was not available. He had winched it up on the spit and it had remained there ever since. "Couldn't afford to run it after gasoline passed 25 cents a gallon," he told Grant. The Bests talked him into staying for dinner and found, through conversation that Grant had worked as a naval designer before and during the war and was still active in designing Fairliner boats in Tacoma, although he had lived in the east from 1930 until 1946. He promised to return soon and bring pictures of some of his designs to share with them. He was as good as his word, returning just a few weeks later, very excited, Mrs. Best said. It seemed that an old acquaintance of his, a Mr. Tom Carstens, owner of a good sized foreign car dealership, had the misfortune of having a fire severely damage a classic Duesenberg Phaeton automobile. Grant wanted to examine the engine in his old boat to see if it was salvageable. Best said he had poured the cylinders full of oil when they laid it up and it was under cover in the cabin, so it might be usable. Grant brought two batteries from the back of his truck, hooked them up with jumper cables and found that the Ghost's engine still turned free. Over the next few days he, Mr. Best and Grant's son, stripped and removed the Duesenberg engine. Grant said that he had bought the damaged Phaeton for a song from Carstens, who was more interested in his sports racing car at that point. Grant went on to restore the Duesenberg and some time later, brought it, along with memoirs of his past and current boat designs, for the Bests to see. They even went for a ride around the Key Peninsula in the grand old car. Among the designs he had accomplished were several 'down east' cruisers, [which are now coming back into style in fiberglass at huge prices], the 81 foot PT boats and 32 foot assault boats of World War Two, the 1947 Fairliner 16 foot Torpedo [the few examples that exist are priceless now] and the popular Fairliners up to the 1960s.

  On subsequent visits he confided that the Ghost, or Sea Bird, was his first design and that he and his partner, a guy named Allen Nelson, actually used it for smuggling liquor during Prohibition. That, in fact, the night he hit the deadhead and arrived on their shore, he was being chased by the Coast Guard, running alone after his partner didn't show up for the run. After leaving the boat with them, he had quit smuggling, gone to Reno, married his wife May, and left to work in the east as a designer. His partner had never been heard of again.

Now, I don't know if it is mere coincidence, but your grandfather, Erik Nelson, the carpenter, had a cousin Al that disappeared in 1930. This Donald Grant also mentioned that the Duesenberg engine was originally modified for marine use by a Ray Moore in Tacoma. Believe it or not, Beckie, that was the name of your great grandfather! I never knew him since my grand mother Carolina divorced him long before I was born, so I can't say it's the same man. Your grandmother, Birdie, pointed him out one day on 25th Street in Tacoma in about 1946, but I don't really remember what he looked like. Another odd coincidence is, that in 1984, I saw that Duesenberg auctioned in Reno for over a million dollars, the first car to attain that price!

I went back to Dutcher Cove last summer to see if the Ghost was still there, but the place has changed a great deal. There's still a lot of driftwood on the spit, but all the old boat hulls are gone. Two nice homes border the cove, leaving no trace of the Best's old cabin. But the place is still spooky with the overhanging cedar branches and the dark, muddy water. I can imagine that on nights like this, when old rum runners can't sleep, one might still hear the deep bellowing exhaust and the scream of the supercharger as the Ghost comes alive to haunt that hidden lagoon. What do you think little one?
Love always,
        Dad

AUTHOR'S NOTES

I hope that Night Runners is an enjoyable break from reality for all my readers. However, a lot of the subjects that I write about have a good deal of truth in them, so hang on and let me tell you the "rest of the story."

All the locations in Night Runners and my previous novel "A Few of the Chosen" [Trafford Publishing, Victoria B.C., 2003] are actual. Contrary to nay sayers on some web sites that I have visited, the Chinese tunnels were a reality, until the City of Tacoma dug through them in many places while installing storm drains several years ago, as noted by pictures in the Tacoma News Tribune at the time. On a personal basis, I went in the Fircrest entrance in 1949, going as far as the first room where branches led to Tacoma and Puget Sound. One tunnel leading toward Tacoma was caved at that time, while two were still open. I later visited the entrance at the Narrows end and it was as described in this story, wooden doors locked and water running from the bottom. It is now obliterated at that end. **Thanks to Don Jacobsen, President of the Fircrest, Washington Civic and Heritage society** for more details of the tunnel complex, the story of his cousin Jack going clear through from Fircrest to Day Island in the 1930s and the story of the 6 foot sword which is also true. [I'm not certain who found it.] Friends of mine found a few coins and small artifacts while exploring, but all I wanted to do was get out of the small opening without suffocating! The real mystery about the Chinese tunnels of Tacoma is: how was such an undertaking accomplished in the late 19th century [without apparent detection] and how did so much of its history become only legend? Nevertheless, many of us old timers were able to visit sufficient portions of it to scare the day lights out of us. Of course, we didn't tell our parents, so perhaps that's how the tunnels disappeared from memory.

Part of the inspiration for the "Ghost" came from seeing a sea sled style boat, with a top made of the same material as Ford roadsters of the late twenties, rotting in the back yard of a member of my Boy Scout Troop in the late 1940s. I was certain it was an old rum runner, with its shallow draft, big engine and ominous look. The "Ghost" is what I would have built in 1929, if I had lived in that era.

Fred Duesenberg died in July, 1932, but he had already designed the centrifugal supercharger that boosted the normally aspirated engine from 265 HP to 320. His brother Augie invented a ram's horn that brought the power to 400 as used in the version in the imaginary Ghost. A similar boat bottom design was used by the Penn Yan company's production cruisers for many years, but harkened to the sea sled idea which I observed as a youth.

Concerning the liquor: Cutty Sark and others did sell more whiskey during Prohibition than previously , just as I sold more gasoline at my Chevron station during the fuel "shortage" of 1980 than I did before or afterwards. People seem to demand what they supposedly can't have!

As to the characters of the story, I had no intention of bringing family into the plot; they just grew there, naturally as weeds, once I started. My grandfather, Ray, owned a garage, he did fool around and lose his family and he died from an unexplained gunshot wound while living with an unnamed woman, while in good health. My dad, Harold, did have his log tow pass him up while navigating Hammersly Inlet one night in 1930 in Foss #29! Aunt Goldie was a feisty little character who partied at Salmon Beach and married Oz at an early age. She was my favorite aunt. We had some fun times in my drinking days and I miss her laugh. Erik Nelson was patterned after my father-in-law who worked at Stadium High and who may have mentioned the tunnel that originally exited there when the building was the Tacoma Hotel. He was an excellent wood worker and could have built a boat as fine as the Ghost. He brewed wine for the family in the basement of their Hilltop area home as attributed to the Ralph Nelson family of the story.

Tom Carstens went from playboy meat packing heir, to auto dealer and sports car racer. I was racing cars then, having bought two from his firm, and enjoyed Tom's great enthusiasm and sense of humor. His vintage Duesenberg burned badly in Tacoma, but was not the one auctioned at Harrah's in 1984 for $1,000,000. My mom, Birdie, talked a lot about Tom, but I don't think Goldie actually dated him.

Chief McGaw was a wonderful character, very much as I described him, as was the old Mack crane truck that later became a water tanker truck for the University Place Volunteer Fire Department. It took a real man to crank that beast and its bark will never be forgotten!

The story of the Best family and their arrival at Dutcher Cove was as they described it to me when I landed on their spit with a sinking 20 foot cruiser in December, 1975. I later rebuilt the treacherous road down the canyon to their cottage and tipped my bulldozer over in the process. They were fine folks and I miss their friendship since they passed on. The ankle biting dog I do not miss.

Al, Don, Jill, and the Tuccis are totally fictional characters as are May Cummings, the Makovich brothers and George Harris, although the latter three names are of people that did exist. Walt and Mabel's place existed after the time frame of the story, but the Tides has been a Gig Harbor landmark for almost a century. The Johnson family of black restaurant owners of the two time periods is fictional, although Roy Olmstead did have a wealthy black, upscale, Seattle restaurant owner as a client in the early 20s. The readers can make up their own minds as to the Kennedy conspiracy, bearing in mind the dubious legacy that Joe Kennedy Sr. left as a liquor baron of the east coast and the tragedies that have accompanied his family down to the third generation. The coins described might come close enough to buy the Hamilton Jet Company, if it were for sale.

Thanks to the La Conner City Library and the Historical Museum there for research concerning the Swinomish Slough. I've run the slough many times, but wasn't sure it was deep enough in 1929-- it was! It's a great place to cruise through tulip fields and pastoral scenery with out resorting to the canals of Europe, though I'll admit that the ride is shorter.

I've done a lot of running at night in boats and even wrote an unpublished [to date] selection of my memories of those foolish accomplishments. It is possible to run at high speed in the dark, rain or fog, but it is unbelievably difficult to do so without some type of bad result. I can highly recommend reading about such adventures over trying them, unless Prohibition is made the law again, at which time you might spot me and the wake of the Ghost speeding down from Canada, hopefully far ahead of any pursuers.

Happy sailing,

Rodger J.

EDITOR'S NOTE: We are pleased that you have purchased Mr. Bille's second novel, but regret to inform you that further contributions from him are unlikely. He was last seen by his wife in early November, 2005 working at his computer station, experimenting with a link to her digital camera. She thought that he had slipped out for a ride on his dirt bike, but no trace has been found to date. A perusal of his computer files showed links to the late 1920s, but the assumption that he tried to travel back in time that some have made is deemed preposterous, except for the addled few who actually believe the stories he has written are more than fictional.

John L. Johnson IV, Victoria B.C., Canada

CPSIA information can be obtained
at www.ICGtesting.com
Printed in the USA
FSOW02n2159060915
10751FS